'This collection of the writings of Aboriginal people engaged in the campaign for basic human, and therefore political, rights adds a great deal to the understanding of the history of Aboriginal Australians. It helps us all, regardless of our race, to remember how much each generation of Aboriginal people owes to those who went before.'
Charles Perkins AO

'This fine collection is remarkable for two reasons. Across 161 years, it gives us the voice of Aboriginal Australians presenting their legitimate request to play a full role in society. It reminds us that this voice has too seldom been acknowledged and far too infrequently acted upon, to all Australians' impoverishment as well as theirs.'
Gough Whitlam AC QC

'I do think this story is very important because there's a lot of people in Australia that think Aboriginal people were so stupid that we did not complain or fight for our rights; this book disposes of that argument.'
Ruby Langford Ginibi

'Fear of the unknown, lack of knowledge and understanding, are barriers to reconciliation between Aboriginals and other Australians. This book should dispel some of the mystery and make understanding easier. I wish it every success.'
Malcom Fraser AC CH

'This compilation of Aboriginal political statements is an important contribution to the education of non-indigenous Australians. The documents remind us all of the courage and vision of Aboriginal leaders who will increasingly and properly be regarded as the heroes of their time.'
Robert Tickner

'*The Struggle for Aboriginal Rights* is timely because of the commitment at the political level to some document of political reconciliation by the year 2000. Most of us have yet to face what it means that Aboriginals are not just another ethnic minority but people with intrinsic rights. If Australians are to come to terms with their present and their future view they need to understand the importance of First Nation status for Aboriginal Australians, a point already reached in Canada, the United States and New Zealand.'
The Hon Fred Chaney

W9-AEF-558

THE STRUGGLE FOR
ABORIGINAL RIGHTS

THE STRUGGLE FOR ABORIGINAL RIGHTS

A documentary history

Bain Attwood and Andrew Markus

ALLEN & UNWIN

First published in 1999 by
Allen & Unwin
9 Atchison Street NSW 1590
Australia
Phone: (61 2) 8425 0100
Fax: (61 2) 9906 2218
E–mail: frontdesk@allen-unwin.com.au
Web: http://www.allen-unwin.com.au

National Library of Australia
Cataloguing-in-Publication entry:

Attwood, Bain.
   The struggle for aboriginal rights.

   Includes index.
   ISBN 1 86448 5841.

   1. Aborigines, Australia—Politics and government. 2. Aborigines, Australian—
History. 3. Aborigines, Australian—Legal status, laws, 4. Aborigines,
Australian—History—Sources. I. Markus, Andrew. II. Title.

323.119915

Set in 10/12pt Times New Roman
Printed and bound by South Wind Production (Singapore) Pte Ltd

10 9 8 7 6 5 4 3 2

CONTENTS

Part 4 1970s–1998   273

Illustrations

Map

Acknowledgements

In the course of undertaking this book we have been assisted by many people. We wish to thank historians in the field of Aboriginal history, other scholars and our students, all of whom helped us in the search for or checking of documents and photographs: Joanne Bach, Peggy Brock, Marita Cullen, Robert Foster, Heather Goodall, Geoffrey Gray, Anna Haebich, Rod Hagen, Steven Kinnane, Kathy Lothian, Jane Lydon, Dawn May and Sue Taffe.

We have been well served by numerous archivists, librarians and other staff at the National Archives of Australia (Canberra, Melbourne and Darwin); Public Record Office of Victoria; National Film and Sound Archives (Melbourne); Museum of Victoria; Archives Office of New South Wales; University of Sydney Archives; State Records of South Australia; Archives Office of Tasmania; Queensland State Archives; Public Records Office of Western Australia; National Library of Australia; State Library of Victoria; Monash University; Koorie Research Centre, Monash University; Mitchell Library, State Library of New South Wales; Mortlock Library of South Australiana, State Library of South Australia; State Library of Western Australia; Australian Institute of Aboriginal and Torres Strait Islander Studies; Rhodes House Library, Oxford University. Staff at *The Age*, the *Australian* and the Fairfax Photo Library patiently answered our inquiries and met our requests for photographs.

Joan Kimm helped find many documents; Donna Carrington, Selena Fernandez, Angela Sullivan and Julie Tisdale assisted with word processing; and Jo Aitken and Vivien Seyler checked the transcriptions. Sue Drummond of the School of Geography and Environmental Science at Monash University drew the map, and Rhonda Joyce and Shannon Mattison of the same unit prepared many of the photographs for publication.

Much of the research was supported by the Australian Research Council. A Visiting Fellowship in the Department of Anthropology at the University of Adelaide gave Bain Attwood the opportunity to undertake research in that city. We spent hundred of hours before word processors; without funds Monash University to assist with typing there would have been many more; advances in computer technology enabled us to scan many documents.

At Allen & Unwin, senior editor Emma Cotter patiently saw the book through its final stages of production. Academic Publishing Director John Iremonger, whose record in publishing indigenous history in this country is unrivalled, wholeheartedly supported the project from the moment we proposed the book to him. We wish to acknowledge his commitment to serious research and informed debate in this field of history.

Gordon Hookey kindly allowed us to reproduce his *Day of Mourning Site* for the cover. Numerous individuals, libraries, archives, government departments, companies and newspapers gave us permission to reproduce material and generously waived their rights to publication fees: National Archives of Australia; Archives Office of New South Wales; University of Sydney Archives; State Records of South Australia; Archives Office of Tasmania; Queensland State Archives; National Library of Australia; State Library of Victoria; Mitchell Library, State Library of New South Wales; Mortlock Library of South Australiana, State Library of South Australia; Australian Institute of Aboriginal and Torres Strait Islander Studies; Rhodes House Library, Oxford University; *Advertiser*, Adelaide; *The Age*; *Australian*; *Canberra Times*; *Courier Mail*; Herald *and Weekly Times*; *Mercury*, Hobart; *Northern Star*, Lismore; *Sydney Morning Herald*; *West Australian*; Beattie's Studios; Education Department of Western Australia; FilmWorld; James Cook University Union of Students; Paul Coe, Roberta Sykes and the Australian Broadcasting Commission; Ted Egan, Len Fox; Michael Gallagher; Trevor Graham; Jack Horner; Alick Jackomos; Cheryl Oakenful; Dr Lowitja O'Donoghue; Dorita Thomson; and James Woodford. We have made all possible efforts to contact the copyright owners of the material reproduced in this book. Anyone wishing to raise a copyright issue should contact us through the publisher.

Finally, we wish to thank Fiona Magowan and Simone Pfau for their encouragement and support, which enabled us to bring this project to fruition.

A note on transcription

We have sought to reproduce documents in their entirety, but in some instances it has been necessary to make excisions for reasons of space. These omissions are indicated by ellipses— ... The spelling and punctuation of the original documents has been retained, except in the case of typographical errors in printed material. Italics indicate emphases in the original. The paragraphing of newspaper articles has in general been altered in order to compress material for publication. Square brackets around ellipses indicate these in the original document. Words have been placed in square brackets where we have thought it necessary to clarify abbreviations, names of people, places, and dates, correct typographical errors, and indicate likely words in illegible originals.

Bain Attwood and Andrew Markus
November 1998

Preface

This book has been produced in the belief that there is an urgent need to document the history of Aboriginal political activism, in part to enable the concerns which occupy a central place in contemporary Australian politics to be placed in historical perspective. In this collection we have sought to bring together Aboriginal voices from the 1830s to the present— voices in some cases silenced, in others unheard or ignored.

For a long time we have been aware of the need for a collection of Aboriginal perspectives and have taken some tentative steps towards this through two previous publications of documents, a compilation of the letters of William Cooper, a leading activist in the 1930s, and a study of the 1967 referendum to change the Australian constitution. We had assumed that the need for a general collection would be recognised and others would work to its realisation before we were in a position to do so. A number of documentary collections dealing with nineteenth century Aboriginal-white relations have been published, but none have dealt exclusively with Aboriginal perspectives; nor has there been an attempt to cover systematically the twentieth century. When there was no sign that a collection such as the one we had envisaged was forthcoming, we began work on this book, a task which turned out to be of far greater difficulty than we had envisaged.

Our first attempt to make a short-list of documents for the collection yielded more than 600, mostly dated from the early 1930s. This we painstakingly reduced to the 200 now published. The process of selection was difficult, as was the task of arrangement. In an earlier version we classified the documents thematically, but found that this suffered from weaknesses which far outweighed the benefits. In such an arrangement the documents lost much of their context, gained through placing side by side documents from the one region or organisation; further, many documents covered a range of issues and could not be easily classified—the option of splitting documents, which would deprive them of their authorial integrity, was never seriously considered. We have thus presented documents roughly in chronological order, the sequence modified by attention to region. We have, however, provided a thorough index, which allows consideration of specific issues— such as the removal of children and rights to lands and sovereignty. We have also indexed key terms to allow changing meanings and contexts to be studied.

Our work in this area has, and will, continue to be questioned by indigenous Australians. Given the realities of contemporary race relations, the work of white historians is often regarded with scepticism and hostility. While we understand the basis of such views, they are ones which we have not allowed to deter our research. We reject the idea that fields of study should be the sole preserve of particular groups or that some sort of certificate of authenticity be required before one can work in a field such as this. It is our view that the historical imagination cannot be thus constrained— that a work needs be assessed on its merits, not on the basis of the ethnicity, race, religion or political beliefs of the author. We have produced this work to the best of our abilities; it is not presented as a definitive selection of documents, for there can be no such selection— all collections will have particular emphases and omissions, their strengths and weaknesses. It is offered in the hope that it will provide knowledge and stimulate discussion, research, and further publication. To this end we are donating the royalties from the sale of this book to fund a bi-annual public lecture on Aboriginal politics.

Abbreviations

AAA	Australian Aborigines Association
AAF	Aboriginal-Australian Fellowship
AAL	Australian Aborigines' League
AAPA	Australian Aboriginal Progressive Association
AFA	Aborigines' Friends' Association
ALP	Australian Labor Party
APA	Aborigines Progressive Association
APNR	Association for the Protection of Native Races
ATSIC	Aboriginal and Torres Strait Islander Commission
CAR	Council for Aboriginal Rights
CPA	Communist Party of Australia
FCAA	Federal Council for Aboriginal Advancement
FCAATSI	Federal Council for the Advancement of Aborigines and Torres Strait Islanders
NACC	National Aboriginal Consultative Committee
NAC	National Aboriginal Conference
NTC	National Tribal Council
SAFA	Student Action for Aborigines
VAAL	Victorian Aborigines Advancement League

Introduction

Stories about the struggle for rights for Aborigines are well known in Aboriginal communities across Australia, being part of an oral tradition passed on one generation to the next. By comparison, other Australians know little of such histories. Many probably regard Aboriginal political activity as a very recent phenomenon—something that only emerged in the heady days of the 1960s and 1970s— and comprising events such as the 1967 referendum, whose significance they often misunderstand.[1] Were they asked the names of notable Aboriginal leaders in the nineteenth century and the early and middle decades of the twentieth century they would be at a loss for an answer.[2] This is a matter of the utmost importance for we will only be able to understand the Aboriginal politics of the last two or three decades if we are familiar with earlier protest by or on behalf of Aborigines. This will allow us to see both the continuities and the discontinuities in the struggle for rights for Aborigines over the last 150 and more years.

Until quite recently, historians had done little to combat this ignorance and instead had helped perpetuate the historical silence about the struggle for rights for Aborigines. Even in the late 1960s when historians began to write what we now call 'Aboriginal history', their concerns were eurocentric. They were preoccupied with understanding relations between Aborigines and Europeans in Australia from the perspectives of the newcomers or invaders. Their focus was upon frontiersmen, racial attitudes, government policy and practice and the destructive and often fatal impact of these forces on Aboriginal communities. Aboriginal viewpoints, let alone Aboriginal politics, were seldom found in these early historical studies.[3] For example, a very useful and much used collection of historical sources compiled by Henry Reynolds in the early 1970s barely made any reference to the subject.[4]

By the early 1980s, however, it was evident that historians had shifted their focus to a consideration of Aboriginal perspectives and agency,[5] and Aboriginal political activity, particularly that of the 1920s and 1930s, was now being considered. In the last two decades Heather Goodall, Anna Haebich and Andrew Markus have told the story of the first Aboriginal political organisations to be founded in the inter-war period, in New South Wales, south-west Western Australia and Victoria respectively; Peggy Brock has described one of the earliest campaigns, that of Aborigines on Poonindie, a South Australian reserve, in the closing decades of the nineteenth century; Peter Read has undertaken a biography of Aboriginal leader Charles Perkins, which includes a study of the 1965 'Freedom Ride'; Reynolds has pieced together a narrative of the demands of Aborigines exiled to Flinders Island in the 1830s; and detailed studies of other particular protests and activists, both indigenous and non-Aboriginal, have also been published.[6] This scholarly work has complemented a steadily increasing number of works by or about Aboriginal and non-Aboriginal activists.[7] However, at the time of writing no general historical account has been undertaken.[8]

In keeping with this scholarly emphasis on Aboriginal perspectives and agency, this collection of historical sources seeks to document the history of Aboriginal politics by recovering Aboriginal voices. Although we are aware that this could misrepresent the story of the struggle for rights for Aborigines, in the sense that it might downplay or marginalise the important role played by non-Aboriginal campaigners, we believe that this approach is valid. Aboriginal people have long been spoken for and spoken about, and non-Aboriginal people have given themselves little opportunity to hear what they have to say (as shown, once more, by the recent native title debate). Furthermore, the non-Aboriginal voices are much better known and relatively accessible, both in terms of printed historical sources and historical studies—for example, through Reynolds' documentary collections and monographs which consider what Richard Broome has called 'that thin strand of humanitarianism' in Australia.[9]

Yet, there are undoubtedly major problems in such an undertaking, mainly because of the relative lack of Aboriginal sources. This is so for two reasons. In the nineteenth and much of the twentieth century, Aboriginal peoples in Australia had less of a political presence than other indigenes, such as Maori in New Zealand and Native Americans. This was the result of several factors: The British denial of their status as landowners and thus the absence of any treaty, itself mainly the consequence of Aborigines lacking the military capacity to force the invaders to negotiate; the extreme depopulation and dispossession that devastated so many Aboriginal communities across Australia; and the paternalism and racism, encoded in beliefs (such as Aborigines were 'a dying race') and government policies and practices, which undermined Aboriginal representation in the political sphere.

On the relatively rare occasions, especially in the nineteenth century, where Aborigines *were* able to represent themselves, their voices often left no historical record. In part, this is due to the fact that Aboriginal culture remained a strongly oral culture, and because many Aborigines were denied the opportunity to learn how to read and write, which meant that often even the most forceful Aboriginal spokespersons were illiterate or barely literate. This is especially true of northern Australia (where the *lingua franca* of contact was pidjin or Creole); Dooley Bin Bin, one of the leaders of the stockworkers' strike in the Pilbara in 1946 is a case in point. Nevertheless, there is a considerable historical record available to the historian wishing to document Aboriginal political campaigns during the nineteenth and twentieth centuries, especially in south-eastern Australia where Aborigines in communities like Point McLeay confidently expressed themselves in the language of their colonial masters.

Research over the last two decades or more has unearthed fragments of this activism—sometimes more than this—in the written record of past generations, and more continues to be found. For example, when Andrew Markus was compiling a collection of the letters of the secretary of the Australian Aborigines' League (AAL) in the 1930s, he found numerous letters in William Cooper's name, nearly all to the Commonwealth and New South Wales governments; later researchers, encouraged by this surprising cache, have located other correspondence, addressed not only to other governments but also to political organisations, campaigners, newspapers and benefactors, in both Australia and England.

However, in some instances, one cannot tell the story of the Aborigines' struggle for rights unless one occasionally has recourse to material created by non-Aboriginal campaigners. This is so for three reasons. First, there are some protests where the only extant records which *describe* what happened are those authored by whites (for example, 13). Second, there are other occasions where the Aboriginal activists' case was only presented orally and was not generally recorded; the Pilbara stockworkers' strike is one such case (66 and 67). Third, in many struggles whites and others played an important role, and in these instances we need to consider not only sources that were co-authored with non-Aboriginal campaigners but also ones that were authorised rather than authored by Aborigines; for example, a study of the text and context of Cooper's letters reveals the hand of the AAL's non-Aboriginal president, Arthur Burdeu, and his role is not only that of an amanuensis (cf. **74–77**); similarly, statements such as that of Davis and Dexter Daniels in 1966 bear the 'signature' of someone else, namely the Communist writer and activist Frank Hardy (**124**). These authorial practices do not necessarily render such sources less authentically Aboriginal, although there are undoubtedly situations where that has been the case. To seek unmediated Aboriginal voices is to search for something that does not exist, since any political expression is always influenced by the prevailing beliefs and attitudes. Our rule of thumb in choosing these documents has been the degree of Aboriginal agency we can discern in the origins of the text and the extent to which the aspirations they express are consistent with those found in texts which have been produced by Aborigines (cf. **72** with **77**).[10]

In this book we reproduce a wide range of written historical sources; there are, for example, letters by or in the name of Aborigines and representatives of Aboriginal organisations to governments as well as to other organisations, campaigners, newspaper editors and the general public; leaflets, pamphlets, flyers and posters authored or authorised by Aborigines; and newspaper and magazine articles bearing the names of Aborigines. However, we have also included many photographs of protests and protesters in the belief that these reveal many of the most important statements by Aboriginal activists, including their Aboriginality which was often more apparent in visual— as it was it oral— forms of politics than in other media. Furthermore, where they are available, we have given priority to the reproduction of documents in which Aborigines *speak*, whether in the form of reported speech, which was recorded by journalists (for example, **88**), clerks at government inquiries such as select committees (for example, **9 51** and **112**), or notetakers at deputations and public meetings (for example, **37** and **76**); or in the form of radio and television interviews (for example, **36** and **143**).

We have chosen not to use oral testimony recorded subsequent to the events they represent. Although we are well aware of the strengths of 'oral history' (and autobiography)— for example, in offering new historical information and different perspectives— we are also cognisant of the weaknesses of such sources for understanding the past.[11] As many historians and other scholars have noted, memory is subject to change and, in remembering, narrators often ascribe meaning or significance to past events that they did not have at the time. This means that oral history, like autobiography, can tell us as much about the time of remembering as of the time being remembered. Such testimony also tends to exaggerate the agency of their subjects as they not only tell what they did but also 'what they wanted to do, what they believed they were doing, [and] what they now think they did'.[12] Furthermore, memory is sometimes littered with inconsistencies and distortions. For example, it is particularly unreliable concerning the time of an event as well as relationships between events. It is true that oral informants do recall some matters of the past more accurately than others— for example, material conditions, everyday practices and routine occurrences— but the recall of values, attitudes and feelings is much more changeable over time, as are ideologies that undergo significant change when the social relationships and consciousness, in which they are embedded, alter. This renders oral histories especially problematic for the historical study of past politics.

To illustrate our contentions, one example should suffice. In researching the history of Aboriginal communities in New South Wales in the twentieth century, Heather Goodall was told by an elderly Dhan-gadi man, Jack Campbell, of the protest mounted in the late 1920s by the Australian Aboriginal Progressive Association (AAPA), one of the first Aboriginal organisations to be founded in Australia. Goodall uses Campbell's recollections to support an argument that 'the prime issue' for the AAPA was land: 'They'd only be spruikin' on land rights, that's all, on land rights.' Goodall, sceptical because she had learned a very different chronology for the 'land rights movement', questioned Campbell: 'But they wouldn't have called it "land rights" then, would they.' He replied:

> Of *course* they was callin' it land rights. 'Why hasn't the Aboriginal people got land rights' they said. 'The Aboriginal's cryin' out for land rights.' They were askin' for Aboriginal land, for the land they was *on*! That's when them whites was chuckin' 'em off. There were places around, thirty-five or fifty acres, sixty acres, what Aboriginal people was *on*, growin' potatoes, pumpkin, corn, stuff like that. But the white settlers went into 'em, they'd just run their cattle through their crops, knock it down, destroy it! They only had dog leg fences then. They were pushin' Lang, at that time, for land rights. That's what it was all about, and to break up the Aboriginal Protection Board.[13]

According to Goodall, Campbell 'was an acutely observant man with an extraordinary memory' who could 'recall fine details of events and people from the 1920s and 1930s'.[14] There is no reason to doubt his account of events, for it is corroborated by the documentary record. In 1938, he wrote to the *Australian Abo Call* :

> Our complaint here is that the A[borigines] P[rotection] Board allows white men to run sheep, cattle, and horses, on the Aboriginal Reserve, and they eat all the feed, so we can't keep horses for our children to ride to school. The fences around the reserve are cut and are falling down. Some of us tried to grow vegetables, corn, potatoes by the river-side, but the white people cut down the fences and let their stock in to trample down and eat what we planted with so much labour. All our work is gone for nothing.

However, Campbell's historical *information* or evidence, like that of any informant, can and should be distinguished from what can be called his historical *statements*—his feelings, evaluations, explanations and ideas concerning what happened[15]—which include his insistence that Aborigines at this time were demanding 'land rights'. For, as the documentary evidence discussed by Goodall and other historians of Aboriginal political organisations of the 1930s shows, the dominant political language they used was that of citizenship rights, and while the loss of reserve lands was undoubtedly a major concern, and their return was an important—for many campaigners the paramount—demand, this was never couched in terms of 'land rights'. This term cannot be found in any documentary sources of this period. This is to argue that oral history tends to produce accounts of the past that emphasise its continuity or sameness with the present (demands)—for example, 'land rights'—rather than its discontinuity with or difference to the past (demands)—'citizenship rights'.

The sources reproduced here cover the period from the first recorded Aboriginal campaigns (in the 1830s) to the present day, but there is a slight bias to earlier periods because we presume that these are less well known to readers. Geographically, there are more sources from south-eastern Australia than anywhere else, but this reflects the historical reality of Aboriginal political activity and is not a matter of historical representation.

II

Aborigines have always resisted colonialism in Australia, mostly obviously on the frontier where clans fought the invasion of their lands, and this has been extensively studied by historians in recent decades. In this study of Aboriginal politics, we are concerned with the activity of Aborigines who, having gained some understanding of the British or Australian political system, have consciously had the purpose of effecting change in their conditions of existence by appealing to or applying pressure on that dominant order, whether it be government or other forms of power such as capital, the media or public opinion.

In a general way Aboriginal political activity has existed in an ambiguous relationship with the state and so is shaped by this; but in a more specific sense the parameters of Aboriginal protest have been determined by the nature of colonial regimes. Accordingly we need to sketch the approaches of Australian governments to Aborigines during the nineteenth and twentieth centuries; these have reflected the varying nature of relations between Aborigines and non-Aborigines at any particular time and place, and are influenced by factors such as the relative population ratios, the economic basis of relations, the prevalent ideas and attitudes in Britain and Australia about Aborigines and the locus of governmental power.

In the areas of earliest colonisation— New South Wales, Van Diemen's Land (later Tasmania) and Western Australia— imperial and colonial government showed little interest in Aborigines. However, in the wake of increasing pastoral expansion and the consequent dispossession of Aborigines, humanitarians in Britain (and, to a much lesser degree, in the Australian colonies) called upon government to consider the rights of Aborigines as British subjects.[16] Consequently, in the late 1830s, Aboriginal protectorates were established in South Australia and the Port Phillip District of New South Wales (later Victoria). Yet, by and large, these measures failed to protect the interests of Aborigines, largely because they were opposed by the pastoralists upon whom the colonial economy rested. Indeed, governments colluded in the dispossession of Aborigines in as much as they refused to recognise their ownership of land, failed to protect their rights as British subjects and sanctioned the involvement of paramilitary forces in punitive expeditions, the latter continuing in Queensland, Western Australia and the Northern Territory throughout the rest of the nineteenth century and the early decades of the twentieth century.

By the early 1850s Aboriginal interests in south-eastern Australia were once more being ignored by the state, and this situation was exacerbated by the granting of responsible government to all the colonies except Western Australia, although a resurgence of humanitarian concern later in this decade resulted in both the re-establishment of missions whose task was to 'civilise and Christianise' the indigenes and some government intervention that aimed to protect and care for Aborigines. Both endeavours, informed by paternalism, often worked to control Aborigines and therefore limit or even deny the rights they had previously enjoyed.

The influence of racial ideas and attitudes, which cast Aborigines as a primitive, childlike race that was doomed to 'disappear', deepened in the closing decades of the nineteenth century, and discriminatory legislation was introduced by several mainland colonies or States— Queensland (1897), Western Australia (1905), New South Wales (1909), South Australia (1911)— which was similar to an Act previously passed in Victoria (1869). These Acts established agencies upon which these governments gradually conferred greater regulatory powers, and so they increasingly determined the lot of a growing number of Aborigines in settled areas. Under these Acts, Aborigines lost basic human rights such as freedom of movement and labour, custody of their children, and control over personal property.[17] In remote Australia, the fate of Aborigines was shaped by demand for their land or labour, and so frontiersmen— rather than government and the rule of law— determined race relations.

The protective and restrictive controls of Aborigines reached a climax in the 1930s, and the post-war era saw the adoption of policies of absorption or assimilation that had first been advocated prior to the war. These policies had, as their premise, the potential of Aborigines, or at least those of mixed descent, to become the same as 'white Australians'. This, among other factors, led to the gradual dismantling of the discriminatory laws, beginning with Victoria in 1957. By the mid-1960s, though, assimilation had fallen into such disfavour in many circles that integration was being advocated, only, in its turn, to be challenged by calls for Aboriginal rights and self-determination.

In considering Aboriginal politics, therefore, we need to bear in mind that considerable variations in government policy and practice and the nature of relations between Aborigines and colonisers could be found between and within colonies, states and territories. For example, in the 1870s and 1880s Aborigines in South Australia and

New South Wales were petitioning government for grants of land, in Victoria they were protesting to retain land previously reserved, in Queensland many were resisting the invasion of their lands, and in the Northern Territory and much of Western Australia most had yet to come into contact with the colonisers.

III

In terms of our definition of Aboriginal politics, the story of Aboriginal protest begins in the mid-1840s, when Aborigines in Van Diemen's Land petitioned colonial and imperial government. That it began there, and continued in the other south-eastern Australian colonies in the latter nineteenth century, is hardly surprising, for these areas of early 'settlement' were not only the ones where Aborigines had been subject to the most rapid and extensive dispossession of their lands but also those where they had been most exposed to new cultural and political influences that gave rise to resources that they could use to protest their fate.

Like Aboriginal protest throughout much of the twentieth century this was intensely local in its focus. It involved Aborigines of a local place or 'country' who, while they often fought in the name of Aborigines in the sense of being the original inhabitants, focused upon their own needs and did not struggle for the interests and rights of other Aborigines (of a colony, state or nation). One should note, though, that a change in Aboriginal consciousness was occurring, in as much as they were beginning to protest in the name of blacks or Aborigines of a colonial formation—for example, a mission station or reserve, as evident at Coranderrk in the 1880s—rather than that of a pre-colonial formation such as a tribe. Likewise, their demands were highly particular: calling for land for themselves or retention of land previously reserved for their use; help to develop that land; better living conditions; and self-government or at least governance sympathetic to their interests. These demands were seldom part of a more general policy or programme that looked forward to or anticipated what they had never had.

By the same token, these protesters were anything but local in the principles (or ideals) which they articulated. Rather, they couched their demands in terms of a widely held political language. This took one or other of two forms although often assumed both. Aborigines legitimised their call for change on *historical* grounds, by reference to their prior occupation of the land of the colony (or state), demanding land and other rights on the basis of that Aboriginality.

In doing so, they often appealed to earlier agreements or promises they believed government had entered into with them but which now had been broken; for example, Aborigines on Flinders Island referred to 'an agreement [to be treated as freemen] which we have not lost from our minds', and at Coranderrk they claimed the reserve had been granted to them by Queen Victoria. Moreover, these protesters rejected any suggestion that they were paupers or slaves who received charity from government, claiming instead that what they received or should receive was just compensation for being dispossessed of their land.

Aborigines, however, did not always speak this language of difference; instead (or sometimes simultaneously) they called for the same ('equal') rights as other human beings— as British subjects, for example— which had no reference to history. So, for example, Aborigines claiming land often articulated their demands in terms of their ability to use land productively and make themselves self-supporting, or questioned their exclusion from the vote on the basis of their being qualified to exercise it wisely like any other citizen.

Whatever the political language these local protesters spoke, though, it is clear they were very familiar with the political discourses of the day. This suggests that such protests often rested on the literacy that some Aborigines had acquired through their intensive contact with missionaries and other teachers. Aborigines involved in protest in the nineteenth century were avid readers of newspapers and so were well informed about colonial politics and, in time, of the protests of Aborigines in other places, thus learning something of how to articulate their demands. More especially, though, the leaders of these local protests tended to be young men and women who often owed their training in politics to Christian missions and/or the protectors who had schooled them in the tenets of humanitarianism and liberalism.

Yet, while the leaders of these protests were invariably of the younger generation the authority they had to represent their people did not always originate in their privileged relationship to the new colonial order, but often depended instead on their connection to the Aboriginal one in the sense that their role was sanctioned by Aboriginal tradition. Such leaders possessed traditional authority, then, at the same time as they had also acquired another manner of seeing and speaking that enabled them to communicate Aborigines' wishes in ways colonial governments could understand.

In their modes of protest these Aborigines were also adept in their use of colonial politics. Much of this consisted of writing letters and petitions to colonial government and forming deputations to wait upon ministers and sympathetic politicians. Another tactic was to appeal to another source of authority, such as the Queen, as Aborigines on Flinders Island did in 1846. But Aborigines also resorted to less legalistic means of protest. For example, Aborigines at Coranderrk went on strike on several occasions during the 1870s and 1880s. In the former mode, white allies were very important, either in advising Aborigines, providing access to politicians, helping to formulate demands or offering refuge to expelled 'troublemakers'.

IV

In the 1920s and 1930s the first Aboriginal political organisations, several of which connected Aboriginal communities over large areas, were founded in New South Wales, Western Australia, Victoria and South Australia: the AAPA, the Native Union, the AAL, the Australian Aborigines Association (AAA), the Euralian Association, and the Aborigines Progressive Association (APA). Most of these organisations had elected office bearers and committees and other trappings of formal organisations, such as constitutions, and were similar in many respects.[18]

Like the nineteenth-century protests we have discussed, their preoccupations could be intensely local. The Euralian Association, for instance, was an expression of the concerns of ' half-castes' in PortHedland, Western Australia. However, most also had a broader focus which at the very least was regional— for instance the mid-north coast of New South Wales for the AAPA and the south-west of Western Australia for the Native Union— and at most was state-wide or even, as in the case of the AAL and the APA, national. The AAL, for instance, developed different policies for Aborigines in settled and remote Australia, sought to establish links with other organisations and Aborigines all over Australia, and made representations to a number of state governments as well as to the Commonwealth; however, like the other organisations, it was not truly national and reflected the grievances of Aborigines 'under the Act' in Victoria, New South Wales and south-west Western Australia. The AAL, therefore, was unable to effectively fight for the interests of Aborigines in northern Australia where the oppressors were not so much government 'protectors' as the bosses of cattle stations. The broadening focus of Aboriginal politics which was none the less evident in organisations like the AAL indicated the increasingly common historical experience of colonialism which many Aboriginal communities had, and the manner in which they were shaping a shared consciousness or identity on that basis.

Where their focus was local and regional, one of the principal concerns of the south-eastern Australian organisations was the removal of children and the retention and development of reserve lands, although, especially with the later bodies such as the APA, the demand for land was usually made on the basis of equal rather than different rights. Moreover, especially in other contexts, the more prominent part of their policy programmes was a demand for citizenship rights and uplift. As a general principle, they argued that Aborigines should be accorded the same political rights, legal position, access to special service benefits and educational opportunities as other Australians. They criticised the protectionist policies and practices of government and rejected, at least in part, the racial assumptions upon which these were based; attacked discriminatory legislation and government control over Aborigines' lives; and called upon the Commonwealth to take over control from the states and introduce a uniform policy—a new deal—which would allow and help Aborigines take their place in society alongside other Australians.

Yet, few, if any, of these organisations should not be seen as assimilationist or absorptionist, since, however much they sought integration and were 'modernist' rather than 'traditionalist' in their outlook, they expressed, albeit inconsistently, a vision of an ongoing state of (Aboriginal) difference. Furthermore, although the dominant trend of political rhetoric of these organisations was liberal and non-racial, there was also another voice that emphasised different rights and made claims on the basis of Aborigines being the indigenous race. This was especially so for the AAPA but also for the AAL. For example, Cooper asserted that 'morally' the land belonged to the Aborigines for they were 'the original owners', and he argued that they were 'entitled to a quid pro quo for the loss of their lands and liberty'. He and other leaders also questioned the legitimacy of the Australian nation and its citizens' 'nationality', as is evident in the following phenomenon: The names Cooper contemplated for his organisation—the Real Australian Aboriginal Society, the Real Australian Natives Society and the Australian Aborigines' League; William Ferguson and Jack Patten's proclamation in 1938 that Aborigines were 'the old Australians'; the AAL's call for representation for Aborigines in the Commonwealth parliament; and the highly symbolic Day of Mourning to mark Australia's sesquicentenary in January 1938. In this regard it is important to

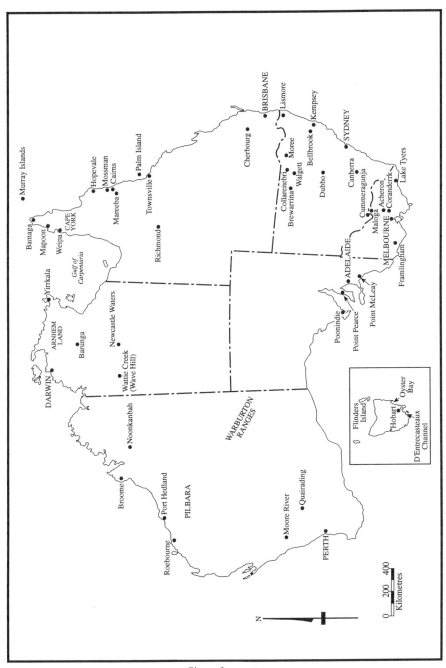

Sites of protest

note that the major organisations of this period restricted full membership to persons 'possessing some degree of Aboriginal blood'; non-Aborigines could join as associate members and were eligible for elected office, but it was held that officeholders should be full members.

Like the local protests discussed earlier, these Aboriginal organisations naturally drew upon and were influenced by the dominant Australian discourses of the day, and they formed alliances with non-Aborigines and non-Aboriginal organisations. All were familiar with the ideals of Christian humanitarianism, British liberal democracy, and/or socialism; and, as we shall see, they were supported by non-Aboriginal men and women in organisations which espoused these ideals. These organisations largely campaigned by means of writing letters and forming delegations to politicians— both state and national— but also by sending letters and petitions to the imperial monarch. In addition, they sought to awaken a sense of responsibility in the general community through writing letters to newspapers and holding meetings. The AAL and the APA also approached other organisations and tried to unify the work of these pressure groups, and appealed to white organisations for help in their struggle. On one notable occasion— a walk-off at Cummeragunja reserve in New South Wales in 1939— these methods were abandoned or suspended by campaigners frustrated by the lack of progress, and direct action was adopted although the walk-off caused divisions within and between the Aboriginal organisations involved.

All these organisations' leaders had travelled, worked and lived in the general community for much of their lives and had largely escaped the oppressive special laws that affected reserve dwellers and others in South Australia, Western Australia, New South Wales and Victoria, although they themselves eventually fell foul of these laws either before or as they took up the fight on behalf of those with less opportunity to do so. Like earlier leaders, these men tended to be mission educated, but now their authority as spokespersons had no traditional basis. However, they all had strong historical links to earlier experiences of oppression and political resistance and, in some cases, such as William Cooper, had been involved in that political action themselves.

The influence on government of these Aboriginal political organisations was negligible— even the protest which is most celebrated today, the 1938 Day of Mourning, had little impact. Of somewhat greater importance was the work of non-Aboriginal organisations and individuals, who either exclusively devoted themselves to Aboriginal matters or who included Aborigines within their range of concerns. From the 1930s, there were a growing number of activists interested in Aborigines, and they ranged across the political spectrum.

The oldest active organisation was the Association for the Protection of Native Races (APNR)—formerly the Association for the Protection of the Native Races of Australasia and Polynesia—which was formed in 1911 when the Commonwealth assumed control over the Northern Territory. The APNR had the objective of persuading the federal government to extend its responsibility to Aborigines throughout the country, but it only began to focus on Aborigines after it was revived in 1927. Its main supporters were members of the Protestant clerical establishment; for example, its long-term secretary, William Morley, was a Congregational minister. It had links with the London-based Anti-Slavery and Aborigines' Protection Society, which, under the guidance of Archdeacon L.E.C. Lefroy, one of the founders of the APNR, took a growing interest in Australia from the late 1920s. Its main focus was on the conditions of Aborigines in Northern Australia, and it drew attention to the massacres and other shocking abuses there in the late 1920s and early 1930s. Soon after, though, influenced by the anthropologist A.P. Elkin, it turned its attention to calling for a 'positive policy' of 'uplift' for Aborigines (see below).

The APNR was more radical than other similarly small, humanitarian organisations, such as the Aborigines' Friends' Association (AFA), founded in South Australia in 1858, the Victorian Aboriginal Group, the Aboriginal Fellowship Group and the Aborigines' Uplift Society—all founded in Melbourne in 1929, 1932 and 1937 respectively—and the Australian Aborigines Ameliorative Association, established in Perth in 1932. They differed in their objectives and methods, but all had a similar emphasis—Aboriginal protection and uplift. Women such as Helen Baillie in Melbourne and Constance Ternent Cooke in Adelaide were prominent in many of these organisations, and in the 1920s and 1930s feminists and women's organisations, such as the Australian Federation of Women Voters, the Australian Women's Service League, the Victorian Women Citizens Movement and the Women's Non-Party Association of South Australia, took an interest in Aborigines. Some of these women had close relations with the British Commonwealth League and the Anti-Slavery Society, and/or with Aboriginal people themselves. Particularly important were the Western Australian missionary Mary Bennett and the feminist Bessie

Rischbieth. These activists, while living in Australia and Britain, campaigned vigorously for rights for Aborigines, often, like Morley, condemning their situation as being one of slavery still. They particularly attacked the sexual exploitation of Aboriginal women by white frontiersmen and the removal of children from their Aboriginal mothers, and argued that Aboriginal women should be provided with protectors who were white women. They sometimes won considerable attention in the London press and they made good use of their connections with organisations there.[19]

Similarly radical was the Aborigines' Protection League of South Australia. This was established in 1925 when Colonel J.C. Genders, a member of committee of the AFA, failed to win that organisation's support for a proposal that emphasised the need for Aboriginal autonomy. An idealist and a romantic, Genders drew up a petition to the Commonwealth in 1927 which proposed an experimental Aboriginal state. He recommended that Arnhem Land be reserved for this, and, if it proved successful, that states be established in other areas where traditional Aboriginal life remained intact and territory be allocated in the south for detribalised Aborigines. Genders further urged that Aborigines in the model state be granted self-government (at some unspecified time in the future); represented in all inquiries dealing with Aboriginal Affairs; and given special representation in the Commonwealth Parliament. As well as obtaining firm backing from members of the AAA, Genders' league attracted the support of a SA Member of Parliament, the anthropologist Dr Herbert Basedow.

From the late 1920s, anthropologists assumed an influential role in Aboriginal affairs, following in the footsteps of the Australasian Association for the Advancement of Science, which had helped found the APNR and had lobbied Government in 1913,[20] and Baldwin Spencer who had advised the Commonwealth government and had served as Chief Protector of Aborigines in the Northern Territory in 1912. Anthropologists argued that government policy should be based on a sound and sympathetic understanding of their culture, which their science could best provide.[21] The most important figure was A.P. Elkin, who assumed the only Australian professorship in Anthropology in 1933 and was elected to the presidency of the APNR in 1934. He was a vigorous campaigner for a positive and uniform policy that would replace the existing fragmented approach which, he believed, consisted 'merely [of] protective measures' that were 'not aimed at advancing the race'.[22]

Elkin became a powerful voice for a policy of assimilation and a trusted adviser to the Commonwealth government.

Elkin had rivals, though, for the ear of government or public opinion: Professor Frederick Wood-Jones of the University of Melbourne, formerly Curator of Anthropology at the South Australian Museum and an outspoken critic of the treatment of Aborigines who attracted much publicity in Australia and Britain in 1937;[23] Donald Thomson, who was commissioned by the Commonwealth government in 1935 to report on problems among Aborigines in Arnhem Land; J.B. Cleland; Norman Tindale; and Olive Pink. They all advocated absolute racial segregation for Aborigines in remote Australia, insisting that physical survival and cultural preservation could only be achieved by creating large inviolable reserves where they could be isolated from contact with Europeans.[24]

These proposals had something in common with the policy of the Communist Party of Australia (CPA) and were strongly endorsed by one prominent trade union official, Tom Wright, vice-president of the New South Wales Labour Council, in a 1939 pamphlet *New Deal for the Aborigines*. In 1931 the CPA, in keeping with the dictates of the Communist International, adopted a fourteen-point programme on Aborigines that included: a call for the abolition of all forms of forced labour; equal wages; abolition of the Aboriginal Protection Boards; the restoration to Aborigines of central, northern and north-west Australia with the rights of independent republics; and the development of Aboriginal culture. Socialists were also active in the 1930s, none more so than Michael Sawtell in Sydney, whose Committee for Aboriginal Citizenship was a critic of the New South Wales Aborigines Protection Board and an advocate for full citizenship rights for Aborigines, and which provided important support for Ferguson's APA.

The role of these white activists and organisations in fighting for rights for Aborigines both helped and hindered the cause of Aboriginal campaigners. On the one hand, their support was crucial, since in many areas of Australia at this time, and indeed for many decades to come, Aborigines lacked the necessary financial resources and were not free to engage in political activity or paid a heavy price for doing so; those living on reserves and dependent on government provision were especially hamstrung as they could be expelled from, refused permission to leave, or ordered on to another reserve. For example, Caleb and Anna Morgan were forced off Cummeragunja in 1907, and Jack and George Patten were arrested and charged in 1939 for inciting Aborigines to leave the same reserve; two of the Aboriginal leaders of the 1946 Pilbara stockworkers' strike were imprisoned for inciting their fellow workers to leave their employment; and Fred Waters was exiled to Haasts Bluff in 1951 after organising a strike in Darwin. In other states, such as Queensland, the reserve system was so repressive that it largely prevented political activity, and those who did protest risked being incarcerated on Palm Island. Where Aboriginal activists were not been nobbled by government 'Protection' Boards or 'Protectors', they had to conduct themselves under the surveillance of the state; for example, Cooper was visited by a detective acting for the Commonwealth Investigation Branch in December 1937; and the Day of Mourning on 26 January 1938 was watched by police. On the other hand, white support often led to government claims that Aboriginal protests were inauthentic or unrepresentative, the work of outside, non-Aboriginal agitators or disaffected Aborigines who did not speak for their people. More problematically, white supporters often failed to listen to or respect the wishes and aspirations of Aboriginal activists and the communities they represented, and sought to impose their own political ideals and programmes on them.

V

In the post-war decades local and regional political action continued much along the lines described already. In as much as there were differences, these can be found in the tactics used and alliances exploited by campaigners, and the growing assertiveness with which they expressed their demands. Causes of spectacular injustice— atomic bomb testing in 1946–47, malnutrition in the Warburton Ranges in 1957, and the trial of painter Albert Namatjira in 1958— were vigorously protested. What came to be called the 'Freedom Ride' in NSW in 1965, which involved picketing clubs, swimming pools and picture theatres, is the best example of this change. Influenced by new models—Martin Luther King, the civil rights movement and the new left in American politics—and working with new and old allies—students and communists—the direct action of Charles Perkins and Student Action for Aborigines received publicity that no previous protest had won. The main point of departure in the post-war era, which was evident by the mid-1960s, arose from the foundation of national organisations, deepening relationships between Aboriginal communities, and a change in

Aboriginal consciousness, and lay in a re-working of the relationship between Aborigines and the Australian state.

One of the most significant developments in the 1950s and 1960s was the founding— in February 1958— of a national organisation, the leftist Federal Council for Aboriginal Advancement (FCAA). A previous attempt to found such an organisation, involving the AAL and the CPA, among others, had failed in 1946–47, and a left-wing organisation, the Council for Aboriginal Rights (CAR)— founded in Melbourne in 1951— been unable to achieve either of its goals: to work out a common 'national policy upon matters involving the living conditions, rights and aspirations of aboriginal people throughout Australia'; and to 'plan, conduct and organise widest possible support for a campaign to obtain justice for all Australian aborigines'.[25] The FCAA, which soon became the most important voice in Aboriginal politics, was led by leaders of its principal affiliate organisations: the Victorian Aborigines Advancement League; CAR; the Aboriginal-Australian Fellowship (AAF); and the Queensland advancement leagues. Although it was dominated by non-Aborigines, it was nonetheless a multiracial organisation which always had Aboriginal leaders, such as Joe McGinness and Kath Walker, and which tried to include and promote Aboriginal perspectives.

In the beginning, the FCAA's programme was largely a non-racial one which emphasised equal (citizenship) rights rather than different or special (Aboriginal) rights for Aborigines; and it is best remembered for its campaign for constitutional change which culminated in the 1967 referendum on clauses in the constitution held to be discriminatory, and which paved the way for a greater Commonwealth role in Aboriginal affairs. It also mounted vigorous campaigns to: repeal the discriminatory legislation enacted in the late nineteenth and early twentieth centuries; to extend and/or restore the right to Aborigines to vote; claim entitlement to welfare benefits; and achieve wage equality for pastoral workers.

What is often overlooked, however, is the way in which the FCAA's agenda underwent change in the 1960s. From its very foundation, there was questioning within the Council of the ideal of assimilation, which the Commonwealth and state governments had adopted as their goal for Aborigines, as Aboriginal leaders asserted their desire to retain their Aboriginality. For example, Doug Nicholls— Cooper's youthful protégé in the AAL in the 1930s— stated in 1958 that Aborigines 'wanted integration, not assimilation'; 'we want to integrate but we want to identify ourselves as a people ...

[We] are fighting to keep ourselves as a people'.[26] Such criticisms of assimilation took root in the early 1960s and influenced organisations like the multi-racial AAF (founded in 1956) so that it changed its original goals as set out in its constitution, as did non-Aboriginal organisations like CAR and the National Missionary Council.[27] In this context, the AAL and APA were revived, thus enabling a stronger expression of Aboriginal voices.

The attack upon assimilation deepened when the Federal Council, led by its first Aboriginal president, Joe McGinness, took up the question of land in 1962-63 in both south-eastern and northern Australia, where governments were trying to force Aborigines off, or diminish, reserves such as Lake Tyers, Mapoon and Yirrkala, in the name of assimilation or economic development. From 1963, at first slowly, then more quickly from 1966-67— when a strike by cattle station workers at Wave Hill in the Northern Territory became a claim for land— the primary focus of Aboriginal politics began to shift away from the ideal of rights for Aborigines as Australian citizens to that of *Aboriginal* rights, the rights of Aborigines as the *Aboriginal* peoples of this continent. For the first time the long-held Aboriginal demand for land was couched in terms of 'land rights'. Whereas previously land had been a concern held and mostly presented at a local or regional level and was marginal to the Aboriginal politics articulated in the metropolitan centres by the major organisations, it now moved from the periphery to become central to Aboriginal politics on the national stage.

At the same time, a major change in Aboriginal consciousness and identity was taking place in association with this, nurtured by the annual national conferences and other networks of the FCAA (which became the Federal Council for the Advancement of Aborigines and Torres Strait Islanders— FCAATSI— in 1964) and improved means of communication. This had a two-fold effect: first, Aborigines across Australia came to have a much greater sense of themselves as a common national group— 'Aboriginal Australians' or 'the First Australians'— with a shared historical experience of oppression; and, second, they came to see themselves as having a shared culture, which was increasingly defined and represented in terms of 'tradition'. This was a process by which the attenuated sense of Aboriginality of Aborigines in settled Australia was renewed or revived through their contact with traditionally-oriented Aborigines in remote areas.

These changes had, in turn, a major impact on the policies and aims of Aboriginal organisations and their relationships with non-

Aboriginal campaigners. For example, in 1968, FCAATSI launched a major national land rights campaign and, in 1968–69, a split emerged within the organisation over the question of who should have power to determine policy—Aborigines (or blacks) or whites—with a breakaway organisation, the National Tribal Council (NTC), in which old-time campaigners Doug Nicholls and Kath Walker were prominent, being formed in 1970, followed by the founding of the Black Panthers of Australia.

There were many similarities between the policy programmes of these 'black power' organisations, on the one hand, and FCAATSI, on the other, but there were also differences. For instance, the protesters who established a 'tent embassy' outside the Commonwealth Parliament in January 1972 not only demanded national land rights and compensation, as FCAATSI had, but also called for recognition of Aboriginal sovereignty. The main differences between the new and the older organisations lay in the methods of protest, their leadership and the language and symbolism they used. Organisations like the Black Panthers and those responsible for the Tent Embassy, for example, had little patience with the legalistic methods long used by their predecessors, preferring more direct protest (emulating the radical political movements in the United States and Europe), such as vigils and sit-ins. The new leaders were much younger and more aggressive, rejected white leadership and tended to spurn association with white organisations such as trade unions and the churches. Their language was more militant, filled with demands rather than requests, and, like the symbols they adopted, was expressive of their difference—their identity as indigenous people. For example, an Aboriginal flag was raised at the Tent Embassy, and 'traditional' headbands were donned elsewhere. This black militancy won considerable attention on the national and even the international stage, although their organisations were relatively shortlived and the shift to black power and indigenous rights severely weakened FCAATSI and its affiliate organisations; the AAF, for example, was disbanded as early as 1969 and the Council itself soon became a pale shadow of its former self.

VI

In the early and mid-1970s, the coming to power of a party undertaking 'to restore to Aboriginal people ... their lost power of self-determination' heralded two major changes in the nature of Aboriginal politics: first, the pressure which Aboriginal political organisations (led

by FCAATSI) had striven to place on government reached a peak, and
the recent wave of black power confrontation receded; and, second,
the struggle for equal rights through the repeal of discriminatory laws,
which had been such an important dimension of Aboriginal political
activity since the 1930s, attained its goal, and the fight for special rights
for Aborigines— whether as disadvantaged Australians or as
indigenes— took its place.

The Whitlam government's major programme for reform— and it is
an approach that has largely been pursued by its successors— worked
to channel Aboriginal political activity in a new direction. This
occurred through the creation of the first Ministry of Aboriginal
Affairs, establishment of Aboriginal Community Services, and the
formation of the National Aboriginal Consultative Committee
(NACC). These initiatives saw the beginning of a process (which has
continued over the last two and more decades) in which many
Aborigines, including leaders such as Charles Perkins, have been
increasingly incorporated into a bureaucracy where they have been
charged with the task of implementing government policy; others
have been absorbed by the demands of managing organisations which
service the needs of Aboriginal communities; and still more have been
embroiled in the consultative processes of nationwide bodies— the
NACC and its successors, the National Aboriginal Conference (NAC)
and the Aboriginal and Torres Strait Islander Commission (ATSIC).
In government eyes the main purposes of the latter bodies have been
merely advisory or/and administrative and so they have been denied
the authority that would provide them with the autonomy and power
which might make self-determination a reality.

As a result, Aboriginal politics have been brought into an
extraordinarily dependent relationship with Australian government,
itself a dimension of a much wider phenomenon that has been called
'welfare colonialism', a term which deliberately juxtaposes citizenship
and its denial. Aborigines and their representatives have been accorded
a place in the Australian polity through the policy of self-
determination, but the regime of the last twenty or so years— which
has been solicitous rather than exploitative and liberal rather than
repressive— has largely remained a colonial one since government
continues to control the future of Aborigines, and does so in
accordance with its own political, cultural and economic agendas.[28]
Aboriginal leaders have therefore been shackled by an increasing
incapacity to disengage from the government structures and funding in
which they have been enmeshed.

A marker of this political weakness is the absence of any new Aboriginal political body which could assume the crucial role of a national organisation like FCAATSI, capable of coordinating the various demands of disparate Aboriginal communities and independent enough to represent these to government. In the place of such an organisation Aboriginal politics have, to some degree, returned to the regional focus which characterised earlier activity, as betokened by the representation of Aboriginal identity in terms of traditional clan names such as Wiradjeri, and generic terms like Koori and Murri. It has been bodies like the Tasmanian Aboriginal Centre and the Northern and Central Land Councils that have proven to be the most important political agencies during the last two decades. They have provided new Aboriginal leaders and there have been coalitions of these bodies and community service organisations. Unfortunately the former have been unable to command nationwide Aboriginal support and the coalitions have only proven to be loose federations that have not been able to perform the roles of a truly national political force.

Since the early 1970s there has been a growing shift in Aboriginal politics towards the presentation of indigenous rights. This emphasis on the rights of Aborigines as the descendants of the Aboriginal inhabitants of the continent has placed enormous importance on history and, in turn, on a closely related form of power, the law. History has necessarily been central to this politics of identity since Aborigines have, quite evidently, been making claims regarding both the precolonial and the colonial past. Land has not been the only focus of this assertion of indigenous rights. There has been an emphasis on the materials of the past which are seen to constitute Aborigines' heritage and, as a result, there has been a struggle with institutions and practitioners perceived to have a stranglehold on 'the remains of the past'—the museums and archives who house them, and archaeologists, anthropologists, linguists and historians who have studied them. In Tasmania, for example, Rosalind Langford and other Aboriginal community leaders have fought to regain custodianship of Truganini's bones and other human and non-human remains.

Aborigines have looked to the courts to prove many of their historical claims and challenge those of the colonial state. In the most notable case the Meriam people won recognition of their native title in the High Court (the Mabo case, 1982–92), thus overturning the doctrine that the Australian was *terra nullius*—a land belonging to no one—and thereby provoked a major crisis amongst conservatives in Australia. More fundamentally, however, there have been challenges to Australian sovereignty, made by those like Paul Coe who took a case to the High Court in 1978.

Such challenges have been central to the programme of the most radical organisation of the last decade or so, the Aboriginal Provisional Government, founded by Michael Mansell in 1990, but other Aboriginal leaders and organisations have also considered matters relating to sovereignty. For example, the NAC proposed a treaty or makarrata in 1979; ATSIC has sought constitutional changes which range from recognition of the prior ownership of the continent by Aborigines and Torres Strait Islanders to the entrenchment of indigenous rights such as native title; and Aborigines, such as Galarrwuy Yunupingu, have been before the courts in cases involving the status of customary law.

Where recourse to the law and other governmental avenues of address have proved unsuccessful, or hopes of progress through governmental programmes have been disappointed, frustrated Aboriginal activists have turned to international forums like the United Nations and the World Council of Indigenous Peoples, as well as to contacts with countries such as China and Libya. Activists pursue these options either to embarrass Australian governments in the eyes of the world or to persuade national governments or international bodies to lobby the federal government. Both approaches can be powerful levers, because Australia seeks to present an image of a racially equal, multicultural nation to the world, and seems to rely on the apparent assent of its Aboriginal subjects.

As this reveals, however, the capacity of Aboriginal people to influence the Australian political process remains limited. Comprising less than two per cent of the population and lacking economic power, Aborigines and Torres Strait Islanders are dependent on both the goodwill of non-Aboriginal Australians and the politics of representation necessary to achieve this. In this regard, large symbolic gestures—largely based on an appeal to abstract matters such as equality and righting the wrongs of the past—assume enormous significance, as the 1967 referendum and the recent question of an apology to 'the stolen generations' reveal, since they provide the underpinning that is necessary for more substantive forms of progress.[29]

In recent decades, an Aboriginality associated with the notion of ancient heritage has been increasingly important to Australian nationalism and so the subject of much appropriation. This has also created a window of opportunity which Aboriginal activists would otherwise not have. Where the valorisation of this ancient heritage has been connected to a better understanding of the last 200 years of Aboriginal history, as was the case with the Keating government, there has been an opportunity for Aboriginal leaders who have been willing to enter into negotiations in order to make some gains for their people.

However, where governments are unsympathetic to Aboriginal interests and other groups are determined to protect their own special interests, many Australians seem to turn against the interests of Aboriginal people. In part, this is probably because they have little historical experience of Aborigines wielding power or any memory of satisfactory co-existence, and so are dismayed by and fearful of the former and sceptical of achieving the latter. Almost certainly they lack the historical knowledge that might enable them to recognise the justness of Aboriginal claims which have long been made in the political arena.

NOTES

1 See Bain Attwood and Andrew Markus (with Dale Edwards and Kate Schilling), *The 1967 Referendum, Or When Aborigines Didn't Get the Vote*, Aboriginal Studies Press, Canberra, 1997, especially chapter 8.
2 By comparison, most Pakeha New Zealanders, for example, would be able to name several Maori leaders.
3 There were notable exceptions but, significantly, the authors were not academically trained historians. The anthropologist Diane Barwick undertook an excellent study of Coranderrk and Cummeragunja ('Rebellion at Coranderrk', seminar paper, Research School of Pacific Studies, Australian National University, 1969, and 'Coranderrk and Cumeroogunga: Pioneers and Policy', in T. Scarlett Epstein and David H. Penny (eds), *Opportunity and Response: Case Studies in Economic Development*, David Hirst, London, 1972, pp. 15–68), and a white activist Jack Horner wrote a fine biography of the Aboriginal leader Bill Ferguson (*Vote Ferguson for Aboriginal Freedom*, Australia and New Zealand Book Co, Sydney, 1974).
4 Henry Reynolds (ed.), *Aborigines and Settlers: The Australian Experience 1788–1939*, Cassell Australia, Melbourne, 1972; cf. Henry Reynolds (ed.),

Dispossession: Black Australians and White Invaders, Allen & Unwin, Sydney, 1989.

5   Henry Reynolds, *The Other Side of the Frontier: An Interpretation of the Aboriginal Response to the Invasion and Settlement of Australia*, Department of History, James Cook University, Townsville, 1981, Penguin, Melbourne, 1982. For a discussion of this shift, see Bain Attwood, 'Aboriginal History', in John A. Moses (ed.), *Historical Disciplines in Australasia: Themes, Problems and Debates*, a special issue of *The Australian Journal of Politics and History*, vol. 41, 1995, pp. 36–38.

6   Heather Goodall, *Invasion to Embassy: Land in Aboriginal Politics in New South Wales, 1770–1972*, Allen & Unwin/Black Books, Sydney, 1996; Anna Haebich, *For Their Own Good: Aborigines and Government in the Southwest of Western Australia, 1900–1940*, University of Western Australia Press, Nedlands, 1988, pp. 125–27, 267–76; Andrew Markus, *Blood From a Stone: William Cooper and the Australian Aborigines' League*, Allen & Unwin, Sydney, 1988, and *Governing Savages*, Allen & Unwin, Sydney, 1990, chapters 10–12; Peter Read, *Charles Perkins: A Biography*, Viking, Melbourne, 1990; Henry Reynolds, *Fate of a Free People*, Penguin, Melbourne, 1995; Su-Jane Hunt, 'The Gribble Affair: A Study in Colonial Politics', in Bob Reece and Tom Stannage (eds), *European–Aboriginal Relations in Western Australian History: Studies in Western Australian History*, vol. VIII, 1984, pp. 42–51; Jack Horner and Marcia Langton, 'The Day of Mourning', in Bill Gammage and Peter Spearritt (eds), *Australians 1938*, Fairfax, Syme & Weldon, Sydney, 1987, pp. 28–35; Erich Kolig, *The Noonkanbah Story*, University of Otago Press, Dunedin, 1987; Peter Read, ' "Cheeky, Insolent and Anti-White": The Split in the Federal Council for the Advancement of Aboriginal and Torres Strait Islanders—Easter 1970', *Australian Journal of Politics and History*, vol. 36, no. 1, 1990, pp. 73–83, and 'Aboriginal Rights', in Heather Radi (ed.), *Jessie Street: Documents and Essays*, Women's Redress Press, Sydney, 1990, pp. 259–66; Russell McGregor, 'Protest and Progress: Aboriginal Activism in the 1930s', *Australian Historical Studies*, vol. 25, no. 101, 1993, pp. 555–68; Michael Hess, 'Black and Red: the Pilbara Pastoral Workers' Strike, 1946', *Aboriginal History*, vol. 18, no. 1, 1994, pp. 65–83; S. Robinson, 'The Aboriginal Embassy: An Account of the Protests of 1972', *Aboriginal History*, vol. 18, no. 1, 1994, pp. 49–63; Noel Loos and Koiki Mabo, *Edward Koiki Mabo: His Life and Struggle for Land Rights*, University of Queensland Press, St Lucia, 1996; Attwood and Markus, *The 1967 Referendum*.

7   Frank Hardy, *The Unlucky Australians*, Thomas Nelson, Melbourne, 1968; Mavis Clark, *Pastor Doug: The Story of Sir Douglas Nicholls*, revised edn, Lansdowne Press, Melbourne, 1972; Charles Perkins, *A Bastard Like Me*, Ure Smith, Sydney, 1975; Kingsley Palmer and Clancy McKenna, *Somewhere Between Black and White: The Story of an Aboriginal Australian*, MacMillan, Melbourne, 1978; Edgar Wells, *Reward and Punishment in*

Arnhem Land, 1962-1963, Australian Institute of Aboriginal Studies, Canberra, 1982; Faith Bandler and Len Fox, *The Time Was Ripe: A History of the Aboriginal-Australian Fellowship*, Alternative Publishing Co-op, Chippendale, 1983; Don McLeod, *How the West Was Lost: The Native Question in the Development of Western Australia*, The author, Port Hedland, 1984; Faith Bandler, *Turning the Tide: A Personal History of the Federal Council for the Advancement of Aborigines and Torres Strait Islanders*, Aboriginal Studies Press, Canberra, 1989; Steve Hawke and Michael Gallagher, *Noonkanbah: Whose Land, Whose Law*, Fremantle Arts Centre Press, Fremantle, 1989; Joe McGinness, *Son of Alyandabu: My Fight for Aboriginal Rights*, University of Queensland Press, St Lucia, 1991; Roberta Sykes, *Snake Dancing*, Allen & Unwin, Sydney, 1998.

8   Political scientists Charles Rowley, Scott Bennett and Christine Fletcher have surveyed the relationship between Aborigines and government (*Recovery: The Politics of Aboriginal Reform*, Penguin, Melbourne, 1986; *Aborigines and Political Power*, Allen & Unwin, Sydney, 1989; *Aboriginal Politics: Intergovernmental Relations*, Melbourne University Press, Melbourne, 1992).

9   Reynolds, *Aborigines and Settlers*; *Dispossession*; *Frontier: Aborigines, Settlers and Land*, Allen & Unwin, Sydney, 1987, *The Law of the Land*, Penguin, Melbourne, 1987; *This Whispering in Our Hearts*, Allen & Unwin, Sydney, 1998; Richard Broome, 'Historians, Aborigines and Australia: Writing the National Past', in Bain Attwood (ed.), *In the Age of Mabo: History, Aborigines and Australia*, Allen & Unwin, Sydney, 1996, p. 55.

10 There has been a tendency among historians in the field of Aboriginal history to both minimise and exaggerate the problems of historical sources—to overstate the lack of Aboriginal sources and to simplify the problems we have in deciphering their significance. Reynolds is a case in point. In *The Other Side of the Frontier* he writes: 'Initially I was convinced, like many previous Australian scholars, that such a study would be impossible to consummate, that the evidence was too fragmentary to sustain serious scholarship ... I became convinced that [this proposition was] awry and in fact [it] gave way ... as the evidence piled up as slowly and inexorably as a sand-drift ... It is clear, now, that the boundaries of Australian historiography can be pushed back to encompass the other side of the frontier. Stretches of difficult country remain but they will become increasingly accessible to our scholarship' (James Cook University edn, pp. 2, 163).

11 For a consideration of the nature of oral history, see Bain Attwood *et al.*, *A Life Together, A Life Apart: A History of Relations Between Europeans and Aborigines*, Melbourne University Press, Melbourne, 1994, Part 3.

12 Alessandro Portelli, 'The Peculiarities of Oral History', *History Workshop Journal*, no. 12, 1981, pp. 99-100.

13 Heather Goodall, 'Cryin' Out for Land Rights', in Verity Burgmann and Jenny Lee (eds), *Staining the Wattle: A People's History of Australia Since*

1788, McPhee Gribble/Penguin, Fitzroy, 1988, p. 181; Goodall, *From Invasion to Embassy*, pp. 160–61. This passage is a composite of the two different transcripts provided.

14 Goodall, 'Cryin' Out', p. 182.

15 This distinction has been made by Michael Frisch, *A Shared Authority*, State University of New York Press, Albany, New York, 1990, p. 7. See also Popular Memory Group, 'Popular Memory: Theory, Politics, Method', in Richard Johnson *et al.* (eds), *Making Histories: Studies in History–Writing and Politics*, Hutchinson, London, 1982, p. 228.

16 R.H.W. Reece, *Aborigines and Colonists: Aborigines and Colonial Society in New South Wales in the 1830s and 1840s*, Sydney University Press, Sydney, 1974, chapters 2–5; A.G.L. Shaw; 'British Policy Towards the Australian Aborigines, 1830–1850', *Australian Historical Studies*, vol. 25, no. 99, 1992, pp. 265–85; Reynolds, *Law of the Land*, and *This Whispering*.

17 For a summary of this legislation, see Andrew Markus, 'Under the Act', in Gammage and Spearritt (eds), *Australians 1938*, pp. 47–53.

18 Goodall, *Invasion to Embassy*, p. 230, notes the differences between some of these organisations.

19 See Marilyn Lake, 'Feminism and the Gendered Politics of Antiracism, Australia 1927–1957: From Maternal Protectionism to Leftist Assimilationism', *Australian Historical Studies*, vol. 29, no. 110, 1998, pp. 91–108; Fiona Paisley, *Ideas Have Wings: White Women Challenge Aboriginal Policy 1920-37*, Melbourne University Press, Melbourne, forthcoming.

20 See D.J. Mulvaney and J.H. Calaby, *'So Much that is New': Baldwin Spender, 1860–1929, a Biography*, Melbourne University Press, Melbourne, 1985, pp. 274–75.

21 See Gillian Cowlishaw, 'Helping Anthropologists', *Canberra Anthropology*, vol. 13, no. 2, 1990, pp. 1–28.

22 *Sydney Morning Herald*, 16 June 1933.

23 Markus, *Governing Savages*, pp. 1–7, 140; Russell McGregor, *Imagined Destinies: Aboriginal Australians and the Doomed Race Theory, 1880–1939*, Melbourne University Press, Melbourne, 1997, pp. 105, 113–114, 226–27.

24 McGregor, *Imagined Destinies*, pp. 224–34, 243.

25 Council for Aboriginal Rights, Constitution, 13 April 1951, Council for Aboriginal Rights (Victoria) Papers, La Trobe Collection, State Library of Victoria, MS 12913/5/6.

26 *Courier* (Ballarat), 15 September 1958.

27 CAR Policy c. 1962, Riley and Ephemera Collection, State Library of Victoria; National Missionary Council, *The Meaning of Assimilation* and *Four Major Issues in Assimilation*, NMC, Melbourne, 1963; John Jago, 'The Australian Aboriginal: Is Assimilation the Answer?', in Aboriginal Affairs of the Methodist Church of Australasia (Victorian and Tasmanian Conference), *Methodist Policy on Aborigines*, National Missionary Council, Melbourne, 1963, pp. 2–3; *Age*, 15 July 1963.

28 See Jeremy Beckett, 'Aboriginality, Citizenship and the Nation State', *Social Analysis*, no. 24, 1988, pp. 3–18.

29 Lois O'Donoghue, 'One Nation: Promise or Paradox?', in ATSIC, *25 Years On: Marking the Anniversary of the Aboriginal Referendum of 27 May 1967*, ATSIC, Canberra, 1992, pp. 13, 14.

1 The nineteenth century

Indigenous politics in the nineteenth century mostly consisted of the struggles of Aboriginal communities fighting to be granted or to retain reserve lands, and battling to govern themselves or be treated fairly and justly by colonial governments and their officers.

Flinders Island

The history of Aboriginal political activity begins in the late 1830s on Flinders Island. Between 1831 and 1834, following a bitterly fought war of resistance against the invasion of their lands which had begun in the mid-1820s,[1] Aborigines had been induced by the colonial government's emissary, conciliator George Augustus Robinson— perhaps by means of a verbal treaty[2]— to surrender to him and abandon the main island of Van Diemen's Land in exchange for safe conduct to Flinders Island where the Aborigines understood they would enjoy a sanctuary and the benefits of 'civilisation' and Christianity as recompense for the loss of their country.[3]

Very soon, however, Aborigines found that they had been led to have false hopes. The food and living conditions at the Aboriginal Establishment, called Wybalenna ('black man's houses'), were poor, and many of the one hundred or so survivors died while others suffered from malnutrition and disease. They also faced a strict daily routine through which they were supposed to adopt the central tenets of Christianity and the standards of European civilisation. After Robinson's departure in 1838 to assume the role of Chief Protector to the Aborigines of the Port Phillip District, the Aborigines at Wybalenna were to experience a succession of unsympathetic commanders, such as Henry Jeanneret.[4]

Although this turn of events often provoked despair among the Aborigines at Wybalenna, younger men and women used their new skills to fight their oppression. These included literacy, as evidenced by the *Flinders Island Weekly Chronicle*, a manuscript newspaper founded by Robinson 'to promote christianity civilisation and Learning amongst the Aboriginal Inhabitants at Flinders Island' and 'be a brief but accurate register of events of the colony Moral and religious' (1).[5] Protests were led by Walter George Arthur, his wife Mary, and Thomas Bruny, among others. Arthur had been separated from his kin before he had learned much of his own culture and language and grew up among colonists, spending a few years in a orphan school in Hobart before being sent to Flinders Island in 1835. He formed a close association with Robinson, leaving the island in 1839 with Robinson and returning in 1842. The protest leaders became committed Christians who were, in the words of one historian, 'confident, even self righteous', embracing 'civilisation' and critical of 'traditional culture'.[6] As a consequence, they drew on several sources in their protest, most of all the humanitarian principles espoused by Robinson and missionaries such as George Walker, who had been influenced by the anti-slavery crusade of English evangelicals and philanthropists. Their protest culminated in 1845-47 (2–5), particularly with a petition to Queen Victoria (3) in which they claimed the colonial government had broken the promises it had entered into when they agreed to go to Flinders Island.

Coranderrk

Aborigines in the Port Phillip District of New South Wales— or Victoria as it became in 1851—were similarly affected by sweeping dispossession of land, frontier violence and, more especially, introduced diseases which caused their numbers to plummet from as many as 85 000 to only a few thousand by the 1850s.[7] The loss of their land provoked appeals to missionaries such as Revd Francis Tuckfield, who reported in 1840:

> And with regard to those tribes who occasionally visit us ... they seem to be acquainted (at least to a considerable extent) with the relative possessions of the Black & White populations— They are conscious of what is going on — they are driven from this favoured haunt & from their other favoured haunts & threatened if they do not leave immediately they will be lodged in gaol or shot. It is to the Missionaries they come with their tales of woe & their language is— "Will you not select for us also a portion of land?". "My country all gone, gone ... The White men have stolen it".[8]

The devastating mortality rates also provoked despair among the traditional landowners. In 1843, a Woiworung elder and signatory to a treaty with John Batman in 1835,[9] headman Billibellary, commented to one of the assistant protectors, William Thomas, that 'no good have them Pickaninneys now, no country for blackfellows like long time ago'. Yet, he also added, 'if Yarra blackfellows had a country on the Yarra ... they would stop on it and cultivate the ground'.[10]

The plight of Aborigines in Victoria worsened with the gold rushes of the 1850s but, by the end of that decade, a humanitarian resurgence resulted in the appointment of a select committee in 1858 'to inquire into the present condition of the Aborigines of this colony, and the best means of alleviating their absolute wants'.[11] Humanitarians, who had been influential in the 1830s and 1840s, believed that Europeans were superior to Aborigines and had a duty 'to colonise the waste places of the earth' (such as Australia), but they also acknowledged 'the great fact' that Aborigines were the 'original possessors' and Europeans were 'intruders' whose 'hostile invasion' had deprived the indigenes of 'their former mode of existence' and almost 'exterminated' them. Accordingly, they believed that Aborigines had an 'inalienable' right to obtain 'the necessaries and comforts of life' and had a 'claim' upon the colonisers; in fact, 'the very first charge' upon colonial government, they argued, should be 'due compensation or provision' for the Aborigines.[12] As in Van Diemen's Land, these humanitarians also recommended that Aborigines should be concentrated on reserves of land where they could be supervised by missionaries who would 'Christianise and civilise' them so they would become useful to 'the state and themselves'. This approach was sanctioned by the Select Committee and later adopted by the government which appointed a Central Board for the Protection of the Aborigines.[13]

Before the Select Committee reported, however, several Woiworung and Taungurong men waited upon the Guardian of Aborigines, William Thomas, who petitioned the government on their behalf (6). Government acceded to the request for land on the Acheron River and soon Taungurong Aborigines were, in Thomas' words, 'wending their way to their Goshen (Promised Land)'.[14] However, the strength of their determination was sorely tested when their hunger for land was thwarted on the Acheron and elsewhere (7) until, in 1863, they and the Woiworung were finally granted land at another traditional site on the Yarra River, a place they named Coranderrk. A month or so later they attended a birthday levee for Queen Victoria (8), and the gazettal of the reserve and a subsequent message from the Queen guaranteeing her 'interest' in 'their advancement and welfare' seem to have established a strong belief that the reserve was the gift of the Queen and the Governor, to be theirs in perpetuity.[15]

The reserve's first decade was one of considerable progress, encouraged by the management of John Green and the leadership of Simon Wonga, William Barak and Tommy Bamfield, whose forebears had been *ngurungaeta* or headmen, and who thus had inherited their traditional authority.[16] Yet the Aborigines remained 'anxious and uncertain respecting the tenure of their land', nervous 'they may be turned away at any time'.[17] In the mid-1870s their worst fears were realised when the Board for the Protection of

Aborigines won greater control over the management of the reserve, forced Green to resign his position as manager, and attempted to close Coranderrk and move its inhabitants to another reserve. This began more than a decade of 'rebellion' by the Aborigines, who resented the loss of Green, the authoritarianism of his successors— Hugh Halliday, Revd W.P. Strickland and William Goodall— and the Board's heavy-handed intervention, and were angered by the threat of banishment.

Their campaign of protest was a relatively sophisticated one. For example, they used their literacy skills to follow colonial politics in the press and write letters to the editors of daily newspapers (12) and to government ministers (14); they formed deputations to wait upon sympathetic ministers such as Chief Secretary Graham Berry (13) and other politicians (11); and they sought the support of humanitarians such as Anne Bon. Their protests were often startlingly effective. The Victorian government was forced to hold two major inquiries— the first, in 1877, to inquire generally into policy on Aborigines and the second, in 1881, to inquire specifically into Coranderrk, at which Coranderrk Aborigines gave evidence and presented a petition (10).[18]

Maloga

In sparsely settled districts of neighbouring New South Wales Aborigines continued to have access to their traditional lands, but in other places they had been thoroughly dispossessed as early as the 1830s and were resettled on missions.[19] On one of these, Maloga, founded on the Murray River near Echuca in 1874 by Daniel and Janet Matthews and the Aborigines Protection Association,[20] Aborigines were, in 1881, to petition the Governor of New South Wales for land in much the same terms as the Woiworung and Taungurong had sought a reserve in 1859 (15); in this they were undoubtedly encouraged by William Barak who was visiting at the time and by other Coranderrk Aborigines who had begun to return to their traditional homelands.[21]

By 1883, land had been reserved adjacent to Maloga— the Cummeragunja Reserve— but Aborigines were expressing their desire to have their own blocks of land and, according to Matthews and others, they were becoming more and more rebellious,[22] probably because they were now very well aware of the looming dispossession of the Coranderrk Aborigines. In 1887, a year after new legislation had been passed in Victoria— the purpose of which was to force Aborigines of mixed descent off the reserves and disperse them into the general community— a deputation presented the Governor with a petition requesting family blocks for 'the former occupiers of the land' and invoking the Queen's authority

(16). Several months later two Maloga men petitioned their local Member of Parliament in similar terms for grants of land. (17); one of these men was William Cooper, who, many decades later, was to become the leader of one of the first major Aboriginal political organisations in Australia.[23] In other areas, too, Aborigines were seeking blocks. For example, a few years later, Aborigines seeking land near Sydney joined forces with Matthews— whose authoritarian control was being rejected at Cummeragunja and who now contemplated founding another mission— to petition the New South Wales Premier for land (18).[24]

Poonindie, Point McLeay and Point Pearce

In South Australia, as in New South Wales, government took little interest in Aborigines beyond the early decades of conflict and dispossession on the pastoral frontier, and responsibility for their welfare was principally, if inadequately, assumed by philanthropists, church bodies and missionary organisations. For example, in 1850, an Anglican archdeacon, Mathew Hale, founded Poonindie on the southern Eyre Peninsula, north of Port Lincoln, and in 1859 George Taplin, employed by the Aborigines' Friends' Association, established a mission at Point McLeay on a traditional site on the shores of Lake Alexandrina, known by Aborigines as Raukkan ('the ancient way'). Other missions were also begun in the south of the colony— for example, Point Pearce in 1868— as they were in the north, by the Anglican and Lutheran churches.[25]

Here, as in Victoria and New South Wales, many of these missions enjoyed an early period of growth and even prosperity, followed by a period when the Aboriginal residents sought greater autonomy and clashed with the paternalistic mission superintendents— such as J.D. Bruce at Poonindie— over governance of the reserves (19 20 and 24). Lack of land and resources frustrated further development of the reserves and saw Aborigines, such as Thomas Adams,[26] requesting small blocks of land they could farm independently (20); and the demands of land-hungry selectors and others threatened the reserves which they had worked for more than a generation (22).

The loss of reserve land such as Poonindie, which was closed in the 1890s, caused much heartache since, as at Coranderrk, the Aboriginal inhabitants had, through tradition or historical association, come to identify these places as their homelands (23), and this displacement provoked petitions begging for land to maintain themselves (21) as well as angry assertions of their right to a very small part of what had originally all been theirs (22). In some instances, however, pressures on Aboriginal reserves seemed to give rise to conflicts between the traditional land owners and other Aborigines, although colonists often understood these in terms of a dispute between 'full-bloods' and 'half-castes' **(24)**.[27]

NOTES

1 See Lyndall Ryan, *The Aboriginal Tasmanians,* University of Queensland Press, St. Lucia, 1981, 2nd edn, Allen & Unwin, Sydney, 1996, chapters 6 and 7.
2 See Henry Reynolds, *Fate of a Free People,* Penguin, Melbourne, 1995, especially chapters 1 and 5; for a consideration of this argument, see Ryan, *Aboriginal Tasmanians,* 2nd edn, pp. xxvii–iii.
3 For Robinson's diary of this mission, see N.J.B. Plomley (ed.), *Friendly Mission: The Tasmanian Journals and Papers of George Augustus Robinson 1829–1834,* Tasmanian Historical Research Association, Hobart, 1966; for an account of the mission, see Ryan, *Aboriginal Tasmanians,* chapters 8–11.
4 See N.J.B. Plomley (ed.), *Weep in Silence: A History of Flinders Island Aboriginal Settlement: With the Flinders Island Journal of George Augustus Robinson, 1835–39,* Blubberhead Press, Hobart, 1987; Ryan, *Aboriginal Tasmanians,* chapters 12–13.
5 *The Aboriginal or Flinders Island Chronicle,* 10 September 1836, George Augustus Robinson Papers, Mitchell Library, State Library of New South Wales, MSS A7073, part 4, CY reel 825.
6 Reynolds, *Fate of a Free People,* pp. 16–17.
7 See R.H.W. Reece, *Aborigines and Colonists: Aborigines and Colonial Society in New South Wales in the 1830s and 1840s,* Sydney University Press, Sydney, 1974, chapter 1; M.F. Christie, *Aborigines in Colonial Victoria 1835–86,* Sydney University Press, Sydney, 1979, chapter 2; N.G. Butlin, *Economics and the Dreamtime: A Hypothetical History,* Cambridge University Press, Melbourne, 1993, pp. 134, 221–26; Richard Broome, 'Victoria', in Ann McGrath (ed.), *Contested Ground: Australian Aborigines Under the British Crown,* Allen & Unwin, Sydney, 1995, pp. 124–32.
8 Revd Francis Tuckfield, Buntingdale Mission, Geelong, to the General Secretaries, Presbyterian Mission House, London, 31 June 1840, Frances Tuckfield Journal, La Trobe Collection, State Library of Victoria, MS 655.
9 For a discussion of this, see Henry Reynolds, *The Law of the Land,* 2nd edn, Penguin, Melbourne, 1988, pp. 125–28; Diane Barwick, *Rebellion at Coranderrk,* Aboriginal History, Canberra, 1998, pp. 20–25.
10 William Thomas, Journal, September-December 1843, Public Record Office of Victoria (henceforth PROV), VPRS 4410, unit 3.
11 Victoria, Legislative Assembly, *Votes and Proceedings,* 1858–59, Select Committee on the Aborigines (henceforth 1858–59 Select Committee), p. iii; *Argus,* 27 October 1858.
12 *Argus,* 17 March and 2 April 1856, 27 and 28 October 1858, 3 February 1859; Victoria, Legislative Assembly, *Votes and Proceedings,* 1856–57, vol. 3, Petition of the United Church of England and Ireland in Victoria.
13 *Argus,* 27 October 1858, 3 February 1859; 1858–59 Select Committee, pp. iv-v; Central Board for the Protection of Aborigines (henceforth CBPA), 1st Report, 1861, pp. 11–12 (Board reports were printed in *Victorian Parliamentary Papers* and

are also held National Archives of Australia (henceforth NAA), Melbourne, CRS B332).

14 *Herald*, 8 March 1859; Thomas to Commissioner of Lands and Survey, 28 March 1859, William Thomas Papers, Mitchell Library, State Library of New South Wales, uncatalogued MS, set 214, item 13; Thomas to Robert Brough Smyth, Secretary, CBPA, 26 July 1860, NAA (Melbourne), CRS B312, item 3.

15 *Victorian Government Gazette*, 30 June 1863; John Dow to Chief Secretary, 3 July 1878, PROV, VPRS 3991, unit 171; Revd Robert Hamilton to Chief Secretary, 23 March 1882, PROV, VPRS 1226, unit 4; Anne Bon to Under Secretary, 29 May 1882, PROV, VPRS 1226, unit 4; see Barwick, *Rebellion at Coranderrk*, chapter 3.

16 Barwick, *Rebellion at Coranderrk*, pp. 9, 84, 125.

17 Brough Smyth to Board for the Protection of Aborigines (henceforth BPA), 2 February 1870, in BPA, 7th Report, 1871, p. 8.

18 The Coranderrk story is told by Barwick, *Rebellion at Coranderrk*.

19 For these missions of the 1830s and 1840s, see Jean Woolmington (comp.), *Aborigines in Colonial Society*, 2nd edn, University of New England, Armidale, 1988; W.N. Gunson (ed.), *Australian Reminiscences and Papers of L.E. Threlkeld*, 2 vols, Australian Institute of Aboriginal Studies, Canberra, 1974.

20 See Nancy Cato, *Mister Maloga: Daniel Matthews and His Mission, Murray River, 1864–1902*, University of Queensland Press, St Lucia, 1976.

21 Diane Barwick, 'Coranderrk and Cumeroogunga', in T. Scarlett Epstein and David H. Scarlett (eds), *Opportunity and Response: Pioneers and Policy*, David Hirst, London, 1972, pp. 36, 45, 46, 47.

22 *Riverine Herald*, 19 November 1886.

23 John Atkinson to Mr J.M. Chanter, 4 November 1887, William Cooper to Chanter, 16 November 1887, AONSW, 1/2667. For a discussion of these petitions, see Heather Goodall, *From Invasion to Embassy: Land in Aboriginal Politics in New South Wales, 1770–1972*, Allen & Unwin/Black Books, Sydney, 1996, pp. 78–79.

24 See *ibid.*, pp. 79–84.

25 See Peggy Brock, *Outback Ghettoes: Aborigines, Institutionalisation and Survival*, Cambridge University Press, Melbourne, 1993, *Yura and Udnyu: A History of the Adnyamathanha of the North Flinders Ranges*, Wakefield Press, Adelaide, 1985; Graham Jenkin, *Conquest of the Ngarrindjeri: The Story of the Lower Murray Lakes Tribes*, Rigby, Adelaide, 1979.

26. Brock has reconstructed his life (*Outback Ghettos*, pp. 51–53).

27 See Barwick, *Rebellion at Coranderrk*, p. 78.

Flinders Island

1. Thomas Bruny, editor and writer, *Flinders Island Weekly Chronicle*, 17 November 1837

Now my friends you see that the commandant is so kind to you he gives you every thing that you want when you were in the bush the commandant had to leave his friends and go into the bush and he brought you out of the bush because he felt for you and because he knowed the white men was shooting you and now he has brought you to Flinders Island where you get every things and when you are ill tell the Doctor immediately and you get relief you have now fine house. I expect that you will not vex one another

To morrow there will be a Market my friends will you thank the commandant for all that he done for you in bringing you out of the bush when you knew not God and knew not who made the trees that where before you when you were living in the woods yes my friends you should thank the commandant yes you should thank the commandant There is many of you dying my friends we must all die and we ought to pray to God before we get to heaven yes my friends if we dont we must have eternal-punishment.

The brig Tamar arrived this morning at green Island I cannot tell perhaps we might hear about it by and by when the ship boat comes to the Settlement we will hear news from Hobartown Let us hope it will be good news and that something may be done for us poor people they are [dying] away the Bible says some of all shall be saved but I am much afraid none of us will be alive by and by as then as nothing but sickness among us Why dont the black fellows pray to the king to get us away from this place

2. Walter George Arthur to Mr G.W. Walker, 30 December 1845

As I understand that Doctr Milligan is to leave Flinders Island and before a new Superintendent is appointed I beg leave to inform you that myself and the remainder of my Country people are desirous of doing all we can to support ourselves upon Flinders without our being any more expense to the Government as we will use our best endeavours to grow wheat and potatoes and gather mutton-Birds and their Eggs, &c. &c.

Mr Clark will do us all the good he can, and assist us, but if the Governor would send down some person to see Flinders after Doctor Milligan leaves it, and before another comes in his place it might save the Government a great deal of money.

Many of the people are improving in reading the Testament we have not enought Testaments for all who would read. But we are doing very well except for the Bad whitemen, the prisoners and Soldiers are no good Sir.

We cannot write to the Governor or else we would tell him how we would work & to assist in feeding ourselves. My wife has learned to read the Testament about the Love of God and the Lord Jesus Christ

and she is very fond of Jesus and his Book and of God and of Jesus and the Holy Spirit and so is two or three more Black men and women. I read a Chapter in the Testament every night before I go to bed to my Family.

And some other of the Blacks who may be in the house my wife earns some Money from Mrs Clark and Mrs Clark and Mr Clark are very good to us.

and advise us what is proper and lend me good books to read the Blacks would all petition the governor to get land and to earn for themselves but they are afraid and when them will not work for other people they are called Idle and Lazy altho' we are paid but very little but indeed Sir we are not so for we work very hard. I cant now write any more but thank you for your kindness to us poor Black people of van Diemens Land.

3. Petition to Her Majesty Queen Victoria, 17 February 1846

The humble petition of the free Aborigines Inhabitants of V.D.L. now living upon Flinders Island, in Bass's Straits &c &c &c.

Most humbly showeth,

That we Your Majesty's Petitioners are your free Children that we were not taken Prisoners but freely gave up our Country to Colonel Arthur then the Govr after defending ourselves.

Your Petitioners humbly state to Y[our] M[ajesty] that Mr. Robinson made for us & with Col. Arthur an agreement which we have not lost from our minds since & we have made our part of it good.

Your Petitioners humbly tell Y.M. that when we left our own place we were plenty of People, we are now but a little one.

Your Petitioners state they are a long time at Flinders Island & had that plenty of Sup^{dts} & were always a quiet & free People & not put into Gaol.

Your Majesty's Petitioners pray that you will not allow Dr. Jeanneret to come again among us as our Sup^{dt} as we hear he is to be sent another time for when Dr. Jeanneret was with us many Moons he used to carry Pistols in his pockets & threaten'd very often to shoot us & make us run away in a fright. Dr. Jeanneret kept plenty of Pigs in our Village which used to run into our houses & eat up our bread from the fires & take away our flour bags in their mouths also to break into our Gardens & destroy our Potatoes & Cabbages.

Our houses were let fall down & they were never cleaned but were covered with vermin & not white-washed. We were often without Clothes except a very little one & Dr. Jeanneret did not care to mind us when we were sick until we were very bad. Eleven of us died when he was here. He put many of us into Jail for talking to him because we would not be his slaves. He kept from us our Rations when he pleased & sometimes gave us Bad Rations of Tea & Tobacco. He shot some of our dogs before our eyes & sent all the other dogs of ours to an Island & when we told him that they would starve he told us they might eat each other. He put arms into our hands & made us to assist his prisoners to go to fight the Soldiers we did not want to fight the Soldiers but he made us go to fight. We never were taught to read or write or to sing to God by the Doctor. He taught us a little upon the Sundays & his Prisoner Servant also taught us & his Prisoner Servant also took us plenty of times to Jail by his orders.

The Lord Bishop seen us in this bad way & we told H[is] L[ordship] plenty how Dr. Jeanneret used us.

We humbly pray Your Majesty the Queen will hear our prayer & not let Dr Jeanneret any more to come to Flinders Island. And We Y.M's servant's & Children will ever pray as in duty bound &c &c &c

Sgd. Walter G. Arthur, Chief of the Ben Lomond Tribes, King Alexander, John Allan, Augustus, Davey Bruney, King Tippoo, Neptune, Washington

4. Mary Ann Arthur to Colonial Secretary, Van Diemen's Land, 10 June 1846

I thank my Father the Govr that he has told us black people that we might write him & tell him if we had any complaint to make about ourselves. I want now to tell the Govr that Dr. Jeanneret wants to make out my husband & myself very bad wicked people & talks plenty about putting us into jail & that he will hang us for helping to write the petition to the Queen from our country people. I send the Gov. two papers one from Dr. Milligan & one from Mr. Robinson of Port Philip to tell the Govr that they know us a long time & had nothing to say bad of us but Dr. Jeanneret does not like us for we do not like to be his slaves nor wish our poor Country to be treated badly or made slaves of. I hope the Govr will not let Dr. Jeanneret put us into Jail as he likes for nothing at all as he used he says he will do it & frightens us much with his big talk about our writing to the Queen he calls us all liars but we told him & the Coxswain who Dr. Jeanneret made ask us that it was all true what we write about him. I remain, Sir, Your humble Aborigine Child, Mary Ann Arthur.

5. Walter George Arthur to Colonial Secretary, Van Diemen's Land, 15 July 1846

I send you with this letter a Statement which I have written of my Imprisonment here in Flinders Jail by Doctor Jeanneret for 14 days and nights will you please to give this letter and my statement to my good Father His Excellency the Governor please tell him His Excellency that I hope he will do for me as if I was a Free white man to send to Flinders two Magistrates to take my informations against Doctor Jeanneret and other People for falsely putting me into Jail— for refusing to take my Bail— for wanting to get £50 from me to let me out— for keeping in Jail without a Committal wanting me to sign a Petition to him to Call myself a bad wicked man— and allso for not sending to the Governor our original Letter about our Petition being true, which we gave him open to read first and ask him to send it to the Governor for us We sent the Duplicate of it among our other letters to the Colonial Sec^ty in June last— Neigther myself or my Wife can live here under Doctor Jeanneret he treats us so badly and wants to make such Slaves of us all and is always revenging what took place when he was here before. I pray his Excellency the Governor will take Care of us poor Black people and send us the Magistrates to whom we will tell our Pitiful Story of what we poor Creatures are suffering different from what Col. Arthur and Mr. Robinson told us when we gave them our own Countrys of Van Diemens Land— the People are now all so frightened from Doctor Jeanneret constant growl and threatenings to put them in Jail and telling them he has full power this time to do as he likes with us all and that his Excellency has no power either over him or the black people that they do not know what to do and they are so watched that they are afraid to write to his Excellency any more as their letters wont be sent by Doctor Jeanneret. they Black People had to send their letters to the Governor in another way than by the Mail. Doctor Jeanneret says we will all be hung for high treason for writing against him he is worst on me for he knows I can speak English and that I do not like to see my poor Ignorant Country people badly treated or made Slaves of. I send you Sir a Certificate for his Excellency to read that I got from Mr. Clark our Catechist for he knows my wife and myself from we were young; and he knows how badly we are all treated here and that I did nothing to make Doctor Jeanneret put me into Jail but because I was

1. As a result of the 1846 Flinders Island petition to Queen Victoria, the British Colonial Office recommended the closure of the establishment, and the following year Walter George and Mary Ann Arthur (right) and their fellow Aborigines were removed to Oyster Cove, a former penal station, in the D'Entrecasteaux Channel. This and other photographs of Aborigines taken in 1860 suggests something of their continuing defiance of and hostility to colonial rule. *(Courtesy Beattie's Studios)*

2. In 1866 or 1867 the Kulin proudly re-enacted on Coranderrk events of the utmost importance to them—their trek to the Acheron reserve several years earlier (above) and their first religious service on their arrival at Coranderrk in 1863. Ceremonies of this nature affirmed their ownership of the land. *(Courtesy Aldo Massola Collection, AIATSIS N6026.1a)*

3. Aborigines on Coranderrk reserve, probably the first to sustain a political campaign, proved to be adept exponents of the methods of British democracy. In 1886, one of their champions, Chief Secretary Graham Berry, who had gazetted Coranderrk as a 'permanent' reserve in 1884, received this deputation of the Kulin men, led by headman William Barak (back row, centre) and his two principal 'speakers', Tommy Bamfield (back row, fourth from the right) and Robert Wandin (back row, far left). As they had done since signing a treaty with John Batman in 1835, the Kulin maintained their principle of reciprocity by presenting Berry with traditional gifts to mark this important transaction regarding land. *(Courtesy La Trobe Collection, State Library of Victoria H141267)*

4. David Unaipon, like many of the Aboriginal leaders in the inter-war period, had been educated by missionaries and tutored in the principles of humanitarianism and liberal democracy. He is pictured here in the repose of a respectable gentleman, discussing matters of import with one of his mentors, the secretary of Aborigines' Friends' Association, Rev. J.H. Sexton, who was responsible for publishing many of Unaipon's writings. *(Courtesy National Library of Australia)*

5. Fred Maynard, leader of the Australian Aboriginal
Progressive Association, pictured in Sydney in the
1920s with his sister Emily. This, like other
photographs of this organisation's representatives, is
suggestive of the influence of the black American
culture of Harlem. *(Courtesy Maynard Family)*

6. The emblem of the Australian Aboriginal
Progressive Association, like that of many
later organisations, reveals that Aboriginal
activists demanded rights on the basis of
their being the original peoples, implicitly
contesting the status of whites as
'Australians'. *(Courtesy National Archives
of Australia (Canberra))*

7. William Harris, founder of the Natives' Union (front right), led this deputation to the Western Australian Premier in 1928: (left to right) Wilfred Morrison, Harris' brother Edward Harris, Harris' nephew Norman Harris, Edward Jacobs, Arthur Kickett and William Bodney. *(Courtesy Steven Kinnane/Western Australian)*

8. A sense of tradition, and the historical claims embedded in this, has been most apparent in indigenous politics where Aborigines have articulated their demands through music, oratory, dance and painting, as the Australian Aborigines' League did at meetings like the one pictured here in 1936, when (from left) William Cooper, Margaret Tucker, Cooper's son Lynch, and Cooper's wife Sarah performed 'corroboree choruses'. *(Courtesy Alick Jackomos Collection, AIATSIS N5344.15a)*

AUSTRALIAN
Aborigines   Conference

SESQUI-CENTENARY

Day of Mourning and Protest

to be held in

THE   AUSTRALIAN   HALL,   SYDNEY

(No. 148 Elizabeth Street — a hundred yards south of Liverpool Street)

on

WEDNESDAY, 26th JANUARY, 1938

(AUSTRALIA DAY)

The Conference will assemble at 10 o'clock in the morning.

ABORIGINES AND PERSONS OF ABORIGINAL
BLOOD ONLY ARE INVITED TO ATTEND

The following Resolution will be moved:

"WE, representing THE ABORIGINES OF AUSTRALIA, assembled in Conference at the Australian Hall, Sydney, on the 26th day of January, 1938, this being the 150th Anniversary of the whitemen's seizure of our country, HEREBY MAKE PROTEST against the callous treatment of our people by the whitemen during the past 150 years, AND WE APPEAL to the Australian Nation of today to make new laws for the education and care of Aborigines, and we ask for a new policy which will raise our people to FULL CITIZEN STATUS and EQUALITY WITHIN THE COMMUNITY."

The above resolution will be debated and voted upon, as the sole business of the Conference, which will terminate at 5 o'clock in the afternoon.

TO ALL AUSTRALIAN ABORIGINES! PLEASE COME TO THIS
CONFERENCE IF YOU POSSIBLY CAN! ALSO SEND WORD BY
LETTER TO NOTIFY US IF YOU CAN ATTEND

Signed, for and on behalf of

THE ABORIGINES PROGRESSIVE ASSOCIATION,

J. T. PATTEN, President.
W. FERGUSON, Organising Secretary.

Address: c/o. Box 1924KK, General Post Office, Sydney.

9. After William Cooper and Bill Ferguson, secretaries of the Australian Aborigines' League and the Aborigines Progressive Association respectively, suggested a day to mark the sesquicentenary of the white invasion of this continent in 1938, right-wing nationalist and publisher P.R. Stephensen lent his support in various ways, including the printing of this poster. *(Courtesy Mitchell Library, State Library of New South Wales)*

10. 26 January 1938: Protesting against the celebration of '150 years' so-called "progress" in Australia', members of the Aborigines Progressive Association were pictured outside the Australian Hall before commencing their conference to commemorate what Bill Ferguson and Jack Patten (far left and far right) were calling '150 years of misery and degradation' for Aborigines. The others identified in this photograph are (left to right): Jack Kinchela, Helen Grosvenor and Selina Patten. *(Courtesy Jack Horner Collection, AIATSIS N4642.11)*

11. Although the first Aboriginal organisations, founded in the 1920s and 1930s, were dominated by men, women like Pearl Gibbs and Margaret Tucker (far left and second from left) played a prominent role in Ferguson's Aborigines Progressive Association and the Australian Aborigines' League respectively, as they did in organisations they helped found in the 1950s. *(Courtesy Mitchell Library, State Library of New South Wales)*

12. In the wake of both world wars Aboriginal activists invoked the military service of Aboriginal men in their fight to be accorded the same rights enjoyed by Australian citizens. In this procession, on May Day in Sydney in 1947, Bert Groves (second from right) and others (left to right) Lila Lord, Tasman Dotti, Alice Groves, Delys Cross and Athol Lester carry placards which also call for the abolition of the hated New South Wales Aborigines 'Protection' Board. *(Courtesy Jack Horner)*

13. In 1949, the Australian Aborigines' League, which had included members of the Aborigines Progressive Association since 1946, decided to represent themselves politically by fielding candidates in the next federal election. 'For the last twenty years', Bill Ferguson—pictured here speaking in the Sydney Domain during his campaign for a Senate seat—reportedly told the press, 'the league had been depending on politicians who had promised better conditions for [A]borigines. Nothing had been done'. *(Courtesy Jack Horner Collection, AIATSIS N4642.13)*

WE WANT TO STOP THIS:

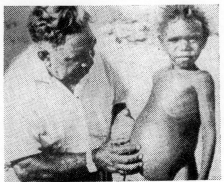

Pastor Nicholls, M.B.E., examining
a child on the Warburton Reserve.

Flies! But too weak to
bother.

HELP US—TO HELP THEM!

14. In 1957 an inquiry led by independent Western Australian MLA Bill Grayden and Doug Nicholls to the Warburton Ranges shot a film and photographs like these, which helped to expose the conditions of Aborigines in the Central Australian Aboriginal Reserve who had been affected by the British rocket bomb testing programme sanctioned by the Commonwealth government. Shocking clips of the film were screened on television in a programme entitled 'Manslaughter', and Nicholls (pictured here) showed the film as he lectured in numerous halls in capital cities and country towns, and the newly founded organisation—the Victorian Aborigines Advancement League—used these photographs in a publicity leaflet. *(Courtesy Riley & Ephemera Collection, State Library of Victoria)*

one of the people who signed the Letter for to be sent to the Governor and because my wife put her name down in it both Doctor Jeanneret and Mrs Jeanneret Called her a Villain and and is making out plenty of bad things about my wife and myself which I can very soon prove are not true. All I now request of his Excellency is that he will have full Justice done to me the same as he would have done to a white man and a freeman and according to the agreement between both Col. Arthur the old Governor and us black people when we were free people and when we gave up our Country and came to live at Flinders Island. 6th June Since I wrote this much the Fortitude has arrived I am too much frighted for Doctor Jeanneret to send my statements which I have write out for to tell the Governor of how I have been treated I must keep it until the Governor writes me leave to send it. I must inclose this letter to a friend in Hobart town to put into the Post Office for me for Doctor Jeanneret says he will send no letters for us I want to tell the Governor that plenty bad salt beef has Issued out for us all for the last month and some of the fresh beef was of the worst kind on Saturday the 1st August we all got for our Ration of meat Stinking Salt Mutton. But these we had to throw out for we must not refuse anything he gives us I am sure the Governor will be sorry to hear that my poor Country-people cry out plenty that they are very hungry from the bad meat Doctor Jeanneret gives them. I again pray the Governor will do some thing for us and not let us be badly treated in the way we are if Governor would send down some person they would very soon find that all I have wrote is true I know Doctor Jeanneret write plenty about us black people to the Governor but I hope Governor will ask ourselves first for we know that he says plenty of things that is not true of us.

I remain, Sir, Your humble Aborigine Servant, Walter G. Arthur Chief of Ben Lomond Tribes.

Please will the Governor give me and my Wife Mary Ann Arthur leave to go up to Hobarttown with Mr. Clark our Catechist when he gose to Town.

Coranderrk

6. William Thomas, Guardian of Aborigines, to the Commissioner of Lands and Survey, Victoria, 4 March 1859

As your Honour will perceive by my communication of the 28th ultimo, that a deputation of the Goulburn tribe of aborigines waited on me to solicit of your Honour a tract of land for their sole use and benefit. I promised to wait on your Honour that day, and to inform them of the result the following morning.

2. Your Honour not being in town, the Surveyor-General gave me every encouragement, that he would receive the deputation in your Honour's absence, which I communicated to the aborigines, and on Wednesday, the 2nd inst., accompanied by the aboriginal deputation, had a favourable interview with the Surveyor-General and the board then sitting, the chief of the Goulburn tribe explicitly made known their request, that the tribe were anxious to secure a tract of land on both sides of a creek which falls into the Goulburn River, named Nak-krom, which the blacks stated was little use to white people, but kangaroos and opossums were abundant there. This creek [Acheron] is in the country of Anglesey, has dividing range to the south, Goulburn River to the north, Muddy Creek and township to the west, and Rubicon Creek to the east.

3. The Surveyor-General very judiciously bid me put the question, 'Would they cultivate?' and further, 'that it was not expected to work like white men, but a little every year.' This was put to them very carefully by me in their own language, to which they replied distinctly, 'That blackfellows and lubras go look out food, but some always stop and turn up ground and plant potatoes and corn.'

4. It was further requested by the Surveyor-General that the number of aborigines be known who were willing to locate on the land that might be appropriated, which I also communicated. The chief gave me the heads of families and children, which amounted to 32.

5. Your Honour will perceive by this brief sketch the application and interview with the Surveyor-General, which the aborigines seemed duly to appreciate.

6. I am not acquainted with the locality required by the Goulburn blacks. There are, I understand, two highly respectable settlers not many miles off, who are both great friends of the aborigines and territorial magistrates, viz., Messrs. Snodgrass and Kerr. I would suggest that the authorities nigh at hand, as a police magistrate or government surveyor, accompany the chief of the Goulburn tribe to the locality they request, when, at the suggestion of the surveyor of the district, the boundary of the aboriginal country might be unmistakably defined and explained to them.

7. As there are 32 aborigines in the number desirous to locate, I would recommend at least one hundred and fifty acres each, not to be divided into 150-acre allotments, but for the chief and his tribe four thousand eight hundred acres, and the dividing range to the south would give them an unlimited range in that direction.

8. The aborigines would require assistance in provisions, implements,

etc., which would be an after consideration, and better arrived at by friends in the locality, who would submit the same for your Honour's approval. A steady, sober, agricultural family on their estate, would be desirable to instruct and encourage them.

7. William Thomas, Guardian of Aborigines, to Robert Brough Smyth, Secretary, Victorian Central Board for the Protection of the Aborigines, 5 October 1860

I have the honor to acknowledge Yours of the 2nd inst, "enquiring information whether it is advisable to retain the Reserve on the Acheron River in addition to the Mohican Station for the use of the blacks on the Upper Goulburn["].

I would by all means recommend that the Acheron River be retained, or else it will soon be taken up by others after the labor the blacks have bestowed upon it— and altercations may arise between them and the Settlers, as the Goulburn blacks will ever consider that as their Reserve.

I am fearful that the Goulburn blacks will never settle satisfactorily upon the Mohican Station, it may serve as back hunting ground and both should now (as it has been purchased) be retained for them.

The Goulburn blacks have waited twice upon me complaining that they have been ordered to remove from the land *they had Settled on and selected,* which I had promised them ever should be theirs— I fear it will be long if ever they are satisfied with their removal, they say, "*that is not the Country they selected, it is too cold and blackfellows soon die there*["].

8. *Illustrated Melbourne Post,* 25 June 1863. Deputation Of Aborigines

The members of the Central Board for the Protection of the Aborigines, headed by Mr Heales, M.L.A., president, Mr Sumner, vice-president, Mr R. B. Smith [Smyth], secretary, and Mr Thomas, J.P., protector, were then introduced. They were accompanied by chiefs of the Goulburn, Yarra, Western Port, and Gipps Land blacks, and several members of the respective tribes to the number of about sixteen, clothed in European costume, but wrapped in opossum rugs and carrying spears. The members of the board having taken a position on either side of his Excellency, with the aborigines in front, forming a semi-circle.

Mr Heales read the following address from the Central Board:–

"To his Excellency Sir Henry Barkly, K.C.B., Governor in Chief of the Colony of Victoria, and Vice-Admiral of the same.— We, the members of the Central Board, appointed to watch over the interests of the

aborigines, beg to introduce to your Excellency the Waworrung, Boono-
rong, and Tarawaragal tribes of Australian aborigines, who desire to congratulate her Most Gracious Majesty the Queen on the marriage of the
Prince of Wales. The proposition to forward a message of congratulation
and presents to her Majesty originated, we are informed, with the tribes
now settled on the Watts River, Upper Yarra [Coranderrk]. The movement was not initiated by the Central Board, but so soon as the fact was
known that two blacks had travelled more than forty miles to ascertain
whether they could be allowed to approach your Excellency for the purpose of presenting an address of congratulation, we rendered every possible assistance to them ... We beg that your Excellency will be pleased
to receive the address, written in the native language and in English, and
transmit it to her Most Gracious Majesty, together with the presents
which the aborigines desire to send. For the board, R. Heales, president.

His Excellency, in reply, said,— Gentlemen, of the Board of Protectors of the Aborigines, I have much pleasure in receiving this address and
have to thank the members of the Board for the great trouble they have
taken on this occasion. I am quite aware of the exertions of the Board for
the welfare of the blacks of this colony, and I am glad to know that their
efforts are attended with so much success.

Wonga, the chief of the Yarra tribe was then presented to his Excellency, and briefly addressed him in the aboriginal language, which was
interpreted by Mr Thomas. His observations were to the effect that the
deputation of blackfellows desired to present an address to her Majesty
the Queen, and to accompany it with presents to her and her son from
the tribes represented.

Mr R. B. Smyth then read the address which was as follows:— ...
Interpretation

Blacks of the tribes of Wawoorong Boonoorong and Tara-Waragal
send this to the Great Mother Queen Victoria. We and other Blackfellows send very many thanks to the Great Mother Queen for many many
things. Blackfellows now throw away all war-spears. No more fighting
but live like white men almost. Blackfellows hear that your first son has
married. Very good that! Blackfellows send all good to him, and to you,
his Great Mother, Victoria. Blackfellows come from Miam and Willum to
bring this paper to the Good Governor. He will tell you more. All Blackfellows round about agree to this. This is all.

His Excellency then said, I shall be obliged to the protector to tell the
natives that I will send the address and their presents across the sea to the
Queen, their great mother as they call her, and to her son. Tell them also
the Queen loves all her subjects, of whatever race, or country, or colour,
they may be, and she will be very glad to hear that the black fellows in

this country love her, and send her a present. She will also be glad to hear that they have given up fighting amongst each other, and live like her white subjects.

Mr Thomas having interpreted this reply, Wonga took from his arm a large and beautifully worked opossum rug which he spread before his Excellency, stating that it was a present from him to the Queen. The other blacks, one of them about eighty years of age, then laid on the rug a number of spears, a wimmera, shield, and waddy, as presents from them to the Price of Wales and Prince Alfred.

His Excellency again thanked the blacks for their presents, and desired Mr Thomas to inform them that the second son of the Queen would perhaps come out and see them. The aborigines then bowed to this Excellency and retired ...

9. Evidence of Thomas Bamfield (also known as Tommy Michie and Punch), 30 September 1881, Board appointed to inquire into Coranderrk Aboriginal Station

The aboriginal Tommy Michie, *alias* "Punch" handed in the following letter:— I report this matter for the welfare of the station. The station has never been improved since the old manager left. No clearing or grubbing done; no potatoes, cabbages, or other vegetables have been grown, and no fencing done since he left. Last time we mustered we counted 300 cattle and horses belonging to the township and cockatoo farmers. Nothing has been put in the orchard, and vegetables have not been grown for the good of our health. Mr. Green was very neighborly, and used to gather young men and women, and old people, and teach them like children, saving them from drinking and fighting; and every year he used to have a gathering. Mrs. Green was like a mother to all the natives, and was good to the women when they were confined, and she used to look after the sick. Under Mr. Green we used to kill our own cattle, and grow our own potatoes, cabbages, onions, carrots, and pumpkins— everything we could grow. We had plenty of milk, butter, and cheese. We get nothing like that now. Nothing has improved since the manager took charge of the station. I do not know what he was put here for. He ought to look around the run and get it made into four or five paddocks for the spring, a paddock for weaners, and a paddock for fat cattle, and kill our own cattle. Clearing and grubbing should be done. The manager is ruining the station. He is not doing his work, only riding about and breaking the Government buggy, and running horses. His daughter rides sore-backed horses; the matter was told to the police, and Captain Page stopped it. Why should not he be fined as well as the poor natives? Why should they take advantage of a poor black because he cannot read and write? I think they have done enough in this country to ruin the natives without taking it from us any more. I went away up the country about the Goulburn for a holiday, and Mr. Strickland sold all my geese, and would not allow me to keep pigs. The pigs and geese kept me in everything I wanted. We can keep nothing. I did not get paid for the geese, and I expect a pound for the lot.

10. Petition, 5 September 1881, Board appointed to inquire into Coranderrk Aboriginal Station

The only complaint we have is this, we all wish Mr. Green back here in Mr. Strickland's position. Mr. Strickland is not a fit man here in regard to work and also to the sick people; he has no idea of tilling the ground or making any improvements on the station, or doing any good for the welfare of the black there; no potatoes or hay here on the station, and the station ought (to) keep itself in meat but it does not; we all have to buy meat. When Mr. Green was here he used to be doing what Mr. Strickland is doing now, that is, he used to preach the gospel and also do the farming work, and also do what Mr. Capt. Page is doing now as inspector, and made a good improvement; and now it takes three men and there is no improvement. If Mr. Green had the use of the money what is laid now since he left, there would (be) something what the station would be able to pay back. We are all sure if we had Mr. Green back the station would self-support itself. No wonder the visitors that come here and go away and say the station ought to be sold, when we won't be allowed to clear the ground; the Central Board, and the manager too, are only leaving this open for to give room to the white people to have something to say about it. The only thing we wish is Mr. Green removed back here, and then they will see that (the) station will (be) improved better, and will also see that those who speak against us will see we have a head manager of us. So that (is) all we all have to say. These are the names of our men what are agreeable and hope to be carried out— Wm. Barak, Thos. Banfield [Bamfield], Dick Richard, Thos. Avoca, Terrick Johnny, Thos. Gillman, Lankey, Willie Hamilton, Alick Campbell, Thos. Dunolly, Martin Simpson, Alfred Morgan, H. Harmony, R. Wandon, J. Briggs.

11. *The Leader* (Melbourne), Supplement, 15 July 1882. Deputation Of Blackfellows At Parliament House

... The interview took place in the great hall of Parliament House, on 5th July, while the Assembly was sitting. Mr. Deakin, member for West

Bourke, introduced them to the Chief Secretary, explaining that the agitation which had been excited at Coranderrk by Mr. Green's removal from the management, about ten years ago, had caused the present deputation to come down to Melbourne, as it had led to similar deputations before, and that their object was to repeat the demands which they have been obliged to make on previous occasions. These demands were that the Central Board may be abolished and brought under the Chief Secretary's department, and that they may have Mr. Green re-appointed as manager. Mr. Deakin pointed out that the Central Board was still adhering to its often avowed intention of getting them removed from Coranderrk, and was also still persisting in its policy of antagonism to Mr. Green; and that consequently the disorganisation and distress prevailing at the station were bound to continue until the board's policy was reversed, and the rights of the blacks were respected and their wishes reasonably considered. Mr. Grant replied that he could not give any promise whatever, but would consult the Cabinet. He would not interfere, he said, with the board on any account, and they must go back and make the best of it; and he concluded by asserting that the agitation was all brought about by outside influence. This the blacks emphatically denied; asserting they had come unprompted by any one; in drawing up their memorial they had been unaided by any one; it was altogether their own idea; and they could only keep on coming down till they got what they wanted ...

12. Coranderrk Aborigines, letter to the editor, *Argus,* 29 August 1882

Sir,— We beg of you to put our little column in you valuable paper please. We have seen and heard that the managers of all the stations and the Central Board to have had a meeting about what to be done, so we have heard that there is going to be very strict rules on the station and more rules will be to much for us, it seems we are all going to be treated like slaves, far as we heard of it,— we wish to ask those Managor of the station Did we steal anything out of the colony or murdered anyone or are we prisoners or convict. We should think we are all free any white men of the colony. When we all heard of it, it made us very vex it enough to make us all go mad the way they are going to treat us it seems very hard. We all working in peace and quiteness and happy, pleasing Mr. Goodall, and also showing Mr Goodall that we could work if we had a good manager expecting our wishes to be carried out, what we have ask for, but it seem it was the very opposite way. So we don't know what to do since we heard those strict rules planned out. It has made us downhearted. We must all try again and go to the head of the Colony.— We are all your

Most Obedient Servants, Wm Barak (X), Thos. Avoca, Dick Richard (X), Thos. Mickey (X), Lankey (X), Lankey Manto, Thos Dunolly, Robert Wandon, Alfred Morgan, Wm Parker. Coranderrk, August 29th, 1882.

13. *Argus*, 25 March 1886. Mr Berry And the Aborigines

Mr. Berry was yesterday the recipient of a somewhat rare compliment, a deputation of pure blacks from the aboriginal station at Coranderrk coming to Melbourne to bid good-bye to the late Chief Secretary. The ceremony took place in the Executive Council chamber at the Treasury-building, the party being introduced by the present Chief Secretary (Mr. Deakin) and Mr. Zox, M.L.A. With the deputation was Mrs. Bon. At the head of the party was Baruk [Barak], a small-statured, grey-bearded native, once chief, and now the sole survivor of the Yarra Yarra tribe. Baruk went up the stone steps of the Treasury with the utmost self-confidence, but the bearing of his followers was generally diffident. Next to Baruk in rank was Bertdrak, chief of the Broken River tribe, but better known as "Punch." A few years ago Punch used occasionally to hold Coranderrk in subjugation with a gun, but when Government officials visited the station he was generally sober and unarmed, and had little chance of doing his race any substantial service. Of late years he has taken to diplomacy, and has given the Aborigines Board and the Government a good deal of trouble. The deputation formed in a crescent round the table, studded with the new portfolios of the Ministry. The natives were dignified and reserved in their demeanour. The gifts brought by the deputation as a present to Mr. Berry were of a varied and characteristic type. In a bundle of native weapons were included boomerangs, newly carved, and the throwing of which was shown in pantomime; a waddy, carved and all ready for use; a gnulla gnulla, or modern shield with the handle nicely lined with wallaby fur. Special presents from Baruk were two long cane spears, which the chief showed Mr. Berry how to adjust in the spear-thrower and to poise for business. A couple of the firesticks by which the tribes were accustomed to light their camp fires were also presented. Baruk was evidently of opinion that all these gifts were intended for use rather than ornament, and on the carpet of the Executive chamber he showed Mr. Berry how to light a fire by placing one stick on the floor, and spinning the other rod between his palms, with the hardened point inserted in a small groove in the stationary stick. The surroundings were not congenial, however, and the fire refused to respond to the friction. In addition to the implements of war, there was an album filled with por-traits of the Coranderrk natives, from a spirited photo of the old chief to the presentment of the most recent "picaninny." A rushwork basket, made by the lubras, was filled with native flowers, with a dahlia and one or two other brilliant aliens added to heighten the effect. A walking-stick, cut from a tree round which a creeper had spirally and symmetrically twined, was another characteristic bush present. The creeper was carved and scaled to represent a snake, and "Punch" suggested that a coat of varnish would heighten the effect. Last of all, one of the party brought a lyre bird's tail.

Prepatory to making the presentation, Mrs. Bon stated that it was 23 years since a deputation had left Coranderrk to attend a *levée* at Government-house, in the time of Sir Charles Darling, and for the purpose of sending a congratulatory address to the Queen on the occasion of the marriage of her son, the Prince of Wales. The aboriginal owners of the soil had never before turned out to do honour to any man leaving these shores. Incidentally she reminded Mr. Deakin that, notwithstanding all that Mr. Berry had one, there was yet plenty for him to do. The natives wished to be relieved of the board, and if the gentlemen composing it had not that sense of honour which should induce them to resign, they ought at least to be relieved of their management of Coranderrk. A lot of money had been misspent in building a large house for the manager, which was locally known as the coffee palace.

The following address, which was said to have been dictated by the chief Baruk, and which was inscribed on illuminated cardboard by Messrs. Fergusson and Mitchell, was read:–

"To the honourable Graham Berry.

"We have come to see you because you have done a great deal of work for the aborigines.

"I feel very sorrowful, and first time I hear you was going home I was crying. You do all that thing for the station when we were in trouble, when the board would not give us much food and clothes, and wanted to drive us off the land. We came to you and told you our trouble, and you gave us the land for our own as long as we live, and gave us more food and clothes and blankets and better houses, and the people all very thankful.

"And now you leave this country, Victoria, to go to England, where we may never see you no more. We give you small present with our love. When you go away keep remembering the natives, for the natives will remember you for your doing good to Coranderrk.

"We had a trouble here in this country, but we can all meet up along 'Our Father.' We hope that God will lead you right through the water, and take you safe to England, and keep you in the straight way, and give you eternal life through Jesus Christ our Saviour.

"Baruk, Chief of the Yarra Yarra Tribe of Aborigines, Victoria, Australia."

The names and native signatures of Bertdrak, Wyerdermn, Kata-warmin, Worteeilum, Ngiaqueon, Pundagoorn, Triabil, and Derranii were also appended.

Mr. Berry, in acknowledging the presentation and the special compliment paid to him, said that it had always been his opinion that the few natives remaining in the colony should be treated with the greatest kindness and consideration, not as paupers, but as a matter of common justice due to the original owners of the soil. He knew that the natives were thinking men, and felt that that was shown in the address presented to him to-day, which was as feeling in its terms, as pertinent in its purpose, and as kindly as any he would receive. He was certain that the inclinations of the natives themselves would be largely studied by the present Chief Secretary. While in England he would be glad to hear of them or from them. Whatever he had been enabled to do for them was through the representations of Mrs. Bon, than whom no people had ever a truer friend.

Mr. Berry then shook hands with each of the natives present and the ceremony concluded.

14. *Herald* (Melbourne), 21 September 1886. The Protection Bill And The Coranderrk Blacks

In the Aborigines Protection Bill now before parliament one of the clauses (No. 5) gives the Board for the Protection of Aborigines supreme control over the blacks. Any aborigines guilty of breaches of discipline may be removed from stations kept up by the Government, or may have their rations stopped by the Board. Previously the blacks have always been able to appeal from the Board to the Chief Secretary, but in the Bill under notice this right of appeal is taken away. The Coranderrk blacks are strongly opposed to this clause, and prepared a petition against it, for presentation to the Chief Secretary ...

The following is *verbatim* copy of the petition, which is signed by the whole of the black male adults at Coranderrk:–

To the Chief Secretary.

Sir,— We wish to ask for our wishes, that is, could we get our freedom to go away shearing and harvesting, and to come home when we wish, and also to go for the good of our health when we need it; and we aboriginals all wish and hope to have freedom, not to be bound down by the protection of the Board, as it says in the Bill (clause 5), But we should be free like the white population. There is only few blacks now remaining in Victoria. We are all dying away now, and we blacks of aboriginal blood wish to have our freedom for all our life time, for the population is small, and the increase is slow. For why does the Board seek in these latter days more stronger authority over us aborigines than it has yet been. For there is only 21 aborigines on the station Coranderrk, including men and women.— Your servants, Chief William Barak, John Logan, Thomas Avoca, John Terrick, Charles Kable, Thomas Banfield [Bamfield], Thomas Gilman, Dick Richard, Lanky Manton, Lanky Gilmore, Edward McLennon, Thomas McLennon, Camgham John, Samuel Rowan, Mooney Clark, Frederick Stewart. Coranderrk, 20th September.

Maloga

15. Maloga petition, 1881

The following is the text of a petition to be presented to His Excellency the Governor:-

"To his Excellency Lord Augustus Loftus, G.C.B., Governor of the colony of New South Wales— The humble petition of the undersigned aboriginal natives, residents on the Murray River, in the colony of New South Wales, members of the Moira and Ulupna tribes, respectfully showeth:-

1. That all the land within our tribal boundaries has been taken possession of by the Government and white settlers. Our hunting grounds are used for sheep pasturage, and the game reduced, and in many places exterminated; rendering our means of subsistence extremely precarious, and often reducing us, and our wives and children, to beggary.

2. We, the men of our several tribes, are desirous of honestly maintaining our young and infirm, who are in many cases the subjects of extreme want and semi-starvation; and we believe we could, in a few years, support ourselves by our own industry were a sufficient area of land granted us to cultivate and raise stock.

3. We have been under training for some years, and feel that our old mode of life is not in keeping with the instructions we have received, and we are earnestly desirous of settling down to more orderly habits of industry, that we may form homes for our families.

We more confidently ask this favour of a grant of land, as our fellownatives in other colonies have proved capable of supporting themselves where suitable land has been reserved for them.

We hopefully appeal to your Excellency, as we recognise in you the protector specially appointed by Her Gracious Majesty the Queen to promote religion and education among the aboriginal natives of the colony, and to protect us in our persons and in the free enjoyment of our possessions, and to take such measures as may be necessary for our advancement in civilisation.

And your petitioners, as in duty bound, will ever pray:— Bobby Wilberforce, Richard (x, his mark), Thomas Williams, Aaron Atkinson, George Cha[r]les, Freddy Walker, Daylight, David Berrick, Peter Stucky, Jacky Wilberforce, Jimmy Turner, Sydney, George Keefe, James Coghil, Sampson Barber, Bagot Morgan, John Atkinson, Peter, Robert Taylor, David Taylor, Jasper Angus, George Aben, Bradshaw, Harry Fenton, Thomas Fenton, Alowidgee, Johnny Golway, Charlie Steward, Ted Robertson, Rochford Robertson, Gibson Platt, Jacky John, Tommy Hawke, Robertson, Boney, Cockey, Barraltaharry, Jimmy Martin, Blucher, Dick Richards, James Edgar, Whyman McLean.

16. Maloga petition, 1887

To His Excellency the Right Hon Baron Carrington, P.C., K.C.M.G.— Your Excellency.— The following of the Aborigines and half-castes on the Maloga Aboriginal Mission Station, and the neighborhood thereof, hereby showeth that while grateful for the benefits conferred upon on them by the liberality of our Government, in aiding the Aborigines Protection Association to provide a home for them and their families, and also recognising their debt of gratitude to that association, they would suggest that on the recommendation of that society those among us, who so desires, should be granted sections of land of not less than 100 acres per family in fee simple or else at a small nominal rental annually, with the option of purchase at such prices as shall be deemed reasonable for them under the circumstances, always bearing in mind that the Aborigines were the former occupiers of the land. Such a provision would enable them to earn their own livelihood, and thus partially relieve the State from the burden of their maintenance. We think that such a provision would be far more in accord with the wishes of Her Most Gracious Majesty Queen Victoria in this the jubilee year of her reign than many of the methods adopted to celebrate that occasion, and also that it would be a fitting memorial in connection with the celebration of the Centenary of the colony. Trusting that your Excellency will see fit to grant our petition, your petitioners will, as in duty bound, ever pray. On behalf of the petitioners.— Robert Cooper, Samson Barber, Aaron Atkinson, Hughy Anderson, John Cooper, Edgar Atkinson, Whyman McLean, John Atkinson (his mark), William Cooper, George Middleton, Edward Joachim (his mark).

17. William Cooper to J.M. Chanter, MLA, 11 November 1887

I most respectfully beg to state that I shall feel deeply obliged if you will be good enough to use your influence toward securing a piece of land for me. I am anxious to get a home and make some provisions for my wife and daughter & as I am an honest hard-working man, the land will be applied to a legitimate use. I want a grant of land that I can call my own so long as I and my family live and yet without the power of being able to do away with the land.

Farming barely sufficient to maintain my family decently I find it therefore impossible to pay for a selection. I shall be perfectly satisfied with 100 acres adjoining the Maloga Aboriginal Reserve if possible. I do trust you will be successful in securing this small portion of a vast territory which is ours by Divine right. We know that grants of land have been made to Aborigines in other parts of N.S.W. and that they have been abused but as there have been no grants made to our tribe I beg you to give us a trial.

Hoping to get a favourable reply.

18. *Sydney Morning Herald*, 12 December 1890. Deputations. The Maloga Mission.

The Revs. Dr. Steel, Dr. Roseby, J.B. Anderson, and Messrs. J. Saxby, J.J. Warr, E. Hogben, and D. Matthews waited upon the Premier yesterday morning as a deputation to ask Governmental aid in carrying out the Maloga mission to the aborigines. The mission, it was explained, was commenced on the River Murray in 1874, and since that time it had been extended to many parts of the colony. With the object of gathering together all the blacks on the coast between Port Stephens and Twofold Bay, it was asked that a piece of land at Jervis Bay should be granted on which might be formed a camp. A petition signed by 16 aboriginals, and in the following terms, was handed to the Premier:— "We, the native blacks about Sydney, ask you if you will be kind enough to give us a piece of land at Jervis Bay, where we can make a home for ourselves and our people. We have been hunted about a good deal from one place to another, and we find it hard to get a living for ourselves and the children, but if we get a chance and some help from the Government we might in time get a living. As it is we find it very hard. Drink and a hard life are killing us off. White people ought to be very good to us for they got our good country for nothing. We don't want them to pay us for it, but they ought to help us to live. We would like our boys and girls to learn to read and write like white children, and we want boats and nets for fishing, so we can get money for our work and learn to live like Christians."

Sir Henry Parkes, in reply, said his experience of the aborigines was that they did not like to be forcibly or in any way removed from the places in which they were born or reared. He sympathised with the object of the deputation, and promised to lay the matter before his colleagues; and until he had taken this step he could give no definite answer.

Poonindie, Point McLeay and Point Pearce

19. Residents of Poonindie to Mr Hamilton, Native Protector, South Australia, 8 January 1887

Dear Friend. We the undersigned to petition to you our most honurable protector to lay out before you our greivances on poonindie. Now our grevance is this Mr Bruce is to us like a tyrant-master.

We the undersigned do make it our business to tell you how Mr Bruce is treating us here he just does as he likes with us and when we tell the trustees about our greivances on poonindie they dont take no notice of us ...

20. Thomas Adams, Point Pearce Mission, to Mr Hamilton, Protector of Aborgines, South Australia, [1888]

I am waiting anxiously to hear from you about the land to know whether I am to have it or not. I should like to have the land I have been asking you for there is only 80 acres in the section that I am applying for but would sooner have it than have 160 any where else as many kind friends of mine who are farmers themselves has offered to start me and help me in every possible way I believe Mr Bruce has been trying to prevent me from having it and makes out that it is to close to Poonindee I believe he has been talking to Mr Blackmore on the matter though I cant say for certain but what I have heard since my return from Adelaide there is every reason to believe that he has and if such is the case Mr Bruce have been treating me very wrong and unjustly it is not to close to the Mission because I have seen natives down Pt McLeay having land within 2 miles of the Station I hope you will try and get me the land it will be a pity if I should lose it after it has been promised to me and I waiting so long when I could have had land which of course is now taken up when the honourable Thomas Playford was commissioner he offered me land up at the Harbour and told me that if I should pick a piece out to let him know and he would reserve it for me but I refused the offer but I told him it was to far then he said to me perhaps you would like to have it nearer my neighbourhood and I told him yes and he looked in the map to see if there was any unleased but there was none or he should have granted it to me I am at present living on Pt Pearce I hope you will let me know as soon as possible

21. Poonindie Petition, 2 February 1894

We the undersigned have been living on Poonindie for a number of years. We are very sorry to hear that the place is to be taken from us. It is very hard to be turned away from what has been our home. We would ask that the whole of the land on the south side of the Tod River, comprising we believe about 3,000 acres more or less of the poorest land on the whole run should be given to us. If this is given we propose to live on it and cultivate and work the land among ourselves. With this and what we can earn by shearing, fishing and getting guano, we can support ourselves and our families. We will do our best to work it and maintain ourselves which we shall be sorry to be turned away from.

22. William Adams, Robert Wanganeen and Henry Angic to the Commissioner of Public Works, South Australia, 19 February 1894

A few weeks ago when the village settlements scheme was being discussed in town Point Pearce was mentioned as a likely spot for a settlement by some of the members of the unemployed and by one member of the Government. Considering that there are from eighty to ninety souls on the Station to feed, clothe, and shelter, the action proposed by the unemployed and one of the members of the Government was little less than inhuman. We, as children of the original owners of the land, presume that we have a right to be considered in the disposal of the land. It was after years of hard labour and self-sacrifice that has made Point Pearce what it is. Besides, what gain would it be to turn one lot of people off to put another on? We consider that the land on Point Pearce is now being put to its best use. It would be impossible for the land to hold any more than at the present time. As it is we are only deriving from the land a mere existence. Compare the land that is on Point Pearce to the millions of acres that are in South Australia; why it is only about the size of a threepenny bit. We are, sir, on behalf of the residents of the Point Pearce Mission Station.

P.S. How is it we are not allowed to vote? As law-abiding and peaceful subjects of the British Crown we don't see any reasons why we should not be allowed to vote. As we are made subject to the laws in South

Australia we deem it only fair and just that we should be allowed to have a voice in the framing of those laws.

23. Tom Adams, Point Pearce Mission, to Mr G.W. Hawkes, 2 April 1895

I write these few lines to thank you on behalf of myself & family & the rest of the few Poonindie natives that are here, dear sir, no one can tell how we felt when we received those kind loving letters from our kind & beloved father, no earthly father as done what he done for us, I wrote to him as soon as I received the letters, I see by the paper's that God as called him home to his Eternal Rest to meet our dear & beloved friend Bishop Short & all our loved one's who have gone before us, please when you write to Mrs. Hale & her family send her our love & tell her that we go with her in mourning dear sir I cant write much to you I feel too sad when I think of Poonindie & our dear father's love & time labour & money that he spent there & I think that the Government as taken it away they may as well have waited until God had called him home to his rest, the natives felt it more for our dear Bishop's sake, it seemed as if they did'ent think of him when they took it away, it is very hard for us to think of our dear old home & white people living there & we've got to pass by like stranger's; we cant help thinking of the times when our dear Bishop Short & Yourself had charge of Poonindie, those were happy days, it was a sad day for us when you left, although I did not belong to Poonindie when it was taken away, still we all love our dear old home, I have been now seven years at Point Pearce. Mr Sutton was here when I came & he proved a good, christian friend to me & my family, the natives of Point Pierce love's him very much indeed, he is a true christian, time's are very hard here at present we are working for our rations, still we are all happy & well; the trustee's are trying to get it out of debt we are hoping for better times after shearing if all is well. Dear Sir the few Poonindie natives that are here wishe's me to ask you if you have any spare time if you could come & see us once more we should be all very glad to see you with love from us all

24. *Advertiser,* 12 April 1907. Point Macleay Natives. Want More Food And Less Prayer

The Premier has received the following petition from 18 aborigines of the Point Macleay Mission Station:– We, the undersigned Naranjeries tribe, and leaders of the Campbell Clan, beg to request your Government to take over the work at Point Macleay, and to carry it on as the Government of Victoria carry on the blacks' station at Korundurk [Coranderrk], in that State. At present the true aborigines of the lakes get little or no benefit from the mission. All the money your Government give us is spent on white officers and the half white population of the place. The real blacks do not get the value of £50 a year out of it all. Of course, the mission does a great lot of preaching and praying, but we old natives of the soil would do with less of that and more of food, clothes, and Better tents. In fact, we are too badly dressed to attend the church, and too ill-fed to think much about praying. But we do pray you to take over the place; we may then be better off. We can't be worse off.

— We are, dear sir, yours (signed on behalf of the clan)— real aborigines— P. Campbell, J. Unipon, L. Campbell, Stonewell F. Blackmoor, A. Blackmoor, W. Newland, F. Waster, A. Harding, G. Harris, N. Pearcis, W. Campbell, J. Lock, E. Rankine, P. Williams, F. Blackmoor, G. Seymour, A.Karloan

2 1920s–1950s

Aboriginal politics in the inter- and post-war decades was characterised by the emergence of political organisations founded and led by Aborigines, yet supported by non-Aboriginal activists. These organisations depended on there being at least a small number of Aborigines who were sufficiently free from government 'protection', and their leaders tended to be men who had not only acquired the rudiments of a European education but had also worked in many areas of Australia— experience that provided them with a broader knowledge of the oppression of their people than that held by most other Aborigines.

These organisations drew their support, however, from Aborigines in particular regions and tended to reflect their concerns, although those founded in the 1930s also strove to represent all Aborigines in Australia. They were formed in response to the impact of increasingly discriminatory legislation and the harsh policies and practices of the government bodies responsible for administering these Aboriginal Acts. During this time, Aboriginal communities were oppressed by Protectors and Protection Boards that variously tried either to push Aborigines onto supervised reserves or to disperse them into white Australian society, thereby threatening their land holdings and families.

New South Wales, Queensland and the Northern Territory

The first of these organisations to be founded was the Australian Aboriginal Progressive Association (AAPA), which was officially established in February 1925, although it had been active during the previous two years or so. The AAPA's focus was the mid-north coast of New South Wales, encompassing Aboriginal communities in towns such as Kempsey and Bellbrook Bridge (26), although the organisation also had a base in inner Sydney where its president, Fred Maynard, lived and worked.

The AAPA's symbol had a motto 'One God, One Aim, One Destiny', but Maynard was influenced less by Christianity— although he had been raised in the church— than by his experiences as a young man as a drover and stockman throughout Australia and later as a wharfie and an active member of the Waterside Workers' Union, and by those of his family who had lost land when it was leased to white farmers. He was assisted by a humanitarian, Elizabeth McKenzie-Hatton, apparently the only non-Aboriginal member of the organisation, who assumed the position of secretary, and heavily supported by a fervent Australian nationalist, J.J. Moloney, a member of both the Australian Society of Patriots and the Australian Natives Association and the editor of a Newcastle newspaper, *Voice of the North* (**25**).[1] The AAPA was largely concerned with the removal of Aboriginal children from their parents and the loss of reserve lands (**25 27 29** and **30**), and it not only articulated a demand for citizenship rights for Aborigines but grounded these claims in Aboriginality—asserting their status as indigenous Australians, and proclaiming a pride in being Aboriginal (**28**).

The organisation grew rapidly during 1925 but seems to have been disbanded in 1928 after an appeal to the federal government that was prompted, in part, by the failure of its protests to the state government as well as to King George V (**29** and **30**). This appeal to the imperial monarch was emulated in 1933 by King Burraga (Joe Anderson) (**31**), a resident of Salt Pan Creek camp in south-western Sydney where Aborigines fleeing the control of the NSW Aborigines Protection Board on the north and south coast had gathered in the mid-1920s. It seems to have been underpinned both by a conviction that their reserve lands had been granted to them by Queen Victoria and an assumption that imperial monarchs continued to have the authority to intervene to protect their indigenous subjects. This emphasis on special or different rights also characterised the call for a model Aboriginal state by South Australian churchmen and philanthropists[2]— a demand which was backed by several Aborigines in that state, such as David Unaipon, but attacked by others (**29**)— and the request for an Aboriginal representative in the Commonwealth parliament (**31** and **32**).

This was much less a feature of the organisation founded in NSW in 1937 by William Ferguson and Jack Patten— the Aborigines Progressive Association (APA)—which represented the demands of its supporters much more by reference to them having the same rights as other Australians and emphasised integration rather than Aboriginality in articulating its programme for change (**35 37 38** and **39**). However, while its concerns were broader than that of the AAPA, they also echoed those of Aboriginal spokespersons such as Joe Anderson and the earlier organisation. This was particularly so for Patten's APA— the organisation split into two bodies with the same name in mid-1938— which was closely associated with the community at Salt Pan Creek and those former AAPA members on the mid-north coast who continued to protest the ongoing dispossession of land (34). The APA led by Ferguson and Pearl Gibbs was similarly regional in its constituency— Dubbo and western NSW communities.[3]

The principal targets for the protest of both these organisations were the feared Act; the hated Aborigines 'Protection' Board of NSW and many of its authoritarian reserve managers; the breaking up of many reserves and the concentration of Aborigines on other ones; the appalling conditions on these reserves; poor schooling; the loss of reserve lands; the denial of social welfare benefits; the removal of children from their parents; and the colour bar in country towns (33 35 37 and 41–44).

In its first year, the APA also attempted to project a political voice onto a broader stage, casting itself as a national organisation. This was particularly evident in the 'Day of Mourning and Protest' it organised to commemorate Australia's sesquicentenary, the ten-point plan it presented to the Commonwealth government immediately afterwards (38 and 39), Ferguson and Patten's *Aborigines Claim Citizen Rights* (37) and a short-lived monthly newspaper, *Australian Abo Call* (48 and 49).

In this endeavour Patten drew heavily on the support of right-wing nationalists P.R. Stephensen and W.B. Miles (36). By contrast, the support among non-Aborigines for Ferguson and Gibbs' APA lay on the left, reflecting Ferguson's long relationship with the Australian Workers' Union and close connections with the ALP and the unemployed workers' organisations, and their relationships with progressive feminist organisations and the Communist Party of Australia (CPA) (35 and 40). Both organisations, however, emphasised the importance of Aboriginal control of the APA, and were critical of humanitarian organisations which claimed to represent Aboriginal interests (41). Yet non-Aboriginal support was crucial: when nationalist supporters withdrew their backing for *Australian Abo Call*, Patten's APA lost much of its force and was disbanded in 1939. The onset of World War II largely curtailed Ferguson and Gibbs' campaigning.

In Queensland there was little political activity. This is perhaps surprising since there were large reserves such as Cherbourg where Aborigines were able to acquire literacy skills— circumstances that underpinned activism in other Australian states. However, it would seem that Aborigines 'under the Act' were powerless to form political organisations because of the extremely repressive state regime— headed by Protector J.W. Bleakley— that oversaw Aboriginal workers' wages through trust funds (45), controlled the large reserves or compounds and removed Aboriginal children from their kin (47–49). 'Troublemakers' were exiled to the notorious Palm Island. These factors made Aboriginal protest very difficult and so relationships with sympathetic whites or Aboriginal organisations were crucial to representation of their plight (46–49). In the Northern Territory, like other remote areas, there is similarly little evidence of Aboriginal protest before the 1940s.

South Australia

It seems that no Aboriginal organisations of any note were formed in South Australia during this period but Aboriginal communities were represented by several mission-educated men— most notably David Unaipon (**50 56** and **57**)— and this enabled various forms of protest, such as holding public meetings and concerts, drawing up petitions, forming deputations to government, and testifying to government inquiries (**50–53**), although these were notably more temperate in tone and even substance than those of the AAPA and APA (**57**).

In part, this moderation probably resulted from the close relationship between the Aborigines' Friends' Association, the most politically conservative missionary organisation in Australia, and one of the mission stations, Point McLeay (**57**). Aborigines on other reserves appealed to Constance Ternent Cooke, the convenor of the Aboriginal Welfare Committee of the South Australian Women's Non-Party Association, one of a number of white women campaigners for Aboriginal rights during the 1920s and 1930s (**54**).

Their concerns were, nevertheless, very similar to those of Aborigines in other states: loss of land; overcrowding on reserves and deteriorating living conditions; Aboriginal representation on the bodies governing their lives; and the removal of children— what one journalist reporting an incident in 1924 called 'stolen' children (**48–54** and **56**).[4]

Western Australia

The first organisation to be formed in this state was founded in the south-west by William Harris, a farmer in the Morowa district who had been attacking the treatment of Aborigines in this area since 1906, and his nephew, Norman. William Harris shared much with the other leaders of the inter-war period: He had been educated— at the Swan Native and Half-Caste Home in Perth— and had travelled widely through his work on cattle stations in the north of the state, thus learning much of the oppression of his people and acquiring a broader perspective on this.[5]

The Native Union and other Aborigines largely protested against the discrimination encountered by Aborigines of mixed descent, whether in terms of exercising the franchise, entering public houses or having their children educated in state schools (**59** and **60**). Likewise, they attacked the authoritarian system of control being established by the Chief Protector of

Aborigines, A.O. Neville, which saw a growing number of Aborigines being brought 'under the Act'; increased interference in their lives; and their 'imprisonment' on reserves such as Moore River, or Mogumber as Aborigines called it (61–64). Nevertheless, William Harris also tried to raise his voice against the massacres of Aborigines by punitive expeditions in the north of the state (61) but, as his nephew noted in correspondence with a sympathetic humanitarian campaigner, it was a difficult task sustaining a political organisation among Aborigines 'under the Act' (64).

The Native Union was short-lived, but Norman Harris and other members of the Harris clan continued to play a role in campaigning against Neville's regime, giving evidence to a 1934 royal commission, where one of the central issues presented by Aboriginal witnesses and Mary Bennett was the removal of children from their parents (64 and 65).[6] Although a small number of Aboriginal women played a role in organisations founded in the inter- and post-war periods, their voices, and the particular interests of Aboriginal women, gained little public representation. This government inquiry provided a forum for the expression of their grievances; among those who took advantage of this were several 'half-caste' women in Broome who petitioned the Royal Commissioner (66).[7]

Aboriginal workers in the cattle industry were similarly disenfranchised, but in the mid-1930s a Euralian Association was founded in Port Hedland with the assistance of a white contractor, Don McLeod, who had connections with various left-wing organisations, including the CPA in Perth. In May 1946 he and two Aboriginal stockworkers, Dooley Bin Bin and Clancy McKenna, coordinated strike action on pastoral properties through the Pilbara (67 and 68). This protest lasted, on and off for three years, and eventually led to Aborigines walking away and establishing a co-operative industry which inspired many other Aborigines and their organisations in south-eastern Australia (70 and 71).

Victoria

The Australian Aborigines' League (AAL) was the most important Aboriginal body in this period, as revealed by its longevity and the breadth of its campaigning. Although it was not formally established until late 1935, those who constituted the organisation were active as early as 1929–30 (72), and while its activities declined in 1940 with the failing health of its principal officebearers, William Cooper and Arthur Burdeu, it was revived in 1945–46 when Cooper's protégé, Doug Nicholls, and Bill Onus— who had been active in Ferguson's APA in 1940–41— joined forces under the AAL banner with Ferguson, Gibbs and Herbert Groves. (In the mid-1950s Gibbs and Groves were to form the Aboriginal-Australian Fellowship.)

The AAL had much in common with the AAPA in as much as it had an emphasis on Aboriginal rights and Aboriginality, as revealed by its call for Aboriginal parliamentary representation in Cooper's petition to King George V (**72 74** and **78**) and its rejection of the policy of absorption (**75**). Yet, it also shared the APA's focus on 'uplift' and citizenship rights for Aborigines (**39 78–80**) and its representation of Australian history (**79**).[8]

The League's scope was much broader than these other organisations, however. This was so from the beginning of Cooper's activism (**72**), as evident in his petition campaign (**64** and **73**), his role in formulating the idea for the Day of Mourning and the League's campaigning in other states such as Western Australia (**81**). Yet the organisation also had an intensely local focus, being particularly concerned with Cummeragunja which, as we have seen, was not only Cooper's homeland (**16** and **17**) but also that of most of its committee including Shadrach James, Nicholls, and Caleb Morgan.

The bitter memory of losing much of the reserve to white farmers is strikingly evident in the condemnation of the NSW Aborigines Protection Board by Morgan's wife, Anna, in 1934 (**75**) and earlier in James' writings (**71**).[9] The regaining and development of this land, as well as the deteriorating conditions on Cummeragunja, were major issues in the League's representations to the NSW government (**77** and **82**).

The AAL campaigns, like those of other organisations and activists considered in this section, met with little success, provoking enormous frustration in the ageing Cooper and his supporters (**78 79** and **84**). This was especially so on Cummeragunja itself, where, in February 1939, many walked off the station, led by Jack and George Patten who had been born and raised on the reserve. Their concerns were the same as those of Aborigines on other reserves in NSW: land: appalling living conditions; maltreatment by the Board's officers; and fear of the removal of their children (**82–85**).

In this they were supported by the CPA and other left-wing organisations (**85**), but the League had previously sought supporters among those like Cooper's mentors—Daniel Matthews and Thomas James—and humanitarians, churchmen and missionaries such as North Queensland missionary E.R.B. Gribble, and had also enjoyed the support of Labor parliamentarians like M.J. Makin (**74**). The League was suspicious of the CPA, despite Margaret Tucker's close relations with members of the party and the faithful support of socialist Helen Baillie (**64**), but the importance of an alliance with left-wing movements was continued during the post-war period with Onus' involvement. Unlike the APA of both Patten and Ferguson, however, these alliances seem to have had little impact on the League's programme. Cooper placed a strong emphasis on what he called 'thinking black' and 'the black man's point of view'.[10]

As the campaigning in the 1940s and 1950s reveals, Cooper's political son, Doug Nicholls, inherited much of this emphasis (86), as well as his concern for Aborigines in remote Australia and his articulation of Aboriginal rights. This is evident in Nicholls joining forces with South Australian churchman Charles Duguid, anthropologist Donald Thomson, pacifist Doris Blackburn and others to fight rocket range testing in the Central Australian Aboriginal Reserve in 1946–47 (88 and 89); his role in attacking the banishment of Darwin strike leader Fred Waters in 1951; and his calling for Aboriginal parliamentary representation (90). Nicholls also emulated Cooper in his political methods (91).

During the 1940s and 1950s land was a less important consideration for Nicholls and the League in Melbourne, even though it continued to be so for Aborigines on reserves, such as Mary Clarke, an executive member of the AAL in the late 1930s (92). Nicholls and Onus focused more on other aspects of Aborigines' welfare in Victoria and elsewhere, such as their living conditions and the colour bar (93 and 94).

NOTES

1   See Heather Goodall, *From Invasion to Embassy: Land in Aboriginal Politics in New South Wales, 1770–1972*, Allen & Unwin/Black Books, Sydney, 1996, chapter 12; see the map on p. 150 showing the communities involved in the AAPA.

2   See Michael Roe, 'A Model Aboriginal State', *Aboriginal History*, vol. 10, pt 1, 1986, pp. 40–44.

3   For a discussion of the APAs, see Goodall, *From Invasion to Embassy*, chapter 17; Jack Horner, *Vote Ferguson for Aboriginal Freedom: A Biography*, Australian and New Zealand Book Company, Sydney, 1974, chapters 4 and 5.

4   *Sun* (Adelaide), 12 November 1924. This report was headlined ' "I Want My Baby!": Aboriginal Mother's Plaintive Cry. State's Shameful Steal: One Law for the White People: Another for the Aboriginals'.

5   See Anna Haebich, *For Their Own Good: Aborigines and Government in the Southwest of Western Australia, 1900–1940*, University of Western Australia Press, Nedlands, 1988, pp. 78–79, 125–26, 156–57, 269–76, 298.

6   See *ibid.*, pp. 330–37.

7   The complete version of this letter has been reproduced in Marilyn Lake and Katie Holmes (eds), *Freedom Bound II: Documents on Women in Modern Australia*, Allen & Unwin, Sydney, 1995, pp. 63–67.

8   Cooper's most powerful articulation of this is his 'From an Educated Black', which is reproduced in Andrew Markus (ed.), *Blood From a Stone: William Cooper and the Australian Aborigines' League*, Allen & Unwin, Sydney, 1988, pp. 85–92.

9   For examples of James' other writings, see *ibid.*, pp. 22–23, 25–27.

10 See, for example, Cooper to Minister for the Interior, John McEwen, 19 April 1939, National Archives of Australia (Canberra), CRS A659, 40/1/858.

New South Wales, Queensland and the Northern Territory

25. **Elizabeth McKenzie-Hatton, Secretary, Australian Aboriginal Progressive Association, letter to the editor, *Voice of the North*, 12 June 1925**

... I have just returned from my third visit along the North Coast Line, where I have visited the camps and settlements of the aboriginal people ...

Everywhere we find them being thrown out, fenced out of the homes that have long been theirs— their lands, which have long been reserved for them, are being ruthlessly taken from them and sold to the highest bidder or leased to white people, already made wealthy by using the labour of these poor coloured people devoid of equitable recourse ...

One aboriginal man reminded me that it is now more than a hundred years since they have been associated with white people, and they naturally want opportunity to develop their affairs along the lines and upon the lessons learned from the white people ...

During the past few months circumstances ... have made the conditions of the aboriginal extremely difficult— the land is being sold, and they are finding themselves on the roadsides or on any corner of "no man's land", where they, in their hapless lot find themselves, homeless, disheartened, and resentful at the injustice which is being meted out to them. They are indeed an unhappy people.

In the hope of doing something to alter these conditions and to prove that they have capacity for organised effort and thrift, they have banded themselves together into an association. The A.A.P.A. has been formed— the letters stand for the Australian Aboriginal Progressive Association, and they have at present two objectives, although the association aims at the uplift of the aboriginal people in the spiritual, social, and all departments of life. The two special reforms they crave for at this time are:

First— That the aboriginal will be given a small portion of land in his own right to build his home upon. A five acre or ten acre lot is asked for in a suitable locality.

Second— They beg that their homes will no longer be despoiled; but that they may be allowed to keep their children with them and develop them along the lines of their own initiative ...

We are surprised to find everywhere such a resentful attitude to the administration now in force. Day after day letters come from the people, pleading for their children, asking me to find their girls, long lost to them—in service somewhere in this State—taken away in some cases seven years ago and no word or line from them. Surely we can do better for these people than this.

I found old women shivering, and cold and hungry, too, who were the original owners of the land which is the garden of the world, and which has yielded such crops recently, that has made our statesmen boast of revenue running into millions, and in our abominable selfishness, still we endeavour to filch the last remaining crumb from the aboriginal people.

26. *Macleay Argus*, 9 October 1925. Gathering Of Aborigines. Conference At Kempsey

A large gathering of aborigines met at the Good Templar's Hall on Saturday to inaugurate the Australian Aborigines' Progressive Association in this district. Mr. Miranda (Frederickton) presided, and handled the meeting very capably. Mr. Maynard, a colored gentleman, president of the Association, was present, and delivered an address on the position, which was greatly appreciated by all present.

Mrs. McKenzie Hatton, secretary, read the report, which was considered very encouraging.

Delegates from Bowraville, Nambucca and Kempsey spoke, while Bellbrook, Nana Glen and Lower Creek were represented.

The day was given over to conference, while the evening was spent in music and song. An interesting feature of the proceedings was the passing of a motion that the Mayor of Kempsey (Ald. H.J. Stewart) be presented with a miniature set of aboriginal weapons of war.

The mayor was invited to be present, but unfortunately could not attend owing to his visit to the Taree eisteddfod. Local natives invited the Vicar of the Central Macleay (Rev. C.J. Chambers) and Mr. McMaugh, and their presence was greatly appreciated.

27. Fred Maynard, President, L. Lacey, Secretary, Australian Aboriginal Progressive Association, to J.T. Lang, Premier of New South Wales, 28 May 1927

We have the honor, on behalf of the members of the Australian Aboriginal Progressive Association, to place in your hands their humble petition for reasonable repatriation in our own land. We respectfully solicit such early alteration in the laws relating to the aboriginals as will make effective the following reforms and which we most sincerely assure you will enable the aboriginals of this State to prove that they are worthy of the full privileges of citizenship, viz:–

A. "That all capable aboriginals shall be given in fee simple sufficient good land to maintain a family.

B. That the family life of the aboriginal people shall be held sacred and free from invasion and that the children shall be left in the control of their parents.

C. That the incapables of the Aboriginal Community (the direct liability of the Government consequent upon neglect in the past) be properly cared for in suitable homes on reserves, the full expense of such establishments to be borne by the Government.

D. That the supervision of all such aboriginal Homes, Hostels or Reserves be entrusted to the educated aboriginals possessing the requisite ability for such management.

E. That the control of aboriginal affairs, apart from common law rights, shall be vested in a board of management comprised of capable educated aboriginals under a chairman to be appointed by the Government.["]

We earnestly commend this request of our united people to your keen and kindly consideration, confident that you and the Honourable Ministers in your Government will recognise the reasonableness and justice of our petition, and that you will, in the next Session of Parliament, restore to us that share of our country of which we should never have been deprived, likewise those family rights which are the basis of community life, and as in duty bound your petitioners will ever pray.

For and on behalf of the Australian Aboriginal Progressive Association.

28. Fred Maynard, President, Australian Aboriginal Progressive Association, to J.T. Lang, Premier of New South Wales, 3 October 1927

I had the honor of addressing you under date May 28th last, and I am now in receipt of a reply from your Chief Secretary, dated 23rd ult., and same was read at the meeting of this association on 1st inst., when I was directed to again communicate with you, as the members of my Board are of opinion that you have not had an opportunity to peruse the document in question as they feel sure you would not have passed same as being the calibre of correspondence befitting a statesman.

I am, therefore, instructed to re-direct your attention to the actual position since same is apparently not comprehended by the author of the

document under review. He appears to be perfectly satisfied with the in-
ference of inferiority and the despicable innuendo which pervades his
remarks concerning the Australian people. I wish to make it perfectly
clear on behalf of our people, that we accept no condition of inferiority
as compared with the European people. Two distinct civilisations are represented by the respective races. On one hand we have the civilisation of
necessity and on the other the civilisation co-incident with a bounteous
supply of all the requirements of the human race. That the European
people by the arts of war destroyed our more ancient civilisation is freely
admitted, and that by their vices and diseases our people have been decimated is also patent, but neither of these facts are evidence of superiority.
Quite the contrary is the case. Furthermore, I may refer, in passing, to the
fact that your present scheme of Old Age pensions was obtained from
our ancient code, as likewise your Child Endowment Scheme and
Widow's Pensions. Our divorce laws may yet find a place on the Statute
Book. The members of this Board have also noticed the strenuous efforts
of the Trade Union leaders to attain the conditions which existed in our
country at the time of invasion by Europeans— the men only worked
when necessary— we called no man "Master" and we had no king.

Our people have, however, accepted the modern system of government which has taken the place of our prehistoric methods and have con-
formed to same reasonably well when the treatment accorded them is
fully considered. We are, therefore, striving to obtain full recognition of
our citizen rights on terms of absolute equality with all other people in
our own land.

The request made by this Association for sufficient land for each eligible family is justly based. The Australian people are the original owners
of the land and have a prior right over all other people in this respect.
The protestations of the British Government and those of the representatives of that Government in this country, as well as the preachings of all
British Christian Ministers, fully support our claim. The equity of the
proposition is so apparent as to need no argument. The remark in your
Chief Secretary's letter concerning the opportunities for the Australian
people to purchase suitable land is refuted by recent proceedings in the
Lands Department when the age-old homes of the native people were
sold over their heads. The further sneer that they are given blankets and
rations is refuted by the refusal of the Government to grant a Royal
Commission to inquire into the conditions under which the native people
live in this State. The recent exposures of refusals of Old Age Pensions to
our elderly people and the statements that these old folks were not receiving any sustenance from the Government have not evidently been
observed by your Chief Secretary, in view of what he writes regarding

help bestowed.

The further statement concerning the home life of the Australian people is again, in our opinion, very wide of the mark. The demand for the Royal Commission was based on this aspect of our family affairs, and the refusal to grant the Commission is answer to the comments of your Chief Secretary.

The condition of our incapables, the direct result of contamination, is another matter which could be best ventilated before a Royal Commission if you will kindly authorise the granting of same, and I am sure that such tribunals have been created to inquire into matters of much less importance than the welfare of the Australian people.

Our request to supervise our own affairs is no innovation. The Catholic people in our country possess the right to control their own schools and homes, and take a pride in the fact that they possess this privilege. The Chinese, Greeks, Jews and Lutherans are similarly favored and our people are entitled to precisely the same conditions for the full and sufficient reasons already enumerated.

I reiterate the opinion of our Board members that you have not been made conversant with the contents of the letter now under reply, and I am also of opinion that being a "City" man, deeply engrossed in the affairs of industrial centres, you are not even remotely aware of the conditions prevailing amongst the aboriginal section of the citizens.

I now, on behalf of my Board, and with every respect, solicit your personal interest in this movement for the complete emancipation of our people, and in any inquiry you may inaugurate you are assured of the fullest support of the members of the Board and the leaders of the people at the various places where aboriginals are located. I am sure that a closer acquaintance with our people will be mutually beneficial, and that you will immediately recognise the wisdom of the action of the Government of South Australia where the aboriginals have been repatriated under model modern conditions. Your investigations will have the effect of placing you in that long and brilliant list of students and scientists who have in recent times acknowledged the rightful place of the Australian Race in the world's history, and who have borne testimony to their worth as lawgivers, as demonstrated by their moral code, and to their worth when judged on the score of loyalty, fidelity, and bravery when conditions have called for the exercise of such virtues.

Assuring you that the members of this Organisation are dwelling on your personal efforts in their behalf, and confident that when you grasp the situation we will experience such a welcome reversal of present intolerable conditions as to ensure your name being perpetuated for centuries as the great benefactor of our race at a critical period of its existence in New South Wales.

29. *Sydney Morning Herald,* 15 November 1927. Aborigines. Want Racial Equality. Appeal To Churchmen. Letter To The King

There was a strange mixture of humour and pathos at a meeting at the Chapter House last night between the Bishop Coadjutor of Sydney (Rev. D'Arcy Irvine), the chairman of the Australian Board of Missions (the Rev. J.S. Needham) and seven aborigines, members of the Australian Aborigines Progressive Association. The natives sought the opportunity of stating their claims to racial equality with the whites and certain other concessions for the less educated brethren. Two of the natives were women, and one of these, Mrs. Duren, astonished Bishop D'Arcy Irvine by saying that she had written to the King.

"To the King?" he asked. "Yes," replied Mrs. Duren. "I addressed it to King George V., England." Certain land, she complained, which had been reserved to the blacks for years, had suddenly been alienated for other purposes, and that had raised her ire. Hence the letter to the Head of the Empire. "Do you think the King received it?" asked Bishop D'Arcy Irvine. "Well", replied Mrs. Duren, "I registered it, so he must have." She admitted, however, that she had received no reply; but the land had not been sold.

For the most part, the president of the Natives' Progressive Association (Mr. F.G. Maynard), a "self-educated aboriginal," acted as spokesman, although his associates punctuated his remarks with interjections. They intelligently pleaded their claims for the repeal of the existing Aborigines Act, and its substitution by another that would be more agreeable to them, and that would make less distinction between them and the whites.

A Fantastic Plan

Mr. Maynard declared definitely against the proposal to institute a native State in the Northern Territory. Some of the less civilised tribes, he declared, would insist upon adhering to their age-old tribal customs, and the place of their birth. In any such project, each State should have representation, he affirmed. When Mr. Needham explained that there was no intention forcibly to remove natives from the usual haunts, but that it was proposed merely to segregate the natives, and secure them from molestation, Mr. Maynard seemed placated. He insisted, however, that the natives should be provided with their own communities, with schools and other public buildings, and should be supervised generally by educated and capable aborigines.

Mr. Needham quoted many instances where natives had been given all opportunities to improve themselves, but with two exceptions— that of the well-known David Unaipon and a Queensland girl— they had disappointed the white protectors who had endeavoured to help them.

Mr. Maynard said that whenever he had come into contact with his people he had discovered the most appalling conditions. At Macleay River he had found 60 natives, men, women, and children, suffering from starvation. The conditions were most horrible. The public did not learn about it because there was a "hush" policy.

Crueller Than Starvation

In reply to Bishop D'Arcy Irvine, Mr. Maynard said that help from the police was not sought, as it was feared that the children would be taken away from the parents. That was considered crueller than starvation.

Mrs. Duren said she had complained to the Minister for Education of the exclusion of black children from the State school at Bateman's Bay. The Aborigines Protection Board was a nice name, she had told officials of that office, but when this kind of thing occurred where did the protection come in? Influence was everything. If one did not have it one got nowhere.

Mr. Maynard also complained that some of the land set aside in the early days of Australia was gradually being alienated from their use; and urged that the liquor prohibition clause in the Act should be abolished, as it was insulting to the aborigines.

Mr. Needham undertook to place the requests before the proper authorities.

30. A.E. McKenzie-Hatton, Secretary, Fred Maynard, President, Australian Aboriginal Progressive Association, to the Royal Commission on the Constitution, 22 February 1928. *(The capitals and elipses are reproduced as in the original.)*

THE MEMBERS OF THE .. A A P A .. ON HEARING OF THE COMMISSION NOW SITTING ... AT CANBERRA. DISCUSSING .. ABORIGINAL AFFAIRS .. HEARTILY ENDORSE THE VIEWS OF THE COMMISSION .. IN THEIR UNITED EFFORTS FOR THE FEDERALIZING OF .. ALL MATTERS .. SUBJECT TO ABORIGINAL CONTROL THROUGHOUT AUSTRALIA ... AND PLEDGE OURSELVES TO STAND .. SOLIDLY .. BEHIND THE WHOLE OF THE .. COMMISSION .. IN THEIR UNITED EFFORTS .. FOR A

GREATER SYSTEM OF CONTROL. RE OUR PEOPLE ...... ALSO WE CLAIM
THAT THE PRESENT SYSTEM OF CONSTITUTED . LAWS AND
ADMINISTRATION .. UNDER THE SIX STATES .. AS NOW CONSTITUTED
.. AS OBSOLETE AND SERVED IT DAYS OF USEFULLNESS ALSO .. A
DOWN RIGHT INSULT TO THE INTELLIGENCE .. OF OUR PEOPLE ...
WE CLAIM THAT AFTER MANY APPEALS TO THE NEW SOUTH WALES
GOVERNMENT .. NO ATTENTION HAS BEEN GIVEN TO THESE
MATTERS .. THE HORRIBLE ABUSE STILL CONTINUES THE RAIDING
OF HOMES OF THE PEOPLE .. WHO HAVE CAREFULLY REARED .. AND
LOVED DEVOTELY .. THEIR CHILDREN .. IS CONSIDERED BY THESE
PEOPLE .. A SHOCKING BREACH OF ALL .. THAT THE AUSTRALIAN
PUBLIC STAND FOR .. YEAR AFTER YEAR .. THESE GIRLS OF TENDER
AGE AND YEARS .. ARE TORN AWAY FROM THEIR PARENTS THEIR
HOMES .. AND PUT TO SERVICE IN AN INVIRONMENT AS NEAR TO
SLAVERY . AS IT IS POSSIBLE TO FIND ...... TRACKED DOWN AND
CAUGHT BY THE POLICE .. AND BY SUCH BRUTAL METHODS .. THAT
NOTHING CAN BE SAID IN JUSTIFICATION OF THE POSITION ..
SIGNED ON TO .. FIVE YEARS OF SERVICE . AT THREE SHILLINGS A
WEEK .. OF WHICH ONLY .. SIX IS PAID WEEKLY .... THESE GIRLS
SUBMIT TO A LIFE OF SLAVERY .. AND MISERY .... AND DISPAIR .. AND
ARE ONLY KEPT IN THESE POSITIONS .. BY THE FEAR OF THE POLICE
.. WHO ARE CALLED IN TO ADJUST ANY DIFFERENCES

(2) the present crisis has been called by the fact that the new south
wales . police .. government are persistantly and steadily pushing forward
a MOST CRUEL LAND POLICY .. IT IS A FACT THAT MANY OF THE
PLACES WHERE THE ABORIGINALS HAVE LIVED . IN SECURITY AND
PEACE .. HAVING CLEARED CULTIVATED AND REAPED FOR YEARS
SUCCESSIVELY .. LAND WHICH THEY HAD LONG REGARDED AS
THEIR OWN .. WHERE THEY HAD LIVED FOR 60 & 70 YEARS .. THEIR
FOREFATHERS BEFORE THEM ...... THE LAND HAVING BEEN GIVEN
THEM BY THE INSPECTORS OF POLICE OF THEIR DAY FOR SERVICE
RENDERED .. AS BLACK TRACKERS ETC .. EVEN APART FROM THEIR
CLAIMS AS ORIGINAL OWNERS .. THEIR LANDS HAVING BEEN
DISPOSED .. WITH NO COMPENSATION .. OR ANY CONSIDERATION
WHATEVER .. THE LANDS SOLD TO THE HIGHEST BIDDER .. WHILE
THESE POOR UNFORTUNATES .. OUR BRO .. AND OUR SISTERS .. ARE
SENT ADRIFT AS VAGRANTS . IN THE LAND .. OF THEIR BIRTH

(3) The fact that the police are the administrators of the aboriginal
protection board . in country places . is a mater of keen disaproval .. with
the members of the association .... unfortunate men women and children
.. the old ones the weak ones .. of the community are insulted bullied ..
when they appeal for help .. which a generous government .. has set aside

for them ... and their use it is quite a common thing TO FIND OLD PEOPLE STARVING .. RATHER THAN APPEAL TO THE POLICE FOR HELP .. AND REAP THE INSULTS INDIGNITIES ... PLACED UPON THEM BLANKETLESS .. RATHER THAN GO TO THE POLICE STATION TO GET THE BOUNTY WHICH HAS BEEN SUPPLIED FOR THEM

(4) the settlements as at present carried on .. are the breeding places of crime .. from earliest childhood the atmosphere of these places .. are that of lying and deciet .... and worse any of the young men .. who have been victimised .. to years of that kind of life .. confess .. that the whole training ..... had tendered to THE DEVELOPMENT OF A BAD CONDITION OF MIND...

(5) and it is affirmed by the women that their first step towards .. a life of shame were at the injunction of those in charge .. in charge ..... of the settlements .. As for the name of a certain inspector .... employed by the aboriginal protection board .... it is passed from one end of new south wales .. with all the invectives of a broken hearted dispairing .. people

31. *Cinesound Review,* **no. 100, 29 September 1933. Australian Royalty Pleads for His People. Burraga, chief of Aboriginal Thirroul tribe, to petition the King for blacks' representation in Federal Parliament**

Before the white man set foot in Australia, my ancestors were as Kings in their own right. And I, Aboriginal chief Burraga, am a direct descendant of the royal line.

The black man sticks to his brethren, and always keeps the rule which were laid down before the white man put foot upon these shores. One of the greatest laws amongst the Aboriginals was to love one another. And they always kept it in law. Where will you find a white man or a white woman today that will say "I love my neighbour". It quite amuses me to hear people saying "I don't like the black man". But he's damn glad to live in a black man's country all the same!

I am calling a corrobborree of all the natives of New South Wales to send a petition to the King, in an endeavour to improve our condition. All the black man wants is representation in Federal Parliament. There is also plenty fish in the river for us all, and land to grow all we want. One hundred and fifty years ago the Aboriginals owned Australia, and today he demands more than the white man's charity. He wants the right to live!

32. King Burraga to Professor A.P. Elkin, President, Association for the Protection of Native Races, 16 January 1936

Being acknowledge by His Majesty King George Vth Wishes to have an interview with your good Society, on behalf of my Coloured people of Australia the Aboriginal, and for the good work you and your Society are doing, for the uplifting of our down Trodden people to improve the poor miserable Circumstances, we have been undergoing, during recent years, the Black man of this Land for some time has never been getting a fair deal, and appeal after appeal have been given very little attention to. Cruel Treatments have been playing a big part all over Australia deprived of all our Rights which had been given to us in the 90s during the Reign of our Good old Queen Her Majesty Victoria. I myself a full Blood Aboriginal of Australia, and 3rd direct descendant of the Challengers of Captain Cook, when he Landed in Botany Bay, In 1770. As near as I can say my Grandfather, whose Native Name was Burraga-Lung, who died some years ago on the South Coast of N.S.W. at the age of 130 years as those that knew Him said he was not a day younger, as some of the early settlers of the South Coast, knew so well as most Aboriginals lived to be a great age before the white man arrived in Australia. He never had any Worries, such as we do of late years, no Elections, no Strikes, no Shortage of food or money. God had given him full and plenty Peace and happiness, that is what we have not to-day. His Customs and Laws, were perfect and so was his Religion, and nothing wanting, but to-day Our people are living in poor miserable conditions through our land under hutters, Squatters, Missionaries, and even the Protection Boards take too great an interest in them. I please ask to excuse, writing and Spelling mistakes, as this Article is written by myself, without the aid of any High School or College Training, but I was proud to sit under a Gum Tree with only a pencil and slate, but the rest of my Education was picked up in my early Travels amongst the different tribes of my people and Others. I belong to the Thirroul Tribe of the East Coast of Australia, and their Bound-ary was from Port Stephens, North Coast, to the Gippsland Lakes known as Lake Tyers on the South Coast. I have been often asked this question don't the Aboriginal Protection Board help you. My answer is no. don't you have free rides in trains no the first thing free they would give me would be a free ride in the P.D. and that is the truth and into Goal I would go or any other Aboriginal. I will be able to give you more information probably, when I meet you and your Society in the near future I trust, and to hear further news concerning the Aboriginal Seat at Canberra, for the interest of my people.

Hoping you will receive this Article No. 1 from me.

P.S. I am enclosing Governor's message please return same as soon as Possible. K.B.

33. Evidence of William Ferguson, Secretary of the Aborigines Progressive Association, 30 November 1937, Select Committee on the Administration of Aborigines Protection Board, New South Wales

I would ask permission to read to the Committee the notes of the speech I made at my first meeting in Dubbo [27 June 1937], as they set out the charges I made against the Board:

This meeting gives me the opportunity of placing before the public the conditions under which our people are living, and also to let you know the hardships and many injustices handed out to them by the so-called Protection Board. In presenting our case I will endeavour to put all my points as clear and concise as possible. I realise that we have all the best learned men and women in the world opposing our claim for freedom, for we have learned by past experience that the scholars and students will recommend that the race be preserved for scientific purposes. What a fallacy! What is there left to experiment with? I will deal with that later on. To begin with, we are asking for the abolition of the Aborigines Protection Board. You ask why should it be abolished? I say that it is not functioning in the best interest of the aboriginal people. The Board appoints managers and protectors to help the people and look after their interests. But the managers have so much power, their power is greater than any other public servant in Australia. I say that no police officer, no magistrate, or no other man, I do not believe the King of England, has power under the British law to try a man or a number of men and women, find them guilty and sentence them without giving them fair and open trial and without producing any evidence to convict, excepting perhaps in countries where there is no law handy such as Papua, New Guinea. I am taking a typical case. At Bulgandramine last August a sheepskin was found on the public reserve adjoining the mission. The manager of the mission took possession of the skin and alleged that someone on the mission had stolen the sheep. He never gave his reason for blaming the dark people. He was not called on to show why he should have suspicion on any of them; he just made his accusations. "Some of you killed a sheep last night, and until such time as the guilty one confesses I intend to withhold the rations of every man, woman and child on the mission." At that time one woman was in bed in confinement. At the end of one week the people presented themselves for rations which were refused. They then held a meeting and sent a deputation to the protector to plead for food for the women and children. They were again refused. At the end of the second week this powerful representative of the Aborigines Protection Board kindly consented to feed them. Now you wonder why the people did not report the matter to the Aborigines Protection Board. They have had experience in the past of making reports against the managers. They fear that dreaded weapon, the expulsion order. This is the most dreadful weapon that could be placed in anyone's hands. It gives an unscrupulous individual the power to brand a man, woman or child with any name which comes under the criminal category, without giving the aborigine the right to deny the charge. I have one out against me, and I have been told by a protector that it is because I am a dangerous man. In years gone by I have been told that the early white settlers had power to shoot or poison the natives, but the Governments thought it was a bit too crude, so they rightly stopped that wholesale extermination. But the Aborigines Protection Board still allows its protectors to use firearms on natives, as in the case at Brewarrina last Christmas, when the manager fired two shots at a man and when asked about it, laughed it off, and said he only fired to frighten him. Was the man a dangerous criminal? If he was, why did not the manager ring for the police and give the man in charge? If he had committed no crime, why did he use a revolver on him? But that is only a little of the power of a protector ... We now pass on to Pilliga Mission, where the Aborigines Protection Board is working a sawmill with "scab" labour. Although there is an award covering that class of work which provides over £4 a week, the protector has men working on the mill, benchmen 25s., tailer-out 22s., and others from 20s. downwards. The mill supplies timber for buildings on other mission stations, thereby coming into competition with other mill-owners who are compelled to pay award rates. For instance, the timber was brought by truck from Pilliga to Dubbo, to build the school at Talbragar Mission, 150 miles. If the timber had been cut by union labour the Board could have bought it cheaper here in Dubbo. I leave it to you to work out for yourselves how the Board, by sweating those men who they are supposed to protect, by the wholesale hiring-out system and supplying cheap labour to wealthy squatters, are using the aboriginal to break down working-class conditions. We are asking for a higher standard of education. We claim that the teachers now teaching our dark children are not qualified to carry out the work they are being paid to do.

How are the teachers appointed? Take the case of Murkins, at Bulgandramine. Let me tell you how he got his job. His brother-in-law was a police constable stationed at Pooncarie. Murkins was staying with him and the constable nominated him for the position at Menindie. The children learned nothing from him in two years, but that did not stop the

Aborigines Protection Board from appointing him manager, protector and teacher at Bulgrandramine. I would like to ask the Board what qualification had Constable's girl at Pilliga to warrant her appointment as teacher. There were girls and boys at Cowra Mission at that time who could teach her. I will deal with other cases later on. That is my answer to those who will ask what do you propose to substitute in place of the Board. The right to educate our people, full citizens' rights, and we will protect ourselves. Surely we cannot make a worse job of it than the Aborigines Protection Board has done. These fluent speakers who will defend the action of the Board, who, with their superior learning and craftily trained minds will try to side-track you probably by personally attacking me, I ask you to keep in mind the injustice meted out to our people, the dangerous power invested in the managers, and if I have succeeded in establishing a case against the Board, I will ask you to vote in favour of the motion which I intend to move at the conclusion of the meeting.

34. Percy Mosely, Burnt Bridge, to Mr J.J. Moloney, Australian Society of Patriots, 1 July 1937

We have again been interfered with. The manager of the A.P. Board came out on the 30th June and took possession of the place and took away the W.C. from the school. Father protested and asked him who had given him permission to remove the buildings and he said we had no right to question him. When he had gone with one load, we nailed up the fence and stopped him from coming in the second time, so he went in and brought the whole of the police force out to help him break the fence. After they had broken down the fence and taken away the second load, the police headed by the Inspector came down to the house and gave the manager permission to take the tank off the place. Then I asked the Inspector what his duty was here to which he replied "Give less cheek or I'll lock you up".

Father has made me his manager because he is not able to manage his own affairs. I told this to the Inspected but he still insisted on seeing Dad.

Now what I want to know is, can the Inspector of Police give the manager permission to take the tank off our home. Please let me know as soon as possible.

35. William Ferguson, 'Give Us Justice!', *Daily Telegraph* (Sydney), 15 October 1937

... As a boy I went to the black mission school although I could have gone to the white one. There I was quite happy and I cannot remember ever worrying about the aboriginal problem until one day when I was going home I saw a number of black fellows grubbing stumps out. When I spoke to them they told me that they were doing it as a punishment. And so I learnt that any station manager could punish my people by making them grub stumps for weeks. When I was 19 I saw the white managers pull a dead starved bullock out of a creek. I watched them skin it and give it out as meat ration to the aborigines.

Suddenly I realised that anything was good enough for the black people. Since that day I have been trying to do something for the aborigine. I love those people. They are my brothers and more than my brothers. I have gone out into the country without even a blanket and every night without question they have fed me. They have sat me by the fire and given me a bed better than their own. You can walk from Victoria to the Gulf of Carpentaria and they will share with you wherever you stop. Yet the white man has ravished our people— disease and debauchery and everything that is evil. We are on a far lower level than when the white men came. You can read in your history books of some of the terrible things they have done to us. I have heard of them from the old men.

Old Mungo told me once of the Murdering Island massacre, from which he was the only one to escape. Listen to this! He told me how a squatter near Narrandera and his men drove a whole camp of blacks on to an island in the middle of the river and shot them down, women and children too, until everyone was dead. Only old Mungo escaped. In those evil days men were given licences to destroy the aborigines. The last licence, it was held by a man named Foster, I think, expired only about 40 years ago. They were legally permitted to shoot and poison us. This is the truth. I know it. Some years ago I was putting up a fence out West. As we dug near a waterhole we came on bones, skulls, hundreds of them. And some of the skulls were little ones, no bigger than my fist. All of them had died where they lay after drinking at the poisoned waterhole.

The missionaries tried to improve things. Then the Government took over the mission stations and about 60 years ago the Aborigines' Protection Board started to look after us. The Board meant well, but we all think the system should go. The natives are living very badly. They are badly fed and they die easily. Diseases bought by the white man are spreading.

I have talked to the black men in their own dialects as a friend, and they have told me horrible things that still go on. Your politicians and your leaders have put us in the background and they want to keep us there. We are a skeleton in the cupboard like the convicts. But the convicts are dead and we are living. The black man cannot speak his sadness, cannot even understand his trouble. Their minds are dulled and the spark of their life put out by the unhealthy control under which they struggle to exist. Floggings are still allowed and the police can chain together captive natives. Or chain them to trees. What an outcry if a white man was chained to a tree! You boast that you have given us the franchise. But you allow us to be carried in cattle trucks, whipped and chained.

Some of your professors write wonderful books about us and our customs. But they are put away on dusty shelves and you never read them or try to learn about us or to understand us. La Perouse is a show window, where tourists can see natives throwing boomerangs. But out in the back country nobody much ever sees them and the public knows nothing of their squalor and misery. All they get is 3/2 a week and huts to live in. Most of the huts have two rooms. Many of these rooms leak, and a lot of them have no flooring. When a station is crowded two families may be put in a hut. Children are often born on bags on the floor. When T.B. comes it runs through a whole station. The natives lose their strength, sometimes their will to live, and they die easily. This is the food they get: Flour, sugar, tea, salt and baking powder to the value of 2/9 a week and, in some places, 1/- a week for meat.

Girls are sent away to be servants on sheep and cattle stations. Often they come back with a half-white baby. In the native stations there are people who are nearly white. They have blue eyes. I have seen them with red hair. But they are called blacks and they live with the blacks. Half-castes are social outcasts.

I think the real end of the race problem must be absorption of the black people. Let them intermarry and intermarry. We are not animals, not vile creatures. Myall blacks can and have been educated to a high standard in a few years. Occasionally one of our people becomes famous. There are thousands of others who could show just as much intelligence and culture if they were given a chance. Yet they educate us only to the third standard in the native schools. We are not given a chance to be anything except laborers. Nobody offered to give me anything but an elementary education. But our main problem is our children. We do not want them to have no future and no outlook as we have had. We do not want anthropological studies and books about the length of our toenails and the size of our heads.

We want you to realise that we are your brothers. That if you treat us as human beings, take away the stigma of color and the idea of the pathetic Jacky Jacky, we will stand by you. That is why I came to this city without any money—to put my people's problems to you. You have taken everything away from us but given us nothing in exchange. Is that right? As one of your scholars has said, you owe us not benevolence, but atonement.

36. Jack Patten, radio interview with P.R. Stephensen, January 1938

Stephensen: Good evening, listeners. Last week I had with me in the studio the Organising Secretary of the Aborigines Progressive Association, Mr. W. Ferguson, of Dubbo, who told you something about the great fight which the Aborigines of Australia are now putting up to obtain equal democratic and citizen rights. Their protest comes very appropriately just now, when we white Australians are preparing to celebrate the 150th Anniversary of white settlement in this country. Now this evening I have another representative of the Aborigines here, Mr. Jack Patten, President of the La Perouse branch of their Association. I am going to introduce Mr. Patten to you, and let him explain his cause, in the brief time available. Ladies and gentlemen, Mr. Jack Patten [...]

Patten: Good evening, listeners.

Stephensen: Now Mr. Patten, will you tell us why the Aborigines are not satisfied with their treatment?

Patten: Well, I have travelled right throughout the country districts of New South Wales, and I have seen the terrible conditions under which my people live. La Perouse is only one of the Aboriginal settlements. Only a few Aborigines live there, about one hundred and twenty. La Perouse is only window-dressing, but there are ten thousand Aborigines and halfcastes living in other settlements and in camps in New South Wales where no tourists go. It is these people, the Forgotten People, that I speak for.

Stephensen: The people who have been kept in the background you mean?

Patten: Yes, ten thousand of them in New South Wales, living in absolutely terrible conditions out West, with no proper chance of education for their children. These are the people on whose behalf I make this appeal to the conscience of the White Australians. You are going to celebrate your 150th Anniversary of 26th January next, but that day will be a day of mourning for us!

Stephensen: A day of mourning?

Patten: Yes, we have no reason to rejoice. You have taken our land away from us, polluted us with disease, employed us at starvation wages, and treated many of our women dishonourably. There are twenty thousand halfcastes in Australia, and this fact cannot be denied. At the same time, you have refused to educate Aborigines and halfcastes up to your own standards of citizenship. You have never extended the hand of real friendship to us.

Stephensen: The whole trouble, Mr. Patten, seems to me that the White Australians have never really thought about this matter very deeply?

Patten: Well, the time has come now, after one hundred and fifty years of so-called "progress", for the white people in Australia to face up to their responsibilities. We are British subjects, but we have no citizen rights. How can you explain that?

Stephensen: It seems to me like British policy.

Patten: Call it what you like, but the fact remains that our people are not getting a square deal, and have never had a square deal at any time in the last 150 years. We now ask for freedom and equal citizenship. Our only hope of obtaining justice is to arouse the conscience of the white people of Australia, and to make them realise how lacking they have been in regard to accepting their responsibilities towards us, the original owners of the land.

Stephensen: Well, what do you want us white people to do about it?

Patten: We don't want to be given charity. We don't want you to study us as scientific curiosities. What we DO want is this. We want to be regarded as normal, average, human beings, the same as yourselves. We ask you not to treat us as outcasts, but to give us education and equal opportunity, which is our birth-right. Don't forget this, we are the real Australians, and we ask the invaders of this country, who brought new ideas to our land, to give us the chance to share in modern progress. Australia ought to be proud of the Aborigines, just as New Zealand is proud of the Maoris, and the Americans are proud of the Indian braves.

Stephensen: The time will come when Australians with Aboriginal blood in their veins will boast of that fact.

Patten: The sooner the better! To speak for myself, I am very proud of my Aboriginal descent. The Aborigines are a virile race, with great traditions. They have helped the white men to colonise this country, and the only reward you offer them is extermination! I repeat we do not ask for charity, we only ask for equal opportunity.

Stephensen: Do you say that the present Aborigines Protection Acts, in the various States of the Commonwealth, are not helpful to Aborigines.

Patten: They are not helpful, because they treat us as inferiors, and so they force us into an inferior position. An aboriginal on a Government Reserve is not taught to be a citizen, he is taught to be submissive, and to accept degradation. This is the official Government policy, which we ask you to alter. We can do nothing ourselves to alter it, because we are deprived of citizens' rights. The Government Protection Boards do not really "protect" us. They merely humiliate us. The Government laws concerning Aborigines have taken away our freedom, which is our birth-right, and have placed us, body and soul, at the mercy of officials, against whom we have no appeal.

Stephensen: The matter certainly calls for a public enquiry.

37. J.T. Patten and W. Ferguson, *Aborigines Claim Citizen Rights! A Statement of the Case for the Aborigines Progressive Association,* 1938

One Hundred and Fifty Years.

The 26th of January, 1938, is not a day of rejoicing for Australia's Aborigines; it is a day of mourning. This festival of 150 years' so-called "progress" in Australia commemorates also 150 years of misery and deg-radation imposed upon the original native inhabitants by the white invad-ers of this country. We, representing the Aborigines, now ask you, the reader of this appeal, to pause in the midst of your sesqui-centenary re-joicings and ask yourself honestly whether your "conscience" is clear in regard to the treatment of the Australian blacks by the Australian whites during the period of 150 years' history which you celebrate?

The Old Australians.

You are the New Australians, but we are the Old Australians. We have in our arteries the blood of the Original Australians, who have lived in this land for many thousands of years. You came here only recently, and you took our land away from us by force. You have almost exterminated our people, but there are enough of us remaining to expose the humbug of your claim, as white Australians, to be a civilised, progressive, kindly and humane nation. By your cruelty and callousness towards the Aborigi-nes you stand condemned in the eyes of the civilised world.

Plain Speaking.

These are hard words, but we ask you to face the truth of our accusa-tion. If you would openly admit that the purpose of your Aborigines Legislation has been, and now is, to exterminate the Aborigines com-pletely so that not a trace of them or of their descendants remains, we could describe you as brutal, but honest. But you dare not admit openly that your hope and wish is for our death! You hypocritically claim that you are trying to "protect" us; but your modern policy of "protection" (so-called) is killing us off just as surely as the pioneer policy of giving us poisoned damper and shooting us down like dingoes!

We ask you now, reader, to put your mind, as a citizen of the Australian Commonwealth, to the facts presented in these pages. We ask you to study the problem, in the way that we present the case, from the Aborigines' point of view. We do not ask for your charity; we do not ask you to study us as scientific freaks. Above all, we do not ask for your "protection." No, thanks! We have had 150 years of that! We ask only for justice, decency and fair play. Is this too much to ask? Surely your minds and hearts are not so callous that you will refuse to reconsider your policy of degrading and humiliating and exterminating Old Australia's Aborigines?
...

Aborigines Protection Acts.

All Aborigines, whether nomadic or civilised, and also all half-castes, are liable to be "protected" by the Aborigines Protection Boards, and their legal status is defined by Aborigines Protection Acts of the various States and of the Commonwealth. Thus we are for the greater part deprived of ordinary civil legal rights and citizenship, and we are made a pariah caste within this so-called democratic community.

The value of the Aborigines Protection Acts in "protecting" Aborigines may be judged from the fact that at the 1933 census there were no Aborigines left to protect in Tasmania; while in Victoria there were only 92 full-bloods, in South Australia 569 full-bloods, in New South Wales 1,034 full-bloods.

The Aborigines of full-blood are most numerous, and most healthy, in the northern parts of Australia, where white "protection" exists in theory, but in practice the people have to look after themselves! But already the hand of official "protection" is reaching out to destroy these people in the north, as it has already destroyed those in the southern States. We beg of you to alter this cruel system before it gets our 36,000 nomadic brothers and sisters of North Australia into its charitable clutches!

What "Protection" Means.

The "protection" of Aborigines is a matter for each of the individual States; while those in the Northern Territory come under Commonwealth ordinances.

This means that in each State there is a different "system," but the principle behind the Protection Acts is the same in all States. Under these Acts the Aborigines are regarded as outcasts and as inferior beings who need to be supervised in their private lives by Government officials.

No one could deny that there is scope for the white people of Australia to extend sympathetic, or real, protection and education to the uncivilised blacks, who are willing and eager to learn when given a chance. But what can be said for a system which regards these people as incurably "backward" and does everything in its power to keep them backward?

Such is the effect of the Aborigines Protection Acts in every State and in the Northern Territory.

No real effort is being made to bring these "backward" people forward into the national life. They are kept apart from the community, and are being pushed further and further "backward."

...

No "Sentimental Sympathy," Please!

We do not wish to regarded with sentimental sympathy, or to be "preserved," like the koala bears, as exhibits; but we do ask for your *real* sympathy and understanding of our plight.

We do not wish to be "studied" as scientific or anthropological curiosities. All such efforts on our behalf are wasted. We have no desire to go back to primitive conditions of the Stone Age. We ask you to teach our people to live in the Modern Age, as modern citizens. Our people are very good and quick learners. Why do you deliberately keep us backward? Is it merely to give yourselves the pleasure of feeling superior? Give our children the same chances as your own, and they will do as well as your children!

We ask for equal education, equal opportunity, equal wages, equal rights to possess property, or to be our own masters— in two words: *equal citizenship!* How can you honestly refuse this? In New South Wales you give us the vote, and treat us as equals at the ballot box. Then why do you impose the other unfair restriction of rights upon us? Do you really think that the 9,884 half-castes of New South Wales are in need of your special "protection"? Do you really believe that these half-castes are "naturally backward" and lacking in natural intelligence? If so, you are completely mistaken. When our people are backward, it is because your treatment has made them so. Give us the same chances as yourselves, and we will prove ourselves to be just as good, if not better, Australians, than you!

Keep your charity! We only want justice.

A National Question.

If ever there was a national question, it is this. Conditions are even worse in Queensland, Northern Territory and Western Australia than they are in New South Wales; but we ask New South Wales, the Mother State, to give a lead in emancipating the Aborigines. Do not be guided any longer by religious and scientific persons, no matter how well-meaning or philanthropic they may seem. Fellow-Australians, we appeal to you to be guided by your own common sense and ideas of fair play and justice! Let the Aborigines themselves tell you what they want. Give them a chance, on the same level as yourselves, in the community. You had no race prejudice against us when you accepted half-castes and full-bloods for enlistment in the A.I.F. We were good enough to fight as Anzacs. We earned equality then. Why do you deny it to us now?

Exploitation of Labour.

For 150 years the Aborigines and half-castes throughout Australia have been used as cheap labour, both domestic and out-of-doors. We are to-day beyond the scope of Arbitration Court awards, owing to the A.P. Board system of "apprenticeship" and special labour conditions for Aborigines. Why do the Labour Unions stand for this? We have no desire to provide coolie labour competition, but your Protection Acts force this status upon us. The Labour Parties and Trade Unions have given us no real help or support in our attempts to raise ourselves to citizen level. Why are they so indifferent to the dangers of this cheap, sweated labour? Why do they not raise their voices on our behalf? Their "White Australia" policy has helped to create a senseless prejudice against us, making us social outcasts in the land of our ancestors!

Comic Cartoons and Misrepresentation.

The popular Press of Australia makes a joke of us by presenting silly and out-of-date drawings and jokes of "Jacky" or "Binghi," which have educated city-dwellers and young Australians to look upon us as sub-human. Is this not adding insult to injury? What a dirty trick, to push us down by laws, and then make fun of us! You kick us, and then laugh at our misfortunes. You keep us ignorant, and then accuse us of having no knowledge. Wake up, Australians, and realise that your cruel jokes have gone over the limit!

Window-Dressing.

We appeal to young Australians, or to city-dwelling Australians, whose knowledge of us is gained from the comic Press or from the "window-dressing" Aboriginal Settlement at La Perouse, to study the matter more deeply, and to realise that the typical Aboriginal or half-caste, born and bred in the bush, is just as good a citizen, and just as good an Australian, as anybody else. Aborigines are interested not only in boomerangs and gum leaves and corroborees! The overwhelming majority of us are able and willing to earn our living by honest toil, and to take our place in the community, side by side with yourselves.

Racial Prejudice.

Though many people have racial prejudice, or colour prejudice, we remind you that the existence of 20,000 and more half-castes in Australia is a proof that the mixture of Aboriginal and white races are practicable. Professor Archie Watson, of Adelaide University, has explained to you that Aborigines can be absorbed into the white race within three generations, without any fear of a "throw-back." This proves that the Australian Aboriginal is somewhat similar in blood to yourselves, as regards inter-marriage and inter-breeding. We ask you to study this question, and to change your whole attitude towards us, to a more enlightened one. Your present official attitude is one of prejudice and misunderstanding. We ask you to be proud of the Australian Aboriginal, and to take his hand in friendship. The New Zealanders are proud of the Maoris. We ask you to be proud of the Australian Aborigines, and not to be misled any longer by the superstition that we are a naturally backward and low race. This is a scientific lie, which has helped to push our people down and down in to the mire.

At worst, we are no more dirty, lazy, stupid, criminal, or immoral than yourselves. Also, your slanders against our race are a moral lie, told to throw all the blame for our troubles on to us. You, who originally conquered us by guns against our spears, now rely on superiority of numbers to support your false claims of moral and intellectual superiority.

A New Deal for Aborigines!

After 150 years, we ask you to review the situation and give us a fair deal— a New Deal for Aborigines. The cards have been stacked against us, and we now ask you to play the game like decent Australians. Remember, we do not ask for charity, we ask for justice.

38. *Australian Abo Call*, no. 1, April 1938. Our Historic Day Of Mourning & Protest. Aborigines Conference. Held At Australian Hall, Sydney, 26th January 1938. Report Of Proceedings

About 100 persons of Aboriginal blood attended the conference.
Proceedings were delayed at the start owing to the Official Sesqui-Centenary Procession.

Telegrams

Telegrams were received from West Australia, Queensland, North Australia, and also a very large number of letters from Aborigines all over Australia, expressing support of the Conference.

President's Address
1.30 p.m.

Mr J.T. Patten, President, said: On this day the white people are rejoicing, but we, as Aborigines, have no reason to rejoice on Australia's 150th birthday. Our purpose in meeting today is to bring home to the white people of Australia the frightful conditions in which the native Aborigines of this continent live. This land belonged to our forefathers 150 years ago, but today we are pushed further and further into the background. The Aborigines Progressive Association has been formed to put before the white people the fact that Aborigines throughout Australia are literally being starved to death. We refuse to be pushed into the background. We have decided to make ourselves heard. White men pretend that the Australian Aboriginal is a low type, who cannot be bettered. Our reply to that is, "Give us the chance!" We do not wish to be left behind in Australia's march to progress. We ask for full citizen rights, including old-age pensions, maternity bonus, relief work when unemployed, and the right to a full Australian education for our children. We do not wish to be herded like cattle, and treated as a special class. As regards the Aborigines Protection Board of New South Wales, white people in the cities do not realise the terrible conditions of slavery under which our people live in the outback districts. I have unanswerable evidence that women of our race are forced to work in return for rations, without other payment. Is this not slavery? Do white Australians realise that there is actual slavery in this fair progressive Commonwealth? Yet such is the case. We are looking in vain to white people to help us by charity. We must do something ourselves to draw public attention to our plight. That is why this Conference is held, to discuss ways and means of arousing the conscience of White Australians, who have us in their power, but have hitherto refused to help us. Our children on the Government Stations are badly fed and poorly educated. The result is that, when they go out into life, they feel inferior to white people. This is not a matter of race, it is a matter of education and opportunity. That is why we ask for a better education and better opportunity for our people. We say that it is a disgrace to Australia's name that our people should be handicapped by undernourishment and poor education, and then blamed for being backward. We do not trust the present Aborigines Protection Board, and that is why we ask for its abolition. (Applause). Incompetent teachers are provided on the Aboriginal Stations. That is the greatest handicap put on us. We have had 150 years of the white men looking after us, and the result is, our people are being exterminated. The reason why this conference is called today is so that the Aborigines themselves may discuss their problems and try to

bring before the notice of the public and of parliament what our grievance is, and how it may be remedied. We ask for ordinary citizen rights,
and full equality with other Australians. (Moved resolution.)

2.00 p.m.

Mr. W. Ferguson (Dubbo): In seconding the resolution moved by the
President, I want to say that all men and women of Aboriginal blood are
concerned in our discussions today. Though some are dark and some are
fair, we are classed as Aborigines under present legislation. The Aborigines Protection Act applies to any persons having "apparently an admixture of Aboriginal blood." We have been waiting and waiting all our lives
for the white people of Australia to better our conditions, but we have
waited in vain. We have been living in a fool's paradise. I have travelled
outback and I have seen for myself the dreadful sufferings of our people
on the Aborigines Reserves. The most terrible thing is that the dreaded
disease of T.B. has made its appearance among our people, and is wiping
them out, right here in New South Wales. Surely the time has come at last
for us to do something for ourselves, and make ourselves heard. This is
why the Aborigines Progressive Association has been formed. I held a
meeting in Dubbo originally, and the way the people responded made me
feel that much could be done. I held meetings in other western towns
and finally came to Sydney, where the press helped to draw national attention to our grievance. We now have a Committee who are bringing
before the public the injustices which our people have suffered. Our
revelations have astounded many white people, who did not realise that
such conditions as we describe could possibly exist in a free country.
Now let me explain that our object is to abolish the Aborigines Protection Board. (Applause.) We are going to abolish that Board, no matter
how long it may take. Everything points to the fact that, within a short
while, many people will support us among the white citizens of Australia.
Our first objective is to organise the whole of the Aborigines of New
South Wales into our Association. For days at the Parliamentary Select
Committee we have had to listen to slanders against our people, especially against our women. Can anyone wonder why we revolt against persons who suppress our people and then accuse us of being "backward"?
If our young boys and girls were given proper education, they would be
able to take their place with other Australians in the community. Unless
we get proper education and opportunity, our people in a very few years
will be extinct. Mr. Cooper of Melbourne will tell you that he has had no
reply to a petition addressed to the King. I say definitely that we do not
want an Aboriginal Member of Parliament. We want ordinary citizen
rights, not any special rights such as that. It is because we ourselves have

begun to organise that public opinion at last is being awakened. We ask for the right to own land that our fathers and mothers owned from time immemorial. I think the Government could at least make land grants to Aborigines. Why give preference to immigrants when our people have no land, and no right to own land? We ask that the Government should give us some encouragement to make progress. It is progress we want, not to be pushed back further and further under the present Aborigines Laws. I say that most of our people in New South Wales have a good practical knowledge of farming, and could make a living as farmers. If not, then the Government should teach our people the principles of Agriculture, and help them to settle on the land, just as they teach and help immigrants from overseas. We are backward only because we have had no real opportunity to make progress. We have been denied the opportunity. In many parts of Australia the white people on the land are helped by Aborigines to such an extent that they could not carry on grazing occupation without Aboriginal aid. The Aboriginal is producing wealth, but not for himself. Yet he is not even allowed to have money with which to buy clothes, and food. If the Aboriginal can help the white man to make money outback, why not give him a chance to make a living for himself? We do not need Government protection. We have had too much protection. Now we ask, not for protection, but for education. We should have trained teachers and nurses of Aboriginal race to go out and help those who are living in darkness. If white people can be trained for this purpose, why not train our own people? The Aboriginal Protection Board system of apprenticing girls for domestic labour is nothing but slavery. All Aboriginal Legislation today is intended to drive our people into the Aboriginal Reserves, where there is no future for them, nothing but disheartenment. From many hundreds of letters I have received from Aborigines all over Australia, I am satisfied that the Aborigines are with us in this movement for progress.

...

39. *Australian Abo Call*, no. 1, April 1938. Our Ten Points. Deputation To The Prime Minister

The following is a full copy of the statement made to the Prime Minister at the Deputation of Aborigines on 31st January last. The Prime Minister was accompanied by Dame Enid Lyons and by Mr. McEwan, Minister of the Interior.

The Deputation consisted of twenty Aborigines, men and women, and Mr. Lyons gave a hearing of two hours to the statement of our case.

Please read these "ten points" carefully, as this is the only official statement of our aims and objects that has yet been made.

TO THE RIGHT HON. THE PRIME MINISTER OF AUSTRALIA MR. J.A. LYONS, P.C., C.H., M.H.R.

Sir, In respectfully placing before you the following POLICY FOR ABORIGINES. We wish to state that this policy has been endorsed by a conference of Aborigines, held in Sydney on 26th January of this year. This policy is the only policy which has the support of the Aborigines themselves.

Urgent Interim Policy

Before placing before you a long-range policy for Aborigines, and while the long-range policy is under consideration, we ask as a matter of urgency:

That the Commonwealth Government should make a special financial grant to each of the State Governments, in proportion to the number of Aborigines in each State, to supplement existing grants for Aborigines.

We ask that such aid should be applied to increasing the rations and improving the housing conditions of Aborigines at present under State control. We beg that this matter be treated urgently, as our people are being starved to death.

The following ten points embraces a LONG RANGE POLICY FOR ABORIGINES, endorsed by our Association:

A Long Range Policy For Aborigines

1. We respectfully request that there should be a National Policy for Aborigines. We advocate Commonwealth Government control of all Aboriginal affairs.

2. We suggest the appointment of a Commonwealth Ministry for Aboriginal Affairs, the Minister to have full Cabinet rank.

3. We suggest the appointment of an Administrative Head of the proposed Department of Aboriginal Affairs, the Administrator to be advised by an Advisory Board, consisting of six persons, three of whom at least should be of Aboriginal blood, to be nominated by the Aborigines Progressive Association.

4. The aim of the Department of Aboriginal Affairs should be *to raise all Aborigines throughout the Commonwealth to full Citizen Status* and civil equality with the whites in Australia. In particular, and without delay, all

Aborigines should be entitled:

(a) To receive the same educational opportunities as white people.

(b) To receive the benefits of labour legislation, including Arbitration Court Awards, on an equality with white workers.

(c) To receive the full benefits of workers' compensation and insurance.

(d) To receive the benefits of old-age and invalid pensions, whether living in Aboriginal settlements or not.

(e) To own land and property, and to be allowed to save money in personal banking accounts, and to come under the same laws regarding intestacy and transmission of property as the white population.

(f) To receive wages in cash, and not by orders, issue of rations, or apprenticeship systems.

5. We recommend that Aborigines and Halfcastes should come under the same marriage laws as white people, and should be free to marry partners of their choice, irrespective of colour.

6. We recommend that Aborigines should be entitled to the same privileges regarding housing as are white workers.

7. We recommend that a special policy of Land Settlement for Aborigines should be put into operation, whereby Aborigines who desire to settle on the land should be given the same encouragement as that given to Immigrants or Soldier Settlers, with expert tuition in agriculture, and financial assistance to enable such settlers to become ultimately self-supporting.

8. In regard to uncivilised and semi-civilised Aborigines, we suggest that patrol officers, nurses, and teachers, both men and women, *of Aboriginal blood*, should be specially trained by the Commonwealth Government as Aboriginal Officers, to bring the wild people in to contact with civilisation.

9. We recommend that all Aboriginal and Halfcaste women should be entitled to maternity and free hospital treatment during confinement, and that there should be no discrimination against Aboriginal women, who should be entitled to clinical instruction on baby welfare, similar to that given to white women.

10. While opposing a policy of segregation, we urge that, during a period of transition, the present Aboriginal Reserves should be retained as a sanctuary for aged or incompetent Aborigines who may be unfitted to take their place in the white community, owing to the past policy of neglect.

40. Pearl Gibbs, *Woman Today*, April 1938. An Aboriginal Woman Asks For Justice

We aboriginal women are intelligent enough to ask for the same citizenship rights and conditions of life as our white sisters. Those of my race who understand our economic conditions have not a great faith in what the white man promises to do for us. We know that we must carry on the fight ourselves.

As the grand-daughter of a full-blooded aboriginal woman, and having lived and been with them as much as I have been with white people, I realise the cruel and unjust treatment, also the starvation that my beloved people, the aboriginals, exist under. I myself have been on compounds that are controlled by the Aborigines' Protection (?) Board of N.S.W. The bad housing and sanitary conditions, the lack of food, the neglect of the aged and sick, no proper education for the children— is there any wonder that my aboriginal people are broken-hearted and discouraged at such shocking conditions!

Ah! my white sisters, I am appealing to you on behalf of my people to raise your voices with ours and help us to a better deal in life [...] Surely you are not so callous as to ignore our plea. Those of my people living in the more civilised parts of Australia are not asking for the stone of anthropology— but for practical humanity, for the opportunity to feed our children properly, to educate them; in a word to grant to them all the rights and responsibilities of DEMOCRACY.

41. Pearl Gibbs, Secretary, Aborigines Progressive Association, to William Morley, Secretary, Association for the Protection of Native Races, 23 July 1938

Having heard from various people of your active, mean unjust and unchristian ideas of what should be done for the aborigines of Australia. May I point out to you that the aborigines are now fit (and have been for many years) to take their places of Full Citizens, We hope to do this by having the Aboriginal Proction Board abolished. If you cannot agree with us, we respectfully suggest that you cease to aid in the demorilising of our race.

42. *Australian Abo Call*, no. 5, August 1938. The Colour Bar At Collarenebri

Collarenebri, on the banks of the Barwon River, is noted for what is called "The Blacks' Cemetery", a collection of graves adorned with broken glass and other ornaments. As a visitor to Collarenebri, I went to see this place. One mile out of town I stopped at the Blacks'.Camp, which is a group of humpies made of flattened kerosene tins and boughs. What I saw at the Blacks' Camp was so interesting that I did not go on immediately to see the Cemetery ...

Noticing a number of children peeping shyly around the humpies, I asked whether they went to school, and was told "No, there is a colour-bar in Collarenebri!" ...

Further enquiries revealed that there are more than twenty children of school age, living in the Blacks' Camp, one mile from the public school at Collarenebri; but none of these children dare present themselves at the public school to ask for education ... because they are classed as "niggers", and would be tormented by the other children. Also, there would be "reprisals" by the white citizens of Collarenebri, if the blacks dared to send their children to the public school.

As the blacks are dependent on the Whites for the right to work (at cheap rates) they do not wish to incur the hatred of the white men. So they keep their kiddies at home, away from school ...

The parents of these children find employment in Collarenebri and district, the men mostly engaged in bush work and some of the women doing laundry work for the people of the town. These people are almost all born at Collarenebri, and they do not wish to leave the vicinity where they are known and can get employment.

Police officers and others have advised the Aborigines to leave Collarenebri and go with their families to Brewarrina or Pilliga Government Reserves, so that the children may be educated at Aboriginal Schools. The parents say they are terrified of the Government Reserves, because their children would be "apprenticed out" to white employers, and perhaps the parents would never see them thereafter. Also, the atmosphere of the Government Reserve would be demoralising to the parents themselves, as they do not wish to live as parasites, drawing Government rations, herded with strangers from other districts.

Serious complaints are made by the Aborigines of Collarenebri regarding official intimidation used by Government representatives in an attempt to force these eight families to remove to a Government Station.

Intimidation

It is alleged that police officers have peremptorily ordered an Aboriginal mother to remove herself and children to a Government Reserve, and have threatened that, in the alternative, the children will be forcibly removed ...

Very few of the Aborigines at Collarenebri draw Government rations or dole, and the Aborigines Protection Board appears to take little or no interest in the welfare of these people ...

It would also seem necessary for the citizens of Collarenebri to learn to be more decent and humane in their attitude to the Aborigines.

It is stated by the blacks that there is a special ward for Aborigines at the local hospital, and also that Aboriginal men, women and girls would not dare to attend a dance in Collarenebri.

The joke is, according to the Aborigines, that many of the so-called "white" citizens of Collarenebri have Aboriginal grandmothers or great-grandmothers, but are not proud of the Aboriginal heritage, as they should be!

Colour Prejudice

Other white men, who pretend to "look down" on the blacks, have attempted to seduce Aboriginal women; and others again do not hesitate to employ Aborigines, both male and female, at far less than "award" wages ...

Even in death, the colour-bar is drawn at Collarenebri. The blacks have a cemetery of their own, out in the bush, the nameless graves covered with broken glass bottles ...

43. *Australian Abo Call*, **no. 6, September 1938. Land Lease Scandal. Is A.P. Board Entitled To Lease Abo. Reserves?**

The Aborigines Progressive Association is investigating the legal position regarding the leasing of Aboriginal Reserves in New South Wales to white men for grazing purposes.

As far as we can discover, the Aborigines Protection Board is trustee for approximately 14,000 acres of land, reserved for the use of Aborigines in New South Wales.

These Reserves are scattered throughout the State, some being only a few acres in extent, and the biggest being Cummeragunja, a Reserve of 5,000 acres in the county of Bama [Barmah], on the banks of the Murray River. With only a few exceptions, the Aboriginal Reserves are poor land, of not much value to white men. Nevertheless, these Reserves were granted by Parliament for the use of our people exclusively, and it was never intended that white men should have access to these Reserves for commercial money-making purposes.

There are approximately 10,000 Aborigines in New South Wales, which means that an average of less than an acre-and-a-half of land is Reserved for each Aboriginal in the land of his ancestors, which, considering the poor quality of the land reserved, is a small enough inheritance for the A.P. Board to keep as an inviolable trust for our people.

In the United States of America, as is well known, oil was struck on Indian Reservations, and, despite attempts by private speculators, the Government stood to its word and insisted that the Indians should get the financial benefit of the oil yield. In Australia, however, there has been no oil struck. The only commercial value of the Reservations is for grass to be used for pastoral purposes.

The position here is that the A.P. Board, as trustees for 14,000 acres of land reserved for Aborigines, has in its wisdom seen fit to lease many of these reservations, wholly or in part, to white men for grazing purposes. In the absence of proper means of testing the Board's authority to do this, we·cannot express an opinion as to the legality or otherwise of this procedure, and we must assume that the Board is legally entitled to do what has been done. At the same time, we think it inequitable that land reserved for Aborigines should be leased to white men, and we intend to investigate the position thoroughly, bringing it before the notice of the Crown Lands Department, and other authorities, who may be able to advise us whether the A.P. Board has exceeded its powers or not in thus having leased to white men land which is usually understood to be reserved for Aborigines only.

44. Pearl Gibbs, radio broadcast, 2GB Sydney & 2WL Wollongong, 8 June 1941

Good evening listeners,

I wish to express my deepest gratitude to the Theosophical Society of Sydney in granting me this privilege of being on the air this evening. It is the first time in the history of Australia that an Aboriginal woman has broadcast an appeal for her people. I am more than happy to be that woman. My grandmother was a full-blood Aborigine. Of that fact I am most proud. The admixture of white blood makes me a quarter-caste Aborigine. I am a member of the Committee for Aboriginal Citizenship.

My people have had 153 years of the white man's and white woman's cruelty and injustice and unchristian treatment imposed upon us. My race is fast vanishing. There are only 800 full-bloods now in New South Wales due to the maladministration of previous governments. However, intelligent and educated Aborigines, with the aid of good white friends, are protesting against these conditions. I myself have been reared independently of the Aborigines Protection Board now known as the Aborigines Welfare Board. I have lived and worked amongst white people all my life. I've been in close contact with Aborigines and I have been on Aboriginal stations in New South Wales for a few weeks and months at a time. I often visit them. Therefore I claim to have a thorough knowledge of both the Aboriginal and white viewpoints. I know the difference between the status of Aborigines and white men. When I say 'white man' I mean white women also. There are different statuses for different castes. A person in whom the Aborigine blood predominates is not entitled to an old-age, invalid or returned soldier's pension. There are about thirty full-blooded returned men in this state whom I believe are not entitled to the old-age pension. A woman in whom the Aborigine blood predominates is not entitled to a baby bonus.

Our girls and boys are exploited ruthlessly. They are apprenticed out by the Aborigines Welfare Board at the shocking wage of a shilling to three and six per week pocket money and from two and six to six shillings per week is paid into a trust fund at the end of four years. This is done from fourteen years to the age of eighteen. At the end of four years a girl would, with pocket money and money from the trust, have earned £60 and a boy £90. Many girls have great difficulty in getting their trust money. Others say they have never been paid. Girls often arrive home with white babies. I do not know of one case where the Aborigines Welfare Board has taken steps to compel the white father to support his child. The child has to grow up as an unwanted member of an apparently unwanted race. Aboriginal girls are no less human than my white sisters. The pitiful small wage encourages immorality. Women living on the stations do not handle endowment money, but the managers write out orders. The orders are made payable to one store in the nearest town— in most cases a mixed drapery and grocery store. So you will see that in most cases the mother cannot buy extra meat, fruit or vegetables. When rations and blankets are issued to the children, the value is taken from the endowment money. The men work sixteen hours per week for rations worth five and six-pence. The bad housing, poor water supply, appalling sanitary conditions and the lack of right food, together with unsympathetic managers, make life not worth living for my unfortunate people.

It has now become impossible for many reasons for a full-blood to own land in his own country. On the government settlements and in camps around the country towns, the town people often object to our children attending the school that white children attend. This is the unkindest and cruelest action I know. Many of the white people call us vile names and say that our children are not fit to associate with white children. If this is so, then the white people must also take their share of the blame. I'm very concerned about the 194 full-blooded Aboriginal children left in this State. What is going to happen to them? Are you going to give them a chance to be properly educated and grow up as good Australian citizens or just outcasts? Aborigines are roped off in some of the picture halls, churches and other places. Various papers make crude jokes about us. We are slighted in all sorts of mean and petty ways. When I say that we are Australia's untouchables you must agree with me.

You will also agree with me that Australia would not and could not have been opened up successfully without my people's help and guidance of the white explorers. Hundreds of white men, woman and children owe their very lives to Aborigine trackers and runners— tracking lost people. Quite a few airmen owe their lives to Aboriginals. I want you to remember that men of my race served in the Boer War, more so in the 1914-18 War and today hundreds of full-bloods, near full-bloods and half-castes are overseas with the AIF. More are joining each day. My own son is somewhere on the high seas serving with the Australian Navy. Many women of Aborigine blood are helping with war charities. Many are WRANS. We the Aborigines are proving to the world that we are not only helping to protect Australia but also the British Empire. New South Wales is the mother State and therefore should act as an inspiration to the rest of Australia. So we are asking for full citizenship and the status to be granted to us. We are asking that the 800 full-bloods in New South Wales be included in the claim— all those who are deprived of all federal social services to be granted, through the state, the old age pension and the maternity bonus until this injustice can be reformed by a federal law. We want an equal number of Aborigines as whites on the Welfare Board.

My friends, I'm asking for friendship. We Aborigines need help and encouragement, the same as you white people. We need to be cheered and encouraged to the ideals of citizenship. We ask help, education, encouragement from your white government. But the Aborigines Welfare gives us the stone of officialdom. Please remember, we don't want your pity, but practical help. This you can do by writing to the Hon. Chief Secretary, Mr. Baddeley, MLA Parliament House, Sydney and ask that our claims be granted as soon as possible. Also that more white men who understand my people, such as the chairman, Mr Michael Sawtell, be appointed to the Board— not merely government officials. We expect more reforms from the new government. By doing this you will help to pay off the great debt that you, the white race, owe to my Aboriginal people. I would urge, may I beg you, to hand my Aboriginal people the democracy and the Christianity that you, the white nation of Australia, so proudly boast of. I challenge the white nation to make these boasts good. I'm asking your practical help for a new and better deal for my race. Remember we, the Aboriginal people, are the creditors. Do not let it be said of you that we have asked in vain. Will my appeal for practical humanity be in vain? I leave the answer to each and every one of you.

45. Albert Hippi and others to J. Mullan, Minister for Justice, Queensland, 1 January 1923

THE HUMBLE PETITION of we the undersigned Aboriginal Natives of Australia at present employed in and about the Richmond District respectfully ask that you as Minister for Justice after reading our petition will enquire into our grievances and assist us in obtaining a reasonable and square deal with the monies that we have justly earned and that have been placed to our credits with the Commonwealth Savings Bank of Australia and which is held by the Protector as trustee.

Each and every one of us look forward after a hard year's work to a holiday at Xmas and only ask that a reasonable amount be given to us or be permitted to draw so much a day during our holiday ...

Each of us have an account in the abovementioned Bank and have requested the Protector's representative here to show us our balances or let us have a copy of statement of pass book, but such request is always refused.

I Albert Hippi am fairly well educated being able to calulate the amounts drawn by me and at present believe I have at least £200 to my credit and think that I should be permitted to draw sufficient to allow me to go away for at least one month's holiday. We do not ask that a big amount be paid to us in one sum but that we be permitted to draw at least £1 a day during our holidays, that is according to the amount to each of our credits.

We ask that some arrangements be made that after we have fitted ourselves suitably to go and have a holiday that we be permitted to draw at the rate of £1 per day up to an amount to be stated, it is absolutely out of the question for the Protector to think we can have a holiday on £10 and as we have the money it is our opinion we should be permitted to spend same in a reasonable manner.

We respectfully ask you, Sir, to obtain for us the following amounts set opposite our names in the manner above described, and also to help us to a clearer understanding of how we stand and what amount of moeny is to our credits.

Trusting you will help us to obtain our rights, We are Sir, Your Obedient Servants.

Names attached: Albert Hippi, Charlie Anderson, Douglas, Jimmy Keyes, Sandy Woolgar, Willie Cooktown, Harry No 2, George Kane

46. *Northern Standard,* 24 March 1936. The Larrakeyah Tribe. Concern Of "Old Men" For Welfare. Deputation To Visit Col. Weddell

For some time past there has been murmurings of discontent among members of the Larrekeyah tribe at the ever increasing numbers of aborigines who are coming to Darwin from surrounding tribes, including Melville and Bathurst Island[s], Daly River, the Alligator Rivers, not to mention aborigines brought to Darwin from various inland centres as witnesses in court cases or to serve out sentences. The lid was lifted a little on this fermentation of discontent on Friday night last week when King Ichungarra-billuk (better known as King George) of the once great tribe of Larrakeyahs, who roamed our foreshores from Point Charles to East Point in the days before the white invasion, hunting fish, dugong, and turtle in their native canoes, called the old men of the tribe together to discuss the matter. The Acting Superintendent of the compound was invited to be present as was also a representative of the "Standard."

The King in opening proceedings said it was their intention to have a deputation to Colonel Weddell but they did not wish to go over Mr Herbert's head. They liked Mr Herbert very much and hoped he would be allowed to remain in charge of the compound. King George pointed out that they had heard reports that the Government intended to shift the present compound to some point inland to make way for more Myilly Point residents.

"The Larrakeyah people are a salt water tribe and would not be prepared to live away from the sea," said King George. "This is all the country we have left, and the Government should leave us on it. Years ago we used to have our camping grounds on Lamaroo Beach and I was born there, as were most of the old men of the tribe. Our water supply was the native well where the present baths are now built. When Doctor Basedow and Dr. Gilruth shifted us to this place they promised us certain things but those promises were never kept. We have cleared the land and built our houses, and we should not now be asked to shift."

Duniuk, another old man, stated that many years ago he had attended school at the Darwin Compound but the Government had long ceased to endeavour to educate the young aborigines. He pointed out with a good deal of bitterness that education was being given to half-caste girls at Darwin and half-caste boys at Alice Springs. "Nothing is being done for our children," he exclaimed sorrowfully.

Another speaker pointed out that he was working and drawing 3/- a week, and another 2/-was going in trust. "How can we buy clothes for

ourselves and keep our families on 3/-," he asked, and our representative
had to admit that it was an economic problem he was incapable of solving.

Several speakers pointed out that the Compound was given to the Larrakeyah tribe, and they objected to members of other tribes camping and living at the Compound. One speaker said that all Point Keats and Daly River blacks should go to the mission in their country. They should not be allowed to come to Darwin as also should the Bathurst and Melville Islands blacks. They also object to the presence of the myall natives coming to the compound and exhibited a real fear for the safety of the members of the tribe. They also complain that the people are filling the place with undesirables from other centres. Another complaint is that the tribe is becoming detribalised and that the children are not learning the language of the tribe but a mixture of the languages of the tribes now resident in the Compound and English.

It was pathetic to see these old men endeavouring to safeguard the interests of their tribe. Asked what they would do if ordered by the Government to shift to another compound, they said they would rather go bush— pointing to the other side of the harbour— than go inland.

A Bathurst Island boy who was in the gathering near the meeting was approached and asked his opinion and he said "Bathurst Island boys will go anywhere with Mr Herbert, who has looked after the blacks well."

One reporter, accompanied by a half-caste, was shown many improvements recently made. These include a large lavatory with 21 seats, divided off to accommodate women and men separately. The place was scrupulously clean. Quite a number of large houses had been erected, while others had been improved by the addition of verandahs. The kitchen had been greatly enlarged and a large "ant nest" oven built. All this had been done with scrap iron and bush timber.

Our half-caste friend explained that it was a big problem to feed the hundreds of aboriginals, not to mention the hundred or so half-caste girls that are housed near by. "Plates," he said, "was the big problem, but this was being overcome by the use of benzine tins which were being shaped to make serviceable."

On the whole the writer was greatly impressed at the work being carried out by the aborigines for their own comfort, and left with the feeling that it would be far better to exclude the outside tribes and allow the Larrakeyahs tribe which has had nearly a hundred years association with the whites to remain in their residence on the small piece of land which they claim was given to them by Dr. Basedow and Dr. Gilruth.

47. Fanny Thorpe to William Ferguson, Secretary, Aborigines Progressive Association, 14 April 1938

I am reporting a little about Queensland. Reports that is cruelty to the Aborigines of Queensland, so therefore I have got a sister who is living at Perger Mission for the where the A.P. Board taken the children away which included 5 girls and 1 boy. they have been away from there mother eight (8) years now. one girl died and the boy got away and came home to his mother. so that leaves four (4) girls away yet. The mother has been trying and trying and as not gone in further a head. The brother go down to the Preice in Beawdesert to get information from them. Well sir I don't no where the girls are. as further as I conserned they are must be died. About three or four week ago I as been over at Woodenbong to see my sister. She said to me how about we writing to the Commission of Police of Queensland about her girls. which we did. I received a letter from my sister yesterday saying that she didn't get any reply from the Police yet. So it a strang thing where have they got those girls at all. So Mr Blakney [Bleakley] is the bottom of all that dirt. When he (Mr Blakney) put the girls out to work they dont like to go back— to Bramba Mission. Then Mr Blakney send the Police man to them to take the girls and send them away. Mr Blakney them away to a place called Palm Island in North Queensland. I don't know where that get any foods at all or left ther to die with starvation. When they go to Mr Blakney for the money he sends them there. So as far as I can under stand that is the jail house for them he as another place where he sends them to called Turaluam jail for the Aborigines of Australia. So what is the reason that the coloured people to like to go back to Queensland to where Mr Blakney. So if possible try and get those girls back for us please.

So this is a little report might help you a long. I hope you would crush the A.P.B of Queensland Mr Blakney to give the poor old Abo of Australia freedom.

So that is all the news

48. *Australian Abo Call*, no. 3, June 1938. A Letter From Clive Martin, Stradbroke Island

I was on a trip to Cherbourg Station on Barambah Creek, and saw "The Abo Call", which I read with great interest. Please send copies to me at Stradbroke Island, as a lot of our people have good education, and want to know all about this great movement.

I will guarantee that you will get all the support you want from this part of the Commonwealth to uplift our younger generation. Conditions here are not too bad, and our children get schooling, but what about our brothers and sisters on those mission stations? It is a disgrace to the Aborigines Protection Board, which we are trying to abolish.

At Cherbourg there is a great deal of favouritism, as the managers favour some, while others have to do without. The teaching is not of good standard. The food issue is very poor. Hundreds of thousands of pounds are held by the Government of Queensland, the earnings of Aborigines, yet our people cannot get decent food and conditions. On Cherbourg the money is spent on building churches and other buildings faster than the population is breeding.

We want proper education for our younger generation. The poor little children at present have not enough food, so they cannot stand up to the strain of school hours with empty bellies. They cannot develop their little minds properly when they are half starved.

A big enquiry is needed in Queensland into the administration of the A.P. Board, same as in New South Wales. We can prove all our charges, and ask for a Royal Commission to visit Barambah and other Missions, to take evidence from the people themselves, without being bullied by managers.

Please make me a Member, also send "Abo Call" each month, as all Aborigines here are eager to know more about this great move for progress.

Your sincere friend, Clive Martin

49. *Australian Abo Call*, no. 6, September 1938. Aborigines' Death Pact. Father and Son

In last month's "Abo Call" we published a statement by Mr. R.M. Watson, a North Queensland grazier, to the effect that Aborigines have been drowned in attempting to escape from Palm Island and other settlements off the coast of North Queensland.

We have ample evidence that Aborigines of Queensland are terrified of being taken away from the mainland to islands off the coast, particularly Aborigines from the far inland, who have never seen the ocean. The Queensland Government's policy of segregating Aborigines on ocean islands is one of the most callous policies ever put into effect by an Australian Government in pursuit of the policy of extermination by "protection".

The Queensland government uses its coastal islands for lepers, criminals, and inebriates, and also for Aborigines, the intention in every case being the same— namely to get rid of pariahs by placing them far away from the sight of the general community. No wonder the blacks are terrified when forcibly taken from their home districts by policemen, and told that they are going to be put on an Island— from which they know they will never escape.

South Australia

50. *Advertiser* (Adelaide), 13 December 1909. The Aborigines. Their Claims On The State. Point McLeay Mission

There are in our country many good citizens who, with every desire to preserve the original holders of the soil, and to do all that may reasonably be expected in the direction of assisting to maintain them amongst the peoples of the earth, are disposed to regard the aboriginal as a creature of whom nothing is to be made. It is generally accepted that the native black is incapable of elevation; that he is without ambition, has no traditions, no records, no past, and no possible future. A night with the concert party of the Point McLeay Mission, now in the city, will be well spent by any Australian who realises that the aboriginal is the real Australian, and that opinions as to the impossibility of doing anything with, or for, him must be submitted to the process of revision.

In the little party now touring the city in quest of funds for the urgent needs of the settlement are boys and girls who, in point of intelligence, appear to be the equal of any of their white countrymen, and some older men who, judging by their addresses at a recent meeting, are competent to debate logically the soundness of the position set up for their acceptance by the constituted authority of the State.

Musical Gifts

... the company under the direction of Mr Reid presents a unique and an enjoyable entertainment, and some of the numbers, especially those in which the words were given in the native language, were full of music ... of the girl Ruth it may be said she sings with expression and occasionally with pronounced feeling ... The boys— lads from 15 or 16 years downward— possess the round alto of boyhood, and some of their voices are sweet ...

An Attractive Speaker

But it was when the adult "David" [David Unaipon] took the platform and spoke of the traditions of his people, of their knowledge of astronomy, their intimacy with the science of botany, their bushcraft and folklore, that the audience gave most attention. In a simple way, and without any attempt at effect, this civilised savage spoke of the similarity of the Greek mythology and the aboriginal fiction. He told of the knowledge of the old people, their idea that the world turned, and that certain stars had their places and their times of appearing. He compared the names of the planets with those given by his people, and told of their tradition that, in the beginning, when the world was in darkness and the men who had lived and died had become animals (a belief which David said was an inversion of the Darwinian theory), the bat, which was formerly a citizen, undertook to provide light, and threw a nulla into the murk. He threw first to the north, then to the south, and next to the west, with no result. "This is my last throw," he said. He threw to the east, "and the sun rose". David spoke of the observation of the growth of the flora, of the movements of the fauna of the wilds, of the changing of the seasons, and, as he proceeded, intelligently commented on the writings of men of science, whose names are familiar rather to the few than to the multitude, to show that the people of his tribe were not always unintellectual and incapable of theorising. He ... held an interested audience for a good ten minutes in a speech unmarked by anything in the way of a faux pas.

A Black Patriot

Then "Philip" took the platform. "Philip" is an older man, and he reviewed the work of the mission, covering a period of many years. He spoke of the education of the people of his tribe, of their moral elevation, and their training to lead lives of usefulness, and told some interesting stories of their ignorance in the pre-mission days. One of these may be repeated ... It was in his per-oration that Philip became convincing and practical. He spoke of the country, of the beauty of it, of its possibilities, and, as he spoke, one forgot he was a black man and a civilised savage. He was an orator and a patriot— this man on the platform. "Where is there another such country?" he asked. And at once there flashed to the memory the lines–

"Breathes there a man with soul so dead
Who never to himself hath said,
'This is my own, my native land?' "

The man felt it all, every word in the lines of the poet. His soul is not so dead but that he knows this is his own, his native land. "It is a beautiful country," he said, "one of the finest on earth— I do not know of any other, but I have read of them. And it cost you nothing. Nothing in blood or treasure; nothing for purchase. It came to you easily, as it went from my people, and, if the Government only gave us a little of the best of it we would not be here to-night asking your help. Instead of that we have to come to you to solicit your assistance towards the purchase of material for roofing our huts. The settlers have burned off or otherwise destroyed, to ensure the safety of their holdings from fire, all the grass we used to employ in thatching our cabins."

It was an anti-climax, a descent from the heights of patriotic enthusiasm to the depths of practical interests. But it fitted the situation and should have been, if it was not, appreciated by the thoughtful in the audience.

51. *Register* (Adelaide), 29 November 1911. Our Black Brothers. A Clever Aborigine. Letter From Mat Kropinjere

The President of the Legislative Council (Sir Lancelot Stirling) has received the following letter written by Mat Kropinjere, a full-blooded aborigine resident at Port Macleay:–

"Dear Sir—Under same cover kindly receive please written matter to Honorable Members of Legislative Council dealing with the urgent requirement of more lands for the Aboriginal mission recently visited by yourself and His Excellency the Governor. Will you please convey my sincerest thanks to the hon. members (on behalf of the other aborigines of the district) and the sincere hope that success may attend their efforts in the acquisition of this land for the mission. Thanking you for what you have done in the matter, and praying a continuance of your utmost endeavour for the well being of our mission. I beg to subscribe myself, Sir, your respectfully, Mat Kropinjere."

The letter addressed to the members of Legislative Council is as follows:–

"Sirs— It is with feelings of great satisfaction that I have read the remarks of several of your members on the Aborigines Bill. I fully agree with those statements, but would like to point out an error, which has crept in some way or other, in which the manager of the Point Macleay Mission is represented to have stated that an additional 3,000 or 4,000 acres of this land offered would make the mission self-supporting. Now, the idea he wished to convey was that the acquisition of the whole of the area offered would produce the effect spoken of. On behalf of the aborigines of the district, I would urge upon you the urgent necessity of much more land for the mission, and would place before you a few facts bearing upon the question. Firstly, I would touch upon the fact of which

you are all aware, and which has been so forcibly expressed by the Hon.
J. Lewis, when he said "that they had taken away their country, and had
given them very little in return." Now you have, through means of education and civilization, enabled us to see this matter in the light just referred to; but we are of the opinion that the Government is not thoroughly acquainted with the results of this transaction, and I will endeavour to throw some light upon the subject. I can very well remember the
times when there were an abundance of the natural foods of the aborigine, as fish and fowl by water, with the kangaroo, wallaby, and opossum
on the lands in abundance; but, owing to the advent of the duck boat, the
gillnet, with various devices for the entrapping of fish, and the kangaroo
hunter's licence, those most necessary requirements for the aboriginal bill
of fare are most conspicuous by their absence, whilst our freedom has
been so much encroached upon that it is now impossible for us to go
anywhere without being reminded of the fact that we are intruders by
those who are so disposed, and are so hemmed around in a very few
hundred acres on our mission at Point Macleay by settlers to the east,
settlers to the west, settlers to the south, with the broad expanse of the
waters of Lake Alexandrina to the north, and the mission which once
proved sufficient to provide for the wants of our people, who now
through the reasons enumerated have been driven into the shelter of the
mission to such an extent that is now totally incompetent to cope with
the demand, owing to the insufficiency of its working area. However, I
feel assured by the tone of the remarks of your members, that you fully
recognise the necessity of more land for the mission, and as this land now
offered is of a nature peculiarly adapted to the aborigine, I will only add
the sincere desire of our people that you will do all in your power to obtain these additional lands for our use, so that there will be no doubt
whatever in regard to our mission being placed upon a self-supporting
basis. So I now leave the matter in your hands, knowing that as you have
given expression to the grievous wrong done to our people, in the alienation of our hunting grounds, and that the sense of British justice, under
which we are so happy and content to abide, will prompt you to make
some reparation; and O! what a grand and glorious opportunity now presents itself for doing so, in a site so suited to all the requirements of the
aborigine.

On behalf of aborigines, yours respectfully, Mat Kropinjere."

52. Evidence of Aboriginal witnesses, 18 July 1913, South Australian Royal Commission on the Aborigines

Alfred Hughes, Point Pearce

2247. You think it is desirable that an able-bodied man like you, who has been sufficiently trained, should have a block of land of his own, and that the Government might consider the advisability of providing you with the means of starting. Tell me what you would be satisfied with in the shape of land, and what conditions you would want?—I think I would be satisfied with 500 acres ...

2258. I have heard in evidence that the aborigines at Point Pierce are very discontented ?—Yes, we are very discontented at the present time.

2259. Will you give the Commission reasons of your discontent?—It is on the land question; we want to get on the land.

2260. What land do you want to get on?—Either this or somewhere else.

2261. This land does not belong to the Government at present, it is land for the aborigines of South Australia for all time, and, unless the Government take it over, that is the difficulty we have to contend with?—We looked upon it as ours, but would be satisfied with land here under the provisions of the 1911 Act.

2262. Is there any other matter with which you are dissatisfied?—No; I do not think.

2263. Have the mission people been treating you fairly and squarely?—We are not quite satisfied. The other farmers came in and we considered we should have been here instead of them.

2264. How did you expect to get in their places?—On the "halves" system.

2265. You would liked to have been on the "halves" system?—Yes.

2266. Where were you going to get the means of working on "halves"?—The mission could supply everything and we could repay them after harvest.

2267. You object to the share farmers coming in and providing the money?—We think we should be there.

2268. Do you think it necessary to have this share-farming going on during the developmental stage of the mission work here?—Some of us had to go away while the work was going on.

2269. Would you have stayed here if there had been work?—Yes. There was nothing here for us to do.

2270. Have you any suggestion to make showing how this share system could have been obviated?—It would have been better for us to have done the work, but we had nothing to go on with.

2271. Had the manager of the mission any plant to give you a start with?—Well, not at the start.

2272. Could they have done it recently? Have their implements and teams been fully employed?— Yes, their plant has been fully utilised.

2273. How could they have put you on when their plant has been fully employed?— We would like to have been in their places— the farmers ...

2282 ... You said just now there was a certain amount of discontent. How long has that discontent been in existence?— Ever since the share farmers came in.

2283. You do not view the European coming in with any degree of pleasure?— ... We do not feel any better for it, although the land has been cultivated. We were better off when they did not touch the land.

2284. Why were you better off?— We seemed to get along better ...

2345. You would rather have a block of land than work under present conditions?— Yes. I would rather have the land.

William Adams, Point Pearce

2357 ... — The land question is what we are most interested in.

2358. What is it that you would like in connection with the land question?— I think that portion of our community should be working blocks of land on their own account instead of on wages.

2359. What is your reason for having that opinion?— We think we are able to work on our own account— to do it for ourselves.

Walter Stansbury, Point Pearce

2469. What is your opinion in connection with the feeling in existence here regarding land?— We are growing more enlightened every year and are anxious to get more into line with modern civilisation. We do not want to stay in the same position all the time; we want to compete in trade like the white man. We think the mission station is for the uneducated. It is only a waste of time having fairly intelligent men here until they die.

2470. Your idea is that you have outgrown the mission. The past work of the mission was necessary and has been of great benefit?— Yes; I admit that, but it does not meet our views at the present time.

2471. How would you improve it?— By placing us on blocks.

2472. What area would you require?— Five hundred acres each— nothing less on this lean country ...

2477. If you had a block of land, would you let it on the share system?— I would work it myself, I would find the means.

Joe Edwards, Point Pearce

2501. Is there anything to prevent you going away and securing employment elsewhere?— We always understood this was our land, and looked upon it as our home.

2502. Your impression is quite wrong?— It may be ...

2504. This is a place to which the aborigines can come, but it is not a place to support you people entirely. You must help to support yourselves as much as you can?— We are anxious to support ourselves. We have grown beyond the mission life, and if we remained here another 50 years we would not be any farther advanced ...

2506. What would you suggest as a means of bettering the conditions of the rising generation?— If you allowed us to have land our children would be bound to benefit. There is nothing for them to look forward to now ...

2508. What do you intend your children to do when they grow up?— It is a hard question.

2509. How is a block of land going to improve your children's prospects?— We always thought that the Government would supply us with teams and implements.

2510 ... If I had a block I could put my children to trades, but I cannot do that now. I think the chances would be much better for them. I really do not know what I can do with my children.

53. *Register* (Adelaide), 21 December 1923. "Give Us Our Children". The Aborigines' Plea. Opposition To New Act

The Aborigines (Training of Children) Act, which was passed last session, has caused much heartburning among the natives, and a deputation of three of them came to Adelaide from Point Macleay to present a petition to His Excellency the Governor, praying for the repeal of the measure. They will return to-day.

Three Ambassadors

The Point Macleay deputies— Willy Rankine, Leonard Campbell and John Stanley— called at The Register Office on Thursday, and explained the aborigines' attitude to the new law. Campbell, the bearer, as he informed an interviewer, of a Scotch name, is a splendidly built man of 47 summers, and he related with pathos, the fear of the native men and women that their young ones will be taken from them. "We don't mind the Government taking them and training them," he said. "We want them to get on and be useful. But we want to feel that we still have full rights over them, and that they are our own children. There are a lot of times when a woman with only one daughter is unable to get about, and if the girl is taken from her, there is no one left to help her, and she has to borrow the daughters of other women. We do not wish to be a burden on the State, but our children have never been State children, and we don't want them to be. The people at Point Macleay would rather give up their mission station than sacrifice their children. We are sorry that we did not see His Excellency, for we think he would have helped us."

A Remarkable Petition

Campbell produced a memorial, which had been prepared and written by E. N. Kropinyeri, at Point Macleay, to express the feeling of the mothers on the question.

The document is reproduced here, exactly as it was written:– PORT MACLEAY, December 16— The hon. members of Parliament of South Australia— Dear Sirs— The Bill has passed, legalising the Act of taking away the children from their parents. This Act, like a mysterious creature of ill omen, is casting a gloom over this our little mission home. Yes, this Bill has passed at last, and the passing of it, provides food for serious consideration. And the first that presents itself to the mind, is the fact that, an Act, which, hitherto had been illegal, and I believe, punished by law, is now legal and supported by law, which produces a reverse effect upon the past legal law, as for instance, in the past, any one taking a child away from its parents without their consent, will be liable to punishment by law. But to-day, any desiring to return and live with their parents, will be dealt with by the laws contained in the Act. Here we have a queer conglomeration of laws, through some unaccountable way, the wild cat of confusion, has effected or gained an entrance into the dovecote of legal harmony, and caused such utter confusion among the inmates, to such an extent, that some, if not all, of them cannot with any degree of accuracy claim, each their respective relationship either to the legal, or illegal origin. However, this is not the matter on which I wish to write. It is mother's love, its claims, its rights, its demands. Now it is understood that a refusal to comply with the demands of an ultimatum of one nation to another, is an acceptance of condition of warfare whatever those conditions may lead to, so the passing of that Bill is a declaration of war between right and wrong. And there is only one, right, and only one wrong, which of the two contending party is right? We will see presently. Mark well, the two forces, arrayed against each other. There stands the advocates, and supporters of the Bill that has passed, strongly fortified, their guns of "intellect" trained and ready for action, they represent "Right." There, on the opposite and facing them is the rank of the enemy, strongly opposing the Bill, a very strange army, possessing no weapons of war, no intellectual powers, no Parliamentary eloquence, not a grain of science in the whole body, that makes the army of motherhood. The only piece of artillery which that army possesses is the weapon called love. And thus equipped, the army of motherhood has taken up their position in opposition to the Bill. The invader of those Godgiven and therefore sacred dominions of mother's love is its claims, its rights, its demands, a possession voted for them in the parliament of heaven, sealed with the image and superstition of His Majesty, whose name is "Love." This army also represents Right. Thus we see the two contending forces each striving for precedence in their claim of Right, and we ask, who is going to win the day? And the reply comes from the ranks of Intellect "victory is ours," and relying on their weapon of attack, Intellect, they thunder forth their intellectual arguments again and again, propelled by the full force of scientific facts. Poor motherhood, how are you going to retain the beauties and glorious possession of motherhood, the right, the claims, the demands of love amid such fearful intellectual bombardment as this, and seeing that you are armed with nothing more than the crude and primitive weapon love, the invention of which dates back in the past eternity. It is true, we are indeed poorly equipped, and we know not how we are going to fare in this fearful struggle, but— and just then, a thin spurt of smoke is seen issuing from the ranks of motherhood, and we knew that love, motherhood's weapon spoke, and that its claims, its demands, and its rights, in their threefold unity is speeding its unerring way to the ranks of the foe, bearing the seal, the hallmark, and the mandate of the majesty on high (the majesty of love) Hon. members (jurymen). The question is asked, Who wins? The bar of eternal justice, truth and righteousness awaits your verdict! What says you?

54. H. Taylor, Point Pearce Mission, to Constance Ternent Cooke, 29 May 1933

I am taking the liberty of writing this note to you in appreciation of the interest you are taking in the control & welfare of the Aborigines generally.

With a feeling of deep interest I have watched the advertiser for the result of the conferences held by the Womens Non-party association together with other bodies and the deputation led by the Hon. Dr. Basedow also the last conference now ended by Women voters and the compromise reached.

It seems just splendid to think that we as a down trodden people *have* such noble Ladies and Gentlemen taking up the cause for the welfare of the Aborigines because I think we would be long waiting on the Government alone for justice.

The question of land has been a long felt wait with some of us to work out our own destiny. Personally I have tried for years to acquire a reserve of land for aboriginals but each time unsuccessful that is I mean the 160 acres each for myself and Wife which is the limit allowed by the Government in The Aborigines Act of the year 1911. Also the inclusion of educated Aboriginal and half castes in a national commission appointed of men and women.

This suggestion came to my mind about six years ago. But how to accomplish it I was at a loss knowing that we are such poor people financially. Though we might have brains enough for the purpose. I do not wish to intrude too much upon your valuable time so will cut a long story short and in conclusion I wish to thank you for the motions moved by you as the representative of SA. also I wish you to convey to the Hon. Dr. Basedow who led the deputation to the Hon. Com. of Public works and other Ladies & Gentlemen who supported him so admirably in our interests my sincerest feeling of thankfulness. I with others feel that at last the cry similar to that which went up from Macedonia. Come & help us in drawing nigh the dark cloud that covered over us lifting away.

55. Petition of Aborigines to the Government of South Australia, 1935

The humble petition of the undersigned *aboriginals* inhabitants of *South Australia* respectfully showeth

1. That the small remnants of the tribes who occupied the State when the *white race* came to *South Australia* have a *strong moral claim* to *proper treatment* from the white race That race today is occupying our lands and in return we are forced to accept charity

Under their rule nearly the *whole* of our race has *disappeared*, and those of us who *survive*, resent to be treated as *paupers* & *outcasts*

We demand fair treatment.

We respectfully ask

1. That in order to deal adequatly with the *aboriginal* & *Half cast* problem a *Board* of *management* be appointed consisting of suitable *represtative's* of the various interests involved

2. That to *represent* the needs of our race *grant* us *power*, to *propose* a *member* in the person of our own blood to be employed by the Government as a member of the *Board*, so that we may have a *voice* in *deciding* the *future* of the *race*

3. That the *white race* which is *charged* both by the *direct command* of those who established these *colonies* & also by every *moral obligation* which can *bind* an *honest nation* shall make a proper effort to redeem us from the *degrading condition* under which we are at present *forced* to live or to give us an *opportunity* to redeem ourselves

So that we will *cease* to be a *burden* of the taxpayers of the *State*

& *Your petitioners* will ever (pray)

56. *News* (Adelaide), 2 November 1936. David Unaipon's Plea For Natives. Lack Of Understanding And Sympathy Alleged. Control Board Of Men Outside Government Service Urged. Problems Of Aboriginal Race

Charging the present and past Governments of South Australia with a complete lack of understanding and sympathy in regard to aborigines, Mr. David Unaipon, the well-known full-blooded native advocate, today urged the appointment of an aboriginal control board composed of men outside the Government service. Otherwise the board members might become protectors of the Government and its interests rather than of the aborigines he said.

He described as apathetic the official attitude toward the "immorality and degeneration" at the Point McLeay Aboriginal Station.

The Aborigines Act Amendment Bill, which provides that the Chief Protector shall be chairman of the proposed new Aborigines Board, will be further debated in the Assembly tomorrow.

Because of his high level of mentality Mr Unaipon, who is a quiet-voiced but sparkling-eyed man, is recognised as an outstanding spokesman on behalf of Australia's 50,000 full-blooded aborigines.

"I should like to be permitted to draw attention to the wishes and feelings of my race in regard to methods of control," he said. "It is our desire that a board should be appointed consisting of men outside of the Government or public departments— men who are sympathetic and understand the circumstances under which the natives live.

"We have been for nearly a century under a Chief Protector. Some of the men who have held that office have acted as 'protector' of the Government. My people feel that their fate should not be left in the hands of any section of the Government service. There should be a new order of administration.

"Living on Government settlements tends to the degeneration of natives and encourages parasitism. Governments appear to think that as long as the natives are fed and clothed that is all they require."

"The real duty of those in control lies not only in feeding and clothing the natives, and contributing to their temporary support when calamities overtake them. The greater duty is rendered when we are led to a higher plane of thought by ideals which stimulate to self-development.

"That can be brought about only by mission institutions under religious guidance, such as the one proposed in the north-west of South Australia by the Presbyterian Church and suggested by Dr Charles Duguid."

Mr Unaipon said that although many people referred to Point McLeay as a mission station, it was actually a Government settlement and to apply the term mission station to it was a confusion of thought. Although there was some religious teaching at the Government stations, he advocated that the whole control should be in the hands of sympathisers who had a deep understanding of the aborigines.

There were schools for the native children at the settlements, but when they left school they were without prospects or outlook in life beyond the ordinary station work, such as milking cows, tending pigs and mending fences.

They were not given definite training as artisans or craftsmen, such as had been given at Point McLeay before the Government took over control of the station from the Aborigines' Friends' Association. During the association's 50-year period of control sheep and cattle were kept on the station and the natives taught to handle stock, shear sheep, and do wool-classing.

They were also trained as builders, carpenters, and bootmakers. A vineyard was established and natives instructed in pruning and the management of vines. When the Government took charge of the station these ventures were closed and irrigation work was destroyed.

"I would prefer that the places where the natives live should not be looked on as Government settlements," Mr Unaipon said. "Governments do not understand the psychology of the aborigines, and are not sympathetic. Whenever there is an opportunity they would rather persecute an aboriginal than help him along.

"If the Government wants to show sympathy now, the best way for it to do so would be by handing over control to men such as those in the Advisory Council of Aborigines, and the Aborigines' Friends' Association, who are longer-experienced and more sympathetic than public servants, who have merely had a clerk's training.

"My people and I will be bitterly disappointed if the Bill is passed in its present form. A compromise in the appointment of the present Chief Protector (Mr. McLean) as secretary of the board might be satisfactory."

Referring to morality at Point McLeay Mr. Unaipon explained that when the Aborigines' Friends' Association controlled the station a system of segregation of the sexes was enforced among the young people by means of dormitories. But the Government had closed the dormitories and taken no steps to discourage promiscuity.

Mr Unaipon does not favour the suggestion made in some quarters that the aboriginal population should have a representative in Parliament.

"I do not ask for social equality or position for my people, but for the opportunity to live our own lives in the best ordered conditions possible" he said.

He does not wish that native artisans should compete with white men and cause resentment by trade unions. But there is always a market for fish, he says, and natives could be assisted to establish themselves in this industry. Several aborigines have their own small dairy farms.

57. *Age,* 18 January 1938. Day Of Mourning. Aborigines Not In Sympathy

The Minister for the Interior (Mr. McEwen) has received, through Rev. J.H. Sexton, honorary secretary of the Aborigines' Friends' Association, a letter from Mr. David Unaipon, a full-blooded aborigine, in which Mr. Unaipon, speaking for the aborigines of Australia, takes exception to the proposal that the opening day of the anniversary celebrations in Sydney should be regarded by Australian aborigines as a day of mourning, Mr. Unaipon is an authority on native legends, on which he has written a book. Mr. Sexton's letter read:—

David Unaipon a well-known native leader in Australia, a full-blooded aboriginal, and a prince of his tribe, has asked me to forward you the enclosed letter for your information. He is not in sympathy with the day of wailing being staged in Sydney on Foundation day. He considers it will only harm Australia abroad, and he says you can make what use you like of his letter. David is the author of a booklet on native legends, and is a good speaker, with an excellent English vocabulary, is very gentlemanly in bearing, and, you will see by his message, a man of common sense. The wailing day will be availed of to criticise Governments and generally finding fault, instead of showing appreciation of the efforts being made to aid the aborigines.

Mr. Unaipon's letter was as follows:—

This day of mourning is a huge mistake, because it is of a political character. The movement is largely an emotional one, sponsored by sympathetic white people and half-castes in order to call attention to native grievances. But the 50,000 full-blooded aboriginals will have very little part in this matter. These will stoically and silently await the coming of a new day.

The signs of this are already on the horizon, for the Prime Minister of Australia has already promised a Commonwealth review of the position. The most effective way of bringing this about is not by traducing Australia and giving it a bad reputation abroad, but by expressing appreciation of what is being done and contemplated for the aborigines. The many hopeful signs of an awakening interest in the native races is a cause for rejoicing, rather than weeping. The most effective way of helping the natives is not in weeping and bemoaning the past, but by acting in the living present. There have been grave faults on both sides, causing misunderstanding and friction, and the exclusion of the natives from the Federal constitution intensified the problem, because this left a national concern to be handled by State Governments.

As a representative of the race, I would like to urge that the 150th anniversary of Australia should be celebrated by the inauguration of a new programme, by which all the privileges of the dominant race should be given to the blacks. The time is past to talk of segregation. Let my people come more fully into the national family. There have been enough scientific investigations already, and no new facts have been brought to light, and yet there is still a plea to segregate the natives, keeping them practically in bush museums for scientific purposes.

The natives should not be kept in the cradle any longer. The aborigines want to be released from the ties that bind them to a decayed system, and want to be associated practically with the whites in the development of Australia, and they ask that the 150th anniversary of the continent may be marked by the wiping off of old scores and the inauguration of a worthy nation programme for the promotion of their well being.

58. Requests submitted by Aborigines, Point Pearce, to the Advisory Council on Aborigines, South Australia, 26 August 1938

1. Better education for our children in the way of technical training and apprenticeship.

2. To help anyone desiring to go on the land by providing them with land not less than 200 acres and a home.

3. Those desiring help in the way of a fully equipped fishing outfit.

4. Help for our unemployed single men in the way of wages or increased ration allowance.

5. That married men employed on Point Pearce Station be paid not less than 7/- a day for 6 days a week and 3d per head for each child in a

family per week.

6. The reopening of our Hospital here at Point Pearce.

7. That the white sharefarmers be put off the Station land and our own native men put on the land.

8. That the 10/- taken out of each mother's bonus be abolished.

9. That the natives be provided with an ambulance to convey our sick to and from the Hospital and if needed to bring our dead home.

10. Also more help for our rationers in the way of butter, eggs and vegetables.

11. The reduction of store and meat prices while wages are so low.

12. That the sons of widows be employed for wages to help the widow.

13. Also the charges for medicine and horse paddocking be abolished.

14. That something be done for the lads between 14 and 16 years.

Western Australia

59. John Kickett to Mr Griffiths, 29 August 1918

I wont A Little Fair Play if you will Be so Kind Enough to see on My Beharfe Since reciving the Letter from the Department *Dated 30th april 1918 that My Children Cannot attend school at Quairading I see that the Education Department as let Johnny Fitsgeralds Children reenter the State School North West of Quairading* they are attending the School four month just now this is not Fair at all they were turned out of the Quairading State School for some reson and let them enter A nother what I here is that Baxter made it right for them Because one of them is at the Front Fighting well Sir *I have Five of my People in France Fighting— Since you were up here for Your Election one as Been Killed* which leave four Cannot my Children have the Same Privelige as Johnny Fitsgerald on thos grounds would you Be so Kind Sir see if they can goe to Dangin or the same school north of Quairading if I send them their Sir I Cannot see why my Children could not attend here at Quairading My People are Fighting for Our King and Country Sir I think they should have the Liberty of going to any of the State I had Fifteen Parents of whos Children are attending the State School here signed my Piteteion Knows my Children well so they could goe to School here But was refused By the Department My Childrens Uncles are Fighting Front Could you do some thing for the little ones well my Apeale Sir would you see Could they goe to Dangin State School or the north of Quairading

60. William Harris, letter to the editor, *West Australian*, 25 September 1925

The proposed enfranchisement of the half-castes produced a lot of insulting remarks from some members of the Opposition in the Legislative Assembly, especially the Leader (Sir James Mitchell), whose statements were very misleading and bitter. Sir James said the bulk of the half-castes were to be found in the sparsely populated parts of the country leading the lives of natives. He knows very well, or, as a public man, he should know, that the natives are living exactly the same as the whites, when possible— by hard work. There is no other way in which they can live. Most of them do contract work; some have farms and are educated, and in that respect they compare more than favourably with the class of Indians that come here. Moreover, the aborigines and half-castes are not aliens; they are in their own land, and some scientists hold that the aborigines are the root stock of the Aryan branch of the human family, and, that given a chance, they are mentally, morally, and physically the equals of any other kind of human being.

I would remind Parliamentarians and others who object to the half-castes having a vote that many of that despised class fought in the Great War. Now they are refused a vote, and they are not allowed to enter a public house, even to take shelter from a storm. Sir James Mitchell caused some amusement by a flippant allusion to the national costume of the aborigines. Even that costume might compare favourably with the skins of animals and blue paint with which the aboriginal inhabitants of the British Isles dressed themselves. One cannot wonder at the viewpoint of Mr. Teesdale and Mr. Angelo on anything connected with justice and consideration for the natives. Both were living for years in a town where aborigines went clanking through the streets chained by the neck to wheelbarrows. Mr. Teesdale says he will walk out of the House when a half-caste enters it. His threat to walk out of the House seems a huge joke, considering the strenuous efforts he has made to keep his seat. His leaving the House may be an awful calamity or not; it depends on how people regard his merits as a legislator; at any rate, the State would survive his desertion. All will admit that a strong sense of justice is necessary in a member of Parliament. The members mentioned are on their own showing deficient in the qualities of justice and mercy, so they cannot be first-class statesmen.

Sir James Mitchell asked if the Government wished to encourage the building up of "the unfortunate half-caste class." Unfortunate! Yes, because of the persistent cruelty and injustice of certain people. Before me is a copy of the Aborigines Act, and I have no hesitation in saying that it is a foul blot on the State of Western Australia, a disgrace to those formulating such Acts and also to the members of Parliament who were responsible for such Acts becoming law. I am certain the majority of the people in this State have no idea how cruelly the natives are treated, or that they are outlaws, and that without doing anything to forfeit their rights to live in freedom in their own land, they can be taken from any part of the State and be compelled to live in prison reserves such as that at Mogumber. But why try to make Pariahs of natives in their own land, people with the civilisation of yesterday, struggling midst adverse conditions to live in the same fields as the whites who have the knowledge gained by thousands of years of civilisation? If the aboriginal must go under, then for humanity's sake give him a fair deal while he is still on the surface.

61. William Harris, letter to the editor, *Sunday Times*, 14 November 1926

Ever since the whites settled in Western Australia the aborigines have not lived in a more cruel and lawless state than they are living today. Since the inauguration of responsible government their condition has gone from bad to worse, and has now become intolerable.

For hundreds of years, in song and story, it has been Britain's boast that under her flag was found justice and fair dealing for all. But in dealing with the aborigines it has been reserved for Western Australia to overturn British Law and justice and that consideration for the weak and helpless that are recognized and held as due by all really civilized people.

I repeat that there is no law for the aborigines in this state. What law or justice can there be for people who are robbed and shot down, or run into miserable compounds? What part or parcel have they in the land in which they have a right to live in? It is true there are reserves marked on the maps, but of what use are they to the natives when the squatter occupies every acre?

Regarding massacres, heaps of human bones mixed with cartridge shells in different parts of the state appear to me to be evidence of the fact of their having been shot down. Most people hearing of the dispersion of natives think that a few shots are fired over their heads to scatter them. This dispersion takes a different form altogether.

The educated aborigines and half-castes in this state are about to form a protective union. As British subjects they claim, and mean to have, the protection of the same laws that govern the white man, not to be persecuted by the Aborigines Department and its officials.

At Laverton we had the spectacle of natives in that district decoyed into the police station on the pretence of being served with food. The doors were closed on them, they were kept under lock and key until the train was ready to start, then taken under armed escort and locked in the train for Mogumber. I have since heard that the Laverton natives broke gaol and got away, except one who is blind. I don't think that anyone knows or cares if they ever got back.

Mogumber is a mixed settlement on the Moore River, where native men, women and children are forced to live along with murderers and other offenders from all parts of this state. Six of these were made police strutting round in all the glory of a uniform, handcuffs and keys to terrorize the others and keep them in the compound. The place also has gaol cells. Why don't they employ respectable police if they must keep the inmates from running away? At night the women are under lock and key to keep them from clearing off. What a nice place it must be for women and children to live in. If all are considered prisoners then the men should be kept in another place.

'Broomeite', writing from the Nor'-West, wants the natives to be shut up in reserves because they will kill and disturb cattle so that they look like hunted devils. How about the Natives? It is not certain that they are the hunted devils, trying in vain to get away from the cattle, with an occasional 'hurry-up' from the stock-man's rifle? Cattle are everywhere fouling the waters, driving off the natives and blotting out their only means of subsistence.

When it is known that the boundaries of a tribe are very limited, can we wonder that desperate, starving natives will at times kill cattle? Those can be punished, but give them a chance to live; don't make their rough, miserable lives worse. Try and win their confidence by kindness; encourage them to work and become useful.

In Melbourne a few days ago Mr Holmes spoke of the dangerous cannibal savages in the North-West. Let me tell Mr Holmes and others that the natives are not the savage and dangerous cannibals he would make out. Of course it must be horribly interesting to people in Melbourne to hear Mr Holmes on cannibalism. It is the correct thing to travelling Nor'-Westers to talk like that.

62. Norman Harris to Jim Bassett, 19 April 1927

We have been looking out for you some time now but I don't think you are much of a swimmer and I know that you haven't got a boat and now that the lakes are running you can't come per road or water and perhaps not by train, so I don't expect to see you this winter.

Now, Jim, we are trying to get some of the natives and half-castes together has a deporation to the Premier has you know what for.

So we can get a vote in the county also one law for us all that is the same law that governs the whites also justice and far play.

I suppose you know that Perth is a prohibiterd around Perth for natives and half cast it is in Saturdays pappie of March 19th, 1927, and last year Tindale Cpt. said that the Government ought to put all the natives out of Australia onto a island out from Kimberly thats rotten what do you say Jim.

Last year in Parliament House they disgust where they should give halfcasts a vote or not anyhow their was hell to pop over that so they would not let them have it.

They are afraid of the native wanting the same has the halfcast why shouldn't he if he is respectable or any person.

Now you see yourself where is the Abo. got a fare go.

He is not alowed in a Pub, not to have a gun, not to camp on revers because squatters stock are there, he is not to have dogs near stock. He is not to grow grapes because he may make wine and get drunk. They bar him in football and cricket must not be in town to long after dark. All Police are in the bush a sort of proctor I have never heard of them protecting the native yet.

In the North has you know they were never given wages just work for kick in the sturn and a little tucker such has it is, and still the same.

A native can't leave this state without getting the permission from the Proctor (Mr. A.O. Neville) a rotten B. The white Police can do just has they like. The native is a prisiner wherever he is. He can be brought from any part of the State put in a Compond such has Mogumber, a rotten prison for alsorts just fancy young girls and boys brought up among them sort and for a certain they dont learn them much *and no moral trainning atal.* Thoes children are there being brought up among all the black cut throats the Police can lay their hands on from all parts of the country. They say they are trying to send them out in the world to do good for themsselves. How cant they when this Aboriginal Act is over them if a girl or boy goes out to work they get the money, if the girls have the misfortune to have a kidie she is got by the Police and sent strait back to Mogumber in most case death release them. So Jim you see they are blocked whatever way they go.

Now it is comonly known that while girls were in Carolup they were tired up floged some time four and five at a time. All thoes that were in

Carolup Mission were brought to Mogumber. They never got payed for
the work they done their. Now this is the question who got that land and
place if it were sold what hapend the money I dont know does anyone
know I never heard of any natives getting a holiday out of the money.

Now Mogumber, a native name Bob Lookenglass tryed to run away
from that prison, he was caught near Moora belted by the Black Police of
Mongumba. Then he got or was brought back to Mongumber he was
tired to a tree and was belted by the white officer in charge put into the
boob that they have ther I think of cause we cant say for a certain he was
brought out of the boob *dead* or nearly.

Yet their are hundreds of halfcast send their children there for
schooling and trainning think they are doing good if they only stop and
think they can see enough. Then again if they dont send them the Police
come along and sends them along to Mongumba or the Prison I should
say The Police can take the children without a warrant or ask their per-
ants permission. They are quite within the Act to take any Aborinal or
Halfcast.

Someone goes up North getting all the half cast girls and boys off all
the stations nitives to if they want them. They have got a motor truck
with seats along the sides and big rings bolted to the centure chains from
rings to natives.

The South Australian League for Natives are trying for a native State
up in the Northern Territory that will be no good because they will have
to keep them their that is the same has Mongumba only on a biger scale.

Mr. Neville gave a lecture in Perth and he said that it was no good
giveing natives land because they would not work it they only use it for
camping ground and he went on to say that he could not name a single
native where he has got land and done good. So you see they will not let
the native have land next. Not letting have land is quite easey when they
make Perth Prohibited against natives and halfcast.

I have got a headache thinking about this Act. Uncle Bill has just gone
from here in to Morawa I am at Dads place now but will be going back
to my place next week. Uncle Bill is going down to Perth at about the end
of the month he is going to Yalgoo now. Uncle Bills is going to have a go
at the Aborigal Department. I think he will smash it up also all these
Componds of cause he wants help from all the natives and h.c. He is not
setting their for his own good because we all can do alright there are
some halfcast yourself and us we get not a bad deal but it not the think
we dont want to be under that Act atal, the one law is quite enough so if
all the natives and halfcast pay a little in to him for a lawyer if we can get
every one it will only run into a few shillings, anyhow thoes who dont pay

what do you think ought to be done to them. So think this is enough about this question.

How are you getting on with your cropping, we haven't started putting any in yet. I was doing some rolling before that rain it settled the burn, although I set it alight last Sunday I may be able to plough it in. We are all doing alright has regards health my little fellow has got two teeth also walking about now so I think I have told you all the news this time hoping I will see you before I die and that you will get a good crop.

Questions within the meaning on the Act

Why should the abo. Act be over us, it is only a By Law?
Isnt the one law good enough it is hard enough to live under?
Why shouldn't a native have land?
The country belongs to him?
Why segregation in his own land?
Why can't he be alowd in a public Hotel?
Why is he a prisnor in any part of the State?
He can be arrested without a warrant.
Why shouldn't he have a voise in the making of the Laws?
How do they suppose keeping natives in a big reserve?
Why shouldn't a native mother demand Freedom for her child?
Why should the Aboriginal Department put quadroons in Morgumba?
How many schollars have they turned out of Morgumba?
Why is it that the fairest are to the blackest?
Why is it that all letters are opened before going and out to?
Is it so that all girls and boy are found a job by the Dept?
Is it so that all from their have to send their money back?
Is it so that girls are lock up in Dormotorys?
Does children have to work?
There are about 300 people in Morgumba what do they do?
Do they get any money for their work?
What dose their food consist of, I bleave Billy Goats?
Do they encourage young people to come their?
Do they stop card playing or gambling their?
Why does anyone who leaves their have to report his movements?
Why is the Act still over anyone who comes from Morgumba?
Why was thoes people shifted from Carrollup to Morgumba?
Who has got Carrollup now how much was it sold for?

Who has got the money for it?

I bleave that girls were tied with chains to get punished.

I bleave that girls were made bend forward while the kick them from behind Jist fancy that.

Why was the name change to Aboriginal Department from a Chief Proctor of Aborigines?

Where does the money go to that is set aside for the Aborigines?

In the early day a white person who married a native woman was aword a bit of land and never lost cast.

Now a white man who is caught near a camp is heavily find or imprisoned.

I could write a lot more but I have got to go on to home this afternoon so will ring off.

Burn this when you are finished with it or send it back to me.

[The above questions were undated, but were forwarded to the government of Western Australia on 21 March 1928, along with other letters between Harris and Bassett, including that of 19 April 1927.]

63. *West Australian*, 10 March 1928. Black Man's Burden. A Novel Deputation. Chief Protector Criticised

Neatly clad and looking slightly self-conscious in the clothes of white men, a deputation, comprising seven full-blooded aborigines and half-castes— the first of its kind on record in this State— waited upon the Premier (Mr. P. Collier) yesterday, and ventilated a series of grievances ...

William Harris, a half-caste, the spokesman of the deputation, stated the deputation's case in perfect English, and showed no small signs of erudition. The Aborigines Act, he said, had always operated to the detriment of the aborigines and lately it had become unbearable. Educated natives were punished under the British law, but otherwise they were treated like wild blackfellows. They should not be debarred from entering the capital city of their own country.

The Premier: Do you think it would be well for the natives if they were allowed to enter the city without restriction? I suggest that the association of natives with the whites has not been altogether beneficial to your people. Mr. Harris: That is due to the absurd regulations of the Act. The restrictions should not be enforced against educated aborigines, who are paying taxes like the white men. Continuing, Mr. Harris said that any man who read the Aborigines Act with an unbiased mind knew it was dead against the natives. Why should the aborigines be dumped into any place the Chief Protector might choose? There was much injustice in the provision that employers must secure a licence before employing aborigines.

The Premier: If there were unrestricted employment of natives, it would encourage sweating by employers. Mr. Harris: Natives south of Carnarvon are quite capable of looking after themselves, although those in the Far North may not be. There were no reserves, he continued, where natives might live in their natural state. Although the reserves were set aside for natives, they were within the area of pastoral leases, and squatters drove the aborigines away. The native reserve at Mogumber was a prison because men were forced to stay there against their will. What was to prevent the natives from living like other free citizens of the Commonwealth?

The Premier: There would be no objection if they were all like you and other members of the deputation, but your whole race could not be allowed to live freely under the same conditions as the whites.

The natives, Mr. Harris resumed, objected to the Chief Protector's transferring families and individuals from their natural districts to settlements like Mogumber, where they were forced to mingle with hostile natives from other tribes. They also objected to native police being placed in control at the settlement, as this led to undesirable practices ...

"These cut-throats from the North," he continued, "have unlimited power. White men should be appointed, if police must be kept there." Another member of the deputation interjected that at Mogumber women and children were forced to associate with gaolbirds from the North. Most of the black police were gaol-birds. "Policemen, white or black, are the terror of the natives," Mr. Harris said. "The natives run for their lives when they see a policeman." The Premier: What do they do when they see a black policeman?— They run twice as fast.

Aboriginals, said the speaker, had no time for the Chief Protector, and were afraid of him. The Premier: Mr. Neville merely administers the laws: he is not responsible for them. I don't think a college education is any advantage to a Protector of Aborigines. A man with practical experience and an early association with natives, who understands their customs and habits, is required. The whole point lies in the administration of the law. Undoubtedly, your people have suffered through want of discretion. White people suffer similar disabilities through foolish administration of the law.

Mr. Harris: We want to live up to the white man's standard. It is no trouble to follow the white man's ideals, although there is room for improvement.

The Premier: Do you suggest that the Chief Protector should live among the natives so that he might be better able to understand their requirements?

Mr. Harris: That would be no good at all. The prohibition against carrying firearms, he continued, was another hardship, as it prevented natives in the North from providing for their needs.

The Premier: I don't think any native will touch a white man without provocation. In any report of the murder of a white man by a native, the white man seems to have been blameworthy.

"If a native State is provided nearly as many soldiers and police as there are aborigines will be required to keep them there," Mr. Harris said. "The department established to protect us, is cleaning us up. We were far better off under administration from England. Under the present Act, Mr. Neville owns us body and soul. There should be discrimination under the Act between full-blooded aborigines and half-castes."

A member of the deputation: Natives living in the North should be subject to control different from that exercised over those in the south …

Mr. Harris said that Mrs. Daisy Bates and Mr. Neville were the worst enemies of the aborigines. The Premier: I understood Mrs. Bates was the saviour of the natives. Mr. Harris: She is doing it for publicity so that people may call her a courageous woman for living amongst the blacks. If she did not encourage the natives to cadge at Ooldea, they would fend for themselves.

Concluding, he said that natives educated up to the standard of white men should be exempted from the Aborigines Act …

64. Norman Harris to Helen Baillie, 15 February 1934

I received your letter and Mr and Mrs Cooper's photo and printed matter a few days ago, and I must thank you very much. I see by your letter that you are very keen in the interest of our native race. There is no doubt us half castes are handicapped and blocked in every direction. I am only speaking of the conditions in this State, in which the law is cruel and intolerable, and we don't seem to have anyone to speak for us. There is an Aborigines Department in this State to care for us, of which the Chief Protector is our "Legal Guardian" and Parliament has given him supreme power to apply the law on our blood caste, and there are only a few of us who manage to escape the foul lick of the tongue of the law. So I hope Mr Cooper will be successful in his venture for better conditions for us. I think he will get it alright if he could only get the support that is due to him by the people mostly affected. I know what it is in this country; it is a very hard job to get the aborigines and halfcastes to organise all together, they don't seem to see the value of it. Those who can see it don't seem to want to do anything for those who are lower, and those who are lower seem to have a policy like "please let us live".

But I have posted Mr Cooper's petition around to quite a lot of different places, so I think I can get some of them to sign the petition. Anyhow we will have to keep on hammering away at them. It is the squeaking wheel that gets the grease.

If the Protectors were to see that we got our full measure of justice, then things would be different. At present in this State, there is no encouragement for any of us to rear a family, because a police officer can come along at any time, without warrant, and send our children away, and we can't say a word because every policeman in the country town is a Protector, and in many cases the police Officers are hand in glove with the squatters, and this State is a squatter-ridden land.

I am very glad a Peace Party has gone to Arnhem Land, and it would have been just what you told Mr Perkins— no party other than one led by the Missionaries would do any good. It has been written down in record that every police party have been a punitive expedition, and the poor natives have been shot down like wild dogs.

It is high time now that the community was educated up to look upon the aboriginal as a human being instead of a zoological specimen. It is encouraging to learn that there are societies growing like the Aboriginal Fellowship Group, and I wish you all the best of good luck in your work in the interest of the aborigines.

There is no doubt it is a very hard job, and one gets little or no support from those most affected. Myself, and a few more of us around here would like to become members of the Aboriginal Fellowship Group, if we can become members I will send our subscriptions along when I hear from you again.

65. Statements of Aborigines, recorded by Mary Bennett. Western Australian Royal Commission to inquire into allegations of the mistreatment of Aborigines, 1934

Mr W., 26 March 1934

... "I am not ashamed to own my aboriginal relations though I have not lived with them. The nearest I have lived to them is 300 to 200 yards, about 20 years ago, when I had permission to camp when I was at

Claremont on the Church reserve; then three natives came along and put up their tents on the reserve; and I was told by Sergeant Thomas, who was the police officer at Claremont then, that I would either have to remove myself, or else move the natives. I would not move the natives away, so I moved myself into a house which belonged to a man named Bishop at Claremont and paid him 10/- a week for it. I have always kept away from aboriginals because I knew that people would try to bring me under the Aborigines Act. The reason I did not want to come under the Aborigines Act is that they take your children and hunt you down and move you for no reason, but just when they please."

He then proceeded to tell me about his interview with the Chief Protector that afternoon. He said:

"When I was in the train this afternoon, my cousin ... caught sight of me, and said he wanted to see me and asked me to go with him to Mr Neville. I went with him, and Mr Neville said to me, 'Dave, you have to come under my laws, you can't get away from them'. I told him that I am not an aboriginal, and that therefore I defy him to call me one. He asked me then, what was my wife? I said, 'a white woman.' He said, 'no, a half-caste', and asked, 'what do you class your wife as?' I told him that [Mr C.], a Welshman, was the father of her. Then he said, 'What do you class your children as?' And I said, 'Clean from the blood of an aboriginal'. He said, 'No, they are aboriginals', and he defied me or anybody else to take them away from him or put them under any other Act' ...

The children were taken away again on Saturday morning and kept in gaol in Pinjarra from Saturday till Monday, then taken to Perth, and kept in Perth gaol from Monday to Thursday, when they were taken to Mogumber by a police constable. They were given a sort of trial at Pinjarra before two justices, a colonel from the Fairbridge School Farm being one of the justices. A justice asked what the children were being sent away for? and the sergeant replied that the children were neglected, and that the Chief Protector had rung the police up and told them to gather the children up and bundle them off to Moore River settlement.

Mrs [W.] said that when she arrived in Perth this afternoon and saw her husband she went to the Aborigines Department and saw Mr Taylor and asked him three times what was the reason for taking the children. "He would not give me an answer," she said, "but went and fetched Mr Bray who said he didn't take them. He said it was between the Sergeant at Pinjarra and the Children's Welfare Department" ...

Mr and Mrs [S.] 31 March 1934, claim:

1., that they are not aborigines,

2., that they have not neglected their children,

3., that they have been self-supporting till the Department interfered to break up their home, and

4., that the Department has caused them the loss of their livelihood.

Mr [S.] ... complains of the following disabilities through being treated as an aboriginal:

(a) exclusion from electoral rolls. (He *was* on the Greenough Roll).

(b) non-payment of maternity bonus. (It *was* allowed for the five elder children, and refused for the sixth.)

(c) disallowance of his claim for sustenance.

...

Mrs [S.] stated that on Friday, May 9th, 1930, at Mullewa, Sergeant McGowan and Constable George Warner arrested her and her husband ... and their five children ... on a warrant signed by Mr Neville and Mr Kitson. Mrs [S.] refused to go with them until they produced the warrant. As far as she could see there was no charge against them on it.

She said: "They bundled us into the police car and didn't give us time to pack up anything or to have our tea. When my husband asked if he could give him time to get a few of the pots and the children's mugs to take with us, the sergeant said, 'Hurry up and get into the car. If you don't hurry up I'll throw you in. You don't need to take those things because you'll be supplied with everything there.' We grabbed our rugs, and a basket with a few plates and forks and mugs, and I put some washing that was drying on the bushes into a suit-case, and we got into the car. We arrived at Mingenew at sundown and they let me go to a shop to get some fruit and then drove to the police station and wanted to lock us all up in a cell. The children were hanging around their father screaming and I rushed off to see if I could get help, but I run into a fence and the policemen caught me and dragged me back to the cell, and my husband said, 'Don't lock us up. We won't run away. The children are very frightened of the cells.' They made us sit in the cell but they left the door open, and went to have their tea. The children were hungry, for we were arrested before tea, so my husband walked across to the police station cooeeing to the police, and asked for something to eat for the children. They brought us out a mutton bone, some bread and some cold tea. We kept on telling the children not to be frightened, and they quietened down after a time."

... [Mr S.] asked the policeman in the train 'what was he taking us for?' and he said that we'd done something and we were going to Moore River under section 12 of the Aborigines Act.' Mr. Mews, of the firm Mews and Winbridge at Mullewa had engaged him to work on his farm at £3/10/- a week, with the use of a house on the farm, and there was a school not a mile away, and he was to start work on the Monday after the Friday that we were arrested; he had let him have ten or fifteen shillings worth of groceries and meat in advance to see them over the time till he started work on the Monday. On the Monday Mr Mews came looking for [Mr S.], and some natives told him that he had been taken to Moore River Native Settlement.

... About a fortnight later Mr Neville came to the Settlement and Mr [S.] asked him why he had been brought there? and said, 'I was brought down by the police with the warrant you sent after me. You took me away from work at £3/10/- a week which you had no right to do.'

Mr Neville said, 'We never wanted you here ... It's your wife and family we want' ...

66. Petition of 'half-caste' women, Broome, January 1935, to the President and Members of the Western Australian Royal Commission to inquire into allegations of the mistreatment of Aborigines

Honourable Gentlemen

With humble respect, we the Halfcastes of Broome, heartily pray you will very sincerely consider this our petition.

It is very difficult to explain fully, to you the unhappy conditions in which we have to live. Through the unfair and unjust treatment meted out to us for one thing most of us do not wish to live with natives and should not be classed at natives.

Because most of us work for white people for a living and by so doing get used to their kind of living. and by being on the Aborigine Act after we are over 14 years of age are still classed as natives. And some of us are over 40 years old. It is called the Aborigine Act and is therefore native with no distinction between the halfcastes and native. We have all been educated and resent this way of treatment.

Re Employment

Our intended employers have to seek the permission of the police to obtain a permit to work us. Many of us refuse to work on that account. We also wish to be able to get reference from our Employers so that if our last Employers leaves the town and a new Employer comes along. We can show the new Employer that we can work satisfactory

Also, if the opportunity for to do daily work for different people in one week (known as charing) we cannot do it because of this permit ...

Marriage

Sometimes we have the chance to marry a man of our own choice. Who may be in better circumstance than ourselves.

A white man or an educated Asiatic but we are again rejected, Because that man does not wish to ask the Chief Protector's consent. We are worse than the aboriginal. They can marry amongst themselves and no question asked, therefore we ask for our Freedom so that when the chance comes along we can rule our lives and make ourselves true and good citizens. Instead of what the Department would and could call us immoral girls. Also it would save our children this disgraceful-position. At present under this system when we get to a marriageable age and we are useful to our employers and our intending marriage is made public. What is there to protect us against that employer sending word along to say we cannot be spared, where as otherwise the Chief Protector might have given his consent to us. Where as the result of such marriage being refused gives some of us fatherless children.

We have supported them by our own earnings and they have not cost the Department anything. The police supervision over us as protectors in the past years has been a very much abused power and as they change every three years, for fear of future years to come we pray that, that will be ended.

It would be a very long and shameful document if we described all their insults nevertheless it is very real.

Some of the police have not hesitated in forcing their way into our homes at any hour of the day or night and grossly insulted us they knowing full-well that we are helpless and too frightened to retaliate.

We have many times been told on such occasions that we would be sent to some settlement or mission if we did not submit ourselves to them.

Now as regards the paid Lady protector, we would like someone who understands us and our native women. One that we can go to when we are in doubt in confidence, one who would talk to us for our good, not a person whose attitude and look would give us the shivers to look at only because she thought we might have done wrong that made us go to her ...

Exemption Papers

Another farce we are told if we are good we could be grated a Certificate. Again under the recommendation of the police, who live here for a short-period. and after obtaining this desired paper should we just make one mistake that might only cost others a fine of 10p by the power of the police could have them cancelled. So we call this a farce for if we all were granted a certificate in January the police could cancel all by December again.

And some of us have no hope of ever getting those papers because in past years we have refused favours to some of these police.

Now both natives and Halfcastes assisted in the great world war of other countries to overthrow the Hun, and it would surprise many did they know of the thousands that died for the British Empire, yet we are treated as if they Hun were in power here.

Anyone of us older women are willing to come up and give evidence if asked and given a promise that we shall not have to suffer any injustice from the Officers after the Commission leaves.

We also ask for a better shelter at the ration camp for our old and infirm natives, most of our mothers have passed out we ought to say are not know by us. Because we educated halfcaste who have been sent to the missions have been taken from either our fathers or our mothers when we were children by the advice of the Department, and by so doing that has been the end of father and mother to us.

Do you not realise the cruelty of this would you white people like to think when you send your children to school, that you would never see them again. That is one more reason why we want our freedom ...

Private Life

We ask for Freedom so that we shall not have to suffer anymore of the indignities that we have done in the past also so that from the same thing. Some of us have fatherless children supported by ourselves that have been brought into this world through no fault of our own, but through fear and should we disclose who were the fathers truthfully. By being on the Act we might not be believed, because the Officers have not to take the word of the mother alone.

And those men who are the fathers of some of those children know this and take good care that the girl they want is alone. And in a place and at a time when no witness for the women is or can be there ...

Marriage Contract

... Finally. Many of us own our own houses and land and many more of us could do so.

We who do own our homes pay the rates when the rate time comes along. We can read, write, sew, crochet, laundry also make our own clothes and for other people too, also other domestic work. So that Sir on that qualification alone we think we should not be classed as natives and kept in bondage by the Act, knowing or at least hearing and reading about halfcastes of other countries of the British Empire that they are not classed with their native.

Again Sir we the Halfcaste population of Broome ask you to give us our Freedom and ask you to give us our freedom and release us from the stigma of a native and make us happy subjects of this our country.

67. A.T.H. Jolley, President, H. Peter V. Hodge, Secretary, Native Rights Defence Committee, to the Secretary-General, United Nations Organization, 13 June 1946

The above Committee desires to bring to your notice facts relating to the imprisonment of two aboriginals, Dooley (native name Bun Bun) [Bin Bin] and Clancy McKenna, and the arrest of Mr. D.W. McLeod, following the dispute between aboriginal station hands and pastoralists in North-West Australia.

Mr. D.W. McLeod, a well sinking contractor in the Pilbarra district of West Australia, was approached by a deputation of six aboriginal station hands at Port Hedland, West Australia, in July 1945. The deputation had been elected by a meeting of some 400 natives. They asked him to represent them in their demands for better conditions on the stations and for adequate provision to be made for the aged, and natives not in employment. McLeod agreed to act for them, and following a conference, wrote to the Commissioner of Native Affairs in Perth. The conference asked that McLeod be appointed as the natives' elected representative and to hold the position of honorary inspector so that he could see that Section 81, Paragraphs a, b and c, of the Native Administration Regulations were carried out by the pastoralists. These read as follows:

(a) Employers of native labour must provide accommodation, including such sanitary conveniences as may be deemed necessary, to the satisfaction of the Commissioner for their native employees.

(b) In all cases, bedding and mosquito nets and ground sheets as required shall be provided to the satisfaction of the Commissioner or an Inspector.

(c) Every employer of native labour shall, if so required, supply native employees with suitable substantial and sufficient food and drinking and bathing water to the satisfaction of the Minister. Saccherine shall not be substituted for sugar, except with the consent of the Commissioner.

It was also asked that a large tract of abandoned land be made over to the natives for a co-operative settlement and £14 was collected for this at the conference.

The Commissioner refused all the requests made by the conference.

It was decided that direct action be taken, after further negative communications with the W.A. Government and on 1st May [1946] 800 native station hands were involved in a strike, their demands being –

(a) The right to elect their own representative,

(b) A minimum wage of 30/- per week.

Some of the pastoralists granted the rise of from £1. per week, to £1.5.0, or £1.10.0, but since then have indicated that this is only temporary during the shearing season.

The police took immediate steps in suppressing the continuation of the strike and arrested Dooley and MeKenna, aboriginal leaders who were subsequently charged and given 3 months imprisonment under Section 47 of the Native administration Act –

"Any person who entices or persuades a native to leave any lawful service without the consent of a protector shall be guilty of an offence against this Act."

McLeod insisted on the demand that the natives be given the right to organize and elect their own representative, and was arrested and charged under Section 47 of the Native Administration Act. He was at first refused bail, but on representation by the above Committee bail was granted.

It is the intention of the above committee to fight McLeod's case and also get a re-hearing of the cases of Dooley and McKenna. If necessary we will take the case to the highest Courts in Australia.

We are also carrying on a campaign on a national scale to have this and many other injustices meted out to Australian aboriginals removed once and for all. Our immediate demands are as follows:

(a) Acknowledgment by the Government of the natives' right to organize and appoint representatives of their own choosing.

(b) A minimum money wage of 30/– per week.

(c) An interpretation, sympathetic to native workers, of Native Administration Regulation 81, Clauses A, B and C, dealing with living and working conditions.

(d) The right of entry of natives' representatives on to all work places to ensure that the regulations are being carried out.

(e) That the Commonwealth Government take over control of all aboriginals throughout Australia and that their affairs be administered in keeping with the principles of the Atlantic Charter, The Australia–New Zealand Pact and the United Nations Organization.

We take this opportunity in bringing to your notice the appalling conditions under which Australia's original inhabitants are living. Economically they are entirely dependent on pastoralists and missions and are virtually tied to the land as serfs. For example, Section 26 of the Native Administration Act reads:

"Any native whom without reasonable cause, shall neglect or refuse to enter upon or commence his service or shall refuse or neglect to work in the capacity in which he has been engaged, or shall desert or quit his work without the consent of his employer or shall commit any other breach of his agreement, shall be guilty of an offence against this Act.

Section 34 of the Native Administration Act reads: "The Commissioner may undertake the general care, protection and management of the property of any native and may take possession of, retain, sell or dispose of any such property, whether real or personal."

Their ration consists of meat, flour, tea and sugar, which is entirely inadequate for their well-being.

Venereal disease, yaws, tuberculosis, leprosy, hook worm, malaria and deficiency diseases are widespread and in some cases universal amongst them, whilst hygiene is non-existent.

Natives serving penal sentences are forced to work for the West Australian Government in chains.

There is no attempt made at education or cultural enlightenment for them.

Their tribal organizations, customs and laws [are] violated, leading to the destruction of their society, whilst no attempt is being made to prepare them for a new economy and culture based on civilized standards.

We appeal to the United Nations Organization to stand behind us in our demands on behalf of Australian Aboriginals generally, and in particular, to the elementary justice necessary to free Dooley and McKenna and save McLeod from a similar fate. We claim that the right to organize is a primary right of free men and its violation is against all the principles fought for by the United Nations.

We appeal to the United Nations Organization to take up the question of securing for the aboriginal people of Australia liberty and rights in line with the principles of democracy.

For coloured Australians of mixed blood and for completely detribalised full-blooded aborigines, full citizenship rights and all measures necessary for the training and absorption of these citizens into industry and rural occupation on the basis of full equality, socially, politically and economically.

For tribal and semi-tribal aborigines, inviolable reserves, the aborigines to have absolute legal ownership of the land of the reserves, together with all mineral and other resources[.] Administration to be centralised in the hands of the Commonwealth Government. Instruction to be given in the language of the tribe, as well as in English. Government aid to be based on gradual economic development with pastoral pursuits, handicrafts etc., and on a co-operative basis and under the control of the aborigines themselves.

68. *West Australian*, **21 June 1946. Natives' Strike. Alleged Counselling. Charges Against White Man**

PORT HEDLAND, June 20— A case of considerable interest, particularly to the people of the North-West began at the Port Hedland Police Court this afternoon, when Donald William McLeod (38) appeared before Mr. M. Harwood, R.M., to answer three charges laid under the Natives Administration Act. The charges against McLeod, which he denies, arose out of alleged attempts to get natives employed on various stations in the Pilbara district to go on strike.

The charges are as follows: (1) That at Nullagine about March 10 he counselled Dooly, alias Bunbun, a native, to persuade natives in the Pilbara district that on May 1 they were to leave their lawful service without the consent of the protector. (2) That at Marble Bar between January and May 1 he counselled Clancy McKenna, a native, to persuade natives to leave their lawful service without permission. (3) That at Port Hedland on May 3 he attempted to persuade natives to leave their lawful service about May 25 without permission.

The case is expected to last until Saturday and will involve the calling of about 20 witnesses, including natives from stations up to 150 miles from Port Hedland. Counsel from Perth have been engaged by both sides, Mr. L.D. Seaton prosecuting for the Crown, and Mr. F. Curran appearing for the defence.

"All Dub In Money"

The first witness called for the prosecution was the native Dooly. Speaking fairly good English, he said that he first met McLeod at Nullagine before last Christmas, when he was working at Mt. Edgar. Later he started working for McLeod. McLeod told him: "All blackfellers not in right, blackfeller wanted to be treated good." McLeod also suggested "All dub in money." McLeod told him to go round and tell the boys to go on strike on May 1. McLeod told him to collect money from the boys, but if they did not have any money it did not matter. He finished working for Don McLeod in March. He went to Marble Bar and saw Ken Duncan, who gave him a piece of paper with seven weeks and three days shown on it. He was shown how to cross one day off each day, and the last day shown was marked "May 1." Telling of a meeting of natives at Marble Bar, he said that he and Clancy McKenna spoke to the natives and that Clancy McKenna collected money. He told the meeting "to strike everybody Wednesday first May, and Don McLeod going to do something good for them." Dooly told of visiting other stations and telling the boys to stop work on May 1. At one station they were "all frightened and don't think they will strike." He collected £6/10/- from the boys at Munda Station.

"Told Blackfellows to Strike"

Early on the morning of May 1, he said, he was at the camp at Marble Bar. He told the blackfellows there to strike that day and to stop for 14 days. All the native men and women in Marble Bar stopped work for three days. Subsequently Constable Marshall arrested him and he was brought to Port Hedland and sentenced to three months' imprisonment.

To Mr. Curran: He was appealing against that conviction. While he was working for McLeod he was paid 30/- a week and had "good tucker." All the boys wanted at least 30/- a week. Mr Curran: Did you want to go on strike last July? Witness: Yes. What for?— Don McLeod.

Witness said that there was no strike on that occasion. There was talk of strike from then on. Last March he asked Don McLeod when would be the best time to strike, and McLeod said that they must all strike together.

Mr Curran: Did you all want McLeod made a protector to look after you? Witness: Yes, we all going to follow Don McLeod.

The second witness, Clancy McKenna, a half-caste, said that he had known McLeod for about two years. He told of discussions at Port Hedland last July. Then, he said, suggestions were made for the purchase of a place for the natives. There was no talk about striking.

"Strike And Be Independent"

McLeod, he said, had previously told him that when they had built the place up they would have a strike and be independent. Later, when he told McLeod at Nullagine that he would get into trouble for collecting money McLeod said that they would have a strike. When he asked McLeod when to have a strike McLeod said May 1 as that was Labour Day. Witness told of visiting various stations, telling them of the strike and seeking money. He arrived at Port Hedland on May 1 to see McLeod. He told McLeod that the strike was going well and that the boys were very strong. When witness expressed some fear McLeod said: "Don't be frightened. We have power behind us." McLeod told him that the strike might last four days and might last a week; it all depended on his people down below.

Mr Seaton: Who was the first to talk about the strike? Witness: McLeod gave us the hint. And you thought it was a good idea?— Yes.

To Mr. Curran: He had originally told McLeod that the natives were not satisfied and wanted McLeod to represent them so that they could get justice.

Mr Curran: Did you tell him you were going to strike if you did not get justice? Witness: Yes. They would have a strike. Did he tell you not to go on strike because there was a war on and that wool was wanted?— That is right.

Kitchener, a full-blood aboriginal gave evidence about a meeting of natives at Port Hedland last July. He said that McLeod told them at the meeting that they should have an organisation and that he would tell them what was right and what was wrong. He later saw McLeod at Bonney Downs just before Christmas, when McLeod told him to be ready for the strike on May 1 ...

Other natives gave evidence of having been told by Dooly to strike on May 1. A native who had been employed at an hotel at Marble Bar was asked by Mr. Seaton why he had gone on strike. "Can't scab on the others," he replied.

The Court adjourned till tomorrow morning.

69. Tom Sampey, Native Co-operative, Port Hedland, Report to the Committee for Defence of Native Rights, 10 February 1947

The police came out this morning to have another try with the Warrawagine boys. Well, he didn't know what to say at times, because some of the boys were firing words after words at him. They all told him plainly that they were not going back any more. He, of course, threatened them that Coverley & the Government wanted men to go back, and if they did not, they would be sent to Mullabulla. Before he finished saying these words, all the boys said that he'd have to shift the 12 mile and Mooleyalla up there too, because we were all one— all joined up as strikers.

Some of the boys told Mason that quite a lot of children have been sent up Moore River, taken away from their mothers, and have never been heard of.

We are all just waking up to the Government laws against us. Just because our colour is black we have not the right to go where we want to.

Mason got beaten left and right, and in the finish he was laughingly telling the boys that he didn't like doing all he did.

As he was leaving the Camp he said he would be out next week again, but was told we could not wait around for him. We want to go out and do our work, instead of waiting for the police; we earn nothing for waiting. He only laughed.

Explanatory Notes [by police]

Warrawagine boys— 40 natives who considered they had been tricked into agreement to return to the stations. Later they refused and joined the Pt Hedland Co-op.

Mullabulla— Government 'reform' station for aborigines.

Mooleyalla— Native co-op working alluvial tin near Pt Hedland.

70. Circular from Peter Coffin, Elsie Lee, Ernie Mitchell, Donald McLeod, Directorate of Pindan Pty Ltd, 12 August 1957

Dear Sir/Madam,

Pindan Pty. Ltd. is the only Company in Australia owned and controlled by Aboriginal Natives.

Pindan is the result of the experience gained by several hundred Aboriginal Native Pastoral workers living in the Pilbara district of North West Australia who, becoming thoroughly dissatisfied with the degrading conditions on the stations where they were obliged to work, went on strike. That was eleven years ago.

They set up their own organisation to struggle for the rights they used to possess before the cancellation of Section 70 of the Western Australian Constitution, and the implementation of the Native Administration Act. Until this occurred the Aborigine in this State was a normal British subject, and his people were entitled to one per cent of the Gross Annual Revenue of Western Australia as compensation for loss of their land.

These were, however, only rights on paper, for due to the illiteracy of these people and constant harrying and unpaid labour, the Aborigines did not know that their rights had been protected. Nor were the facts made known to the public generally for it was always intended that the original owners should be tricked out of possession of both their land and their just compensation.

If the facts had been clearly known public opinion would long ago have demanded justice for the original inhabitants, and no Government or group of employers would have been able to pursue the unprincipled scheming which has for so long been a feature of the so-called native problem.

To prepare the Aboriginal Natives for their place in primary industry as cheap, often entirely unpaid, menial labour, the Church and the State have set up Missions. These are supported by restrictive legislation designed in the first place to ensure that the inmates could not escape, or if they did escape could be arrested.

In these institutions intensive efforts were applied first to disunite the family, and then to disrupt and demoralise a culture inherited and sustained, not to say cherished, for so many thousands of years. This was called persuading the Aborigines to accept our ways. The only ways of ours that they had opportunity to follow were the most menial, arduous and humiliating.

It is no credit to the Australian people as a whole, and particularly to those who support these activities, that no enquiry has been made to determine why these institutions consistently turn out broken and shiftless men and women.

It is no credit to the Trade Union Movement of Australia that no enquiry has been made as to why so many Labour Governments in the various States have supported this policy.

Even the most cursory enquiry will reveal that the Aborigines of Australia possess the same mental and physical capacity as any other race. There is no reason why they should be treated with discrimination.

It is true that for some time the public was assured that the Aborigine for some mysterious reason was doomed to die out, and as a result any sympathy or interest on his behalf would be a waste of effort. In such circumstances the work of the good Church people who were easing his dying pillow was all that was required.

Today this canard is entirely discredited, to a large extent due to the efforts of the members of Pindan Pty. Ltd. After the strike of 1946 they were able to maintain their organised, self-supporting unity against the most bitter and sustained attacks by the West Australian Governments. They have shown their embattled fellows throughout the length and breadth of Australia that it is possible to break the bonds which have proved so soul-destroying and complete. The decline in numbers has been halted.

It is our responsibility to support them in their demand for the rights and privileges we demand for ourselves. We must ensure that just compensation is given not to some Department of State or Church Mission or any other inefficient source, but to the Aborigines themselves.

Only if this is done can we claim to cherish and practise the equality, dignity of freedom and independence within a system of Democracy, available to each and every one irrespective of religious belief or colour of skin.

This is the essence of the Native Question.

Victoria

71. Shadrach L. James, 'Help My People!', *Herald* (Melbourne), 24 March 1930

It is gratifying to note that another gracious and courageous friend has stepped into the arena to fight our battle. The article on this question, which appeared in The Herald on Saturday [Donald Thomson, 'A Plea for a Vanishing Race'], is a momentous one, and will, undoubtedly, lead other sympathetic friends to do likewise and expose the injustice and wrongs under which my poor, helpless, downtrodden people are being hustled into an untimely grave.

No sooner had the white man invaded our land than the extermination of our people began, and it has gone on, and is still going on, under various guises. It is an undeniable fact that the early colonists, not only dislodged our people from their hunting grounds, but, with the help of the police, shot down hundreds of them. It seems the police can do so still with impunity, although not going to the same measure of excess. Their wickedness in this respect knew no bounds; they armed and taught our men to go on a pleasure excursion occasionally, shooting down their own people for the squatters' rum and "bacca."

Attitude of Whites

The whole attitude of the white man towards the aborigine has all along been to dis-spirit and humiliate him, to extinguish his self-respect, to suppress his ambition; in short, to kill his hope. To his natural disabilities the white man has added other disabilities which I cannot enlarge upon here, and which make the conditions of life seem so hard that the very atmosphere in which he lives appears hostile, and the consequence is he has no will to live.

Our so-called protectors are diligently attending to the care of my people, with the full conviction that they are slowly but surely passing out. "Let us," say they, "make them as comfortable as we can before they pass out." Hence all their efforts for the care of my people are mere palliatives, only sop. There is absolutely nothing, as a matter of fact, in all their activities, feeding, clothing, housing and caring, which can be counted as of vital interest to lift us up by education and other means to aspire to the dignity of citizenship. Other colored races in Fiji, New Zealand, Samoa, New Hebrides have been raised to the dignity of teachers, lawyers, doctors and clergymen.

The mentality of my people, according to the late Sir Baldwin Spencer, the greatest authority on this question, is not inferior to the white man's. While the efforts put forth for the advance of the colored people, I have just mentioned have been attended with success, because they have been carried on with confidence, earnestness and assiduity, there have been no serious attempts for our advancement in Australia.

The Race Changing

Do not think of the future fitness of the aborigines to improve intellectually, socially and morality in terms of the past. The aborigines of today are different from those of yesterday. They are more industrious, more ambitious, more intellectual, more provident and less vicious. They are eagerly but patiently waiting for the time to come when the white people now occupying our land and enjoying the inestimable benefits it yields (I mean the white people in power, who are still possessed of a live conscience) will shake off their indifference and heartlessness and wholeheartedly arise to give our cause the hearing and consideration it deserves. We are the descendants of the people you have unjustly disinherited of their land, and of their privileges.

We are not unreasonable in asking you to secure for the us the best prospects of free development and to provide for us a full opportunity to display our capacities, and so legislate that we should know that we live and move and have our being in Australia as right, not on sufferance. We are at present— shame on the Governments of this land— landless and homeless wanderers. We ask you to secure land and homes for us by public law and not by regulation of the Aboriginal Protection Board.

Native M.P. Wanted

As one who thoroughly knows his people, their thoughts and feelings, their likes and dislikes, I may be privileged to suggest that the aborigines should be placed under the supervision of the Federal Government. They should have a native representative in Federal Parliament and a native protector with an advisory council comprising whites and aborigines in each State.

We strongly deprecate the policy of placing us under the supervision of the police. Many of my people shun the aboriginal stations controlled by the Aborigines' Protection Boards because of this and its gaol-like conditions. Police and gaol are inseparables in the mind of an aborigine, and this association does not tend to elevate, but depress him.

72. William Cooper, letter to the editor, *Age,* 16 March 1933

I desire to draw attention to the inhuman treatment of aborigines in Central Australia. These aborigines live under primitive conditions. But they are not allowed to live in peace. White men, who call themselves civilised, go among them with firearms, and often use them on unarmed aborigines. Aborigines have a right to receive the utmost consideration and best of attention from the whites. They lost much when the whites came to Australia, and surely it is the duty of whites to protect them from attacks by armed men.

We read in newspapers of 3rd February, 1933, of a grave charge against the police for alleged acts of brutality against aborigines. These charges were made by Mr. R.S. Schenck, of the Mount Margeret Aboriginal Mission Station, Morgan, W.A. He stated that for no apparent reason members of the police force shot natives down. It is the duty of the Government and all white people to take up this matter, and to provide tribal sanctuaries for the aborigines. It is against the nature of the aborigine to move from his home country, and he should be well cared for in his natural environment. If carefully educated in right surroundings aborigines would soon accustom themselves to the ways of decent white men. Scientists, anthropologists and sociologists are doing nothing to bring about just conditions for these aborigines, but simply look upon them as material for investigation and experiment. During the war many aborigines were among the first to offer for enlistment in the A.I.F., to protect the British Empire. Surely, then, it is our duty to protect the remainder of their race from inhuman treatment.

When the first white settlers arrived 145 years ago there were hundreds of thousands of aborigines here. But brutal extermination followed, and the number of full-blooded natives was reduced to 17,000. The killing of natives is continuing to-day, and if it is not soon stopped the Australian aborigine will become extinct.

Of course, all whites are not destroyers of natives. And not all whites give no consideration to them. There are many, for instance missionary workers, who go into the unpleasant parts of Australia to assist the natives. They suffer many tortures and inconveniences, but, realising the duty of the white race to the natives, they continue their work uncomplainingly. They who devote their lives to the preservation and uplift of the aborigines will be remembered forever, and given a honored place in the history books of the future. Surely, then, it is the duty of every white person in Australia to follow their example. Of course, all cannot go into Central Australia, but all of us can bring pressure to bear on the Government to have the aborigines protected from armed men, and to provide sanctuaties in the areas in which they now live.

73. William Cooper, Petition to the King. *Herald* (Melbourne), 15 September 1933

"Whereas it was not only a moral duty, but also a strict injunction included in the commission issued to those who came to people Australia that the original occupants and we, their heirs and successors, should be adequately cared for; and whereas the terms of the commission have not been adhered to, in that (a) our lands have been expropriated by your Majesty's Government in the Commonwealth, (b) legal status is denied to us by your Majesty's Government in the Commonwealth; and whereas all petitions made in our behalf to your Majesty's Government in the Commonwealth have failed: your petitioners therefore humbly pray that your Majesty will intervene in our behalf and through the instrument of your Majesty's Government in the Commonwealth grant to our people representation in the Federal Parliament, either in the person of one of our own blood or by a white man known to have studied our needs and to be in sympathy with our race."

74. William Cooper to Revd E. R. B. Gribble, 17 December 1933

Dear Sir you will please find inclose, a letter I received from Mr Makin M. P, who I asked to approach the Goverment for Premission to allow all Aborigines to signe the Petition that is to be forwarded to the King when Completed. I asked for Queensland NSW and Victoria so there is no need for the Natives to be afraid to signe, as you will notice on Mr Makins letter, if any of the authorsitys should interfear you will Please noteafie me at once, I forwarded one Copy of the Petition to you about the 1/8/33, trusting you have received it safly. I am anxious to hear from you soon, I May Mention I have received Premission from south and westren Australia also from Northern Territory, these states I have received a large number of signatures, I am Pleased to say the Church Missionary Both here and South Australia have taken up this good Cause, my People also in South Aust have formed a very strong Group for the Purpose of trying to get Better Conditions for all, and other Bodys are taking up this Great work for the Betterment of our People, also if you can give me Mr James Nobels adress I would be glad, as I wesh to get in Touch with him as soon as Possiable, you will Please ask my People if they would have any objection of a Deputation to the Government in the Comminwealth, to approach them for our Conditions befor forwarding the Petition to the King as we think it is the right thing to, I would like all signatures to be in hand about the 15 of June next. trusting to get a Early reply ...

P.S. Excuse my Poor writing

75. Anna Morgan, 'Under the Black Flag', *Labor Call*, 20 September 1934

What flag flies over the Australian Aborigines? Some say it is the British flag. We say that we live under the Black Flag of the Aborigines "Protection" Board. We have not the same liberty as the white man, nor do we expect the same justice. For twelve years we lived on a mission station in New South Wales. My husband was given a 30-acre block of land; he cleared and fenced it, and then waited for implements to break it up. There were only two teams of horses to do all the work for ten such farms, and no assistance from outside was allowed. When at last we did get in a crop the Board took away the land from us. We wanted to remain on the land and make our living however we could. But, no; the Board would not have that; we must live on the mission station.

After the men had cleared and fenced about 90[0] acres of virgin soil the manager wrote to the Board, saying that the men were too lazy to work the land. Those who protested against this injustice were classed as agitators, an expulsion order was made out against them, and it was served by the local police. My husband was among the victims. Soon after, he went away, but because we had no way of removing our belongings, we left some at his father's place.

A few months later we came, prepared to take our belongings away. We stayed one night at his father's place, and the next day my husband got a summons for trespassing. He was taken and gaoled for fourteen days. Did he break any of the British laws? No. He broke the laws of the Black Flag. When a white man is charged with a crime, he is taken to court and judged. If innocent, he is allowed to go home to his family, and there the matter ends. A black man is expelled from the mission—the land reserved for him and his people—and can never go back to his own people again. Perhaps the family, unwilling to be separated from him, shares his exile until it pleases the mighty "Protectors" of the aborigines, or their managers, to give them a gracious pardon, and allow them to return home again. My husband and I have been expelled for all time.

Here we are! Taken from the bush, placed in compounds, told, "This is your home and your children's as long as there is an aboriginal left"; put under managers, scarcely allowed to think for ourselves. We were suppressed. We were half-educated. We lived on what white people call "sustenance." We bought our own clothes. We cleared Crown lands. At the age of fourteen our girls were sent to work— poor, illiterate, trustful little girls to be gulled by the promises of unscrupulous white men. We all know the consequences. But, of course, one of the functions of the Aborigines' Protection Board is to build a white Australia. Those who pride themselves on "British fair play" should think of us who live under the Black Flag. We want a home. We want education. You have taken our beautiful country from us— "a free gift."

Even a worm will turn, and we, the down-trodden of the earth, at last raise a feeble protest, and dare to ask for better conditions and the abolition of the rule of the "Black Flag." Will you help us?

76. Notes of a deputation representing Aborigines to the Minister for the Interior, 23 January 1935

... *Mr. Cooper* presented the following statement which was read on his behalf by Mr. James:–

"This deputation has the honor to represent the aboriginal population of Australia.

We, on behalf of the descendants of the aborigines naturally are greatly concerned in everything affecting our people. We consider that it is one of the most pressing problems of the day, yet it does not seem to seriously trouble the mind of the Government.

Therefore, on behalf of the aboriginal population of Australia we appeal for a constructive policy with better conditions than those existing and under which our people have to live. We respectively remind the Government that a strict injunction to the effect "that the aborigines and their descendants should be properly cared for" was included in the Commission issued to those who came overseas to Australia, and we trust the present Government will take every lawful means to extend the protection to the native population, who are His Majesty's subjects, and the Government must punish, with exemplary severity all acts of violence and injustice which may in manner be attempted or practiced against the aborigines who are to be considered as much under safeguard of the laws as the white people under the British Flag.

Believing the British Empire to stand for justice, order, freedom and good Government we pledge ourselves as citizens of the British Commonwealth of Australia to maintain the heritage handed down to us by the Creator which we believe to be true, and we, therefore, with confidence, desire moderation and forbearance to be exercised by all classes in their intercourse with native inhabitants, and that they will omit no opportunity of assisting to fulfil His Majesty's most gracious and benevolent intention to them by promoting advancement in civilization under the blessing of Divine Providence.

This injunction has not been carried into effect for our people have been driven further and further into the barren wastes on which it is impossible to live for much longer, consequently, the native people are faced with extinction.

Many of our civilised aborigines have not been given the status of citizens of the Commonwealth.

Many have no voice in its Government and no vote in the election of Parliament, and are apparently cut off from all opportunity of becoming good citizens and a valuable asset to the country.

I wish to point out having had 60 years' experience of a fruitless task and waste of good energy on an Aboriginal Settlement on which no useful industries have been given to enable them to become useful and independent of the support of the Government.

The aborigines should not be blamed because it is not their fault but the fault of the policy pursued by the various Governments in not adopting the suggestions mentioned before.

The Maoris of New Zealand have had Parliamentary representations since 1867, therefore, the Parliamentary representation of the Australian aborigine is long overdue.

In view of these facts, we, on behalf of the native races of Australia, respectfully submit the following requests:–

(1) That we be allowed aboriginal representatives to protect our interest in the State and Federal Parliaments;

(2) That a Federal Department of Native Affairs be established to unify the aboriginal work of all States so that Australia may work out a national policy for her native race;

(3) That a sympathetic officer be appointed for this Department to do for the aborigines what Sir Hubert Murray has done in New Guinea.

77. William Cooper, Secretary, AAL, to B. Stevens, Premier, New South Wales, 15 November 1936

There are two communications from my league to you which have not been acknowledged and one which received a somewhat evasive answer, or so it seemed to me. The dates of the communications were for the first two, February 19th. of this year, and of the latter May 16th. I am quite certain that the delay has been due to your overseas visit, and am just as sure that had the matters come to your notice in the normal way, you would have received them, and have given them your careful consideration. I am summarising the communications and request your earnest kindly consideration.

I requested that you hear a deputation from this league on some occasion when you are in Melbourne, as doubtless you will be from time to time. The requests are:–

(1) That full citizen rights be accorded to all aborigines whether living on a settlement or not. This to include sustenance where aborigines are not able to secure work.

This league appeals for full rights as enjoyed by white people and naturalized aliens, these rights being civic, political and economic. We claim the right to work for full wages or the payment of full sustenance (dole) if unable to work. We contend that our women should receive the maternity bonus in cases of childbirth. In short, we claim the removal all disabilities so that an aboriginal person shall have the same status as the white person, a maori or a naturalised alien. In our deputation we would seek to convince you of the capacity of every member of our race in N.S.W. for full citizenship.

(2) That no-one be expelled from an aboriginal station without an enquiry to be conducted by the A.P. Board and that the aboriginal charged in such cases be entitled to assistance (legal or otherwise).

We contend that many men and women have been expelled for no good reason as agitators. Some of these have been good christians of unblemished character. We do feel that some, at least, have been irregular, being done by the manager without reference to the Board, or without the full case being presented. The cruel operation of expulsion is particularly felt when the person is old and desiring to go home in the evening of life. We appreciate the need of discipline, but this is aided when an inquiry takes place, as, if there should be any offence, due notice can be taken of it. The person will, if given a hearing, have the feeling of justice done. The assistance is asked for as one with a good case would be given the opportunity of presenting it satisfactorily.

(3) That lands occupied by aboriginals developed by them, suitable instruction and necessary equipment being provided. When men are adequately trained, that opportunity be given to dark men to cultivate land

for their own profit.

We will be able to show you that our men have been able to succeed in the past, and given a chance we are sure that many of them will succeed in the future. All we ask is that the lands now in use as aboriginal stations be fully exploited. When a native has proved his capacity for successful work, and capacity to manage his own affairs, he be allowed to settle land for his own profit. We are aware that reasons will be given to show the impracticability of this proposal, but we have a complete answer to any objectors. We feel that the native will be assured of some income, and that the costs of the A.P. Board will be reduced if a fair try out is given to this proposal. A definite preliminary proposal is set out at some length later in this letter.

(4) That the schools now provided for aboriginal children be raised to the standard of schools provided for white children and that the curriculum of native schools be the same as that in the schools of white children.

It is an open secret that dark children are not to receive education beyond the third grade and they are not getting it in the schools conducted by the department. We claim that our children should get the full opportunity of attaining the fullest primary education and for secondary education where the capacity is evident. Our people say that they want their children to be able to become doctors, nurses, teachers, etc., just as it has been possible for other natives, Fijian, Indian, etc., in other parts. We claim that our race is just as capable and you will appreciate that we only ask the chance of doing so where competence is present.

(5) That parliamentary representation be allowed to aboriginals in the same way as the maoris of New Zealand are catered for.

The maoris have four members in their legislature. Until the time that there is no aboriginal problem we do feel that a member in the House to present their case and conserve their interests is but fair.

In the matter of the development of aboriginal lands we submitted a proposal for a try out at Cumeroogunga, named because of its ideal situation on the Murray, with abundance of good water, with land easily irrigible, with fertility of soil and convenience to markets. We proposed as follows:– ...

The labour for the work requiring to be done will be, of course, by the natives, who would work for sustenance received, receiving also a part of the profit according to the labour given.

Cumeroogunga is potentially wealthy. The people are very poor. We feel that such poverty in such potential wealth is wrong. We suggest that the needs of the people be related to the capacity of the soil for mutual advantage of the administration and the natives.

In submitting this I would be pleased if you would regard it as an earnest of the desire of the aboriginal to co-operate for his own uplift. I would suggest that our League can be, and is, willing to be of material aid in the uplift of our race. We therefore ask your most favourable consideration.

78. William Cooper, Secretary, AAL, to T. Paterson, Minister for the Interior, 16 June 1937

I am addressing you personally for the matters I have to communicate are so important from the Aboriginals' point of view that we wish to know that the matters have your own personal consideration.

You may have heard that I have a petition to the King signed by some 2000 members of my race, setting out our disabilities and praying the intervention of His Majesty to intervene for the prevention of the further extinction of our race and that we be granted representation in the Federal Parliament.

This petition was ready for despatch some two years ago and I had already consulted the Military Secretary to the Governor-General as to its presentation to His Excellency for Despatch to His Majesty when the promise was made that the future of our race would be considered at the next meeting of the Premiers, to be held in August 1936. Because we felt that there was a generally improved attitude toward the former owners of the land and in view of the definitely sympathetic attitude of the Hon. the Prime Minister and yourself we held over the presentation of the petition till this meeting could consider the matter. This meeting proved abortive, as far as the aboriginal cause was concerned, consideration being deferred to a meeting of departmental officer to be held in February 1937. This meeting was postponed till April and though it was held then, the only announcements in the press are the usual matters, which, coming from the Administration whose reaction to the aboriginal problem we find objectionable, is all we could expect. We feel that all the delay, all the expense, all the talk is just to result in "As you were". We looked to the political field, representative of public opinion, and we were shuffled on to the Administration, which has never been sympathetic, but always repressive.

Frankly, I am disappointed. We did look to this move as marking an epoch in our history. We asked bread. We scarcely seem likely to get a stone. We are not surprised that the Administration gave scant notice, in the lack of expressed public opinion, to organisations of white people, who are not sufferers, but we did expect that when the native voice was organised to speak for itself, being actual sufferers, some notice would be taken.

Imposed on, defrauded, exploited, oppressed, we have no redress because our oppressors are private people but when it is a matter of administration we feel that we can claim British justice, which should remedy our wrongs without further delay.

I am aware that the old bogey of Finance will be urged but with the passing of the depression every other class of the community demands and gets relief. The greatest sufferers should be the first relieved but we claim *"THAT ABORIGINAL UPLIFT CAN, AND SHOULD BE MADE SELF-LIQUIDATING"*.

For five long years our league has been functioning and seeking the removal of the 150 years old oppression. We have got nothing definite excepting the refusal of our claim for representation in the Federal Parliament—no result but a refusal—and no prospects but continued exploitation. 80,000 aborigines in Australia, deliberately kept from uplift and refused one representative in Parliament. Yet in New Zealand the same number of natives have four members and one minister for Native Affairs. Our need is greater because our people are scattered. We only ask for a member with the same status as the Member for the White Population in the Territory. We quote this separate representation as a precedent but urge our much larger numbers as a better reason for representation than has the white population of the Territories.

We did the reasonable thing in withholding our petition to His Majesty for two long years, but unless we are assured that something definite will be done without further delay we will go ahead and solicit the intervention of His Majesty, which we believe we have the right to do and which prerogative the King has the right to exercise.

The aboriginal is poor, desperately poor, and designedly kept poor and no white man of means is sufficiently interested in our cause to spare of his means something for our uplift. If we had the means ourselves, or if it was made available we are sure that the first expense would be the greatest and that progress would be possible by the profits of the venture. We claim that the native has a right to live in the "Land of His Fathers". We claim he has the right to this without the need for working for it but we know that this is not desirable and would do harm to the race. We therefore claim the right to work for our living under modern conditions. We want the right to full education, academic, cultural and industrial and to be able to take our place beside the white race in full equality and responsibility. We ask the right to be fully British. In claiming this we protest with all our might against the discrimination between the full blood and the half caste. All are aboriginals and prefer to be so. Even near whites are more disposed to lean to the aboriginal side of the ancestry than the white.

The whole attitude of the administration is framed without regard to native opinion and from the assumption that the dark man admits the superiority of the White and desires incorporation in that race. This is most decidedly wrong.

The two races, side by side yet distinct, cannot be with any prejudice to the white race for our numbers are so inconsequential beside the number of whites. Equality in law will not mean actual equality as we know we must still suffer the disability of a minority and of color but equality in law is what we are asking.

Given time you will find that the dark race will prove an asset to Australia, being British to the core and loyal to a man.

While I have necessarily had to speak candidly, you will know that it is not personal. We know how well meaning the Prime Minister and yourself are and this we appreciate. We are further withholding the petition for a little longer while we ask what is the utmost you are prepared to do in the way of remedying our injustices.

79. *Herald* (Melbourne), 7 August 1937. Aborigines Petition the King, by Clive Turnbull

Australia has never given her native people a fair deal. In this interview, Mr. W. Cooper, spokesman of the aborigines and secretary of the Aborigines' League, pleads for opportunity, by education and general help, for the aborigines to become a citizen fit to take his place in the forefront of Australian life ...

"Education and opportunity will overcome the problems of the aborigine," he said.

"Our aims are set forth in the constitution of the Australian Aborigines League. The immediate programme of the league is the progressive education of the aboriginal race by education and training in the arts and crafts of European culture.

"For primitive aborigines, while they remain primitive, we ask the unalienable possession of adequate reserves to which white men shall have access only by authority from the Chief Protector.

"We ask that offences by white men against aborigines shall be punished by similar penalties to those for similar offences against white men, and to ask for special courts recognising tribal laws. We ask for education and industrial training.

"For the semi-civilised and detribalised natives we ask for reserves of agricultural land, the right to work and provision of full rations when no work is available, full rations to aged and infirm natives, and free education in State schools or in special schools.

"For civilised natives we ask the provision of agricultural land machinery, the right to work, invalid or old-age pensions, and complete educational and political rights.

"We are human. We may be uneducated by white standards: we are fully educated by our own. I do not know whether all colored peoples are the same, but we have a very high moral code and the principles of Christianity are part of our life.

"We want to get up to the same standards as the whites. But we are coming to the end of our tether. Now we are sending a petition to the King."

MR COOPER took down a great roll of signatures. "If we cannot get full justice in Australia we must ask the King," he said. "Some tell us that the King has no power now in these things, but we shall try anyway. There are 2000 signatures here, from aborigines all over Australia, not only in the towns, but at Palm Island, Bathurst Island and other distant places. Those who could not sign their own names have made their marks."

... "Up till the present time the condition of the aborigines has been deplorable," Mr Cooper said. "Their treatment was beyond human reason until the Lyons Government came in. I speak of a man as I find him, and I find Mr Lyons a gentleman. His Government is the first in the history of Australia to take up the cause of the aborigines. But it is not enough.

"Before that things were bad indeed. I am very very sorry that the white people of Australia must carry the bloodstains of the aborigines for evermore. It was the doing of uneducated white people and criminals in the first place, and the tradition of cruelty was handed down from white generation to generation to the present day.

"Fortunately the present generation of white people is becoming more sympathetic. That is very encouraging to me. I sit here working hour after hour in correspondence with my people thinking. How can we save them?

"I feel for my people as anyone would. Now the shootings, poisonings, and extermination have ceased, so far as I can tell. I get letters from Palm Island, from Mount Isa, from Central Australia, and all parts of Australia from my countrymen, and there is a great improvement in their treatment. We must give the present Government credit for that.

"But for our principal needs, what is done? We talk to politicians, and they say, Yes, they'll do this, and do that, but the years go on, and what is done?

"We need education, and we need industry. You will never bring our people forward without those things. The policy of the Governments at present will keep them laborers all their lives. You may read the views even of sympathetic white men. But they are not our views. We are the sufferers; the white men are the aggressors.

"We need a modern technical school for our people. You may ask where is the money to come from. But we have lost countless millions to the whites— the whole wealth of Australia. Are we not entitled to this? Must we lose our money as well as our lives?

"Our people should be given the training so that they may become doctors and nurses and teachers and teach our tribes the rules of hygiene and the best ways of living. But instead of lifting our people up, the early comers to our country destroyed them.

"They were destroying people better than themselves! If we had been a treacherous race they might have been excused. But there is no excuse for the murders which were committed upon us. There is no excuse for taking a man's life away without cause.

"Yet if these people had been different, how different already might have been our story! Then you would have had already a colored race that Australia could be proud of. We should have been soldiers, doctors, airmen. We have the courage and the resource.

"Now our people have nothing: all was taken from them. They will never have anything so long as the present state of things endures. They will be laborers, rabbit-trappers, casual fishermen perhaps.

"Nor do I think you can ever bring the present generation of aborigines up to the highest standard. They have a horror and fear of extermination. It is in the blood, the racial memory, which recalls the terrible things done to them in years gone by.

"Even now they do not like to say much. They think, 'If we open our mouths we will lose even what little we have.' But the next generation of aborigines: you can bring them up to any standard you like.

"In Fiji, not very long ago, the people were cannibals. Now they have their own doctors and lawyers and professional men. Is it not shameful that Australia should be so backward in training her native people?

"Now we hear much of developing the north. Why should not our own people develop it? Why will the Government not let us have a chance to do it, to make our own State in our own country?"

80. William Cooper, Secretary, AAL, to J.A. Lyons, Prime Minister, 23 May 1938

I am informed that some of the natives of Cumeroogunga, who previously voted at elections, were excluded on the last occasion, for reasons not known to them. We remember that this has been the experience of Western Australia natives and would request to be informed if there is any connection between these actions. Apart from Western Australia, of which State we are fully informed is there any exclusion of natives previously on the electoral roll from the exercise of the Franchise. If so, what are the details. Will you also advise as to the men who were excluded at Cumeroogunga.

We stand for, and desire, that all natives who are civilised whether they are full blood or half-caste, should have all the privileges of community services, including the right to be enrolled as voters, and that those who are not yet in the condition that they can intelligently vote should have special representation in Parliament. Till we secure what we desire we are in definite protest against any withdrawal of rights now enjoyed.

Hoping to hear from you soon.

81. William Cooper, Secretary, AAL, to the Chief Secretary or Minister for Native Affairs, Western Australia, 17 July 1938

At a meeting of this league held on saturday the resolution as set out attached was adopted and in forwarding it I desire to say that we aborigines keenly feel the repressive legislation under which the condition of our race in Western Australia has been worsened. Conditions have always been worse in Western Australia than in the rest of Australia and while we did not think it was possible for them to be worse than they were we have found that they have been worsened. It passes our comprehension why a Labor Government could be the instrument of forging our chains to be heavier and at a time when the Federal Government (non-Labor) is steadily improving our conditions and the Labor Government in Queensland is showing deeper concern for our welfare. The Labor policy for aborigines in New South Wales surpasses everything else contemplated in Australia, yet Western Australian Labor is out Hitlering Hitler in the way of hounding a harmless and well meaning race and regimenting the religious teaching and education we are to receive. Frankly we do not believe that the legislation enacted and the regulations under the act are the will of labor and we plead that the whole matter be referred to the party with a request that Labor express its voice in the matter. We do feel confident in the result if this be done.

Motion adopted at a meeting of the Executive of the Aborigines' League, held on Saturday, 16 July 1938.

Resolved that:– The Australian Aborigines' League, the organised voice of the Natives of Australia, having watched the trend of the repressive legislation in respect of aborigines in Western Australia and the regulations made under the act, with the serious effect of both on our people strongly protests against many features of the Act and the regulations particularly those prescribing:–

1. The obligation of natives to seek a permit to visit Perth and to produce such permit on demand.

2. The obligation of natives to obtain a license to enable them to be eligible to work for a white man.

3. The intrusion of the Department for Native Affairs into the personal life of aborigines, requiring that it shall be consulted and its approval obtained before our girls are allowed to be married to men of mutual choice.

4. The obligation of natives to cut adrift from their own kith and kin not exempted from the operations of the Act in order that they may be eligible to obtain exemption from the operations of the act themselves.

We also strongly protest against the regulation requiring missionaries and educationalists to be licensed to preach to or educate our people and that licences which may be granted may be revoked at any time without the right of appeal from the decision of the Department. This we consider to be a menace to the right of Free speech, hampering our friends in their stand for justice for our people.

We further consider that too much power is vested in one person, the Commissioner for Native Affairs, and we advocate the formation of a Board for the Protection of Aborigines, on which our people shall have representation.

We appeal for the vetoing of the Regulations made under the Act and the amendment of the Act itself to enable the removal of obnoxious clauses and we call on all people who love justice to stand by our people in their present need.

A copy of this resolution is to be sent to the Hons. the Minister for Native Affairs in Western Australia and the Minister for the Interior, Canberra.

82. William Cooper, Secretary, AAL, to the Chairman, Board for the Protection of Aborigines, New South Wales, 28 November 1938

While conditions in some parts of Australia are improving, for a long time I have been receiving complaints about conditions at Cumeroogunga. What impressed me was that complaints were made by men of sterling character, people of fine type. Some of the complaints I was not able to verify, not being on the spot and in respect of others I told those concerned that the League would have to have something definite before we could take up the matter. I felt that there was a good backing for some of the statements made but our league is careful in what it says and does not want to lose its good name by irrational statements. I wanted to be able to prove the statements made.

Later I received a petition, which I forward herewith, and which you will see is very representative of the people living on the settlement. On receipt of this I made personal enquiries and herewith is set out the complaints of the people. They are prepared to substantiate them to you personally or to a board of enquiry you may appoint. They are not satisfied that the Inspector (Mr. Smithers) or some other officer conduct an informal enquiry. This in the past has never been satisfactory and it is as much a protest against such officers as against the management. They and this league ask for an enquiry which will seek to know facts with a view to a remedy.

1. The manager and the matron call all the married women only by their christian names. The married men object to this and the women support their protest. The women say that they are required to always call Mrs. M'Quiggan Matron and they feel that she and the manager should call them Mrs. Jones, or as the case may be.

2. Natives are not allowed under any circumstances to travel in the cab of the station truck. This rule is never varied, no matter what the weather, even with convalescents returning from the hospital. Native women, known to be tubercular, have been compelled to sit on the back of the truck, in the cold and wet, while there is room in the cab for these delicate people. The natives contend that the truck was supplied for the use of the station and that it is unreasonable to force delicate women out into the cold and wet while there is room in the cab for them.

3. The houses near the river do not get sanitary clearances though they are but a short distance from the centre of the township. The occupants bury the nightsoil. When the River rises over the land this nightsoil is disturbed and the water of the river is polluted.

4. The meat issued to the natives is from sheep so badly conditioned

as to fit only for boiling down. The carcases average only 20 to 25 lbs. in weight. The meat is secured from the Echuca Freezer and is starving stock. It is unfit for human consumption and much is thrown to the dogs.

5. Many of those to whom clothing was issued under previous administrations do not now receive it which is now only issued to old people. A wider issue was made prior to Mr. M'Quiggan being appointed.

6. The manner of Mrs. M'Quiggan to the women is most offensive. She goes to the homes when she likes and says what she likes. If things don't suit her she bounces the women. If they pick her up for the way she speaks the rations are stopped or, if they are old people, their curry and pepper are stopped.

7. The natives ask that the Health Inspector visit the place and report on its condition.

8. Open night pans are infested with flies, which also pollute the food. A more suitable type of W.C. is necessary or, preferably, a septic tank system should be installed.

9. The streets are in bad order. In heavy rain, people are up to their knees in mud and water.

10. The rooms of the houses are too small and the number of rooms too few for the size of the families. Overcrowding results and there is much dissatisfaction.

The complainants are ready to submit evidence to a Board of Enquiry or yourself. They are not prepared to do so to the Inspector or other Officer of the Board responsible for the conditions.

The League supports the claim for a full, free and impartial investigation.

83. Telegram (from Jack Patten), 3 February 1939, Barmah, Victoria

MR STEVENS
PREMIER PARLIAMENT HOUSE
SYDNEY

ABORIGINAL MEN WOMEN LEAVING RESERVE CUMMERA-GUNJA CAUSE INTIMIDATION STARVATION VICTIM-ISATION DEMAND INQUIRY IMMEDIATELY ... PATEN

84. William Cooper, Secretary, AAL, to B. Stevens, Premier, New South Wales, 20 February 1939

On November 28th I forwarded a letter, copy herewith, to the Chairman of the Board for the Protection of Aborigines, covering a petition of the natives of Cumeroogunga for the removal of Mr. and Mrs. M'Quiggan from the charge of the aboriginal station. To this communication I did not receive a reply but it was received for the names of the petitioners were posted at the Station, inviting those who wished to remove their names to do so. I submit that this is not in accordance with British tradition and would not be done for a fully white community and in itself constitutes a further grievance. The conditions which were so objectionable became more aggravated until the victimisation experienced forced a number of the people to leave New South Wales for Victoria, where they are living under very hard conditions.

I submitted our grievances and the people would have been satisfied if the enquiry had been granted, unless that enquiry was conducted by the very officers we are protesting about. We felt that in inviting the Chairman of the Board to arrange for this we were not going past those who had the administration of aboriginal affairs. Our people were prepared to submit their complaints and to support them with evidence and we felt that it was only necessary to do this when the will to do a fair thing would give some amelioration.

We aborigines are not agitators. We feel we have a right to British Fair Play and do make our representations in the right quarters, often with considerable satisfaction to ourselves, particularly in the Federal sphere. We ask only what we feel that the White public is willing to concede to us, for it is our experience that the general public is sympathetic to the native cause. We feel we have grievances, not against the Government, nor so much against the Board itself as those who are employed by the Board and who act in a way the Board would not agree to, if it knew the facts. It never does know the facts for the only source of information by the Board is that submitted by the very officers we are protesting about. We are not an enemy people, and we are not in Nazi concentration camps. Why should we then be treated as though we were?

In regard to the present exodus from the station. This is our only way of protesting and of directing attention to the wrongs we are compelled to endure. It has had the effect of doing this and now that we have been able to bring the matter to the notice of the Government I trust we can expect that fair deal we seek. This is no ordinary strike, seeking conditions that employers will not concede. It is merely drawing attention to conditions which neither Government, Parliament nor Public would suffer, if they but knew them and to seek the conditions which we believe all three above mentioned would be glad to accede to.

A contented aboriginal population will be an asset, and we are satisfied with very little, and we realise that the Government would like us to be happy and contented ...

The setting out of the above facts will show that we feel that we labor under disabilities that should not have to be suffered. We trust we have satisfied you that an enquiry is justified. May we therefore ask that you make it possible for the people to return to their homes because if they do so under present conditions they know they will be subjected to worse treatment still than they have suffered in the past ...

85. "Half Caste Aborigine" [Margaret Tucker], 'Conditions at Cummeroogunga', *Workers' Voice*, 1 March 1939

"As a constant reader of the "Workers' Voice", and a half-caste aborigine who has experienced conditions at the Cummeroogunga Mission Station, I should like to confirm the article in your issue of February 11," writes "Half-caste Aborigine" to the "Voice".

"The conditions at Cummeroogunga are shocking. The rations issued by the administration are often rotten— not fit for pigs to eat. Housing and sanitary conditions are vile. Cows that supply the aborigine children with what little milk they receive drink at a damn in which sanitary pans are washed. Some of these cows are tubercular, and should be destroyed. Giving evidence before a Commission in N.S.W., a former sister at the mission said that trachoma [an eye disease— Ed.] is rampant in the settlement.

"The Mission has many acres of land which we could work up ourselves, but rather than give it to us the Aborigine 'Protection' Board leases it out for grazing purposes Aboriginal men working on the Mission some years ago were 'given' blocks of densely timbered land. As soon as they had cleared the land it was taken away from them.

"The people at Cummeroogunga lived in constant fear of their children being taken from them by the Board, and being placed in homes. Wholesale kidnapping (it was nothing less) occurred on the Mission only a few years ago. The Manager sent the aboriginal men away on a rabbiting expedition.

"No sooner had they left the station than car loads of police (who had been waiting) dashed in and seized all the children they could get their hands on. These children were bundled into the cars and taken away for the Board to dispose of. Many of them never saw their parents again. [The seizure of aboriginal children by State authorities is still legal in New South Wales and Western Australia.— Ed.]

"These are only some of the terrible things that confront our people. I appeal to all 'Voice' readers to help us in our fight for liberty and free-dom. Help us to protect ourselves from the clutches of the Aborigine Protection Board."

86. *Uplift* **(publication of Aborigines' Uplift Society), November 1940, report from** *Sun* **(Melbourne), November 1940. "White People Must Think Black".** **Aboriginal Spokesman's Eloquent Plea For His People**

Australians were raving about persecuted minorities in other parts of the world, but were they ready to voice their support for the unjustly treated aboriginal minority in Australia? Mr. Doug. Nicholls, aboriginal preacher, and former League footballer, asked the question at the Unitarian Church yesterday.

"We want to say good-bye to compounds and native reserves," he said. "We want to live in co-operation, to help as Australia progresses.

"I saw my people on the Nullabor Plain, when I was crossing by train, running to and fro by the carriages, begging for food, crying 'Gibbit, gib-bit [...]'. They seized pieces of apple peel, scraps of bread that were thrown out the windows and doors. I can never forget it.

"White people must learn to think black".

"When you took this land from us you took us with it. We are your re-sponsibility. Although we try to live as good citizens and pay our taxes, we are denied all the privileges of nationhood. We cannot vote. In New South Wales our children cannot go beyond the third grade in school. The authorities may close the schools to them; but they cannot close the schools of human experience."

Aborigines capable of expressing themselves on current matters can-not reasonably be treated as stone age people. This is what our admini-stration is doing.

87. *Daily News*, **28 March 1946. Native JP Attacks White Rule**

Following recent reports that aborigines had been chained and flogged in Central Australia, the Aborigines' League plans to send an aboriginal ob-server, with a movie camera, into South Australia, the Northern Territory and Western Australia to secure evidence of how the black man is being treated.

Announcing this at a meeting of the league State President W. Onus, J.P.— himself an aboriginal— also attacked State administration of natives and church missions. Said he: "The missions have failed to help our people. They have taken a primitive people and tried to get them to live by the law of the Ten Commandments. But how can an aboriginal learn a moral code by which the white people themselves cannot live?"

He added that natives were taught religion by different sects, and were thus set one against the other. Before the white man came there were no prisons and no divorce courts in Australia. It was useless to try to teach religion without a proper cultural education, and nobody seemed to want the aborigines to be educated beyond a low standard.

The few who had made good positions in life for themselves had done so in the face of direct opposition from the State Aboriginal Control Boards.

Delinquency

He said there was admittedly delinquency among natives, but it all arose from the system. In New South Wales, for instance, children were educated to the fourth or fifth grade and then sent out to farms and such places. There they worked from daylight to dark for 1/6 a week, which was held in trust for them. Many of the boys rolled their swags and left in disgust, and a lot of these learned bad habits on the road.

It was worse for the girls, whose plight was dreadful. They had to work in many cases for arrogant housewives, who clothed them in their cast-offs. "When these girls see the white girls beautifully dressed, with money, and a boy-friend on their arm, and the aboriginal girl has cast-off clothing, no money and no boy friends, is it any wonder that so many of them have turned to prostitution," said Mr. Onus.

He said that in Victoria on the mission stations, aborigines were paid 3d an hour for work. One protested recently, and was expelled.

Natives expelled from missions usually put up hessian and tin humpies on the outskirts of towns. "They would get into bad habits and be moved on— ending as nomads, going from town to town."

War Records

Rehabilitation was not proving much help to the aboriginal. These soldiers, many with magnificent war records, were not sufficiently educated to take advantage of rehabilitation facilities. "They are simply offered jobs digging or breaking stone," said Mr. Onus. "This is happening in all States, and our books are full of such cases."

Dealing with natives who are still tribalised, Mr Onus said: Much of the wealth of pastoral Northern Australia is based on the exploitation of aborigines; Anthropologists do not want the aborigines to become absorbed; they regard them as too valuable an object of study; Politicians would not be concerned to see them die out, for it would end an active worry for them; Missionaries only wanted to teach them religious formalities.

Mr. Onus challenged Minister for the Army Forde to debate him in public on whether aborigines were fit and proper types for the Army in Japan.

88. *Herald* (Melbourne), 4 October 1946. Native Protest On Australian Bikini. Rocket Test Opposed

It was incumbent on the people of Australia to protest loudly against an Australian Bikini, said the secretary of the Aborigines' League (Mr. D. Nicholls) today. If tests were necessary for the rocket bomb they should be made elsewhere—maybe in mandated territory, where the lives of peaceful people would not be affected.

Mr. Nicholls, who is an ordained aboriginal minister and former well-known Association footballer, endorsed the view expressed in the London Times by Dr. Charles Duguid, noted Adelaide surgeon, that shifting Central Reserve tribes to other areas would sign their death warrant.

Tragic Theft

Thousands of "poor primitive defenceless aborigines" in Central Australia were threatened with another tragic theft of their hunting grounds by the proposal to use the central reserve for the tests, said Mr. Nicholls. Only those who knew how the tribes lived in Central Australia could anticipate the results of forcing them to leave their food caches, hunting grounds, and chains of water holes. He had no record of the number who would be affected, but some thousands of nomads were still wandering through areas where their forefathers had lived for centuries before the arrival of the white man.

Central Australian tribes had so far, escaped the fate of aborigines in other parts of Australia, whose only legacy from contact with the white man was loss of their possessions and free way of life. Now it seemed an experiment was to be used as a reason for depriving them of their lands and food.

Women and children, who might remain in the reserve while the rocket bomb tests were made, would be scared to death by the noise. The coming of this terror must also affect the game on which they lived. There had been no adequate compensation for losses of aboriginal territory in the past—there could be no real recompense for the Central Australian tribes if they were driven away from the land of their forefathers.

Native Rights

It was likely that the general rights of aborigines would be considered at the Federal congress of the Returned Servicemen's League on October 28, when delegates would discuss State branch protests against the Defence Department embargo on aborigines serving with the occupation forces in Japan. Several State branches would seek a franchise for aborigine ex-servicemen. Mr. Nicholls said the Aborigines' League demanded that every aboriginal should have the same right to vote as any other citizen.

89. William Onus, President, AAL, to Dr Donald Thomson, 7 January 1947

Have read of recent dates your articles in the Herald for which I must congratulate & thank you on behalf of my people. Very pleasing to see men of your calibre take up the fight on our behalf, I feel sure that your efforts will meet with considerable success, However it as given the above League impetous. My League will be Convening a General Meeting to be held in the Assembly Hall Collins St on Friday 28th Feb 47, 8. pm. & would you be so kind to come along & be our Guest Speaker for the night. Would be very grateful if you would oblige, We are banking on a distinguished set of speakers. Mr Allan Marshall will attend & an invitation as been sent to Dean Langley & an aboriginal speaker. This meeting will be well attended & many Trade Union Representative's will be there So hoping you will accept this invitation & to reply as soon as possible to enable us to give the due amount of publicity.

90. Doug Nicholls, Secretary, AAL, to J.B. Chifley, Prime Minister and Leader of the Australian Labor Party, R.G. Menzies, the Leader of the Australian Liberal Party, and A.W. Fadden, the Leader of the Australian Country Party, 1 July 1949

I write to ask your support on behalf of my fellow members of the Australian Aboriginal race for our request that we be accorded representation in the Australian National Parliament.

The request is that provision should be made for the election to the House of Representatives of a representative of the Australian Aboriginal race to be elected upon the vote of all aborigines enrolled under the current Commonwealth franchise.

We wish that this proposal should be effected by compiling an electoral roll, including the whole of Australia, of all full-blood aborigines, or part aborigine blood, covering all other than those who have always been entitled to the normal franchise by virtue of being 50% or more white blood. I desire to make it quite clear that this proposal does not envisage giving electoral rights to aborigines still living in the tribal state or who are ineligible under the law for enrolment as Commonwealth electors at the present time.

The request is simply that, in order to provide an opportunity for a spokesman for my people in the National Parliament of their own native land, there should be compiled into one electoral roll all the aborigines at present entitled to the franchise, and that they should vote, not in their respective electorates, but as for one electorate to choose their own representative.

I am not in a position to know whether the numbers so eligible would be of a strength warranting a request that the elected representative should have equal voting rights in the House of Representatives. My attitude, and the attitude of my people on this point, would be to take the reasonable view that, if the Aborigine 'Electorate' approximated in numerical strength that of any of the newly created House of Representatives Divisions, then we would expect our representative to have the right to vote.

If, on the other hand, the electoral strength of our race proved to be very substantially below the strength of the normal electoral divisions, then we would for the time being be content to accept the same status as the Member for the Northern Territory, and the intended new Member for the Australian Capital Territory, with comparable limited voting entitlement.

Would you be kind enough to consult the members of your political party, or your organisation as the case may be, and advise me whether your Party will support our request.

We feel that we are not asking more than the minimum to which we are entitled in requesting one spokesman for the native Australian race to sit in the Australian National Parliament where the white people of our native country will have 180 representatives in the next Parliament.

An indication of your Party's attitude to our request will be awaited with eagerness, and I trust will be decided as a matter of urgency.

91. *Argus*, 22 January 1951. Oldest Australians Mourn The Jubilee

A "Day of Mourning" to lament this year's Jubilee is being considered by the Australian Aboriginal League. It would mark the anniversary of the white man's entry into Victoria. Mr. Doug Nicholls, pastor of the Church of Christ's Aboriginal Mission, Fitzroy, revealed this last night at a meeting of Melbourne aborigines.

"Our voice, long silent, is now raised in protest against the exclusion of Old Australians from the Jubilee celebrations," he said. "Australian aborigines have little to be thankful for about the advent of the white man."

Pastor Nicholls said the "Day of Mourning" could be held on the Yarra bank, where the signing of the treaty between John Batman and the Truganini tribe could be re-enacted. A rally in the Town Hall, portraying the great part aborigines had played in Australia's development could follow.

Aboriginal athletic champions, including boxers Dave Sands and Jack Hassen, and aborigine ex-servicemen could take part. Aboriginal art could be represented by Albert Namatjira, the great painter from Central Australia.

A delegate suggested that a rally on the Yarra bank could be preceded by three floats. The first, carrying full-blooded aborigines, would represent the aborigine before the coming of the white man. The second, with a chained aborigine guarded by a white man with a whip, would represent the introduction of Western "civilisation." The third, with aborigines in European dress, would represent the present day.

Other suggestions for aboriginal participation in the Jubilee were:
- Boomerang throwing exhibitions.
- A procession of aboriginal sportsmen who "have distinguished themselves in every field except tennis and golf."
- A large corroboree.

The meeting decided to ask the Jubilee committee for a "place for aborigines in the celebrations."

92. *Argus*, 22 February 1951. 'Leave Us A Tiny Corner'. Native Plea

Mrs Mary Clarke, of Framlingham, descendant of Truganinni, last of the Tasmanian aborigines, made an impassioned plea for the aborigines last night.

She spoke at a meeting in The Australian Church, Russell Street, against the eviction of a half-caste woman and her children from a home at the aborigines' settlement at Framlingham, near Warrnambool. During the discussion it was stated that the Aborigines' Board probably would not give effect to its previous decision to evict the woman and her family from a home which it had considered she wrongfully occupied.

"Police came out to collect our rent," Mrs. Clarke said. "The Aborigines' Protection Board think it is important for the colored people to pay rent. But the white people never thought of paying US rent for the whole country that they took from our ancestors."

"Give Us A Go"
"Leave us this tiny corner where our homes are," said Mrs. Clarke. "Why should we pay rent for it at all? We regard that little bit of land as ours still. You have never given us a fair return for this country [...] Give us a go in our own country."

Resolutions were passed unanimously objecting to the Framlingham eviction. The Government was urged to restrain the Aborigines' Board from selling or removing any cottages from the Framlingham settlement.

The meeting also asked for a more constructive Government policy aimed at the welfare of aboriginal people, and expressed the opinion that the time had arrived for administrative changes for the welfare of the aborigines.

93. Doug Nicholls, Vice-President, Council for Aboriginal Rights, 'Natives In Victoria Are Suffering, Too', *Argus*, 16 January 1957

Revelations of the conditions under which West Australian aborigines are living have shocked Australia— but we need not go so far afield to discover such conditions. They exist in Victoria. In Dimboola, Shepparton, and Mooroopna particularly, many are living in hovels and humpies, trying to fight against the conditions shanty life inevitably brings about.

With little hope of a better life it is little wonder that most of them give way to despair and drift into a way of life that is deplorable. Drinking, shiftlessness and loose behaviour always follow debased living conditions, and the only chance of repair lies in these aborigines being given more help by the authorities and greater consideration by the communities in which they live.

Apart from the apathy of the authorities, these people, so often condemned for shortcomings that are thrust on them by the depressed life they lead, are treated as inferiors by many white people, as naturally their own sense of inferiority shows out in their easy falling away into delinquent habits. It would be impossible to paint too dark a picture of the conditions in which at least a half of Victoria's aboriginal population live.

The report of Mr. McLean, who was appointed by the Government to investigate the living conditions of the State's aborigines, may bring some relief. That at any rate, is our fervent hope.

Destroy The Color Bar

Mr. Bill Onus, president of the Aborigines' League, believes that Victoria must destroy its "color bar" before the native population can be redeemed and its future made certain and happy.

"Victoria's aborigines number probably 2,000. At least a half of them are living in worse than slum conditions, or in houses not fit for habitation," he said. "The excuse for this is that aborigines will not adapt themselves to life in good homes. But this has been disproved in New South Wales— where better homes are provided, our people react well to their environment.

"We hear a good deal about the way the natives of our north and north-west are treated as the scum of the earth. They suffer the same treatment here. Merely to say a man or a woman is an aborigine is to stamp them with inferiority, and any psychologist will tell you what happens to an individual when a feeling of inferiority becomes ingrained. No, Victoria has certainly nothing to be proud of in its treatment of its native people.

"I believe that the aborigines should have direct Federal representation, that this country should adopt the method employed by New Zealand, which has given the Maori the high civic and human dignity he has today. Given the chance, he can become an eminently fine citizen. And today, Victoria's aborigines, as well as the aborigines of other parts of Australia, are pleading for that chance."

94. *Tribune*, 1 May 1957. Tears Over Aborigine Film. Petition Launched On Aborigines

There were cries of disgust and horror and people openly wept when a film showing the plight of Aborigines was screened in the Town Hall on Monday. "We hear plenty about what happens in Hungary but not too much about what is being done to these people" commented Rev. W. Childs, an Anglican Minister who was on the platform.

The film was made by Pastor Douglas Nicholls, of Victoria, on a recent tour of the Warburton Ranges in Western Australia. It showed Aborigine children too weak to brush flies from their faces; the bones of an Aborigine who had died of thirst; and others in various stages of emaciation and starvation.

The screening was a feature of a meeting called by the Aborigine-Australian Fellowship to protest against the ill-treatment of the Aborigines Pastor Nicholls was chairman.

15. The emphasis of organisations such as the Aboriginal-Australian Fellowship, which affiliated to the Federal Council for Aboriginal Advancement after its founding in 1958, was upon the status of Aborigines as fellow human beings and fellow Australians. This is revealed by the cover of this 1957 Victorian Aborigines Advancement League leaflet, although the iconic image of the 'traditional elder' might be interpreted as an expression of Aboriginality. *(Courtesy Riley & Ephemera Collection, State Library of Victoria)*

He is an AUSTRALIAN!
You as an Australian, can help the Aborigines!

16. May Day 1959: The Aboriginal-Australian Fellowship and other organisations used the case of Albert Namatjira, the federal government's exemplar of assimilation, as a means of protesting against discriminatory laws that denied Aborigines 'basic human rights'. *(Courtesy Len Fox)*

17. May 1963. At a demonstration organised by the revived Australian Aborigines' League and the Federal Council for Aboriginal Advancement to protest against the threatened closure of Lake Tyers reserve, the march began at Batman's plaque on Flinders St—signifying that the Aboriginal campaigners believed that their rights to land had been recognised at the beginning of British colonisation—and ended on the steps of Parliament. It was headed by Doug Nicholls and Lake Tyers leader Laurie Moffatt (foreground), and Joe McGinness, the Council's President (second row left), and supported by about a hundred Aborigines marching behind a banner 'Lake Tyers for the Aborigines'. *(Courtesy* Herald *and* Weekly Times*)*

18. In August 1963—following a visit by Labor frontbencher Kim Beazley snr and Federal Council for Aboriginal Advancement Vice-President Gordon Bryant, in the course of which it was suggested they petition the Commonwealth parliament to protest the loss of reserve land—the Yolngu people of northeast Arnhem Land presented a 'bark petition' to the Commonwealth parliament. When the authority of the men who signed this petition was questioned by the Minister for Territories, Paul Hasluck, they presented a second one. *(Courtesy AIATSIS N4.11)*

THE FACTS ON WAGE DISCRIMINATION AGAINST ABORIGINES

19. This cover of a leaflet prepared by the Federal Council for Aboriginal Advancement's 'Equal Wages for Aborigines' committee shows part of a contingent of 'nearly 400 Aboriginal men, women and children' who, according to the Communist newspaper *Tribune*, 'made history by marching with the trade unions in Darwin's May Day parade' in 1964. Their placards read 'Pay My Dad Award Wages'; 'Citizenship Without Economic Equality is a Farce'; and 'Wards Employment Ordinance ... R.I.P.', and they marched behind a Council for Aboriginal Rights (Northern Territory) truck, which bore two placards: 'Open the Door Equal Work Equal Rights Equal Pay Banish Cheap Labour', and 'White Brothers and Sisters We Need Your Help'. *(Courtesy Riley & Ephemera Collection, State Library of Victoria)*

20. & 21. Above and below: 'Freedom Ride': On 16 February 1965, Sydney University students picketed the Walgett Returned Servicemen's League for several hours in protest against the club's refusal to allow Aboriginal men to be members. They proceeded to another New South Wales country town, Moree, where, the following day, Charles Perkins led SAFA and local Aboriginal children in an attempt to desegregate the municipal pool. Reports and images of Perkins and other 'freedom riders' being verbally and physically abused by local townsfolk and led away by the police made racial discrimination a headline story in the Australia media. *(Courtesy* Sydney Morning Herald*)*

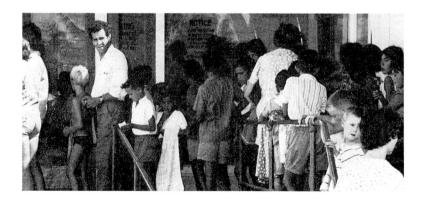

22. Following a strike which began on Newcastle Waters cattle station in the Northern Territory, a speaking tour organised by trade unions and FCAATSI saw two representatives of the Aboriginal workers—Dexter Daniels, secretary of the Northern Territory Council for Aboriginal Rights and former organiser of the Australian Workers' Union, and Gurindji stockman Captain Major (Lupgna Giari), who led the initial strike—address meetings of trade unionists and others in capital cities in eastern Australia. At this meeting of workers on the Australia Square project in Sydney, the 51-year-old Captain Major described his poor wages and called for 'a fair go for my people'. *(Courtesy State Library of Victoria)*

23. The power of the written word: Soon after the Gurindji abandoned their strike camp to occupy land at Wattie Creek, they called on Frank Hardy (front row, fourth from left) to draw up a petition to the Governor General, as well as a sign; Pincher Manguari (front row, far right) told him: 'Well, maybe we put that Gurindji word there, we never bin see 'em that word, only have him we head.' This photograph by Bill Jeffrey, the local welfare officer and one of their supporters, includes Gurindji leaders (front row, left to right): Long Johnny Kitgnaari, Gerry Ngalgardji, Mick Rangiari and Vincent Lingiari.

24. Bill Onus (foreground) and Stan Davey (to Onus' right) prepare for a rally in Melbourne on 26 May 1967, the last day of a decade-long campaign by the Federal Council for Advancement of Aborigines and Torres Strait Islanders to repeal discriminatory clauses in the Australian constitution. The organisation's special 'Vote Yes' committee presented the referendum as a campaign for citizenship rights for Aborigines and federal control of Aboriginal affairs, and used Aboriginal children in much of its campaigning in order to symbolise hope for the future. *(Courtesy* Herald *and* Weekly Times*)*

25. On 27 May 1967 the fight for constitutional change, which had been led by the multiracial organisation FCAATSI, won the 'overwhelming' victory it needed in order to force the Commonwealth to embark on a programme of reform. This occasioned much jubilation among members of organisations like the Aboriginal-Australian Fellowship, who are pictured here toasting the director of the New South Wales campaign, Faith Bandler. Others include Revd Alf Clint (left and behind of Bandler), Bert Groves (far back left row) and Harriet Ellis (back row, second from right). *(Courtesy AIATSIS N5002.27)*

KOORIE

BOOGAJA

26. By the late 1960s, the growing emphasis on Aboriginal rights and Aboriginality had influenced organisations such as the Victorian Aborigines Advancement League, now led by Bruce McGuinness. This, a cover of one of their leaflets produced at this time, draws attention to the Aboriginal culture of southeastern Australia. 'Koorie', it explained, was the way Victorian Aborigines named themselves, while 'Boogaja' meant 'heading for a special place'. *(Courtesy Riley & Ephemera Collection, State Library of Victoria)*

27. Led by Frank Roberts and Doug Nicholls (pictured front left) and Kath Walker, about 200 Aborigines and non-Aborigines commemorated the 200th anniversary of Captain Cook's landing, at La Perouse Aboriginal reserve, across from Botany Bay, by holding another day of mourning. Standing on the water's edge. Walker, wearing a red headband, read a version of her poem 'Oration', while wreaths were thrown into the water, watched by Aborigines carrying placards bearing the names of surviving and destroyed Aboriginal clans. Other protesters wore badges declaring 'I support Aboriginal land rights', while there were stickers proclaiming 'Cook is bad news for Aborigines'. *(Courtesy* Sydney Morning Herald*)*

28. The turn to indigenous rights coincided with an emphasis on 'black power' which drew its inspiration not from American Indians but American blacks. The Black Panther Party in Australia drew heavily on its counterpart in America, not only for its programme but also, as is evident in this photograph, for its style. The caption for this photograph read: 'The Black Power salute from Black Panther field marshalls Gary Foley (foreground), Billy Craigie (right), an anonymous field marshall (left) and Dennis Walker (centre).' *(Courtesy* Australian*)*

The meeting decided to launch a petition for a Referendum to make Aborigine Affairs a Commonwealth responsibility—thus depriving the Commonwealth Government of the alibi it uses to excuse its past and present neglect.

Petition Appeal

Mr. Leslie Haylen (Labor) MHR for Parkes, appealed for the maximum number of signatures and promised to submit the petition to Parliament.

...

3 1950s–1970s

The late 1950s saw the emergence of the first national organisation to represent Aborigines, the Federal Council for Aboriginal Advancement (FCAA), later the Federal Council for the Advancement of Aborigines and Torres Strait Islanders (FCAATSI). It dominated the struggle for Aboriginal rights until the late 1960s, when its authority was challenged by Aboriginal leaders, particularly a younger generation of activists, whose methods of protest, ideals and policies differed to some degree.

FCAA(TSI)

The Federal Council, a leftist organisation, was formed by non-Aboriginal and Aboriginal leaders in 1958. This followed the establishment of Advancement Leagues in Melbourne and other capital cities and the Aboriginal-Australian Fellowship (AAF) in Sydney (which comprised its principal affiliate bodies), protest over the condition of Aborigines in the Warburton Ranges led by WA parliamentarian Bill Grayden (93), and calls for a national organisation by, among others, the feminist campaigner Jessie Street.[1]

Its programme was a wide-ranging one that emphasised the rights of citizenship rather than Aboriginal rights (95), although it was to call for special rights on the grounds of Aborigines' disadvantages (117). Melbourne Aboriginal leader Doug Nicholls played an important role from the beginning, aided by a close working relationship with the Council's secretary Stan Davey and one of its vice-presidents, Labor MHR Gordon Bryant—both prominent figures in the Victorian Aborigines Advancement League (VAAL); so too did Queenslanders Joe McGinness, who assumed the Council's presidency in 1962, and Kath Walker.

In keeping with its first principle, the FCAA assumed leadership of the continuing fight against the discriminatory policies and practices that were represented by the State and Territory Aboriginal Acts. In this the Council followed in the footsteps of a Melbourne campaigner Anna Vroland and the AAF by drawing up petitions in 1958 and 1962 which called for constitutional change (**93 94 102** and **103**), a campaign which culminated in the 1967 referendum (**117** and **118**).[2] It also used other methods to contest the discriminatory regimes (**113**); for example, the Council appealed the conviction of painter Albert Namatjira in 1958 for supplying alcohol to one of his kinsmen, in order to challenge the validity of the Northern Territory Welfare Ordinance which had made nearly all Aborigines there 'wards of the State' (**96**). This task actually fell to the VAAL when the new organisation proved unequal to the task,[3] but by 1962 the FCAA had been strengthened and was showing the value of a national body in helping vulnerable Aboriginal activists fighting oppression on reserves and intimidation and violence in country towns. (**98–101**).

In calling for the repeal of these discriminatory laws, the FCAA and its affiliates were demanding the right to integrate into mainstream society, but Aboriginal activists and many of their non-Aboriginal supporters were critical of the policy of assimilation where it implied that Aboriginality would be extinguished (**97**). As early as 1958, at the Council's inaugural conference, Herbert Groves reportedly stated:

> What does assimilation imply? Certainly, citizenship and equal status—so far, so good; but also the disappearance of the Aboriginals as a separate cultural group, and ultimately their physical absorption by the European part of the population ... We feel that the word 'integration' implies a truer definition of our aims and objects.[4]

The AAF President and other leaders increasingly attacked assimilation in the 1960s (**103** and **116**), particularly as the issue of land returned to the agenda of Aboriginal organisations (**107**). In 1961, McGinness and the FCAA began a major campaign against further alienation of reserve lands in North Queensland when the Queensland government threatened Mapoon mission on Cape York peninsula by leasing much of the reserve to the mining company Comalco (**104 105** and **114**). Soon after, Davey, Bryant and the Council joined forces with the Yolngu people of Yirrkala mission and its superintendent, Revd Edgar Wells, to fight the Commonwealth government's leasing to miners of a portion of their north-east Arnhem Land reserve on Gove Peninsula. This protest saw bark petitions being presented to the federal parliament and, subsequently, a parliamentary select committee into the Yolngu's grievances which recommended that compensation be paid (106 110-12). Aborigines in south-eastern Australia had already renewed their fight for their reserve lands,[5] spurred on by the threat to reserves such as Lake Tyers (107 and 108), but this struggle gained a deeper significance when the FCAA began to draw connections between the alienation of land in both settled and remote Australia (107 and 109). A campaign for 'land rights' soon began in which 'proprietary rights' and 'entitlement' to land constituted a radical new agenda (115).

Freedom Ride

The Federal Council's major campaigns, such as that for constitutional change, drew attention to the plight of Aborigines but, prior to the 1967 referendum, no protest had as much impact on public perceptions as a bus trip through the country towns of western New South Wales by a group of University of Sydney students in February 1965. This protest was organised by Student Action for Aborigines (SAFA) with the twin goals of conducting a survey of Aborigines' conditions and exposing racial discrimination (119 and 122).

Led by Charles Perkins, one of two Aboriginal students on the tour, what was quickly dubbed as a 'Freedom Ride' attracted extraordinary publicity. Regional and national newspapers, radio and television covered the SAFA's dramatic picket of the RSL Club in Walgett and the municipal swimming baths in Moree (120), and made Perkins a national figure. Following the advice given to them by one of their advisers, an American lecturer who had been on a freedom ride in Missouri— 'The real key to this whole thing is to get some visual image across'— the SAFA succeeded in pushing Aboriginal affairs onto the political stage as it had never been before. One political scientist was to observe later: 'Possibly this was an important turning point. Once the Aboriginal situation became a matter for political action ... it became essential for governments to develop a national strategy.'[6]

Later in 1965 smaller groups of freedom riders returned to some of the country towns to establish contact with and support local Aboriginal groups, such as in Walgett where a branch of the recently revived Aborigines Progressive Association had been founded and where protestors staged a noisy demonstration to desegregate the picture theatre (123).[7]

The Gurindji and Gove

'Land rights' began to assume a greater significance for FCAATSI and other bodies prior to the 1967 referendum. In May and August 1966 Aboriginal stockworkers had gone on strike on Newcastle Waters and Wave Hill cattle stations in the Northern Territory, in protest over an Arbitration Court ruling to postpone the payment of equal wages for Aboriginal pastoral workers for three years. The strike was organised by Dexter Daniels, the North Australia Workers' Union and the Council for Aboriginal Rights (Northern Territory), and supported by FCAATSI and a host of other bodies (**124** and **125**). However, by October that year, this industrial action had been transformed into a claim for land by the Gurindji who, led by Vincent Lingiari and assisted by Frank Hardy, among others, were soon to petition the Governor-General and walk off Lord Vestey's Wave Hill station and sit down at Wattie Creek (Daguragu) (**126**).[8]

This protest captured the imagination of many Australians and further advanced the fight for 'land rights', as evidenced by FCAATSI launching a major petition campaign in 1968 (**127**). The Gurindji struggle became of crucial significance to the cause of land rights, as did that of the Yolgnu on Gove Peninsula, when, in 1969, they sought to challenge the doctrine that Australia had been a 'terra nullius' in 1788 and prove that they had owned their land 'since time immemorial' (**128**), a bid which failed to convince Justice Blackburn of the Federal Court (**129**). Through these highly symbolic causes, a sense of national Aboriginal identity was developed further, as was evident in mid-1971 when traditional clan leaders joined together in a common struggle for Aboriginal land rights (**130**) and Aboriginal radicals founded a tent embassy in the nation's capital the following January (**141**).

Black Power and Aboriginal identity

Bolder political methods such as the Freedom Ride and the championing of Aboriginal rights in the call for land were among the factors that had a major impact on the question of political alliances for Aboriginal activists and the matter of Aboriginal identity in the late 1960s and early 1970s. In 1968 and 1969 Charles Perkins, old-time campaigners like Doug Nicholls and Kath Walker, and a radical Quaker who was sympathetic to Aboriginal control, Barrie Pittock, challenged what they saw as white domination of FCAATSI (**131** and

132), raising the cause— or in the eyes of moderates such as OPAL's (One People of Australia League) Neville Bonner the spectre— of 'black power'(134-36). This was to result in a split in the organisation and the founding of the National Tribal Council in the following year (138). Simultaneously, these and other campaigners like Bruce McGuinness, began forcefully to articulate pride in Aboriginal history and culture, deploying old and new symbols of Aboriginality (133 137 and 138) and, later on, attacking white control of the Aboriginal past, such as skeletal remains (151 and 152).

In a parallel move, young militants, attracted by the programme and the image of the Black Panthers in the United States, founded an organisation along similar lines (139 and 140). These advocates of black power gained even greater prominence, when Michael Anderson, Bill Craigie, Gary Foley, Bobbi Sykes and others— along with older campaigners like Chicka Dixon— responded to Prime Minister William McMahon's rejection of Aboriginal land rights on Australia Day 1972 by establishing an embassy in front of Parliament House (141 and 142). The embassy brilliantly symbolised Aborigines' sense of being foreigners in their own land, all the more so when the Commonwealth government ordered police to remove the protestors (144 and 145). The embassy also heightened the demand for Aboriginal autonomy while expressing an argument that hitherto had not been voiced or at least barely heard in Australian political discourse— a claim to Aboriginal sovereignty— which Paul Coe among others was to champion (143 and 147).

These younger militants not only called upon white campaigners to stand aside but also criticised older Aboriginal leaders and organisations such as FCAATSI, both for their alliances with whites and for being too moderate. This, and their sometimes militant methods of protest (149), provoked various reactions from older Aboriginal leaders, which included sympathetic understanding and condemnation (146, 148 and 150).

NOTES

1   See Bain Attwood and Andrew Markus (in collaboration with Dale Edwards and Kath Schilling), *The 1967 Referendum or When Aborigines Didn't Get the Vote*, Aboriginal Studies Press, Canberra, 1997, p. 21.

2   See *ibid.*, chapters 3 and 5.

3   *Smoke Signals*, July 1959, p. 2.

4 Cited by Len Fox (compiler), *Aborigines in New South Wales*, AAF, Sydney, 1960, p. 23; see also *Herald* (Melbourne), 1 September 1958.

5 See Heather Goodall, *From Invasion to Embassy: Land in Aboriginal Politics in New South Wales, 1770–1972*, Allen & Unwin/Black Books, Sydney, 1996, chapter 22.

6 C.D. Rowley, *Outcasts in White Australia*, Penguin, Melbourne, 1972, p. 388; Charles Perkins, *A Bastard Like Me*, Ure Smith, Sydney 1975, pp. 74, 85–86; Peter Read, *Charles Perkins: A Biography*, Viking, Ringwood 1990, pp. 95–113, 117; see also Peter Read, 'Darce Cassidy's Freedom Ride', *Australian Aboriginal Studies*, no. 1, 1986, pp. 45–53.

7 See Read, *Charles Perkins*, pp. 113–17.

8 For Hardy's account, which includes the testimony of Daniels, Lingiari, Captain Major (Lupna Giari) and others, see *The Unlucky Australians*, Thomas Nelson, Melbourne, 1968.

FCAA(TSI)

95. *Smoke Signals,* May 1958 (publication of Victorian Aborigines Advancement League). **Federal Council For Aboriginal Advancement**

February 1958, an historic conference of organisations actively working for the advancement of aborigines was held in Adelaide. Delegates from nine organisations from five States voted unanimously to establish a Federal Council for Aboriginal Advancement. This body is to act as a means of interstate co-operation for the advancement of aborigines throughout the Commonwealth.

Officers of the Federal Council

The following delegates were elected to form the "Continuing Committee" for the Federal Council: Dr. C. Duguid (S.A.), President; Vice-Presidents: Mr. H. Groves, J.P. (N.S.W.); Mr. W. Graydon, M.L.A. (W.A.); Miss A. Bromham (Qld); Secretary; Mr. S. Davey (Vic); Members: Mrs. M. Blackburn (Vic), Miss S. Andrews (Vic).

Aboriginal Delegates to Conference

Of the 12 official representatives from State organisations, 3 were aborigines; Pastor Doug Nicholls, M.B.E. (Aborigines Advancement League, Vic); Mr. Herbert Groves, J.P. (Aboriginal-Australian Fellowship, N.S.W.); Mr. Jeff Barnes (Aborigines Advancement League, S.A.). Each made valuable contributions to the discussion and the formation of the General Principles which were unanimously adopted by the Conference.

Five Basic Principles

Conference unanimously adopted the five following principles as the basis for a common policy for the advancement of aborigines throughout the Commonwealth.

Principle 1: Equal citizenship rights with other Australian citizens for aborigines.

To implement this principle it was agreed that member organisations would work in their respective States: (1) For the repeal of all legislation, both Federal and State which discriminates against the aborigine. (2) For the amendment of the Federal Constitution to give the Commonwealth Government power to legislate for aborigines as for other citizens.

Principle 2: All aborigines to have a standard of living adequate for health and well being, including food, clothing, housing and medical care not less than for other Australians.

It was agreed that in implementing this principle each organisation would press for their respective State Governments and the Federal Government (1) To make immediate plans for improved housing for all detribalised aborigines. (2) To see that the feeding of aborigines on Government Stations, Missions, Sheep and Cattle Stations is not less than the new ration scale recommended by the Federal Department of Health, June 1957.

Principle 3: All aborigines to receive equal pay for equal work and the same industrial protection as other Australians.

Principle 4: Education for detribalised aborigines to be free and compulsory.

Principle 5: The absolute retention of all remaining native reserves, with native communal or individual ownership.

96. *Herald* (Melbourne), 23 December 1958. Namatjira To Serve Gaol Term

Darwin. Aboriginal artist Albert Namatjira lost his appeal against his conviction on a charge of having supplied liquor to a native ward. But his gaol term was cut from six to three months.

In the Supreme Court in Darwin today, Mr Justice Kriewaldt dismissed Namatjira's appeal against his conviction, but allowed has appeal against the sentence. He said the sentence would begin 15 days after the first sitting of the High Court in 1959 ...

Appeal Support Pledge

"We are deeply shocked at the judgment," aboriginal Pastor Doug Nicholls said today. Pastor Nicholls, field officer for the Aborigines' Advancement League, and Mr Stan Davey, secretary, said the league would support an appeal to the High Court. "We are shocked that an Australian citizen should be sentenced on what is obviously discriminatory legislation." they said.

"The Welfare Ordinance which provides the basis of this charge and places Namatjira in an impossible position"— between two worlds— is an inhuman, discriminatory piece of legislation."

"Press On"

"The Judge's statement concerning liquor indicates the greater concern over the consumption of liquor than basic human rights.

"The Namitjira appeal should have been postponed until after the hearing of the writ issued on behalf of the four Aranda tribesmen testing the validity of the Welfare Ordinance. We will support an appeal to the High Court. In the meantime the League intends to press on with proceedings with the writ against the Northern Territory Administration and the Commonwealth Government to prove full-blooded aboriginals free citizens."

97. *Smoke Signals,* October 1959. The A.A.L. and Integration

The second objective of the A.A.L. Reads: "To work towards the complete integration of people of Aboriginal descent with the Australian community with full recognition of the contribution they are able to make".

The term "integration" is used in preference to assimilation on the grounds that it implies the ability of the smaller group to retain its identity while living within and in harmony with the National community. "Assimilation" which means "to be made like" implies the total absorption of the lesser into the larger community. For the Aborigines, racial genocide.

For integration to take place aboriginal groups must have the opportunity to establish themselves wherever practicable as socially and economically independent and self-reliant people. On the other hand where individuals and families desire to be totally identified with the white community, they too should be assisted to this end.

Co-operatives and Community Centres

It would seem that the establishing of consumer and producer co-operatives and community centres for people of aboriginal descent are ideal aids to enabling them to become economically and socially independent and self reliant. Consequently the A.A.L. seeks to encourage the formation of co-operatives and community centres, not as a means of segregation but as means through which aboriginal people with self confidence and self respect can take their place on equal economic and social terms with other Australians.

N.B.— "Integration" is the term used by the I.L.O. Convention 107 which sets an international standard for the treatment of indigenous peoples. A.A.L. policy is in agreement with this standard.

98. Gladys O'Shane, President, Aborigines and Torres Strait Islanders Advancement League, Cairns Branch, to Stan Davey, Secretary, FCAA, 11 May 1960

We wish to put the following facts before you as a matter of urgency in the belief that they concern the rights of the ordinary citizen and of any democratic organisation. Equally they concern the very limited rights of the Aboriginal and Island people.

In February last allegations were made of brutal behaviour by police towards some Aboriginal women in the town of Mossman.

Demands for proper investigation and an open inquiry into these allegations have been made by our League and by the Cairns Trades and Labour Council.

When the Queensland Minister for Mines, Mr. E. Evans was in Cairns in February, a deputation from the League and the Trades and Labour Council waited on him to press for a proper investigation and public inquiry.

Instead of any such inquiry resulting, during recent weeks Cairns police officers have visited the homes (or a neighbour's house) of those comprising the deputation, and of other people, for the purpose of interrogation.

We are informed that when a deputation of trade unionists on May 8th last, interviewed the Inspector of Police at Cairns to demand that police visits to homes cease, this officer stated that the interrogations were intended to obtain evidence for laying a charge of libel against the person or persons who originally made the allegations. A few days later, armed with a warrant, police searched the home of a League member and removed material which we contend has no connection with the Mossman allegations. A receipt for this material was denied the householder.

We also contend that such police activities are intimidatory and that the intention is to cover up the real issues involved, namely police behaviour towards Aborigines in Mossman, particularly since criticism of and concern at the use by North Queensland police of their powers under the Aborigines Protection Acts is increasingly widespread. Otherwise, if police conduct in Mossman has been and is proper and even legal, and the allegations are untrue, why is the demand for a public inquiry refused?

We therefore ask if you will make these facts known as widely as possible and enlist the strongest support for our demand that police visits, raids and intimidation cease, and that an open inquiry into

Mossman police behaviour towards Aboriginal people be held immediately.

These facts and our demands have been put before the Premier Mr. Nicklin and the Minister for Police and Native Affairs, Mr. Pizzey. May we suggest that your organisation add its protest and support our demands.

99. Press Statement, Aborigines and Torres Strait Islanders Advancement League, Cairns Branch, 14 May 1961

The Aborigine and Torres St Islands Advancement League re-affirms the charges laid against the Superintendent of Hopevale Mission, Mr. Kernick, in that he directed and inflicted corporal punishment on Jim Jacko, by flogging him twelve times with a loya cane, and that he directed that Gertie Simon be flogged and also that he instructed the cutting off of her hair.

We re-affirm that the reason that Jacko and Simon ran away from the Mission was because Mission Authorities imposed a penalty of two weeks work without pay because they appeared together at a football match after the girls parents had given consent to their courtship.

We completely reject the findings of Dr. Noble's investigation, as reported in the Press, not only because the findings are grossly incorrect but because investigations by the D.N.A. in the past have been far from truthful. We refer in particular to the exposure by the Anglican Bishop of Carpentaria of conditions at the Mitchell River Mission after a whitewashing report by Dr. Noble.

We deny that any tribal customs as known and practised by the Australian Aborigines exists at Hopevale Mission. This rules out any suggestion of tribal punishments for either Jacko or Simon. Punishments inflicted were at the direction of the Mission Superintendent.

Jacko and Simon were not tracked down, they returned to the Mission themselves. At no time did Jacko's possession of a gun constitute a danger to life or person. The fact is, the Mission does not provide meat to the people and it is necessary for them to have guns to hunt game to eat. When Jacko left the Mission he took his gun with him to provide food.

The Court referred to by Dr. Noble, would no doubt refer to the Mission Council, which is invariably appointed and dictated to by the Superintendent of the particular Mission. Dr. Noble's statement that Mr. Kerneck thrashed Jacko to save him from greater punishment is not a fact. The Superintendent inflicted the punishment after another native had refused to carry out the flogging directed by the Superintendent.

The continued reference in the finding of Dr. Noble's to "tribal punishment, tribesmen and tribal elders" brands the whole investigation as a concoction, because they just do not exist.

This League along with other organisations, now demands that Dr. Noble have this whole matter investigated by an open public inquiry on which this League and the Trade Unions should be represented.

100. Joe McGinness, Secretary, Aborigines and Torres Strait Islanders Advancement League, Cairns, to Stan Davey, Secretary, FCAA, 29 June 1961

I arrived back in Cairns on Tuesday evening. We had a meeting last night to report what took place at the enquiry. This meeting was held with the T. & L.C. at the Trades Hall and was well attended, over 60 people being present.

Publicity has been very limited, although there was a Courier-Mail reporter present at the enquiry.

As in my previous letter all our allegations were proved correct.

The terms of reference of the enquiry was confined to the treatment of Jacko & Simon in the month of April only, so you can imagine how narrow the enquiry was. This was to prevent the true facts of the Administration of the mission being made known. But evidence prove that the Aborigine "Act" was ignored completely when Simon & Jacko were dealt with. It also proved that Dr. Noble was very misleading in his public statement about the whole case.

87 typed pages of foolscap was used for the evidence, and due to the press silence about the Case it is our intention to publish a pamplet for distribution to the Public. This will take a bit of time as you can imagine, as we hope to use all of the transcript published. As soon as we have the job done I will forward you same.

I asked Pauline Pickford to contact you Stan. She will be able to give you a more detailed account of things, it was quite an experience for her, and she was astounded of what went on up here among the Aborigine people.

I forgot to mention in my last letter that I recieved the £50 through Pauline's organisation [Council for Aboriginal Rights]. I understand this was from a request by you. I was to furnish a report to her organisation as to how I used the money but I will have to do this later, as we will have to look at our expenditure with the T. & L.C. We still have the Solicitor's fees outstanding plus a few small accounts. We hope to raise enough to cover expenses through the various Unions here.

I asked Jacko to consider coming to Cairns to work the cane season, but he preferred to stay in the Cooktown area and he had prospects of a job there. I had a short conversation with the Deputy Director of Native Affairs as to Jacko's future, but he was non-commital he appeared embarrassed to see Jacko represented by Council at the enquiry. He did not expect to see Jacko at all, I think he really expected the enquiry to be over in a day and "white washing" the whole affair and holding us to ridicule.

A Resolution from the meeting last night was— Calling for the removal and the prosecution of the Superintendent for his part in the treatment of these young couple.

101. FCAA, Police Bashings Mareeba (Qld.) Aborigines Assaulted. Special Bulletin issued by Stan Davey, Secretary, 8 May 1962

(The following allegations have been received from the Aborigines and Torres Strait Islanders Advancement League, Cairns Branch. Members of the League visited Mareeba, 36 miles from Cairns and were provided with this information by Aboriginal residents living on the Council Reserve. The names of the police offices concerned have been provided but are withheld from this publication for obvious reasons).

On Tuesday, 24th April, beginning at 1.30 a.m. and ending approximately at 3.10 a.m., these incidents are alleged to have occurred:-

1. While apparently under the influence of liquor, Constables "A" and "B" went to the Mareeba Council Aboriginal Reserve and bashed in the door of the home of Aboriginal, Jack Cummings;

2. Pulled Daryl Richardson, Witty Kawane and Colin Simon out of bed and forced the three men into a car and took them some distance down the road and then ordered Witty Kawane and Colin Simons to fight.

3. When they refused, Constable "A" bashed their heads together.

4. Witty Kawane escaped and rang the Mareeba Sergeant, who told him his men would return when they had done their duty.

5. Colin Simons also managed to escape and rang Sub-Inspector McDonald of Cairns, who advised him he would come to Mareeba later. (He arrived at midday).

6. After the 3 young men had escaped the 2 policemen returned to the Reserve and forced their way into another home. Two girls, Doreen Second, aged 14 years, and Janet East, 15 years, were dragged out, slapped, punched and kicked. While the girls were being hit, Constable "A" brandished a butcher's steel, (now in the possession of a member of the Cairns League) and with abusive language, threatened to cut their throats.

7. The two policemen returned to the home of Jack Cummings, threw beds outside after tossing the occupants out of bed, threw table and chairs about, broke fern baskets, orchids and pot plants.

8. The residents of the Reserve, thoroughly aroused, went and asked the police what it was they wanted. The police then commenced to fight them, but the residents refused to be intimidated.

Sub-Inspector McDonald interviewed 14 men from the Reserve on Tuesday evening at the Sergeant's residence Mareeba. These people were told that the police would handle everything but they were asked not to say anything to anyone about these matters. (The 2 policemen had not been suspended from duty eleven days after the alleged incident).

Call For Open Inquiry

Subsequent to the above information, the Cairns' League sent the following telegram to Premier Mr. Nicklin, the Leader of the Opposition, Mr. Duggan, the Minister in Charge of Police, Mr. Pizzey and the Commissioner of Police, Mr. Bischoff.

"Aborigines' Advancement League protests illegal unprovoked entry of homes and assault on two Aboriginal girls and several men at Mareeba Council Reserve on April 24th by Police "A" and "B". We demand immediate suspension of "A" and "B" and full open inquiry."

N.B. Request for action. Organizations and individuals are urged to take similar action to the League. An open inquiry is essential. The 2 police officers concerned should be suspended immediately. Queensland maintains a police State for its Aboriginal residents which is contrary to the Australian way of life. The occurrence of such blatant acts of injustice demands that responsible Australian citizens take action to cause the Queensland Government to alter its Aboriginal policies.

Stop Press: 18th May: Report to hand that Police suspended—
open inquiry to be held.

102. FCAA, Petition leaflet, 1962

Petition for a Referendum to Remove Discrimination Against Aborigines from the Federal Constitution

The Australian constitution at present provides:–

Section 51—Legislative Powers of Parliament: "The Parliament shall, subject to this Constitution, have power to make laws for the peace, order and good government of the Commonwealth with respect to:–

Clause XXVI—The people of any race, *other than the Aboriginal race in any State*, for whom it is deemed necessary to make laws."

Section 127—Census: "In reckoning the numbers of people of the Commonwealth or of a State, or other part of the Commonwealth, *Aboriginal natives shall not be counted.*"

The Council maintains that these examples of racial discrimination should be removed.

Aborigines are people, despite Section 127, and they have the right to peace, order and good government under the Commonwealth Parliament.

Section 51, Clause XXVI: Means that laws with respect to Aborigines are the responsibility of the States, apart from those living in the Northern Territory.

The effect of this clause is that there is little uniformity in the laws governing Aborigines in the States and Territory.

RIGHTS ENJOYED BY ABORIGINES ON SETTLEMENTS AND RESERVES
IN 5 STATES & THE NORTHERN TERRITORY

	N.S.W.	VIC.	S.A	W.A.	N.T.	QLD.
Voting Rights (State)	Yes	Yes	Yes	No	Yes	No
Marry Freely	Yes	Yes	Yes	No	No	No
Control Own Children	Yes	Yes	No	No	No	No
Move Freely	Yes	No	No	No	No	No
Own Property freely	Yes	No	Yes	No	No	No
Receive Award Wages	Yes	No	No	No	No	No
Alcohol Allowed	No	No	No	No	No	No

Such variations and inconsistencies can hardly be justified and must cause a great deal of confusion. Consider, for example, the case of an Aboriginal transferring from a settlement in N.S.W. to one in the neighbouring State of Queensland.

The types of benefits should depend on the degree of education and integration enjoyed by the Aborigine and not on the State or Territory in which he resides.

The Federal Government has no power to make laws with respect to Aborigines and yet must try to defend in the United Nations and other International bodies the varied assortment of Rights and Restrictions practised by the States.

This clause has been used to justify the practice of not paying Federal Award Wages to Aborigines. These awards should apply to all workers in the relevant industries.

The only practical way in which these variations can be removed is for the Commonwealth to *Possess and Exercise* the power to make laws with respect to Aborigines.

Section 127— Census: Implies that Aborigines are not people or at least not people of any account.

Apart from its institutionalised insult to Aborigines, this section has some practical implications.

I. Reimbursements to the States of money collected as Income Tax are based on their populations as obtained in the Census. The States thus receive no reimbursements for the Aborigines in their communities but are expected to provide basic services such as Education, Housing and Hospitals. On the other hand, the Commonwealth collects Income Tax from Aborigines in the States, but has no power (under Section 51) to make laws to assist them and cannot under Section 127, reimburse the States with this money.

This anomaly can be corrected by deletion of Section 127.

II. Aborigines may now vote at Federal Elections, but are not counted in the Census, which is used to fix electoral boundaries. The exercising of this right will increase the size of the electorate and so decrease the effectiveness of their vote. Both Queensland and Western Australia probably lost a seat in the House of Representatives because of this section.

III. Australia has a responsibility to educate Aborigines and integrate them into the economic life of the community. This responsibility is recognised by both the Commonwealth and the States. It is difficult to see how this responsibility can be met if accurate information is not obtained as to how many Aborigines are living in each

locality.
FOR BOTH MORAL AND PRACTICAL REASONS, SECTION 127
MUST BE REMOVED FROM THE CONSTITUTION ...

103. Council for Aboriginal Rights, Report by Kath Walker on her National Tour launching the petition of FCAA and her speech in Sydney on 6 October 1962

In Sydney we made history, there was an Aboriginal speaker from each State on the platform, with Mr. Gordon Bryant M.H.R., representing the white race as Chairman.

I spoke to job meetings, universities, various organisations. The rally was off to a good start; we had the public behind us and I left Sydney in a blaze of publicity through Radio and T.V. It was rather a shame that the papers at this stage had decided to ignore us. In Victoria the tour was on the same lines as that in New South Wales, with the public very keen to help. I visited Lake Tyers ... also I met the Aborigines at Lakes Entrance and found them living in tents in very appalling conditions. They told me they wanted to return to Lake Tyers but had been refused permission to go back. I told them that the only way they could get anywhere was to organise themselves into meetings and groups and try to work their way through in a bunch. Now at Lake Tyers I was not able to give a public speech ... I was, however, allowed to speak to some of the women there ...

The people told me that they wanted to stay together, that they were interested in co-operatives, the co-operative system, and they were *very* interested in the Petition and I *knew* that they understood everything about it. When I had explained it to them and what it meant they were very keen to help me. They wanted to help by signing the Petition.

In South Australia—I was very disappointed with South Australia, I rather think that the South Australian Aboriginal Advancement League did not quite understand what we wanted of them, I was only able to speak to the Aboriginal Advancement League ... From Adelaide I went through to West Australia and I was met with terrific enthusiasm from my own people as white people, who wanted so much to do something around the work for the Aboriginal people. The itinerary covered many, many things, I even went into the country where I was met by the Press, Radio, and the T.V., and I got quite a reception from them. My own people were on the station to meet me, which pleased me very much because West Australia is wanting to do something, especially the Aboriginal people themselves, and much can be done in West Australia. I found that West Australia was the most interesting part of the tour, because there was the tension in the air that I was going to give hope back to my people. I could see that from the start when my people were waiting for me to arrive to show them the way through. There were many places I went to, but unfortunately I was placed in a position where I found myself instead of advertising the Petition, I was defending my people and trying to do something about the drink law ... Of course the moment I crossed the border into West Australia, I came under West Australian Aboriginal rules and the main thing on the books is that when you are of Aboriginal birth you can not have a drink—even if you *do* happen to have citizenship rights in the other States. I have citizenship rights in Queensland because I am exservice and am entitled to citizenship rights. If I wanted to claim citizenship rights in West Australia, I would have had to apply for a licence. This is known to my people as a dog ticket, I refuse to wear it and I said I would get the drink without it. Much publicity went around about this ...

I spoke on all platforms and got once again a tremendous reception from both my own people and the white race. All the way through, I found that the white race, the white Australian, has a very high sense of fair play; he wants to help, I shocked him all the way along the line, my greatest problem was educating the white race, they do not know anything about us and I had to put them right on quite a lot of things.

The ignorance of the white race is very, very apparent and I found this out on the tour ... I could see that by the time I had finished the West Australian tour that my people had got a "shot in the arm", there was a tension in the place, everyone was talking about the hope that there could be in the future, this was very, very evident, my people were looking for someone to start the ball rolling and now that the ball has rolled, I'm hoping that they will keep it rolling. There was much sadness when I left, my people desired to hold on to me and keep me there, this has happened in all States, they have begged me to return and I have promised that I will return with one idea in my head; to find the leaders in each State because this is the missing link between the white man and the Aboriginal. We must now put the missing link into the chain and if the governments wish to help my people, they will start listening to the leaders within the Aboriginal ranks themselves ...

And now I would like to give you a summary of my platform speech which I used in all States. I spoke about the Petition, Section 51, Clause 26 and Section 127, explaining to them what was expected, what we wanted the public to do, and then went on to talk about the specific scheme that the Federal Council for Aboriginal Advancement would like to bring forward in preference to the Acts which now govern the Aboriginal people.

We desire that the Acts be wiped completely out and that a specific scheme, such as you have for your ex-service men and women, be placed into operation. Such a scheme could b[r]ing the Aboriginal people forward ... Such a scheme must be voluntary, my people must have it only if they themselves desire it. If they wish to take advantage of it, then let them do so, if they do not, then let them go through of their own accord ...

Now, the scale of rights is what I'm going to speak about next, to give you an idea of just what we are up against. Now, rights enjoyed by Aborigines on settlements, reserves, etc. (this is in the five States and the Northern Territory) now I must emphasise the fact that this is on reserves and settlements and does not apply to those outside ...

I feel now that I must bring in two very important words, they are integration and assimilation. There seems to be much confusion around these two words, the policy of the government up till now has been that of assimilation for my people. Now, boiled down, assimilation means the swallowing up by a majority group of a minority group. My people, the Aboriginal people are the minority group and they can only be assimilated by the final wiping out of this minority group. Now it is not our desire to have this happen, they have tried hard to do this, but it has not been successful and we feel that this is the most inhuman way of bringing my people forward, we feel that something must be done about it, so picture if you can, in my attempt to explain to you these two very important words, picture if you can a river which we will call the river of ignorance with two banks, the one on the right side we shall call the civilisation side of the bridge, the other side— stone age. Imagine a span from the civilised side of the bridge up and we shall call that span assimilation. Now my people on the stone age side of the bridge have to jump the big gap to the assimilation side span of the bridge. Some made it, I was fortunate enough to be one of them, to have made this big jump, but there are thousands of my people who did not, and they fell to the river bank below and were forced to live like scavengers on the rubbish dumps of the white race. These are our fringe dwellers, they have come too far and cannot climb back to what used to be, but they have not yet reached the stage where they can stand side by side with the white race. Of all my people, I'm most upset about the fringe dwellers. Much help is needed for them. How then, can we help the fringe dwellers?

Now then, let us put the other span of the bridge in, the span from the stone age side of the bridge, and we'll call it integration. Integration means the bringing forward of a race of people with their own identity and their own pride intact. They would come forward onto the integration side of the bridge with such things as their culture and their language. No doubt the old people would want to stay at the integration side of the bridge, so let it be. Let the choice be that of my people, they should be allowed to stay there. But the young people who are forever pushing on, would no doubt cross to the assimilation side of the bridge and so on to the assimilation side of the river. But when they crossed this bridge, the young people would do so, proud of the fact that they were of Aboriginal blood, happy to be what they are, and not going forward as replicas of the white race. Assimilation can only bring us forward as replicas of the white race; this is not what we desire, we desire to be Aboriginals, proud of this fact, and when they stood on the other side of the bridge amongst the civilized people, the white people, they would stand there as a friend and neighbour alongside the white man, respecting his way of life and expecting him in return to respect the Aboriginal's way of life. Now I find in my tour through, that the Aboriginal's knowledge is much greater than that of the white man in one respect. He knows more about the white man than the white man knows about us, and this is something that we must get together and rectify. We took time off, we, the Aboriginals took time off to understand what the white man wanted and to respect his views, this has not happened on the white man's side of the bridge and now the time has come when he himself must get to know us and understand us and respect us for what we want. I know that the present generation is not responsible for the past, I cannot blame the present white man or woman nor will I hold him or her responsible for what has happened in the past. I care not about the past, but the future I am worried about. The future is what we want, a bigger and brighter future for both races. I will however, and I feel I'm justified, I will hold the present white man and woman responsible for what happens to my people in the future. This I feel is their responsibility as well as mine.

Now I would like to tell you some facts about the Acts and I am going to quote the Queensland Act, it is the worst Act of all the

States and I am going to give you a rough idea of what the Aboriginal people are up against ...

Now in summing up the position, I feel (1) The Australian public wants to help the first Australian to a better way of life. (2) Our greatest obstacle is the ignorance of the white race, much education is needed for both races. (3) Authorities must be made to realise that the only way they can succeed to help us is to use the missing link in the chain, that is the leaders within the groups of the Aboriginal people themselves, for no one understands the Aboriginal more than the Aboriginal himself. (4) A new system must be introduced and the old system wiped ... In formulating such a scheme, the keynote should be full citizenship rights and integration *not* assimilation. I feel a follow up tour is necessary, with a campaign organiser staying long enough in each State to help Aboriginals to organise and work together with the leaders in each State ...

104. *They Have Made Our Rights Wrong*, pamphlet authorised by Joe McGinness, Secretary, Aborigines and Torres Strait Islander League, Cairns, 6 November 1962

"They have made our rights wrong. Is there any law that can force us away from Mapoon? When we asked why, we didn't get a straight answer ..."

". . .We all here are standing very strong. We all said we won't shift from here ... Uncle, you must try and help us fight strong ... "

". . . If we could get help we are willing to back those who try and help us. Please hear this call. We want to hold this place Mapoon, the place wherein wee were born into the first Gospel of Christ. This is all I ask on behalf of my people at Mapoon."

— Letters from Mapoon Mission to the Aborigines and Torres Strait Islanders Advancement League, Cairns.

The Struggle for Mapoon

At Mapoon, high on the west coast of Cape York Peninsula, a hundred and seventy-six people are firmly resisting official efforts to make them leave their ancestral lands and go to Bamaga, farther north.

They are calling for help from all who respect human rights.

In the last two years, seventy-six Mapoon people have been removed to Bamaga or "exempted" from the Act and sent to fare for themselves in unfamiliar towns.

Bitterly regretting the change, spokesmen from among them are joining with those standing firm at Mapoon in challenging attempts by representatives of the State Government and of the Presbyterian Board of Missions to make the people leave their homes and hunting grounds.

Neither Government nor mission authorities have made any clear statement about the matter.

Commonwealth Aluminium Corporation Pty. Ltd. (COMALCO), which has been granted a lease of more than a third of the Mapoon mission area, is silent.

About Mapoon

Mapoon was established by the Presbytarian Board of Missions in 1891. At one time the mission area covered about 3345 square miles but, as the June 1959 Report of the Queensland Department of Native Affairs disclosed, 1230 square miles were excised on lease to Comalco ...

Threatened closure

In 1959 the Rev. Sweet, an official of the Presbytarian Board of Missions, visited Mapoon and told the assembled aborigines that the mission was to be closed down and they would have to shift.

Allan Parry, a spokesman of the Aboriginal Council and elder of the church, said his people wanted a reason why they should leave Mapoon. "There is no such law to make us leave," he protested.

But no satisfactory reason has yet been given. Spokesmen for the Government have blamed the Church, and vice versa.

Despite visits from officials such as Dr. Noble, Minister for Native Affairs; Mr. P. Killoran, Deputy-Director of Native Affairs; and the Rev. J. Stuckie, President of the Australian Board of Missions, the people refuse to be persuaded.

Any correlation between the closure of Mapoon and the presence of Comalco mining operations in the area has at all times been denied.

But the question remains, what does the Government intend to do with Mapoon once the people have been expelled from the area?

People Bewildered

When told they must leave their tribal grounds, without good reason, the Mapoon people, though bewildered, decided to stay.

At the 1959 meeting with the Rev. Sweet, Allan Parry pointed out that his people were able to live independently of the mission. They kept themselves in food from their own gardens and by hunting and fishing. For commodities requiring money, they could get income from mining, station work, crocodile shooting, etc.

"We thank the Church for the teaching of the Gospel and the schooling of our children and their three meals a day, and we thank the Government for the medical— but that is all, because with our own bare hands we do the rest."

Authorities then threatened to close the church, school and store, and to cut the ration boat from Thursday Island. And then, if the people still would not shift, "the mining people will come with their bulldozers" ...

Alternatives to Mapoon

A general vote by Mapoon residents showed they did not want to shift. But they were told they had no choice except exemption from the Act, which meant that the Government washed its hands of them, or staying under the Act and moving to the Bamaga district ...

Bamaga

Cape York Government Settlement, established in 1948, with an area of only 152 square miles and a population now of 837, has had a most unhappy history.

It consists of Bamaga village, and its nearby satellites, Cowal Creek and Red Island Point. They have been used by D.N.A. officials as a sort of dumping ground for unwanted or "unmanageable" people from missions and reserves farther south.

Jim Jacko, of the notorious Hopevale Mission flogging case, was, in spite of assertions to the contrary, sent to Bamaga.

Bamaga has a reputation among Aborigines and Islanders as a penal settlement. Stories are told of neglect, unemployment, hunger and bashings.

Besides being attached to "their own" country and distrusting Bamaga administration, Mapoon people have a very sound economic reason for preferring to stay at Mapoon.

Game and fish are plentiful there, and they successfully "live off the land."

Bamaga is "different country" ...

Substandard conditions

At Bamaga village about 400 people are distributed among 41

houses, which are substandard in size and amenities, although better than many of the houses on missions in other parts of Cape York Peninsula ...

A new settlement, officially named Mapoon Village (sometimes called Hidden or Happy Valley) is being established between Red Island Point and Bamaga Village and at present has seven houses, also substandard.

Educational, medical and recreational facilities are also inadequate ...

Promises and Reality

The Queensland government says it intends to develop Bamaga as a self-supporting settlement with an increasing standard of living.

If this can be done at Bamaga, why not Mapoon and other Peninsula settlements? Why should the people be compelled to leave their homelands? Have not those who broke up their old tribal way of life the moral duty to enable them to live better without having to leave their homelands?

A critical examination shows that the so-called plans to make Bamaga a worth-while place are hollow ...

Secrecy Harmful

The facts presented here have been gathered with great difficulty because of the secrecy surrounding Queensland Government Aboriginal policy and administration, especially in Cape York Peninsula.

The Aborigines and Islanders who supplied the facts risked punishment, jail, chronic unemployment, or exile to a corrective settlement.

The facts show that the Government's talk about "assimilation" and "protection" of Aborigines is a smokescreen for cruel racial discrimination.

Ostensibly to protect detribalised Aborigines from undesirable contact with white Australians, the Queensland Protection Act prohibits any person entering or remaining within the limits of a reserve without the Superintendent's permission "for any purpose whatever." Permission is given readily enough to people prospecting for minerals and with other business interests, but it is very difficult for people really concerned about Aboriginal welfare to get in.

Aborigines from outside a reserve have to obtain permission even to visit relatives or friends. This is not always granted.

Such "protection" provides a very convenient cloak for safeguarding administrative methods within missions and settlements from observation and criticism. It has also served to keep the "protected" Aborigines backward.

The Government should grant right of unrestricted entry into Mapoon, Bamaga and other settlements by interested persons, including officers of the various Aboriginal Advancement Leagues.

Such persons should be enabled to consult the Aboriginal people about their own wishes, in an atmosphere free of intimidation or deception ...

Aborigines Speak Up

Of recent years, with the assistance of the trade union movement and other organisations which respect human dignity, Aborigines and Islanders have undertaken increasing activity on their own behalf. They have found their own spokesmen, who can state what their people need very capably, and in no uncertain terms.

Their demands have been shaped and expressed in a series of meetings and conferences.

At the Fifth Annual Conference on Aboriginal Affairs held in Adelaide last April, the majority of the delegates were of Aboriginal and Island descent, 42 in all from five States. This Conference produced a Programme of Action.

It demanded that reserves, missions and settlements be granted unconditionally to the native residents. Residence should be voluntary, restrictive regulations repealed and management placed in the hands of elected committees of residents.

Any project making a profit from existing reserves (such as Comalco, pastoral companies) should pay royalties to a fund for development of Aborigines on the particular reserve.

In these demands lies the only just answer to the problems and the future of the people of Mapoon.

Until Aboriginal communities own and control the lands they live on, they will never be free of the danger of dispossession.

Significance of Mapoon

The struggle for Mapoon is a particularly significant part of the whole struggle of Australia's oppressed Aboriginal minority.

If public outcry is strong enough to halt dispossession of Mapoon people, the Government will be forced to pause before taking similar action on other missions and settlements and before allowing further alienation of Aboriginal lands to mining and pastoral interests.

It is urgent that the demand be raised *now* for Mapoon people to be allowed to remain on their lands and for exiles to be allowed to return if they wish. The State Government should also be urged to allow a thorough investigation by competent people, free of racial prejudice, into ways and means of developing Mapoon in accordance with what the people themselves want.

We urge all who read this story to protest and campaign on behalf of the Mapoon people, whose hearts beat strong in the faith that they do not stand alone in their struggle for simple human rights.

Support the national petition for a referendum to alter the Commonwealth Constitution so as to include Aborigines in the Census, and make the Commonwealth Government responsible for them.

105. Joe McGinness, President, Aborigines and Torres Strait Islanders Advancement League, Cairns, to Mr Frank Nicklin, Premier, Queensland, and Mr Jack Pizzey, Minister for Police and Native Affairs, Queensland, 21 February 1963

At our Leagues' Conference held here in December 1st & 2nd, (a copy of findings enclosed) a recommendation was adopted that we write your Government and request certain reforms which should improve the existing unsatisfactory conditions and social status of Aborigine and Torres Strait Islanders.

The Aboriginal Preservation and Protection Act, and Torres Strait Island Act, has been agreed by your Government to be outmoded, and now have appointed a Committee to investigate certain aspects of the Act, with the view of revising same.

Conference indicated strong opposition to the Governments proposal to any revising of the present Acts, as this implies that discriminatory legislation against Aborigines and Islanders would still remain. Discriminatory law is not in keeping with the United Nations Charter of Human Rights, and certainly is an embarrassment to Australia.

In order to clarify our position, we therefore request your Government to repeal the two Acts, and to replace them with legislation providing special benefits for Aborigines and Torres Strait Island people, along the lines of special Commonwealth legislation for repatriation and rehabilitation of ex-service men and women. In preparation for this, to approve a Committee immediately, to conduct a Public Inquiry into the needs and wishes of the Aboriginal and Island peoples.

Such a Commission to have among its members, strong representation of coloured people from north, centre and south Queensland and the Torres Islands, and to include elected representatives of the Trade Union movement. The Public Inquiry to be conducted along the same lines of the Federal Inquiry into Voting Rights, and special care to be taken to see that Aborigines and Island witnesses can speak fully and freely, without fear of consequences.

In the proclamation of the Public Inquiry and in the course of the Inquiry itself, it should be made clear to the people concerned, that it will in no way be compulsory for people to accept the benefits of the new law. They should have the right to decide for themselves, in each case, whether or not to seek aid.

We also request the State Government to hand over ownership and control of all existing centres of Aborigine settlements to the residents of each, operating through elected Committees. Royalties from industries which have been operating on Aboriginal Reserves, should be paid to Aboriginal Committees of the respective areas. The Federal Government saw fit to do this regarding the Government Bauxite Corporation when granting prospecting rights to them of the Arnham [Arnhem] Land Aboriginal Reserve.

Perhaps at this juncture you will agree, owing to the recent widespread outbreak of dysentry among Aborigines throughout the state, which resulted in death for several aborigines, that the present Protection and Preservation law, is of no real value to our people. Further, articles that have appeared over the past two weeks, in the Sunday Truth regarding the unfortunate plight of Aborigines at Lockhart River Mission, clearly indicates that Missionaries are no longer prepared to accept the responsibility of caring for the Aborigine people as a favour to your Government.

We suggest to meet the immediate needs of the people who may need guidance in their own administration of reserves, that advantage should be taken of the United Nations, where expert advice could be sought in order to create employment and training, and in some cases establishing industries on the areas granted to Aborigine or Island people. An auxillary organisation of the United Nations, the International Labour Organisation, has done work of this nature among the indiginous races of other other nations, with satisfactory results. We therefore recommend your Government give this very serious consideration, in regards to granting ownership of existing Reserves to the people.

We purpose to raise other matters related to Aborigine and Island welfare, in future correspondence.

Copies of this will be forwarded to other interested organisations.

106. Narrijin and others to Mr H.E. Giese, Director of Aboriginal Welfare, Northern Territory, March 1963

Mr Gise who looking after for all the Aborigines in the N.T. We want to help us belong to this country Yirrkala, please Mr Gise? Because the Maining campany will be here soon. All the Aborigines in Yirrkala are wondering about this country. What we are going to do Mr Gise? You think us a funny? or you think us a good people. You going to help us Mr Gise? or no. These maining people will chasing us to other places, we don't like that. Please sir? We like Yirrkala best. This is a word for all the people in Yirrkala. We want Yirrk. open country. So we may go hunting for meat. We don't like the maining campany will come close to the Mission area, please Mr Gise? Our children are in school. They will grow up belong to this country. They may us what they were learned in school. They will help the fathers, mothers, sisters, brothers, or their relations about the white man laws, white man way to living, white man ways to eat. White man way to cook, and wash our plates. This time we don't understand about the white man ways yet. We going to ask you for this country Yirrkala. We are don't like to come near to the Mission. If the maining people like to use this country, alright they will stay away from the Mission, Mr Gise? This is a words for Narrijin and all the Aborigines in Yirrkala Mission, says this.

Thankyou Mr Gise, Goodbye.

107. Joe McGinness, Address to 'Save Lake Tyers' meeting (Melbourne), 22 May 1963

"The Purpose of this Meeting is that Aborigines wish to present their views as to what should be done for their future welfare on Lake Tyers.

And this is one of the very rare occasions where we have been organised sufficiently to publicly present these views.

The present Government Policy of Assimilation denies Aborigines throughout Australia the right to plan their own destiny.

In all States of the Commonwealth restrictive legislation operates, where Aborigines are under the control of "*protection* Acts".

In the Administration of these Acts, which deal with Aborigines, we find people with titles such as Commissioners, Directors, Protectors, Chairmen and other Petty Government Officials.

In States such as Victoria there is an Aborigine Welfare Board. We have Aborigine members appointed as members of the Board. The Aborigine members of the Board do not necessarily present the views or wishes of the Aborigine People, but are there to help implement the Board and Government policy of Assimilation and this could be termed as "Sham Democracy".

We realise of course that some Aborigines are prepared to accept assimilation, but what we object to is "*forced assimilation*".

I've seen this Policy of forced Assimilation in all its viciousness, degrading rottenness *being* applied elsewhere, particularly in Queensland where the "Protection Acts" have been applied to Aborigine leaders within the Reserves where Aborigine people reside, which have resulted in preventing Aborigines developing leadership and Groups from making demands for reform and raising their Standard of living.

Family life has even been disrupted by the Authorities and leaders isolated, to prevent the Aborigines from organising effectively against the treatment they receive on these reserves.

It appears that it is quite O.K. for Aborigines to remain on reserves living under Sub-standard conditions and being assimilated, providing they are not attracting any Public attention as to their true plight.

The people of Lake Tyers have been for the past 12 months, advocating for a new deal in their own little way.

This has prompted the Government here to step up their Assimilation policy, with promises of Housing and Employment in Towns surrounding Lake Tyers. Some people have accepted this offer, but again we don't want this forced on the people who do not wish to leave Lake Tyers, and we feel that this could be the result of these false promises and hopes of a better deal elsewhere, while Lake Tyers could easily be developed by the people themselves with the sympathetic assistance and understanding of the Government.

Our national organization—the F.C.A.A. has been most concerned over the filching of Reserves in other States and we would not like the same thing to happen to Lake Tyers and the people dispossessed."

Using a map of Australia to illustrate his point Mr McGuiness listed the threatened Reserves, Yirrkala, Weipa, Mapoon, Mona-Mona and Lake Tyers.

The following resolution was carried by the meeting:–
"This Public Meeting called by the Australian Aborigines' League affirms the right of the Aboriginal People to own and develop Lake Tyers Reserve.

We demand that the present Government take immediate steps to implement the Demands presented by the Aborigine Delegation at Parliament House today.

We also call upon all interested individuals, and organizations to actively support these demands until such time as Justice has been achieved to the satisfaction of the people of Lake Tyers".

108. Doug Nicholls, letter to the editor, *Age*, 27 May 1963

In expressing our appreciation of Dr. Donald Thomson's public statement ('The Age,' 23/5) of the position we have known he maintains, may I give some illustrations from my own experience.

Our birth place means much to our people.

Whenever possible I return to my home at Cummeroogunja, on the Murray. Like the people of Lake Tyers, we, too, wished to develop our land.

On each visit as I walk across the small part of the reserve still available to us, I see again the fine old people who were our parents, I remember the pride they had in their flourishing wheat fields, grown on land they had cleared.

Many families owned their own horse and jinker. We were proud of our homes, our church and our school.

Gradually the N.S.W. Government made it clear we had not titled right to the land. White neighbours were leased sections of the reserve.

We became dispirited and depressed. As the station commenced to break up the blame was put on to the people and it was said we were lazy and irresponsible.

Destroyed

It was the Government's policy and bad administration which destroyed us.

A self-respecting, independent people became dependent on charity and hand-outs.

Many families, refusing to live under the Government's system, attempted to make their way in the white community. Descendants of these folk now walk the streets, live on the fringes of nearby towns and the banks of the Murray.

Other families who put up with conditions were ultimately offered homes in the nearest country centre, where, it was alleged, employment would be available and their children would receive a better standard of education.

The three families who accepted the offer found how difficult life is for unskilled aboriginal laborers in white society, in spite of assistance from well-intentioned people.

They became demoralised and disintegrated. Their children finished up in Government institutions.

This is what I have seen and I will fight to the end to prevent it happening to the Lake Tyers families.

The retaining of Lake Tyers as a basis for creation of employment through community development must be seen as a practical humane plan which can offer security, shelter and stability to family life.

109. *Age,* 27 June 1963. Aborigine's Cable Seeks U.N. Inquiry

The Aboriginal Advancement League yesterday cabled the United Nations and asked for an inquiry into alleged "further alienation of aboriginal reserves."

Pastor Doug Nicholls, the leader of the advancement league, signed the cable.

It said: "Australian Government ignoring minority rights of aborigines. Two million acres of reserves alienated since 1959, further half million threatened. Residents moved without consent or compensation. United Nations inquiry requested."

Pastor Nicholls said the assimilation policy of the Victorian Aboriginal Welfare Board was not the answer to the problem.

"We want to see reserves such as Lake Tyers, in Gippsland, developed by the aborigines themselves on a community basis," he added.

110. FCAA, press release, 12 August 1963

The F.C.A.A. has taken legal action on behalf of Aboriginal residents of Yirrkala, Gove Peninsula to oppose the French, Pechiney Aluminium Company's application for lease land at Point Dundas on Melville Bay, Arnhem Land, Northern Territory.

Mr. R.C. Ward, barrister of Darwin, will appear on behalf of the Federal Council at the hearing in the Mine Warden's Court on

August 16th.

Objections to the application for the lease have been lodged as follows:

1. Neither the Northern Territory Administration nor the Mine Warden Court has the authority to deal with the application.

2. The Mining Ordinance and Regulations have not been complied with.

3. The land applied for is not Crown land.

4. The land belongs to the resident Aboriginal people.

5. The application is not just or equitable.

6. The granting of the lease is contrary to public policy.

7. The land is a part of an Aboriginal Reserve.

The Federal Council executive decided on this action following the recent visit to Yirrkala district by Mr. Gordon Bryant, M.P., vice president of the Council. Mr. Bryant's enquiries revealed that the Aboriginal residents had been in no way consulted. Since returning to Melbourne he has received letters from the elders of the people requesting help to "get back our country of Yirrkala and Melville Bay".

The executive felt compelled to take legal action to protect the rights of the residents as the Northern Territory Administration, whose statutory responsibility it is to protect the people, had neither consulted nor advised them concerning the alienation of their land.

A community of 500 persons has been compressed into an area of one square mile as a result of Government negotiations with Pechiney Company.

Issued by: Stan Davey. General Secretary.

Following are copies of letters received by Mr. Bryant from Yirrkala people, dated July 23rd, 1963.

Dear Mr. Bryant, We want you Mr. Bryant to help us get back our country of Yirrkala and Melville Bay. You can act for us for land title. Yours faithfully, Djalalingba.

Dear Mr. Bryant, We undersigned people of the tribes living in the Yirrkala district ask you to help us to keep hunting land and food gathering land which we believe we will lose when land which is our place of living is handed to companies for mining. We are hurt that the Government told us nothing of this before it took place. We do not believe that your Government would treat white people this way. We believe our occupancy of this land was lawful. We believe that our old age occupancy of this land gives us rights which should not be brushed aside. We are afraid of the fate of the Larrakeah people a few years ago, will be our fate in a few years if we lose our rights here. We ask for your action to help us. Yours sincerely, Signed: Djalaingba, Dhuygala, Wulanybuma, Daymbalipu, Paiyin, Wawuygmarra, Diayila, Manunu, Nyabilingu, Lundywuy Larrakan, Milippkum. (The latter letter was written first in the native Matha language.)

111. Yirrkala petition to the House of Representatives, August 1963

The Humble Petition of the Undersigned Aboriginal people of Yirrkala, being members of the Balamumu, Narrkala, Gapiny and Miliwurrwurr people and Djapu, Mangalili, Madarrpa, Magarrwanalinirri, Gumatj, Djambarrpuynu, Marrakula, Galpu, Dhaluaya, Wangurri, Warramirri, Maymil, Rirrtjinu tribes, respectfully sheweth.

1. That nearly 500 people of the above tribes are residents of the land excised from the Aboriginal Reserve in Arnhem Land.

2. That the procedures of the excision of this land and the fate of the people on it were never explained to them beforehand, and were kept secret from them.

3. That when Welfare Officers and Government officials came to inform them of decisions taken without them and against them, they did not undertake to convey to the Government in Canberra the views and feelings of the Yirrkala aboriginal people.

4. That the land in question has been hunting and food gathering land for the Yirrkala tribes from time immemorial; we were all born here.

5. That places sacred to the Yirrkala people, as well as vital to their livelihood are in the excised land, especially Melville Bay.

6. That the people of this area fear that their needs and interests will be completely ignored as they have been ignored in the past, and they fear that the fate which has overtaken the Larrakeah tribe will overtake them.

7. And they humbly pray that the Honourable the House of Representatives will appoint a Committee, accompanied by competent interpreters, to hear the views of the people of Yirrkala before permitting the excision of this land.

8. They humbly pray that no arrangements be entered into with any company which will destroy the livelihood and independence of

the Yirrkala people.

And your petitioners as in duty bound will ever pray God to help you and us. (English translation)

Bukudjulni gonga'yurru napurrunha Yirrkalalili Yulnunha malanha Balamumu, Narrkala, Gapiny, Miliwurrwurr nanapurru dhuwala mala, ga Djapu, Mangalili, Madarrpa, Magarrwanalinirri, Djambarrpuynu, Gumaitj, Marrakula, Galpu, Dhabuayu, Wangurri, Warramirri, Maymil, Ririfjinu malamanapanmirri djal dhunapa.

1. Dhuwala yulnu mala galki 500 nhina ga dhiyala wananura. Dhuwala wanga Arnhem Land yurru djaw'yunna naburrungala.

2. Dhuwala wanga djaw'yunna ga nhaltjana yurru yulnungunydja dhiyala wanga nura nhaltjanna dhu dharrpanna yulnu walandja yakana lakarama madayangumuna.

3. Dhuwala nunhi Welfare Officers ga Government bungawa lakarama yulnuwa malanuwa nhaltjarra nhuma gana wanganaminha yaka nula napurrungu lakarama wlala yaka'lakarama Governmentgala nunhala Canberra nhaltjanna napurruga guyana yulnuyu Yirrkala.

4. Dhuwala wänga napurrungyu balanu Iarrunarawu napurrungu näthawa, guyawu, miyspunuwu, maypalwu nunhi napurru gana nhinana bitjarrayi näthilimirri, napurru dhawalguyanana dhiyala wänganura.

5. Dhuwala wänga yurru dharpalnha yurru yulnuwalandja malawala, ga dharrpalnha dhuwala bala yulnuwuyndja nhinanharawu Melville Bathurru wänga balandayu djaw'yun nyumukunin.

6. Dhuwala yulnundja mala yurru nhämana balandawunu nha mulkurru nhämä yurru moma ga darangan yalalanumirrinha nhaltjanna dhu napurru bitjarra nhakuna Larrakeahyu momara wlalanguwuy wänga.

7. Nuli dhu bungawayu House of Representatives djaw'yn yulnuwala näthili yurru nha dhu lakarama interpreteryu bungawawala yulnu matha, yurru nha dhu djaw'yun dhuwala wängandja.

8. Nunhiyina dhu märrlayun marrama'-ndja nhinanharawu yulnuwu marrnamathinyarawu. Dhuwala napurru yulnu mala yurru liyamirriyama bitjan bili marr yurru napurru hha gonga' yunna wangarr'yu.

(Australian matha)

[Here follow the signatures]

112. Evidence of Milirrpum, 1 October 1963, Select Committee into the Grievances of the Yirrkala

Milirrpum, an Aboriginal, Yirrkala Mission was called and examined.

Gentlemen, you are very welcome to come here. We are very pleased this afternoon that you have met together for this business—to come to a meeting here. Thank you very much.

Mr. Dean

386. Do you think it is a good idea for the mining people to come here and work on some part of the area? Do you think that this will bring advantages to your people?— We did not know what people came here. First of all, aboriginal people not get whisper nowhere. Other people really plunder this country— only take from this country. We did not know, first of all, why they came. But later on, we soon get a little bit of word. But all aboriginal people did not get the word from mining people to mission. After that, when mission get little bit of word from mining people and mission tell us they went to all the marks. After mission tell us, we were worrying a little bit about our country. All aboriginal people did not know anything about why they mine bauxite. That is why the people little bit worry. They see men plunder this country. We were worrying about our children and our country. We want to hold all the country. All generations of our people here. The people here little bit worry because of all this whisper, and that is why we people come together this afternoon for this business.

If this country taken, we want something else from mining people. This aboriginal people's place. We want to hold this country. We do not want to lose this country. That is how the people are worrying about this country. We want to get more room for our hunting and our fishing, because later on we get more people. Our children are to come. All my children at school in this country. They want to hold this country. We fought the law for our children for all this country. Please, we do not want to lose this country. We stand on this country. The aboriginal people were the first Australians here. Then you people come along. Please, that is my word I am telling you. That is my last word. Thank you ...

Mr. Barnes

386. You say that you are frightened of losing this country. What

do you use the country in the area of the mining lease for mainly?— Later on, when the people have more and more children, we not have enough room to live in—to hunt. That is why the people want to hold this country. We do not want to lose it. You can come. You can help. We listen to what government people tell us. We remember the word the last two or three months when they came here and tell us. Also, we remember Mr. Evans tell our people. When we hear about that we very glad. You want us to sell this country, you know. But no, please. It is my father's country. This country belong to my father. This always belong to my fathers ...

Mr. Beazley

423. I should like some clarification of a point which arose out of Mr. Chipp's question. My question is to find out whether they do think that all Arnhem land belongs to them. Does Groote Eylandt belong to the Yirrakala people or to other Aborigines?— (*Interpreter*) It belongs to the Aborigines generally even although they speak a different language and are in a different group.

424. Does Roper River belong to Yirrkala or to other Aborigines?— (*Interpreter*) It belongs to the Yirrkala people but it belongs to everybody.

425. Does Yirrkala belong to the people of Groote Eylandt and the people of Roper River?— (*Interpreter*) Yes, it belongs to the whole lot even though their languages are different.

426. Does he believe that the Aborigines are one people?— (*Interpreter*) Yes, they are aboriginal. They are one.

427. Can he go to Roper River and Groote Eylandt to hunt?— (*Interpreter*) There are Yirrkala people at Roper River and at Groote Eylandt now doing that. Yes, they can do it.

428. Evidently there is a common kin with the people in that direction. Is there any finish anywhere to the Yirrkala people's country? Does it finish at Melville Bay or at Caledon Bay? Does he know where it finishes?— (*Interpreter*) He says that the various places Mr. Beazley mentioned belong to various clans. For example, Caledon Bay belongs to the Djapu; but when I mentioned Groote Eylandt, he said it belonged to the Groote Eylandt people particularly although they are able to come here. They are able to do that too but this is their country really ...

Mr. Beazley

455. The witness spoke at one part of his evidence a good many

times about his father. Would you ask him whether his father is buried in this land?— (*Interpreter*) Not actually here, but at Mata Mata, which is in the area near Caledon Bay.

456. Does he believe his father's spirit to be in this land?— (*Interpreter*) I believe he is thinking mainly of the clan, his father's song belonging to the clan and his totem. It is the clan's territory, his father's territory. And his father before him. It is patrilineal descent. It is not particularly his father, but just the territory of their clan.

457. His ancestors?— (*Interpreter*) Yes.

458. Does he believe that the spirits of his ancestors are in this land?— (*Interpreter*) Yes. A relation ancestor died and his spirit went back into a rock which belongs to his clan, the Rirratjingu clan. That is where the spirit is. They are the sacred features of the land.

113. Queensland Council for the Advancement of Aborigines and Torres Strait Islanders, *The Existing Aboriginals Preservation Act, Amendments Which Should Be Made and Why*, 1964

The treatment of Aborigines in general in Queensland is discriminatory and violates fundamental human rights as laid down in the United Nations Charter of Human Rights.

The conditions of the 27,000 Aboriginal people under the existing Act are particularly scandalous. The following proposals apply to this section of the people.

We Advocate:–

Land and Property: Full land and property rights. No further alienation of Reserve, Settlement or Mission lands. *Because:* Aborigines are not now allowed to own property, real or personal. They have no title to lands they live on or to their homes.

Freedom of Movement, within, and in and out of Reserves, etc. *Because* permission is now necessary to visit a Reserve, even for relatives of Aborigines living there. An Aborigine can be forcibly removed from a Reserve; detained on a Reserve; or moved from one Reserve to another.

Freedom for the Family as for all other citizens. *Because:* Aborigines must now get permission to marry. Children may be taken from their parents without neglect or cruelty being proved. The "age of consent" for an Aboriginal girl is at puberty.

Removal of Censorship. Because under the existing Act mail, both inward and outward, may be censored.

Wages and Conditions Equal to Those of White Workers. Because: Aborigines on settlements and missions and in the pastoral industry, and most Torres Straits Islanders, are paid sub-standard wages.

* An Aborigine may be worked up to 32 hours a week without payment on Government Settlements and Church Missions. Nearly 5000 station hands are paid little more than half the wages of similar white workers.

* Wages are not paid direct to the Aborigine but held "in trust." He has to ask permission to withdraw (often refused). He has no pass book, so no proof of his bank balance.

* Aborigines cannot choose their job, or leave it if dissatisfied. They cannot organise in a union— and it is an offence for anyone to attempt to persuade them to do so.

* Aboriginal workers under the Act get sub-standard rations, accommodation, etc.

Removal of Extra Taxation from Aborigines' Earnings. Because a compulsory deduction of 5% for married men and 10% for single men is made from Aborigines' wages (on top of the usual taxes paid by all citizens).

Justice Before the Law: Abolition of the dictator-like powers of Superintendents of Settlements. Under these an Aborigine can be punished for "any act subversive of good order or discipline."

In contravention of established principles of British justice–

* The Superintendent or his representative is both accuser and judge.

* The Aborigine has no right to a defence lawyer.

* Onus of proof is in some things placed on the accused.

Full Civil Rights. Because: Exemption from the Act is granted arbitrarily on the decision of the Director of Native Affairs and can be revoked at any time. Aborigines should have full civil rights. Special assistance need not mean special restrictions.

Special Measures Needed. We Advocate:–

* *Federal and State Government grants and interest-bearing loans to Aborigines* to allow them to exploit for their own benefit the mineral and other resources on Reserves.

* *Financial and technical assistance* for Aboriginal enterprises.

* *Educational courses specially adapted* to Aborigines' background (not of a lower standard). Use of their language where it exists, as well as English.

* *Professionally trained social workers* (not just one, but many) to assist Aborigines to develop modern communities.

What You Can Do To Help Ensure The Above Measures

Write, phone or see your local State Member of Parliament and ask him to seek the above amendments when the Government brings down its new Bill in the near future. Pass on this leaflet to all who will read it.

114. *Tribune*, 8 April 1964. Shameful Story Of Mapoon

"We are ashamed that our efforts have failed to prevent the forced abandonment of Mapoon settlement, at Cape York, Queensland," said Mr. S. Davies [Davey], general secretary of the Federal Council, at the conference.

"Nowhere in Australia during the past years has there been a more blatant breaking of promises and denial of human rights," he said. "Following the forced removal of Aboriginal leaders to Bamaga at the tip of Cape York peninsula, the burning down of most of the remaining cottages, the Committee has placed the matter in the hands of a solicitor with a view of testing legal action against the Queensland Department of Native Affairs."

Dragged Away

Mrs. Jean Jimmy, one of the Aboriginal leaders of Mapoon, told how force and police were used to drag them away. "The D.N.A. and the Church were not fair to us. When we refused to leave our homes in Mapoon they closed the school, they left us without a flying doctor for seven months.

"The D.N.A. ship came with police aboard. They gave us an hour to pack some belongings and took us to sleep at the mission cottage guarded by four policemen, like criminals. Next morning the D.N.A. ship took us to Bamaga. There were no homes. People took us in. I was given a room. We were told we would have a laundry and shower, but we wash our clothes like the old pioneers. It's hard for our boys to be employed. Those who work get only £9 a fortnight. This is not enough for a family. We were forced to leave old Mapoon and everybody had tears. My people sent me here to represent them."

As Mrs. Jimmy sat down Conference broke into a heated debate and resolved to protest to the D.N.A. Queensland on the methods used to disband Mapoon, called for the appointment of an individual Commissioner to investigate what happened, hear the views of the Mapoon people and restore the status quo if they require it.

Mr. R. Hancock (BWIU) explained that a big slice of Mapoon had been given to Comalco, the huge aluminium monopoly, who, he said, were given enough bauxite deposits to last for 300 years. "But they had to grab the mission site as well," he said.

115. *Australian,* 14 March 1966. Aborigines Ask For Land Rights

A proposal to give Aborigines in New South Wales land rights to prevent their land being steadily whittled away will be put to the Sate parliamentary joint committee on Aboriginal welfare.

The submission claims that in the 25 years to 1964, 9000 acres of land belonging to Aboriginal stations were taken from them, while only 151 acres were added. The submission, made by the Aboriginal-Australian Fellowship, will be discussed by the committee.

It says: "The Australian Aborigines' Welfare Board have no title to Australia whatsoever. All Aboriginal reserves and missions are Crown land and State boards have alienated much reserve land—and occasionally added to it since the 1880s. The reserve land is neither sold nor leased to Aborigines but it has often been sold or leased to European farmers. The NSW Department of Lands disposes of whatever reserve land the Aborigines' Welfare Board does not regard as being used (part or whole of a reserve), particularly when families are induced to give up reserves for a better life in their own houses. Reserves being Crown land, the authorities remind the residents they do not own them. Yet vast acres of the old Brewarrina and Cummeragunga reserves were released for sale or lease to Europeans. Efforts by people at Cummeragunga reserve to own it and farm wheat by means of a company to be backed by the Aborigines' Advancement League have received no support from the welfare board."

Strong Feeling

The submission says Aboriginal feeling on land rights is so strong that a conference of Aborigines last year decided to seek an injunction to prevent the welfare board alienating any land set aside for Aborigines until a committee elected by Aborigines investigated the legal position ...

The submission proposes:

NEW LEGISLATION to prevent land being alienated from Aborigines without stringent rules on compensation. An Aboriginal land court would be set up to deal with compensation.

ABORIGINES should be given title to some reserves with certain inalienable safeguards.

OTHER RESERVES in poor physical condition should be inspected and the people consulted before any decision is made to dispose of them through the proposed Aboriginal land court.

The submission cites examples of land being taken away from Aborigines.

116. Evidence of Herbert Groves, President, Aborigines Progressive Association, 5 April 1966, New South Wales Joint Committee of the Legislative Council and Legislative Assembly upon Aborigines Welfare

980 ... if I understand you aright, your association wishes these people to remain as a group. In other words, you believe in integration in the community but not in general assimilation?— W. I am opposed to assimilation because there are so many different definitions that you can get of "assimilation". I do commend the Hon. Paul Hasluck for his definition. I thought it looked very good on paper, but in practice quite a number of welfare officers are inclined to favour the other interpretation that may be arose from a survey that was made by Professor Watson in Adelaide. He stated conclusively that aborigines could be absorbed into the white race in three generations without fear of throwback. Welfare officers are inclined to favour this definition of assimilation, but it seems to me it would mean the disappearance of a race of people. I do not think it was the Creator's plan that a race of people should disappear. In my mind I feel that assimilation is a modern term for extermination. To condense my argument, in my book it is a form of Chauvinism. We should accept aborigines on the basis of equality, and also help retain their culture ...

982 ... I myself am very much in favour of aborigines pursuing their culture and carrying on with it. I think there is something beautiful in aboriginal culture. People from the respective universities who work in this field also agree with me. I have been very concerned about the preservation of the aboriginal language, which is rapidly disappearing ...

990. But you do not disagree with the present policy of assimilation, which is that the aborigines shall choose to do so. Would you agree with that?— W. Yes, I think the freedom of choice is one of the fundamental principles of democracy.

991. That does not cut across your integration ideas, that you think you should retain your cultures, customs and so on, which you can only retain to a very limited degree in an Australian community. The fact that you agree to assimilation does not cut across your idea of preserving aboriginal culture and customs?— W. Assimilation by those and for those who want to assimilate, but you will find that a lot of people do not favour assimilation. Surveys that I have made in there or four States indicate that the views on assimilation are that Europeans feel that it will create an indigestible lump of colour in society, and it is not generally acceptable. The same thing applies to the aborigines. A lot of them have no desire to assimilate through inter-marriage. This is where there is quite a lot of confusion about assimilation. There are different definitions of it. But I favour integration because integration means to become part of the community and not to be absorbed by the community, as in assimilation.

992. You say in your submission that assimilation is almost gen[o]cide. Surely it would be possible for you to be ordinary members of the Australian community and still, if you wished to be called an aborigine or a person of aboriginal descent, couldn't you?— W. Yes. Well, I suppose there is a possibility of that, too. I myself can adapt myself in any community, but that does not go for all aboriginal people. It is just as easy for me to go and live off the land, the same as my ancestors did, as it is for any other full-blooded aborigine.

993. You go on to say that the policy is one of relegating the future descendants of our people to an under-privileged, low-income group. If you do not wish to become full members of the community, are you not encouraging what you are trying to combat? In other words, you will always be in the low-income, separated group if you do not aim to become full members of the community in every sense of the word.— W. I do not agree with that because if aborigines want to remain in groups and build up co-operatives and remain in their respective groups they should be able to do so. We have such groups in Australia today in Italian colonies in Queensland and also Maltese colonies. These people have no intention or idea of assimilating, but they mix very freely and they do preserve their national dances and culture and their own way of life. There

does not seem to be any objection to what they are doing, so why should the aborigines be regarded in a different light if they want to do it? ...

1000. You do not favour intermarriage?— W. I do not favour disappearance of a race. I do not think it is right that aborigines should be encouraged to inter-marry, but if they wish to do so, it is their democratic privilege to do what they want to do.

1001. I may be on the wrong track, but it seems to me that when you say you object to a policy that will bring about total obliteration of Australian aborigines and their culture, the only way you can preserve that is by retaining this group within their own confines. Is that what you want to do?— W. It is something that the Italians and the Maltese are doing. They are remaining, some of them, in groups of their own. Many Italians have gone out into all sectors of the community, as you well know, but you still get an element that remains together to preserve their culture. Of course, they join together for parties and for their respective celebrations ...

1118. Very well. But as soon as it comes to living conditions, you suddenly want to take them all back out of the integrated society and put them into areas where aborigines live together.— W. Not necessarily. I said that there are many aborigines who have no desire to be Europeanized. This will be prevalent for a long time to come. They have no desire to participate in assimilation or integration. They want to remain in groups.

1119. This is the free choice of anyone.— W. Is there any reason why they should not remain in groups?

1120. No. And I do not think anyone is trying to force them into anything else.— W. Why not make it possible so that some scheme is available so that they can develop their communities?
...

117. Referendum on Aborigines (Background Notes), prepared by the National Directorate, Vote Yes Campaign (FCAATSI), 31 March 1967

On 27 May all enrolled voters in the six States of Australia (but not in the Australian Capital Territory and the Northern Territory) must answer 'YES' or 'NO' to each of two questions. These questions are 'Do you approve the proposed law for the alteration of the Constitution entitled "An act to alter the Constitution so that the number of Members of the House of Representatives may be increased without necessarily increasing the number of Senators"', and 'Do you approve the proposed law for the alteration of the Constitution entitled "An Act to alter the Constitution so as to omit the words relating to the people of the Aboriginal Race in any State and so that Aboriginals are to be counted in reckoning the population".

The questions will be in the above order and must be answered separately by 'YES' or 'NO' in the appropriate boxes. An informal vote on one question will not invalidate a formal vote on the other.

Our concern here is with the second question which concerns Aborigines. The relevant Act would omit from paragraph (xxvi) of Section 51 of the Constitution the words 'other than the Aboriginal race in each State', and would repeal Section 127. It was passed unanimously by both Houses of the Commonwealth Parliament.

Section 127 reads, 'In reckoning the numbers of the people in the Commonwealth, or of a State or other part of the Commonwealth, Aboriginal natives shall not be counted'. This section was originally included in the Constitution for two reasons, both of which are no longer valid. Firstly, some sixty or seventy years ago there was genuine difficulty in counting Aborigines because many were nomadic, which is not the case today. Secondly, Aborigines were at that time not considered worthy of a vote, and therefore were not to be counted in the numbers determining electoral boundaries. Today Aborigines are entitled to vote in all States and Territories of the Commonwealth and therefore ought to be counted in the census which determines the size of the electorates. There is no reason for the retention of this Section of the Constitution and ... all parties are agreed on the desirability of its repeal.

Section 51 reads 'The Parliament shall, subject to this Constitution, have power to make laws for the peace, order and good government of the Commonwealth with respect to (xxvi); the people of any race other than the Aboriginal race in any State, for whom it is deemed necessary to make special laws'. The proposed deletion of the words 'other than the Aboriginal race in any State', will thus have the effect of enabling the Commonwealth to make special laws in relation to Aborigines anywhere in Australia.

The Commonwealth power to legislate on Aboriginal affairs would be a power held concurrently with the States, and need not conflict in any way with State powers. Indeed Commonwealth power ought to complement the State Powers, facilitating, for instance, Commonwealth financial assistance for State projects such as Aboriginal housing or vocational training. This would particularly benefit those States, such as Western Australia and Queensland which have large Aboriginal populations.

In addition, Commonwealth power would enable the Commonwealth to take the initiative in setting up such bodies as an Aboriginal Education Foundation (along the lines of the very successful Maori Education Foundation in New Zealand and an Aboriginal Arts and Crafts Board (similar to the Indian Arts and Crafts Board in the United States) which would be most effective on a nationwide basis.

In its original form, Section 51 (xxvi) was apparently designed to protect Aborigines from Commonwealth laws discriminating against them. However, with the change of Australian (and world) opinion on the rights of racial minorities it is now apparent that any Commonwealth laws in relation to Aborigines would be favourable to Aborigines. In view of the special disadvantages of lack of capital, education and 'know-how' suffered by the Aborigines, the well known principle of justice that 'it is as unjust to treat unequals equally as to treat equals unequally' is a strong argument for special legislation to enable Aborigines to overcome their disadvantages.

This principle is widely applied to other classes of peoples, for instance, ex-Servicemen under the Repatriation Act. Something similar is needed for Aborigines.

Australians are held collectively responsible for the treatment and conditions of the Aboriginal people by world opinion. Proper race relations is a national and international issue which therefore ought to be dealt with by Australia at a national level as well as at the State and local levels. Australia ought, for instance, to be able, at a national level, to ratify Convention 107 of the International Labor Organisation which deals with the right[s] of indigenous minorities such as the Aboriginal people. At present there are six different Aboriginal administrations with six different policies, and only one (South Australia) is endeavouring to satisfy Convention 107.

Aborigines are a national responsibility. We must see to it that the National Parliament is able to accept that responsibility. We can make this possible by voting 'YES' for Aborigines on 27 May.

118. *Age*, 11 April 1967. No Vote Fear On Rights Issue

"I am not at all confident Australians will vote Yes in the coming referendum on Aborigines' rights," the president of the Aborigines Advancement League (Mr Bill Onus) said last night. Mr Onus ... was officially opening the league's campaign for the May 27 referendum. "Australians in general are apathetic towards the Aborigines' problems", he said. "Although they agree on the morality of full rights for the Aborigines, they do not feel inclined to do anything about it."

Mr Onus said it had been suggested that the Aborigines' referendum was strictly a political issue ...

"But this is not a question of politics. It is a fundamental question of human rights, the case of one man being equal to the other" ...

"It is essential that the public be told clearly of the moral and social consequences of the referendum where it affects the Aborigines," he said.

Mr Onus said Australians must vote to give the Aborigine full citizenship rights. It was a basic question of human rights.

"The referendum must be passed," he said. "The image of Australia throughout the world is at stake. If it is not passed, Australia will be held up to ridicule."

Freedom Ride

119. Charles Perkins to Mr A.G. Kingsmill, Chairman, New South Wales Aborigines Welfare Board, 18 January 1965

Following our discussion at your office and at your request I have therefore summarised briefly the principles and aims of Student Action for Aborigines.

I am the Chairman of this group which has a membership at the present time of over 80 full time students who attend the University of Sydney. Members come from varied societies and groups within the University thus representing a wide cross section of University interests ...

S.A.F.A. intends to tour by a chartered bus (45 passengers) the West and North Coast of N.S.W. This tour will last two weeks and will take in all towns which have a fairly substantial Aboriginal population. We hope to visit, with the Board's permission, all reserves plus missions, and town homes of Aboriginal people. We wish to view all facets of Aboriginal assimilation and accumulate statistical data on the same.

The route to be taken will pass through the towns mentioned here:

Wellington, Dubbo, Walgett, Moree, just over the border into Queensland and then on to Lismore. From Lismore to Sydney we hope to visit all major Aboriginal settlements.

The main objective of the whole tour would be a comprehensive survey of Aboriginal life in the main towns visited. This would be under factors such as: (1) Housing (2) Education (3) Employment (occupation—income) (4) Health (5) Attitudes—European and Aboriginal.

We will be directed in this survey by the Rev. T.D. Noffs who did a similar survey in America.

We believe the material compiled would be of great benefit to all organisations dealing with Aboriginal welfare. It will possibly give some a guide to future action and indicate both Aboriginal and European attitudes to problems of assimilation.

S.A.F.A. proposes also to integrate certain theatres, swimming pools etc which discriminate against Aboriginal people. The tactics will follow the pattern set by the Rev. Martin Luther King. It is passive non-violent action, and to complement this fact I enclose an article written by King which contains the thesis of this principle.

We do not intend to create confusion or disturbances that will lead to violent action. We merely wish to stimulate *both* Aboriginal and European towns-people into doing something practical themselves about the situation.

I personally feel that this tour will channel student action and eventually University action into doing something constructive for eleviation of this particular social problem. Too long have students complained of South Africa and such. I feel it is time they channelled their efforts to doing something for their own depressed coloured group.

The tour is scheduled to begin on the 13th February and finish on the 27th February.

As Chairman of S.A.F.A. I would appreciate the co-operation of the Board in allowing us access to Reserves as I believe this is a constructive and worthwhile project.

120. *Sun*, 17 February 1965. Students May Set Up Pickets

Sydney University students may picket Moree Council baths and the public school today, as a protest against alleged racial discrimination. The students' leader, Charles Perkins, 29, a part-aboriginal Arts student, said this in Moree today.

Mr Perkins said the group had found signs of discrimination against the Moree aborigines during a survey yesterday. However, all facts will be double-checked early today, before any action is taken, he said.

"The two main places where discrimination is practised are at the baths and school. We found yesterday that aboriginal children from the mission settlement receive half an hour less schooling each day. This is because the bus which picks them up collects European children first, and delivers them to school before going to the mission. In the afternoons, the aboriginal children are let out 15 minutes early to get the bus home." Mr Perkins said local authorities promised to rectify the matter, but nothing has been done so far.

"We also found that there is discrimination against aborigines at Moree baths, run by the local council," he went on.

Europeans "Reluctant"

"Some aborigines apparently are not allowed to swim in the baths. There are also other minor things, but these are the main points at the moment."

He said discrimination at Moree is not as bad as in Walgett, and there had been no incidents so far. Our main problem has been the reluctance of the local Europeans to cooperate with us. "We have spoken to the local police inspector, and he has agreed to co-operate with us as long as the demonstrations are passive.

"Although Moree is not too bad, we don't want discriminatory action of any kind against aborigines in any place."

121. *Australian*, 22 February 1965. Race Tour Bus Driver Walks Out

Sydney university students involved in racial violence at Moree, northern NSW, on Saturday, were left stranded yesterday when their hired bus driver walked out because he said their anti-segregation tour was too dangerous ...

The driver left the students' chartered bus at Grafton, refusing to go on to Lismore and Kempsey where the students planned further efforts for Aboriginal rights ...

Mr Charles Perkins, the students' leader said: "We do not blame Mr Packenham for deciding to leave the tour. He has been intimidated into leaving for fear of danger to the bus and to himself."

Mob of 500

At Moree on Saturday the bus was pelted with eggs and rotten fruit as it pulled up in front of the municipal baths to take on the students after their 3½-hour demonstration. Four men have been charged with offensive behaviour. Three are Moree residents and one is of no fixed abode.

During the demonstration one student was punched to the ground, a former alderman was dumped in the gutter, and one of the girl students was spat on. The students blocked the entrance to the baths after they were refused permission to bring in nine Aboriginal children. A mob of 500 gathered around them shouting insults and throwing fruit. The mayor, Alderman William Lloyd, grabbed three students by their shirts and led them away.

Kept Out Again

Council employees carried away another student Mr Chris Page, 20. The students returned and blocked the doorway again. They left after the Mayor agreed to introduce a motion to rescind a 1955 council regulation barring Aborigines from the baths. The council will hear the resolution tonight and is expected to vote on it next week.

The crowd at the baths grew so violent that police had to escort the bus out of town. Aborigines were again excluded from the baths yesterday.

122. *Star* (Lismore), 23 February 1965. Students Arrive In Lismore. To Make Survey Today

A "socialogical survey" relating to the treatment and acceptance of aborigines, will be undertaken in Lismore today by 30 members of the Student Action for Aborigines Council who arrived in Lismore last night.

The group— 21 young men and nine girls— all Sydney University students— arrived by charter bus about 9 p.m. from Grafton. The men spent last night in a pavilion at the Lismore Showground and the girls were billeted with a number of Lismore residents.

Leader of the group, 29-year-old third-year art student, Mr. Charles Perkins, said the survey in Lismore would follow a pattern set in other centres the group had visited. However, he did not expect any trouble in Lismore. In fact, he said, the trouble which had been encountered at centres such as Walgett and Moree, had not really been expected. But, in both these centres the troublemakers had been members of the minority "hooligan element," and did not represent the feeling of the majority of the community.

Mr. Perkins said the group's first activity today would be to visit the aboriginal settlement at Cabbage Tree Island at 9 a.m. Later in the day the "socialogical survey" would be undertaken in Lismore streets. Members of the group would interview people at random on matters relating to health, housing, employment, education and population. Similar questions were being directed at aborigines during their tour, he said. Mr. Perkins said it was hoped to leave Lismore for Coffs Harbour about 3.30 p.m.

Mr. Perkins said he had been surprised by the amount of publicity the group had received. Most of this had been brought about by violence and this, too, had been completely unexpected.

Concern

Mr. Perkins said he had heard today of statements attributed to the Mayor of Moree, relating to the lifting of the "colour bar" at the town's swimming baths. He said if this and other promises made by the mayor were kept, it would be considered the visit to the town by the group had achieved its purpose.

Although he felt the remainder of the tour would be free of violence, some concern was held for the visit to Kempsey. This was mainly because the Kempsey swimming pool was not integrated, he said. In addition, there was a colour problem at Kempsey as far as a number of hotels were concerned.

Mr. Perkins said the group was "not completely happy" with the title of "Freedom Riders". He said this had become a label, but the group preferred to be known by its proper title— The Student Action For Aborigines Council.

The group was met on arrival in Lismore last night by Pastor F. Roberts, Jnr., and escorted to Lismore Showgrounds. The boys then began to prepare their own meal while the girls were taken to billets in Lismore.

One member of the group said the bus charter had cost £360— about £200 of which had been raised through folk concerts in Sydney. Additional cost to each member was about £20, mainly for food.

123. *Churinga* (publication of the Aborigines Progressive Association), December 1965

The Delegation arrived in Walgett on Friday, 13th August, and received a warm welcome from Mr. Harry Hall who gave us a full account of recent events. He assured us that he and Mr. Ted Fields, A.P.A. Vice-President, with the support of the local Aborigines and the majority of the town's people, were determined to break the colour bar at the Luxury Theatre on the following Saturday night.

Although the press reported the colour bar was off, a written agreement prepared by the theatre proprietor, Mr. Conomos, stated that discrimination would not cease until 1st September, and until that date only "regulars" who attended the theatre three times a week would be admitted to the lounge.

Mr. Harry Hall received word that A.P.A. leaders would not be admitted.

Miss Iris Hall said the young people of the town were most affected by the colour bar in the Luxury Theatre lounge, because they all mixed happily in other social activities of the town, but all sat together downstairs rather than be separated when they went to the cinema.

This was confirmed by the actions of the young non-Aboriginal people who waited outside the police station for the release of those arrested, with hot Bonox and biscuits for the comfort of their friends. All those arrested were kept in custody for about four hours, including the two girls who were under age, who are released on verbal bail into the custody of their fathers, until the case is heard on the 1st September.

The Delegation, accompanied by Mr. Harry Hall and Ted Fields, visited the four main Aboriginal localities around Walgett. After discussing the arrests with the people here and in the town main street, it was evident that the arrests had strengthened the people's determination and not stifled the movement. On the contrary the A.P.A. leaders gained more support from the local people.

An Aborigine who had been away from town working, after hearing of the A.P.A. leaders' intentions, took a handful of uncut stones from his pocket saying he had no money on him but he wanted to support the movement and the stones could be sold for funds for the fight. Mr. Eric Woods pinned a badge of membership on him.

Mounting tension in the town was increased by the arrival of Inspector Chalker and police reinforcements from Bourke, who interviewed Mr. Harry Hall in their car in the main street of Walgett. The police were concerned about the need for additional forces in the event of the theatre proprietor not admitting Mr. Harry Hall and Mr. Ted Field to the lounge of the Luxury Theatre.

Earlier the local police Sergeant Gleeson, stated that as the Government policy was to assimilate the Aborigines, the A.P.A. leaders must be protected during their attempts to desegregate the local theatre.

Saturday night a large crowd of excited people and a number of police gathered outside the theatre to see if Mr. Harry Hall and Mr. Ted Fields would be admitted to the theatre lounge.

After they were admitted many aborigines queued up for admission, some were refused for various reasons.

After the A.P.A. leaders' victory by gaining admittance, the crowd gathered in surging groups vigorously discussing the colour bar and whether the attempts to break it, successful or not, would have harmful results in other ways, such as losing their jobs from employers, many of whom had come to town and warned their employees not to become involved in the activities of Harry Hall and A.P.A.

Mr. Harry Hall said, "Must we and our children live all our lives being told what we can do, by our employers? They need our labour as much as we need employment, and for our children's sake, we must change things now."

At the interval the crowd was joined by many theatre patrons who considered it more interesting outside than the entertainment inside.

More and more people became involved in the vigorous discussion between Aborigines and non-Aborigines, employers and employees, until it was evident that only a few Aborigines and a hard core of town employers supported the colour bar.

At the peak of the discussion Mr. Harry Hall addressed the crowd. He thanked the students for their unfailing efforts to reveal the colour bar to the public. He thanked the delegates from Sydney for journeying so far to give moral support for the activities initiated by the Walgett A.P.A. He also thanked the police for their protection and co-operation, saying, "I hate to think what would happen to that little student surrounded over there if the police were not here to protect us." Following this the crowd dispersed and the colour bar in the Luxury Theatre was broken.

The Gurindji and Gove

124. Northern Territory Council for Aboriginal Rights, Program for Improved Living Standards for Northern Territory Aborigines, leaflet, 1966

The following resolution was unanimously adopted at the fourth Annual General Meeting of the Northern Territory Council for Aboriginal Rights held at Rapid Creek, Darwin, on 24/7/66:–

"The present living standards of native workers in the Northern Territory is a disgrace to Australia and a clear breach of the Charter of Human Rights. We therefore resolve:

1. That the native workers on pastoral properties and in other employment come within the wage Awards and receive equal pay this year, not in three years as decided by the Court.

2. That the "slow worker" provisions of the recent Court findings be abandoned.

3. That the present bad and illegal arrangement under which some Station Managers, Welfare Settlements and Missions handle Social Service payments cease, and all Maternity Allowances, Child Endowment, Pensions and other Social Service payments be made direct to Aborigines.

4. That housing conditions on pastoral properties, Welfare Settlements and Mission Stations be brought up to the standard as set down in the Social Welfare Ordinance and further improvements be made.

5. That an adequate variety of foods be available on pastoral properties, Welfare Settlements and Missions to ensure a balanced diet for native employees.

6. That adequate educational and medical facilities be provided.

7. That the Aboriginal native race of Australia be protected by federal Law and native women be given full protection of existing laws.

8. That the use of abusive and offensive terms of racial prejudice such as "nigger" and "boong" be made a criminal offence.

9. That natives have full control and ownership of reserves.

10. That natives be granted full citizenship rights inside as well as outside reserves.

11. That the Northern Territory Council for Aboriginal Rights

will work with the trade union movement and other interested organisations to bring this program into effect."

On behalf of the Northern Territory Council for Aboriginal Rights and its members— we ask for your support.

Davis Daniels, Secretary; Dexter Daniel, President.

125. Dexter Daniels, President, Northern Territory Council for Aboriginal Rights, press release, Aborigines and Northern Territory Cattle Stations, 25 October 1966

(Refer statement Sydney Morning Herald, 25/10/66, p. 7).

Mr Morris can try to replace his Aboriginal stockmen if he wants to.

At present in the Northern Territory there are about 160 white stockmen, including 60 head stockmen.— (The 22 white employees at Wave Hill include book-keepers, mechanics, carpenters, etc.) At least 1000 of our people are employed as stockmen. We are not frightened by the pastoralists threats of disemployment. With equal wages some of our people may be put off but we can care better for them on proper wages.

Mr Morris and Mr Chisholm are welcome to find whitemen who will work 12 hours a day, 7 days a week, live for months in isolation from their families, live in humpies and not resent being spoken to as animals.

How long does it take to train a stockman?

How long does it take a whiteman to know our country as my people know it? Who will find the Jackeroos and train them to ride?

Perhaps Mr Morris would like to live in the conditions his company has provided for my people and work for $6.00, or even $14.50 per week.

Mr Morris may be assured that what is now happening on pastoral properties will also happen to Welfare settlements and Missions which fail to provide proper wages and living conditions.

The pastoralists and Welfare have kept my people as slaves for 50 years or more. This must stop.

126. Gurindji petition to Lord Casey, Governor General, 19 April 1967

MAY IT PLEASE YOUR EXCELLENCY

We, the leaders of the Gurindji people, write to you about our earnest desire to regain tenure of our tribal lands in the Wave Hill-Limbunya area of the Northern Territory, of which we were dispossessed in time past, and for which we received no recompense.

Our people have lived here from time immemorial and our culture, myths, dreaming and sacred places have evolved in this land. Many of our forefathers were killed in the early days while trying to retain it. Therefore we feel that morally the land is ours and should be returned to us. Our very name Aboriginal acknowledges our prior claim. We have never ceased to say amongst ourselves that Vesteys should go away and leave us to our land.

On the attached map, we have marked out the boundaries of the sacred places of our dreaming, bordering the Victoria River from Wave Hill Police Station to Hooker Creek, Inverway, Limbunya, Seal Gorge, etc. We have begun to build our own new homestead on the banks of beautiful Wattie Creek in the Seal Yard area, where there is permanent water. This is the main place of our dreaming only a few miles from the Seal Gorge where we have kept the bones of our martyrs all these years since white men killed many of our people. On the walls of the sacred caves where these bones are kept, are the painting of the totems of our tribe.

We have already occupied a small area at Seal Yard under Miners Rights held by three of our tribesmen. We will continue to build our new home there (marked on the map with a cross), then buy some working horses with which we will trap and capture wild unbranded horses and cattle. These we will use to build up a cattle station within the borders of this ancient Gurindji land. And we are searching the area for valuable rocks which we hope to sell to help feed our people. We will ask the N.T. Welfare Department for help with motor for pump, seeds for garden, tables, chairs, and other things we need. Later on we will build a road and an airstrip and maybe a school. Meanwhile, most of our people will continue to live in the camp we have built at the Wave Hill Welfare Centre twelve miles away and the children continue to go to school there.

We beg of you to hear our voices asking that the land marked on the map be returned to the Gurindji people. It is about 500 square miles in area but this is only a very small fraction of the land leased by Vesteys in these parts. We are prepared to pay for our land the same annual rental that Vesteys now pay. If the question of compensation arises, we feel that we have already paid enough during fifty years or more, during which time, we and our fathers worked for no wages at all much of the time and for a mere pittance in recent years.

If you can grant this wish for which we humbly ask, we would show the rest of Australia and the whole world that we are capable of working and planning our own destiny as free citizens. Much has been said about our refusal to accept responsibility in the past, but who would show initiative working for starvation wages, under impossible conditions, without education for strangers in the land? But we are ready to show initiative now. We have already begun. We know how to work cattle better than any white man and we know and love this land of ours.

If our tribal lands are returned to us, we want them, *not* as another "Aboriginal Reserve", but as a leasehold to be run cooperatively as a mining lease and cattle station by the Gurindji Tribe. All practical work will be done by us, except such work as bookkeeping, for which we would employ white men of good faith, until such time as our own people are sufficiently educated to take over. We will also accept the condition that if we do not succeed within a reasonable time, our land should go back to the Government.

(In August last year, we walked away from the Wave Hill Cattle Station. It was said that we did this because wages were very poor (only six dollars per week), living conditions fit only for dogs, and rations consisting mainly of salt beef and bread. True enough. But we walked away for other reasons as well. To protect our women and our tribe, to try to stand on our own feet. We will never go back there.)

Some of our young men are working now at Camfield, and Montejinnie Cattle Stations for proper wages. However, we will ask them to come back to our [own] Gurindji Homestead when everything is ready.

These are our wishes, which have been written down for us by our undersigned white friends, as we have had no opportunity to learn to write English.

Vincent Lingiari. Pincher Manguari. Gerry Ngaljardji. Long-Johnny Kitgnaari. Transcribed, witnessed and transmitted by Frank J Hardy. J.W. Jeffrey.

127. Aboriginal Land Rights Campaign 1968, pamphlet issued by FCAATSI and the Abschol Department of the National Union of Australian University Students

WHAT WE SEEK

1. Aboriginal Ownership of Existing Aboriginal Reserves.

Full legal recognition by the Commonwealth Parliament of the rights of permanent tenure or secure title, fully compensatable at law, of all Aborigines having a traditional association with such land, and all descendents of such Aborigines, as represented by a legally incorporated body in the case of each area concerned, over all existing land throughout the Commonwealth which at present is reserved, temporarily or otherwise, for the use or benefit of the Aboriginal natives of Australia.

2. Recognition of Aboriginal Ownership of Traditional Tribal Land at Present Owned and Leased by the Crown.

The recognition of Aboriginal ownership of all existing Crown land having Aboriginal groups living upon or in association with it, where traditional occupancy according to tribal custom can be established from anthropological or other evidence in relation to the Aboriginal groups concerned. Such land is to include land at present leased by the Crown to pastoral interests. Ownership is to be vested in legally incorporated bodies representing each Aboriginal group concerned and constituted as far as possible according to their desires and customs.

In the case of existing leases these are to be re-negotiated with legal representatives of the Aboriginal owners, with full compensation by the Commonwealth for any variations, including compulsory resumption of such areas of leased land as may be desirable, so as to ensure an economically viable, independent, and dignified life for the Aboriginal owners pending expiration of the leases. Rentals are to be paid by the lessees to the Aboriginal owners, as is the practice with Maori land in New Zealand and some Indian land in the United States of America.

3. Aboriginal Consent for the Benefit from Mining and Other Development.

The development of mining and other economic enterprises on all Aboriginal lands as defined under 1. and 2. above by other than the Aboriginal owners must be subject to the informed consent of the Aboriginal owners and to any reasonable conditions which they may determine. Such consent and conditions should be determined by the decision of elected representatives of the Aboriginal owners as a legally incorporated body, and their legal advisers. Agreements for such development must be drawn up by negotiation between the legal advisers of the Aboriginal owners, Government, and the developers, and be legally binding on all parties to such agreements. Such royalties as would normally stem from such development are to go to the Aboriginal owners as a legally incorporated body, for disposal as that body may decide.

WHY DO WE SEEK ABORIGINAL LAND RIGHTS?

1. Common justice requires that no group or class of people should be deprived of their rightful inheritance.

Sir Thomas Buxton, Chairman of the Aborigines' Committee of the British House of Commons recognised this as long ago as 1834 when he wrote "In order to do justice we must admit first that the natives have a right to their own lands." This view was supported in regard to the Yirrkala Aborigines of Arnhem Land by the Select Committee appointed by the House of Representatives, which in its report in 1963 said "your Committee believes that a direct monetary compensation should be paid for any loss of traditional occupancy, even though these rights are not legally expressed under the laws of the Northern Territory." Again, in relation to the Gurindji claim to part of the Wave Hill pastoral lease in the Northern Territory, a Committee of the N.T. Legislative Council reported, in November 1967, "your Committee is most impressed with the strong moral claim that these people have to this small portion of a much larger area, that from time immemorial, they have considered to be their's". We seek to have this long recognised moral right given legal force as an expression of a more just attitude towards the Aboriginal people.

2. International opinion and precedents demand it.

As long ago as 1594 the Spanish "Laws of the Indies" said: 'We command that the farms and lands which may be granted to Spaniards be so granted without prejudice to the Indians; and that such as may have been granted to their prejudice and injury be restored to whoever they of right shall belong."

This and related principles incorporated in the "Laws of the Indies" became the basis of modern international law, which unfortunately is not enforceable in our courts. Nevertheless there is strong moral and political pressure on Governments to abide by such principles. For example Convention 107 of the International Labour Organisation, adopted in 1957 but not yet ratified by Australia, reads "The right of ownership, collective or individual, of the members of the (indigenous) populations concerned over the lands which these populations traditionally occupy shall be recognised", (article ii).

Such rights have been recognised in New Zealand, the United States, and other countries, and even by Australia in relation to Nauru and the Territory of Papua and New Guinea. In an official publication the Australian Government in 1960 stated "Respect for native land ownership was laid down as a basic principle of Australian administration in Papua over 80 years ago".

It is nonsense to claim that Aborigines do not qualify because they are a "nomadic people". Anthropologists are agreed, as Prof. R.M. Berndt has put it, that "In Aboriginal Australia generally, land was inalienable" or as Prof. A.P. Elkin wrote in 1938 "The local group owns the hunting and food-gathering rights of its country; members of other groups may only enter it and hunt over it after [...] permission has been granted".

Are we to continue to discriminate against Aborigines to the point of making them the only native people in modern history to be completely deprived of their land?

3. It is vital to the economic well-being of the Aborigines and to future race relations in Australia.

Aborigines and part-Aborigines at present live in over-crowded sub-standard conditions, under-educated, under-employed, and without control of any capital resources with which to change this situation. Prof. C. Rowley has described part-Aborigines in N.S.W. and parts of S.A. as living in a "culture of poverty", while Dr. F. Lancaster Jones has found child mortality rates in the N.T. amongst the highest in the world. Yet approximately 50% of the Aboriginal and part-Aboriginal population is under 15 years of age, and their number is expected to double in 20 to 25 years.

Clearly in the northern third of Australia, where Aborigines are a substantial fraction of the population, a growing number of people who are both poor and racially distinct will lead to a dangerous racial situation unless major changes are made. Aborigines are increasing in number faster than they are being "assimilated", as shown by the increase in the number of "pure Aborigines", principally because poor people are difficult to assimilate (or integrate) into an affluent society.

For the sake of all Australians, the Aboriginal people must be helped to rise out of poverty. This can best be achieved by giving them control of capital resources, renewed self-respect and initiative, and bargaining power with respect to employers and industrial developers. The way is open to achieving all these aims by giving Aborigines back control of their own land, for then Aborigines will be able to bargain on equal terms with employers and developers so as to get maximum benefits in terms of wages, conditions, on the job training schemes, and even share-holding and proprietary rights. This is already happening with American Indians. It can and must happen here.

4. It is important for the psychological well-being of the Aborigines.

It is a sociological fact that every human being needs a sense of belonging to a group with which he shares common beliefs, traditions, and attitudes to life. Such groups should be a source of pride, confidence and self-respect.

Most Aborigines, because of their appearance, are forced to see themselves as part of an Aboriginal group, so that it is vital psychologically that Aborigines as a group have traditions and achievements to be proud of. Land is an important symbol of Aboriginal grouphood, and a vital link with old traditions and an honourable and proud history. The final dispossession of the Aboriginal people would cut that link and be a symbol of defeat and the death of a tradition. Deprivation of land thus leads to restlessness and a degrading lack of self-respect, initiative and pride.

WHO IS BEHIND THIS CAMPAIGN?

Essentially this campaign started when for the first time a sympathetic white Australian listened to the pleas of Aboriginal Australians for control of part of their own land.

Aborigines and part-Aborigines all over Australia have pleaded for the remnants of their land for over 100 years. For example, in 1870 the secretary of the Victorian Board for the Protection of Aborigines informed the Board that the Aboriginal men on Coranderrk Aboriginal Station, near Healesville "are still anxious and uncertain respecting the tenure of their land" and recommended that the Board try to "get a grant of the land now reserved for the use of the Aborigines". Coranderrk was finally abolished in 1948.

In 1963 a petition from the Yirrkala people of Arnhem Land to the House of Representatives finally led to the appointment of a Select Committee which made recommendations which recognised the moral validity of the Aboriginal plea. Another petition, from the Gurindji people to the Governor General was rejected in 1967, but in 1968 the new Commonwealth Minister in Charge of Aboriginal Affairs indicated, after visiting the people, that he would assist them. At the 1968 Conference of the Federal Council for the Advancement of Aborigines and Torres Strait Islanders a plea was also received from the Elcho Island people for "land with full rights to timber, minerals and fishing" along the coast of Arnhem Land.

At the same conference the "All-Aboriginal Session" (at which only Aborigines are present) passed the following resolution, "That F.C.A.A.T.S.I. launch a national campaign [...] urging the granting of Aboriginal land rights, and in particular the granting of full title and rights to compensation with respect to all existing Aboriginal reserve land throughout Australia, and the provision of land for all Aboriginal individuals and groups seeking to live on, use, and develop land in their traditionally occupied areas". This was later adopted by the full Conference of F.C.A.A.T.S.I.

F.C.A.A.T.S.I. itself is a body which meets in a Conference once a year at which delegates from affiliated organisations elect an Executive, pass resolutions, and discuss Aboriginal Affairs. Besides Aboriginal Advancement organisations, affiliated organisations include some church, trade union, and student organisations.

In a recent statement on "The Future of Aboriginal Missions", the Division of Mission of the Australian Council of Churches said "the best interests of the (Aboriginal) people [...] includes their right to ownership of the land and the minerals within it, on the basis of prior occupancy or natural right." We members of F.C.A.A.T.S.I. believe that this is the position which all thoughtful non-Aboriginal Australians must come to if they are people of good will.

WHAT WILL IT COST?

Compensation to pastoral lesees, in those cases where excision is necessary may run into some millions of dollars, spread over a number of years, but in many cases it should be possible for the leases to be re-negotiated in modified form, with the Aborigines as owners. In that case compensation would only be needed to cover variations in the leases, which could be much less.

Financial and technical assistance to the Aborigines will also be necessary, and where this is not possible by agreement with private enterprise, Government assistance will be needed. However, such assistance and development will of course be aimed at the development of self-sufficient and profitable Aboriginal enterprise and the elimination of the present widespread hand-outs of food, supplies and other "welfare" provisions.

Such costs must be weighed against the present (1965-6) expenditure on Aborigines and part-Aborigines *of more than $20 million per year* which has been increasing at more than 10% per year since 1958. More importantly, such costs must be weighed against the long-term prospect of failing, if we follow past policies, to solve our racial problem. *We cannot afford to fail.*

WILL ABORIGINAL LAND RIGHTS RETARD DEVELOPMENT OF THE NORTH?

We believe that once Aborigines in the North see that development of their own land, on their own terms, and in their own interests, is both possible and fruitful, we shall see a great rush forward.

At present Aborigines are resentful, suspicious, and apathetic towards development because they see it only as bringing in more strangers and depriving them of more and more land.

Aborigines are a large, well-adapted, local work force, ready and eager for on-the-job training and participation in a true developmental partnership. Given the bargaining power of land ownership and the need for their consent they could reach agreement with prospective developers on the conditions under which they would enter with enthusiasm into new moves leading to an eventually integrated economic and social partnership.

If there are resources on Aboriginal land worth developing, there will be developers willing to do so on the Aborigines' terms.

WILL IT LEAD TO SEGREGATION OR APARTHEID?

NO. Aborigines through their legally incorporated governing bodies will be able to lease land to non-Aborigines for pastoral uses or for other developmental purposes such as the siting of industries or towns. Aborigines will be free to come and go, move into non-Aboriginal areas or employ or invite non-Aborigines on to Aboriginal owned land. It simply means that Aborigines will at last inherit, own, and control some capital resources, as do most Australians. It should lead to a lessening of the economic barriers between the races and thus to faster eventual integration between Aborigines and non-Aborigines.

WHY SHOULD ABORIGINES BE SPECIALLY FAVOURED OVER ROYALTIES?

The Commonwealth Government already levies double royalties when granting mining rights in the Arnhem Land Reserve and pays them in to a special trust fund for the benefit of Aborigines, on the grounds that Aborigines should share in the benefits arising from development on the Reserve.

We also view it as direct compensation for the disruption of traditional ways of life which mining and other development inevitably brings about, and as an important source of income to be used in helping to cope with the necessary changes. Because these reasons relate directly to the local Aboriginal community so affected, we believe such royalties should go to their direct benefit rather than into a more general fund. Such an arrangement is already in force on Groote Eylandt thanks to the policy of the Church Missionary Society, and the money is being put to good use.

Funds from Mineral royalties have led to many desirable developments on Indian Reservations in the United States, for instance scholarships, tribally owned motels, factories and a timber mill.

WHAT EFFECT WILL IT HAVE ON THE PASTORALISTS?

Many pastoral lesees will not be affected as no Aborigines remain with close connections to the land in question. In other cases lessees will be able to re-negotiate leases with the Aboriginal owners, with Government compensation for any loss incurred.

Undoubtedly many pastoralists will find their traditional Aboriginal work force more independent than hitherto, but such a growing independence is already evident, and in view of the pastoralists' threats of large-scale dis-employment of Aborigines when equal wages come into force, this is hardly undesirable.

Mr J.H. Kelly in his book "Struggle for the North", which is fully documented, amply demonstrates the long-standing inefficiency of many large absentee-owned pastoral leases in Northern Australia. It is thus hardly appropriate for the pastoralists to cry out about a feared "reduction in productivity". Smaller, more highly developed leases may well be more productive.

Problems of access and provisions can readily be solved by turning private airstrips and roads into public ones, and the establishment of independent or government stores where appropriate. Such developments may well benefit the independent pastoralist, and certainly contribute to more rapid development of the North.

ARE WE BEING REALISTIC?

The Minister in Charge of Aboriginal Affairs at the Federal level has already indicated his support for increasing Aboriginal independence and initiative, and a moving away from the welfare paternalism of the past.

The Division of Missions of the Australian Council of Churches clearly supports our aims, and that body represents the major mission administrations involved in day-to-day Aboriginal affairs.

International precedents show it is right and realistic, international opinion and politics makes it a matter of great practical importance for Australia's external relations, and the international repercussions of racial conflict make it vitally important that Australia set its internal race relations on a proper footing before racial strife spreads to Australian shores.

Are questions of morality and national interest to determine the issue, or are we going to be swayed by a few vested interests?

128. Milirrpum and Others v Nabalco Pty Ltd and Commonwealth of Australia, Supreme Court of the Northern Territory. Amended statement of claim, 16 March 1970

"1. (a) The Plaintiff Milirrpum is the head of the Rirratjingu clan of the Australian aboriginal natives and brings this action on behalf of himself and other members of that clan.

(b) The Plaintiff Munggurrawuy is the head of the Gumatj clan of the Australian aboriginal natives and brings this action on behalf of himself and other members of that clan.

(c) The Plaintiff Daymbalipu is the head of the Djapu clan of the Australian aboriginal natives and brings this action on behalf of himself, those other members of that clan, and those members of the following clans of Australian aboriginal natives, namely the Marrakuli, Galpu, Munyuku, Ngamil, Wangurri, Djambarrpuyngu,

Manggalili, Dhalwangu, Warramirri and Madarrpa clans, who normally reside on the land in the Melville Bay to Port Bradshaw area of the Northern Territory commonly referred to as the Gove Peninsula.

"2. Nabalco Pty. Ltd. is and was at all material times a body corporate capable of being sued in its own name.

"3. The aforesaid aboriginal clans are groups of natives, each group or clan being bound together by common patrilineal descent from early ancestors, each child at birth becoming a member to the clan to which its father belongs.

"4. Pursuant to the laws and customs of the aboriginal native inhabitants of the Northern Territory, each clan holds certain communal lands. The interest of each member of the clan in such communal lands is a proprietary interest and is a joint interest with each other member of the clan. Each such individual interest arises at birth and continues until death.

"5. Pursuant to the said laws and customs, the interest of each clan in the land which it holds is inalienable and its incidents include—

(a) the right to occupy and move freely about the said lands;

(b) the right to exclude others from the said lands;

(c) the right to live off the waters and the plant and animal life of the said lands;

(d) the right to dig for and use the flints, clays and other useful minerals in the said lands; and

(e) the right to dispose of any products in or of the land by trade or ritual exchange.

"6. Pursuant to the said laws and customs, the Rirratjingu and the Gumatj clans hold and exercise the said rights over, and have from time immemorial held and exercised the said rights over, all that land comprising a peninsula generally North of Port Bradshaw and East of Melville Bay in the Northern Territory and commonly referred to as the Gove Peninsula. The whole of the land referred to is hereinafter called 'the said land'. Further particulars in the form of a map showing the approximate boundaries of the areas held by the said clans respectively will be supplied before the hearing of this action.

"7. Until the happening of the events referred to in paragraph 28 hereof, the Rirratjingu and Gumatj clans had remained in quiet and undisturbed possession of their respective portions of the said land.

"8. In or about the year 1788 the British Crown asserted sovereignty over much of the Eastern and Central parts of the Australian continent, including the said land.

"9. By reason of the matters referred to in paragraph 8 hereof the ultimate or radical title to the said land became vested in the British Crown. However, the proprietary interests of the Gumatj and Rirratjingu clans, referred to in paragraphs 4, 5 and 6 hereof, remained undisturbed and were and are recognized by the common law of England and Australia.

"10. In order to extinguish the aforesaid proprietary interest of the said clans it would have been necessary for the Crown—

(a) to obtain their consent;

(b) further or alternatively, to pay compensation;

(c) further or alternatively, to extinguish the said interests by express enactment or other act of state.

"11. The said clans have at no time consented to the extinction of their said respective interests in the said land.

"12. The said clans have at no time received any compensation for the extinction of their said respective interests in the said land.

"13. No enactment or other act of state has ever extinguished the said interests of the said clans either expressly or by necessary implication.

"14. Alternatively to paragraphs 9-13 hereof the said clans acquired title to the said land by possession adverse to the Crown by reason of the fact that they exclusively occupied and intended to possess their respective portions of the said land from 1788 for a period in excess of 60 years.

"15. Further or alternatively to paragraphs 9-14 hereof, by Letters made Patent by King William the Fourth on the 19th February, 1836 whereby South Australia was erected into a province, it was provided in the proviso to the Letters Patent, 'that nothing in these our Letters Patent contained shall affect or be construed to affect the rights of any Aboriginal Natives of the said Province to the actual occupation or enjoyment in their own persons or in the persons of their descendants of any lands therein now actually occupied or enjoyed by such Natives'. The said proviso operated within South Australia as an order under the authority of, or having the force and effect of, an Act of the Imperial Parliament ...

"28. Nabalco Pty. Ltd. has wrongfully entered the said land with bulldozers, excavators, trucks and other machinery and a number of servants and workmen and broken down the native bush, erected structures, taken valuable bauxite ores, destroyed or damaged plant life and destroyed or driven away animal life (on both of which the persons referred to in paragraph 1 hereof depend for their food, art beliefs and way of life) and violated sacred areas and objects of the Rirratjingu and Gumatj clans. Particulars of the said sacred areas and objects will be supplied before the trial of this action ...

"34. By reason of the matters herein alleged the secondnamed defendant had and has no interest in the said land enabling it effectively to grant any leases or other rights over the said land in pursuance of the said Ordinance or agreement ...

"And The Plaintiffs Claim:—

(i) Damages against the Defendant Nabalco Pty. Limited.

(ii) An Injunction to restrain Nabalco Pty. Limited from repeating or continuing any of the acts complained of.

(iii) A Declaration that the abovenamed clans are entitled to the occupation and enjoyment of the said land free from interference.

(iv) A Declaration that the Minerals (Acquisition) Ordinance 1953-1954 is *ultra vires* and void in so far as it purports to have compulsorily acquired for the Crown in right of the Commonwealth bauxite ores and other minerals as defined in that Ordinance, existing in their natural condition in the Northern Territory.

(v) A Declaration in the terms of paragraph 34 above.

(vi) Such further or other orders as the Court may think fit."

129. Yolngu Statement in the Gupapunyngu Language, presented in Canberra to William McMahon, Prime Minister, 6 May 1971

Translation

The people of Yirrkala have asked us to speak to you on their behalf. They are deeply shocked at the result of the recent Court case. We cannot be satisfied with anything less than ownership of the land. The land and law, the sacred places, songs, dances and language were given to our ancestors by spirits Djangkawu and Barama. We are worried that without the land future generations could not maintain our culture. We have the right to say to anybody not to come to our country. We gave permission for one mining company but we did not give away the land. The Australian law has said that the land is not ours. This is not so. It might be right legally but morally it's wrong. The law must be changed. The place does not belong to white man. They only want it for the money they can make.

They will destroy plants, animal life and the culture of the people.

The people of Yirrkala want:

1. Title to our land.
2. A direct share of all royalties paid by Nabalco.
3. Royalties from all other businesses on the Aboriginal Reserves.
4. No other industries to be started without consent of the Yirrkala Council.
5. Land to be included in our title after mining is finished.

Signed R. Marika, Daymbalipu Mununggurr, W. Wunungmurra

130. The Gurindji Blues, written by Ted Egan and sung by Egan and Galarrwuy Yunupingu, introduction by Vincent Lingiari, RCA Records, 1971

My name be Vincent Lingiari, came from Daguragu, Wattie Creek Station. [Speaks in Gurindji.] That mean that I came down 'ere to ask all this [fella] here about the land right. What I got, story from my old father or grandpa, that land belong to me, belong to Aboriginal man before the horse and the cattle come over on that land, why I'm sittin' now. Well, that's what I bin keepin' on my mind. Now, I still got it on my mind. That's all the word I can tell you.

Poor bugger me
Gurindji
Me bin sit down this country
Long time before Lord Vestey
Allabout land belongin' to we
Poor bugger me
Gurindji

Poor bugger blackfeller this country
Long time work no wages we
Work for good old Lord Vestey
Little bit plour, chugar and tea
For Gurindji
From Lord Vestey
O poor bugger me

Poor bugger me
Gurindji
My name Vincent Lingiari
Me talk about allabout Gurindji
Daguragu place for we
Home for we
Gurindji

But poor bugger blackfeller this country
Gov'ment boss him talk long we
Build you house with electricity
But at Wave Hill for can't you see
Wattie Creek belong to Lord Vestey
O poor bugger me

Poor bugger me
Lingiari
Still me talk long Gurindji
Daguragu place for we
Home for we
Gurindji

Poor bugger me
Gurindji
Up come Mr Prank Hardy
ABSCHOL too and talk long we
Givit hand long Gurindji
Buildim house and plantim tree
Long Wattie Creek for Gurindji

But poor bugger blackfeller this country
Gov'ment law him talk long we
Can't givit land long blackfeller see
Only spoilim Gurindji
O poor bugger me
Gurindji

Poor bugger me
Gurindji
Peter Nixon talk long we

Buy you own land Gurindji
Buyim back from Lord Vestey
O poor bugger me
Gurindji

Poor bugger blackfeller Gurindji
Spose we buyim back country
What you reckon proper fee
Might be plour, chugar and tea
from Gurindji
to Lord Vestey
O poor bugger me

Black Power and Aboriginal identity

131. *Churinga*, February 1968. New National Group Urged For Aborigines

A conference of Aboriginal leaders has decided to seek the establishment of a new national organisation for Aborigines.

In a statement issued yesterday, they condemned the Federal Council for the Advancement of Aborigines and Torres Strait Islanders as not representative of Aborigines *or genuine Aboriginal opinion.*

The statement said the aim of the new association would be to allow Aborigines national expression.

Election

The conference, held in Sydney on Friday, was called by *Pastor Doug Nicholls*, of Victoria, *Miss Maude Tongarie*, of South Australia, and *Mr. Charles Perkins*, of Sydney, manager of the Foundation for Aboriginal Affairs.

It was attended by 35 Aborigines *from all States* representing various Aboriginal organisations.

The new organisation, if formed, will be called the *National Aboriginal Affairs Association*.

The conference recommended a sub-committee be formed to investigate the possibility of establishing the organisation.

It also resolved that no member of the council should have been elected to office without reference to its general body or to the Aboriginal people.

"This had happened in recent weeks," the statement said, "with the election of *Mrs. Faith Bandler as general secretary, Mr. Clive Williams as State secretary, and Mr. Jack Horner as national co-ordinator.*"

The statement said a second conference of Aboriginal leaders *would be held in Canberra soon and submit recommendations to the Prime Minister, Mr. Gorton.*

Last night Mr. Perkins said the council was "incompetent".

"It does not truly represent the Aboriginal people *as was originally intended,*" he added.

132. Kath Walker, 'Black-White Coalition Can Work', *Origin*, 18 September 1969

When the Federal Council for the Advancement of Aborigines and Torres Strait Islanders was formed in 1958, it was expected to be a fighting organisation, consisting of Aborigines and white Australians who would work together with such allies as they could influence on the national scene.

It was to be a coalition in the interest of Aborigines' and Torres Strait Islanders' advancement.

Unfortunately, the coalition today is seen as 'patting on the backs' of selected Aborigines (selected by whites) whom they call leaders.

Aborigines have never recognised all the top black Australians as their leaders. White people in the movement have always dictated to the black Australians.

Looking back, the only major improvement has been the 93% 'Yes' vote of the referendum of May 1967; but this improvement did not benefit the black Australians though it eased the guilty conscience of white Australians in this country and overseas.

It can be regarded therefore as a victory for white Australians who formed the coalition with black Australians. Black Australians must be seen as stooges of the white Australians working in the interest of white Australians.

If black Australians are to become masters of their own destiny, white Australians must recognise them as being capable of formulating their own policy of advancement ...

White Australians must understand that what is good for them does not necessarily follow as being good for black Australians ...

Most white Australians, even those who attempt to communicate and cooperate with black Australians, do not see racial inequality in the same way as black Australians do ...

The political and social rights of black Australians have been and always will be negotiable and expendable wherever they conflict with the interests of the white Australians ...

As long as black Australians remain politically dependent upon white political machines, their interests will be secondary to those machines.

White Australians establish their own goals and demand that black Australians identify with them. When black reformers begin to expound theories and goals in the interest of their people, whites decry them as being ambitious ...

These reformers are classed as being unacceptable by the white Australians and they define them as being of no use to their own people. White Australians feel they are better judges than the black Australians in selecting black leaders.

133. Charles Perkins, letter to the editor, *Australian*, 8 April 1968

I would like to enlighten E.J. Smith, who asked in a letter to *The Australian* on March 27 why part-Aboriginal people such as myself identify as Aboriginals.

Firstly we were usually born on Mission Stations, Government Reserves or shanty towns. We received aid only as far as it was convenient for the white people. We were therefore identifiable to ourselves as well as white people as "the Aboriginals".

Secondly we were related by kinship, blood and cultural ties to our full-blood parents or grandparents. This tie can never be broken merely because the degree of "blood" may vary, or if white authority or individuals wish it so. An example of this is the Northern Territory where before 1956 an Aboriginal was any person with one drop of Aboriginal blood in his veins—the definition was reversed by law only some ten years ago. Very convenient for the lawmakers, but imagine its affect on the Aboriginal family. Aboriginals are not like white people. They love their children, whatever shade. Generally, in the past, the white people never really wanted us. When they did it was usually on their terms for sexual, economic or paternal reasons.

Thirdly many thousands of our people were forced to carry passes—much like passports—if ever we wished to mix in the white community. This carried our photograph, plus character references. We were labelled as fit and proper Aboriginals to associate with

white people. I was one of the few Aboriginals in Adelaide who refused to carry a pass or "dog ticket" as we called it. All my life, before I graduated from the University of Sydney, I was categorised by
law and socially as an Aboriginal. Now that I have graduated I am
suddenly transformed by people such as Smith, into a non-
Aboriginal.

This conveniently puts me into a situation where I must, according to official assimilation policy, forget my people, my background,
my former obligations. I am now "white." I therefore am not supposed to voice an opinion on the scandalous situation Aboriginal
people are in nor am I entitled to speak any longer as a "legal Aboriginal." All this because I have received my degree and am in a position to voice an opinion. Or could it be that I, and others like me,
could influence the unacceptable social-racial status quo in Australia?

Fourthly there can be no real comparison between a nationality
and race. A nationality is a mere political or geographic distinction
between people. Race on the other hand goes much further into the
biological (color) and cultural (kinship, customs, attitudes) field.

The Aboriginal people in Australia today— full-blood and part
blood— do not want the sympathy of white people with an attitude
such as Smith's. We have had enough of this in the past.

What we want is good education, respect, pride in our ancestry,
more job opportunities and understanding.

It seems people such as Smith carry a guilt complex of past mis-
treatment, and would want to now stop the truth from being revealed, and hence control Aboriginal advancement.

If Australians would delve into our social history in a truthful
manner they would be horrified at the result of the investigation.

The story is not a nice one and Aboriginals have suffered as a
consequence.

All our lives Aboriginals have lived in a secondary position to the
white Australian.

I no longer wish for this situation. Therefore I, and approximately 250,000 others like me, claim our ancestry. We are Aboriginal Australians— proud of our country and our race.

134. Neville Bonner, President, OPAL, letter to the editor, *Courier Mail*, 25 September 1969

Opal disassociates itself from Mrs Kath Walker's brand of Black
Power, that which used solely as a disruptive tactic.

Opal however firmly believes in the type of creative power which unites with force, God given existing in each and every Queenslander regardless of color, to work towards good, for the benefit of all those living within our State.

135. Victorian Aborigines Advancement League, Statement on Black Power, 1969

To use the words of Jean-Paul Satre [Sartre], "Not so very long ago, the earth numbered two thousand million inhabitants: five hundred million men, and one thousand five hundred million natives".

That is white power.

Since the end of World War II, many of the coloured peoples who live under white colonial rule have gained their independence and coloured minorities in multi-racial nations are claiming the right to determine the course of their own affairs in contradiction to the inferior state under which they had lived.

That is black power.

Black power is not one single style of action. It does not necessarily mean violence or black supremacy, although in some expressions it has used violence and sought black supremacy. Those expressions have gained publicity because of their dramatic nature.

Black power also means what Dr. Barrie Pittock has described, as follows: "The Black Power idea in essence is that black people are more likely to achieve freedom and justice for themselves by working together as a group, pursuing their goals by the same processes of democratic action as any other common-interest pressure group such as returned servicemen or chambers of commerce. Up to this point Black Power is hardly controversial, and the idea, whether known by that name or not, is widely accepted amongst Aborigines who are active in their own cause."

In fact, several expressions of that kind of black power can be seen, in which Victorian Aborigines are involved. The take-over of the Easter conference of the Federal Council for the Advancement of Aborigines and Torres Strait Islanders by the Aboriginal delegates was one. The Victorian Aboriginal Tribal Council is another. The United Council of Aboriginal Women is another.

The Aborigines Advancement League supports the principle of black power, without necessarily condoning all the ways by which it expresses itself in various parts of the world, or indeed, in Australia.

It is inevitable and healthy that there will be differences in the ways Aboriginal people understand black power and in the methods which they are prepared to use to obtain their ends. The League is able to provide a forum where all views can be discussed.

The League exists for the benefit of Aboriginal people. Its Aboriginal members are in a position to tell the League what it should be and do to best serve the interests of the Aboriginal people. Its non-Aboriginal members will stand back while those decisions are being made, and will work to put them into effect in collaboration with the Aboriginal members.

136. Dulcie Flower, Harriet Ellis, Faith Bandler, Ken Brindle and Pastor Frank Roberts, 'Why we believe that Aborigines and Islanders should have allies in their fight for rights and advancement', 1 March 1970

Dr. A. Barrie Pittock, convener legislative reform committee of FCAATSI has circulated a statement which he calls *"Why I believe only Aborigines and Islanders should decide FCAATSI policies"*.

In putting his views before a wide group of people, Dr. Pittock did not consult one Aboriginal or Islanders Member of the Fccatsi Executive. He may be falling into the trap he warns Aborigines and Islanders about— paternalism!

Wouldn't it have been more considerate to leave this issue to be debated, in the first place, by the All Aboriginal Session of the Federal Conference?

That may have been a mistake and a mistake understandable from one in Victoria where Aborigines are few in number.

There are other points raised in Mr. Pittock's appeal that need the views of people of Aboriginal and Island descent.

FCAATSI came into existence as a forum and common front of black and white people who *opposed the destruction of aboriginal rights*. It did not come into existence, as he says, "to help, represent and speak for Aborigines and Islanders" nor to "decide what is good for them". It represented an attempt to unite *white organisations supporting Aboriginal rights with Aborigines and Islanders demanding those rights*. FCAATSI has opposed racialism, whether it be black or white.

Whom did it unite?

Many church groups that did not accept the old ideas of mission-owned and mission-controlled Aborigines and Islanders.

Many trade unions that called for *equal rights and advancement* for Aborigines and Islanders with people of European descent.

Many individual Australians of Aboriginal and European descent who supported *equality in all things for Aborigines.*

Some of the student organisations, particularly within the NUAUS and its scholarship body ABSCHOL.

Some Federal and State Parliamentarians who raised the demands of FCAATSI in the Parliaments of Australia.

The emphasis was always on *uniting the greatest number of white organisations with aboriginal and islander organisations to win the demands of the rights and advancement movement.*

None of the policy-decisions of FCAATSI have ever asked for or sought to achieve one thing of benefit to white organisations. Could an all-black organisation have achieved what has been achieved? Could what has been achieved have been achieved without a multi-racial organisation?

Dr. Pittock refers to the Conference which FCAATSI called in November last on Aboriginal Power, Rights and Advancement. What did that conference show and what did FCAATSI Federal Executive set out to do as a result of it?

It said that white control of Aboriginal Areas like Palm Island and hundreds of others through the North should be ended. Who controls them? FCAATSI or the Federal and State Governments?

The conference said most of the Northern Territory should go to the control and ownership of the Aborigines.

Who controls it and disposes of it to overseas interests? The Federal Government, not FCAATSI and its affiliates.

It is only through the unity between Aborigines and Islanders and supporting white organisations that the rights and advancement of Aborigines has *any hope at all.*

Some may see the future in State and Federal Governments handing out what seem large sums of money to Aborigines in organisations.

What has that to do with the problems of the hundred thousand Aborigines *who won't be employed and supported by the state and federal government?*

What about the Queensland Wages Trust Fund?

What about Aboriginal land ownership?

What about Northern Territory Wards Ordinance? Wage Rates?

What about the health problems?

What about the housing problems? etc [...]

137. Kath Walker, 'Oration' (poem), presented to FCAATSI for use at Parliament House, Canberra, 27 March 1970

Here, at the invaders talk-talk place,
We, who are the strangers now,
Come with sorrow in our hearts.
The Bora Ring, the Corroborrees,
The sacred ceremonies,
Have gone. All gone.
Turned to dust on the land,
That once was ours.
Oh spirits from the unhappy past,
Hear us now.
We come, not to disturb your rest.
We come, to mourn your passing.
You, who paid the price,
When the invaders spilt your blood.
Your present generation comes,
Seeking strength and wisdom in your memory.
The legends tell us,
When our race dies,
So too, dies the land.
May your spirits go with us
From this place.
May the Mother Of Life,
Wake from her sleeping,
And lead us on to the happy life,
That once was ours.
Oh Mother Of Life,
Oh spirits from the unhappy past,
Hear the cries of your unhappy people,
And let it be so.
Oh spirits— Let it be so.

138. National Tribal Council, Policy Manifesto, adopted 13 September 1970

Preamble:
    We representatives of the Aboriginal and Islander peoples of Aus-

tralia reaffirm our pride in our own history, culture, and achievements as peoples. Our peoples have been shamefully treated at the hands of white settlers and governments right up to the present day. This had led to the degradation, dispossession, and pauperisation of many of our people. Despite this, we are proud of our race, and of the many achievements of our people, in their adversity.

Today we assert our right to stand in full economic, legal, and social equality beside white Australians, with whom we wish to live in peace and harmony. We solemnly commit ourselves to the struggle to achieve such equality and justice. In this struggle we welcome allies, but not masters.

We stand for self-reliance. We hope for aid both morally and financially, but cannot be dependent on it. We depend on our own efforts, on the united stance of our own people.

Towards these ends we assert the need for the following broad policies to be adopted and implemented by the Australian people and their governments.

1. Federal Responsibility and Action:

In view of the abject failure of the various state and Northern Territory administrations to mete out economic, legal, and social justice to our people, we assert that the time has come for the Federal Government to use its constitutional power to legislate on behalf of Aborigines and Islanders throughout Australia, so as to implement the policies being developed by the Commonwealth Office of Aboriginal Affairs. We want an indigenous national administration, elected by the indigenous people of Australia, and responsible for the administration of all government monies to be spent on Aboriginal and Islander Affairs.

Towards this end we call for the immediate setting up of an all-party Standing Committee of Federal Parliament to enquire into the needs and aspirations of the Aboriginal and Islander people of Australia with power to recommend all necessary legislative and Constitutional changes. We pledge to work towards the election of direct Aboriginal representation at both Federal and State levels.

2. Land and Mineral Rights:

We call on the Federal Government to adopt immediately a policy of full recognition of the right of Aborigines and Islanders to the ownership of their traditional land, of just compensation for all land taken from them, and for royalties to be paid to those communities which are affected by mining, forestry, or any other outside exploitation of their land and culture. All land upon which Aboriginal and Islander communities still reside or with which they still have traditional links, should be returned to them. Compensation must be paid for all other land. We see this as the only just and politically feasible way of avoiding the future pauperisation of the Aboriginal and Islander people, and of obtaining the capital necessary for their economic development.

We further call for the effective and absolute protection of all sacred sites and objects of the Aboriginal and Islander peoples.

We recognise that some of these things are being done already in some areas, usually as the result of specific protests or politically embarrassing revelations, but call on the Federal Government to ensure that in future these things are done automatically in all areas, as a matter of established general policy.

3. Education:

Results of a recent study of the 1966 Census statistics show that Aborigines enter school later, progress slower, quit sooner, and terminate at a lower level than white Australians. The Aboriginal population as a whole, and despite equal ability, is inadequately educated to cope with an agricultural economy of the late 19th century, much less an industrial economy of the late 20th century such as is being forced upon them.

This has an enormously bad effect on the whole network of Aboriginal life, opportunities and achievements.

The time has come for a massive attack on all the factors leading to this unsatisfactory situation. This is one of the first tasks for an elected indigenous national administration which can be expected to take into account the cultural differences involved, and the need to develop an educational pattern appropriate to the Aboriginal and Islander background needs and desires.

4. Consultation and Power:

The avowed Australian policies of "consultation" with Aborigines and Islanders, while still in embryonic form, are meaningless and useless unless white decision makers are prepared to give credence to what Aborigines and Islanders say is in *their* best interests. So-called "consultations" which fail to materially affect policies and decisions are farcical and counter-productive.

Aboriginal and Islander Councils, or other legally incorporated

Aboriginal and Islander bodies, should be given actual policy-making and administrative roles, including the management of real and financial resources, economic development and planning. Such roles must involve real power to make decisions and to act upon them. It is only when this is done that Aborigines and Islanders as a whole will become independent and self-supporting members of the Australian community.

At the national and state levels this can best be done by the formation of elected indigenous national and state administrations, as outlined in Section 1, which will take over the functions of the present State and Federal Aboriginal administrations.

5. Legal Aid and Protection:

Aborigines and Islanders in Australia need more lawyers than welfare officers. The time has come for the formation and encouragement of legal incorporation within Aboriginal and Islander communities for their greater protection and bargaining power. There is a great need here for financial, technical, and legal assistance both from the Federal Government and from voluntary agencies both within Australia and from abroad.

It should no longer be possible for petty officials, mining companies, or others to push Aboriginals and Islanders off their land or otherwise deprive them of their rights. Where the rights of Aborigines and Islanders are at stake, lawyers should intervene to ensure that justice is done. So-called "gentlemen's agreements" are not good enough.

Amongst the rights in desperate need of protection are the rights of public access and freedom of movement and association on reserves, missions, settlements, and particularly in company towns such as Weipa (Qld.) and Yirrakala/Nhulumbuy (N.T.) where at present the white administrations can obstruct or remove any person they find to be objectionable irrespective of the wishes of the Aborigines and Islanders who live there.

A Federal law prohibiting all forms of racial discrimination is urgently required both as an indication of the commitment of the Australian people to racial equality and as a practical measure designed to discourage and overcome individual instances of discrimination and prejudice.

6. Health:

There is abundant, well-documented evidence of a tremendously high level of Aboriginal ill-health. Infant mortality and morbidity rates rank amongst the worst in the world. Emergence as a thriving community is not possible with such a deadening burden of ill-health.

Emergency nutritional, medical, housing and public health measures are urgently necessary. It is not good enough for administrators to take refuge in the common excuse that "we are doing further research" (however desirable that may be) while yet another generation is decimated and invalided by death and disability.

We do not want to see more of our people killed or crippled by disease. We demand that this genocide should cease at all costs.

7. Employment:

Past Government policies have ensured that the Aborigines and Islanders as peoples, are too poorly educated to obtain decent jobs. White authorities on Aboriginal communities have consistently failed to provide adequate vocational training.

We therefore demand that an extensive and adequately financed and effective On the Job training programme using Aborigines and Islander staff be set up for all Aborigines and Islanders who wish to participate. Where industries or technical colleges are set up in areas heavily populated by Aborigines or Islanders, preferential employment should be given to the local indigenous inhabitants, and training schemes provided where necessary.

We further demand that full award wages be paid to all Aborigines and Islanders regardless of where they live and work. Discrimination against Aborigines and Islanders in employment is widespread in Australia and we call for an end to this discrimination.

Where necessary finance must be provided to ensure meaningful employment in areas where Aborigines and Islanders live.

8. Cultural Pluralism:

Australian governmental policies of lip service to the worth and value of Aboriginal and Islander traditions and culture should be made a reality by encouraging, not discouraging, programmes, seminars, and courses which aim at the re-acculturation of Aborigines and Islanders. There is a growing desire by many people of Aboriginal and Islander descent for study programmes which will teach them what they need to know in order to find their true identities as Aboriginal and Islander Australians.

Governments must abandon the failed policy of assimilation which amounts to cultural genocide and encourage the growing desire for bi-culturalism in a genuine and voluntary plural society.

If Aborigines and Islanders decide that the maintenance and development of voluntary and distinctive Aboriginal and Islander cultures and communities is in their own best interests, this decision should be accepted, respected, and encouraged by white Australians. Freedom and equality cannot otherwise be realities in Australia.

This is not to say that we are advocating the complete return to a semi-nomadic hunting and food-gathering economy, which is clearly not possible on a large scale, but that modern adaptations of traditional cultures are possible even though they may not coincide with the white Australian culture in all respects.

9. Freedom from Prejudice and Discrimination:

We call on all Australian governments to ensure that steps are taken to eliminate racial prejudice from all school text-books and curricula, and to ensure that text-books and curricula are developed and used which will engender mutual respect and understanding between the races while taking fully into account their differing cultures and history. All materials relating to Aborigines and Islanders in all formal education curricula should be subject to the scrutiny and approval of a board composed of Aboriginal and Islander people.

Racial discrimination in all existing laws and in all public activities and pursuits must be eliminated by effective Federal and State legislation as soon as possible.

10. Justice and the Rule of Law:

The administration of justice in the courts, and the rule of law on settlements, mission stations, and in company towns, should be in accordance with the standards laid down by the United Nations Organisation and its agencies, and by the International Commission of Jurists. In particular, defendants should have the effective right to legal representation by independent lawyers, and must be made fully aware of their legal rights and of the details of legal proceedings in the courts in a language in which they are fluent, even if this requires the presence of trained interpreters.

For too long people have been bewildered by legal jargon in an unfamiliar language, and had pleas of "guilty" entered for them by their so-called "protectors". Such proceedings make a mockery of the law and must be stopped. We call on the International Commission of Jurists to report on Aborigines, Islanders, and the rule of law, as it has done so effectively in other countries where similar conditions prevail.

139. Black Panthers of Australia, Platform and Programme, 1970

What We Want
What We Believe

1. We want freedom. We want power to determine the destiny of our Black Community. We believe that Black people will not be free until we are able to determine our destiny.

2. We want full employment for our people. We believe that the federal government is responsible and obligated to give every man employment or a guaranteed income. We believe that if the white Australian businessmen will not give full employment, then the means of production should be taken from the businessman and placed in the community so that the people of the community can organise and employ all of its people and give a high standard of living.

3. We want an end to the robbery by the white man of our Black Community. We believe that this racist Government has robbed us and now we are demanding restitution for the armed robbery of our land, which is the social, culture and economic base of any people. We will accept land and mineral rights for the existing black communities, and monetary restitution for those dispossessed victims. The Germans are now aiding the Jews in Israel for the genocide [of] the Jewish people. The Germans murdered 6 million Jews. The Australian racist has taken part in the slaughter of over a quarter of a million Black People (This entails 75% of the total population and total genocide of Tasmanian Blacks). We feel that as the number of Jews murdered represented only a small portion of the Jewish population as compared with the significant attempted genocide of the black people of this country, we feel that it is a modest demand that we make.

4. We want decent housing, fit for shelter of human beings. We believe that if the white landlords will not give decent housing to our black community, then the housing and the land should be made into co-operatives so that our community, with government aid, can build and make decent housing for its people.

5. We want education for our people that exposes the true nature of this decadent Australian society. We want education that teaches us our true history and our role in the present-day society. We be-

lieve in an educational system that will give to our people a knowledge of self. If a man does not have knowledge of himself and his position in society and the world, then he has little chance to relate to anything else.

6. We want all black men to be exempt from military service. We believe that Black people should not be forced to fight in the military service to defend a racist government that does not protect us. We will not fight and kill other people of colour in the world who, like black people, are well victimized by the white racist government of Australia. We will protect ourselves from the force and violence of the racist police and the racist military, by whatever means necessary.

7. We want an immediate end to *police brutality, murder & rape of black* people. We believe we can end police brutality in our black community from racist police oppression and brutality. There is a need to make policemen out of the "Pigs" that are presently acting as law enforcement agencies. It's only way that this can be done is to give the communities control of the *police*. Without this the *"pigs"* will continue to be used as tools of the Fascists system. When the Government becomes a law breaker the people must become the law-enforcers.

8. We want freedom for all black men held in prisons and jails. We believe that all black people should be released from the many jails and prisons because they have not received a fair and impartial trial.

9. We want all black people when brought to trial to be tried in court by a jury of their peer group or people from their black communities. We believe that the courts should follow the Law. The Law gives a man the right to be tried by his peer group. A peer is a person from a similar economic, social, religious, geographical, environmental, historical and racial background. To do this the court will be forced to select a jury from the black community from which the black defendant came. We have been, and are being tried by all-white juries that have understanding of the "average reasoning man" of the black community.

10. We want land, bread, housing, education, clothing, justice and peace. And as our major political objective, a United Nations-supervised plebiscite to be held throughout the black colony in which only black colonial subjects will be allowed to participate, for the purpose of determining the will of black people as to their national destiny. When, in the course of human events, it becomes

necessary for one people to dissolve the political bands which have connected them with another, and to assume, among the powers of the earth, the separate and equal station to which the laws of nature and nature's God entitle them, a decent respect to the opinion of mankind requires that they should declare the causes which impel them to the separation. We hold these truths to be self-evident, that all men are created equal; that they are endowed by their Creator with certainness. That, to secure these rights, from the consent of the governed; that, whenever any form of government becomes destructive of these ends, it is the right of the people to alter or to abolish it and to institute a new government, laying its foundation on such principles, and most likely to effect their safety and happiness. Prudence, indeed will dictate that governments long established should not be all changed for light and transient causes; and, accordingly, suffer, while evils are sufferable, than to right themselves by abolishing the forms to which they are accustomed. But when a long train of abuses and usurpations pursing invariably the same object, evinces a design to reduce them under absolute despotism, it is their right, it is their duty, to throw off such government, and to provide new guards for their furture security.

140. *Australian*, 5 December 1971. Simon Townsend Talks To The Leaders Of The Black Panthers

... Two leaders of the Black Panther Party, known as field marshals, are Gary Foley, 21 and Paul Coe, 23. They claim a membership of about 30.

Foley and a third field marshal who asked to remain anonymous, talked freely with *The Sunday Australian* last week. They are uncompromising and dogmatic, but intelligent, articulate and intense.

Foley, married, says he has not worked for two years and would not divulge his source of income. He was a draughtsman: "But every job I had they would stick me up the front where everyone fell over me—I was the token Aboriginal." He spends much of his time now involved with the Aboriginal Legal Service and Medical Service at Redfern, Sydney.

"We're going to train a select group in urban guerilla tactics and use of explosives. We'll be ready to move in a month, and then all hell will break loose" ...

Won't you attract people interested solely in violence?

"You've got to expect that," Foley says. "But the re-education usually sorts that kind out."

Women play a key part in the party. "In the tribal culture everyone had a specific role. If someone fell down on their role, the whole system fell down. This is more or less the system we operate within the party."

Who would be unsuitable?

The third field marshal says: "Someone who's in it for kicks, thrills, who's got an ulterior motive like publicity or getting a few birds. It's a very disciplined party. People who don't face up to the discipline are generally sifted out."

Recruits see films, hear lectures and are given books to read, then they are asked to discuss them at a subsequent meeting. New recruit meetings are held about once a month in a house in Redfern. The re-education programme takes about three nights a week for the month.

The Panthers consider their enemies to be white society at large, Aboriginal Uncle Toms, the Nazi Party (from whom they fear violence) and white radical groups (who would use them for their own purposes).

Foley says "We don't like the Communist Party, although we're friendly with a few individual communists. They're fighting a class struggle, but we are not even up to that, because we're fighting for survival as a black race.

"The Australian Government has reduced Aboriginals to the same level as flora and fauna by saying we belong to the land, but the land doesn't belong to us. We want land rights now and then the black man can assimilate, integrate or live separately. But he must be able to choose for himself," Foley adds.

The Black Panthers claim they will bomb symbolic targets and gradually work up to more significant targets such as the property of employers and unions which discriminate against Aboriginals.

What about the backlash?

Foley says violence is natural to an Aboriginal because he has been subject to it from birth: "Violence is their means of survival. All the Black Panther Party is doing is utilising and redirecting this violent feeling.

"When we go into action the government is going to get off its behind and do something, not publicly because that would be admitting they're bowing to the pressures of radicals. But changes will come, quietly and subtly."

The anonymous field marshal says publicity is important to the cause. "Mainly we need coverage overseas because the Australian Press will never give the Aboriginal a fair go. We look to overseas because it's the only way of embarrassing this bloody government into doing something."

He says Aboriginals identified with the American Indian. But they took the American name Black Panther for the glamor surrounding it. A party committee is now working on finding a fully Aboriginal name and symbol ...

They don't have any rule, like the American Panthers, forbidding fraternisation with whites. Foley adds "we do have a very strict ruling that no one be drunk or on drugs when carrying out party work."

No white can join because, says Foley, no white could understand the experiences of a black man in a white society.

Dennis Walker, son of Aboriginal poet Kath Walker, is probably the foremost guiding spirit of Black Power. He arrived in Sydney from Brisbane on Thursday and leaves for Melbourne tomorrow for discussions on extending the Black Panther Party to Brisbane and Melbourne.

Walker, 25, a tall ex-sailor, was financial co-ordinator of the Aboriginal and Islanders Council in Brisbane, until its Government grant funds ran out. Walker says he has deserted his wife and four children because he can't support them. He refuses to work except with blacks or for blacks, so the Commonwealth won't pay him unemployment benefits.

He describes the Panthers as a political education and self-defence group. "Its defensive violence of the people versus oppressive violence of the system, or survival versus money," he says.

"In the United States, the people have the constitutional right to arm themselves. We can't carry guns here but the police can, which puts Aboriginals at a distinct disadvantage."

Walker sees a danger in the Panthers becoming black racist. He adds: "Going out and killing people haphazardly would make us just a terrorist group. We must be strategic."

...

141. *Age*, 28 January 1972. Natives Open 'Embassy' Of Their Own

Canberra—Three young Aborigines have set up an "Aboriginal Embassy" on the lawns opposite Parliament House to protest against the Government's decision not to grant tribal land rights. They hope about 100 Aborigines from all parts of Australia will join them in the next few weeks.

One of the Aborigines, Mike Anderson, 20, of Walgett, NSW, said yesterday the group planned to stay "indefinitely". He said: "We mean business. We will stay until the Government listens to us." Mike, who wearing a Black Power badge, is vice-chairman of the all-black NSW Aboriginal Lands Board, which seeks land ownership rights of reserves for Aborigines.

In his Australia Day statement on Aborigines the Prime Minister (Mr. McMahon) said the Government would not give Aborigines land rights on reserves based on traditional association.

Mike said the Aborigines would discuss a policy submission and put it to the Government. He predicted that the Government's decision on land rights would lead to violence.

"If we destroyed a church we'd be put in prison, but when white men destroy a spiritual place like Arnhem Land we can't put them into prison," he said. "I look to Arnhem Land as a place where we can start to dig our roots in and restore the pride of the Aboriginal culture. If they destroy that we have no place."

Notices outside Aborigines' red tent said "Why pay to use our own land?" and "Which do you choose—land rights or bloodshed?"

Mike said he was associated with "last-resort" minority organisations that would favour "getting out into the streets" and destroying something belonging to the white man if he destroyed Arnhem Land.

He said Aborigines should be compensated for all the land outside the reserves that had been taken away from them. The compensation should be used to start a trust fund so Aborigines could buy back land they wanted.

142. Aboriginal Embassy Land Rights Policy, '5 Point Policy'

We Demand
1. Full State rights to the Northern Territory under Aboriginal ownership and control with all titles to minerals, etc.
2. Ownership of all other reserves and settlements throughout Australia with all titles to minerals and mining rights.
3. The preservation of all sacred lands not included in Points 1. and 2.
4. Ownership of certain areas of certain cities with all titles to

minerals and mining rights.

5. As compensation, an initial payment of six billion dollars for all other land throughout Australia plus a percentage of the gross national income per annum.

Authorised by Aboriginal Embassy Cabinet Committee.

143. Transcript of *Monday Conference*, ABC Television, 20 March 1972

PAUL COE, a 23 year old law student and a founder of the Aboriginal Legal Service in Sydney. BOBBI SYKES, a freelance journalist and travelling delegate for the Aboriginal Embassy in Canberra. Interviewers Robert Moore, Brian White, Dominic Nagle.

...

MOORE: Miss Sykes, when we speak of land rights, what land, for which Aborigines, where are we talking about? In other words, what do we mean by land rights?

SYKES: I think the acknowledgement of land rights of the people who were here pre-existing before Cook arrived. The people who already are still in their own areas want the land titles to those areas, that's the missions and the reserves. The number one demand on the policy from the Aboriginal Embassy is statehood for the Northern Territory, under preferably black leadership ...

MOORE: Mr. Coe ... supposing white Australians, or the white Australian government or whatever we say, admitted or acknowledged that it had taken Australia from the Aborigines by conquest; supposing it admitted this in whatever form, in the form of a treaty or, I don't know, a document of some kind. What in practical terms would Aborigines do then? What do you want then?

COE: Well the first thing is recognition in some form of treaty. There was a time when Aboriginal people weren't even regarded as people, more as the flora and fauna, that in fact Australia was not even a settled continent and that the British settlers had every right and every justification to come in and take over control of Australia. Now in such we want ... acknowledged ... the resistance the Aboriginal people put up to counteract the invasion of the white man. Well the treaty would acknowledge this— the resistance, the part the Aboriginal people played in combating the white man, and also the destruction of the Aboriginal society as it stood [...]

MOORE: And the claim that it acknowledges would be [...] ?

COE: Well I was getting to that point. The claim that it acknowledges that aboriginal people as such that since they've been deprived of something which they own, they should be entitled to compensation for this; but more so they should be entitled to compensation in the way that they have the right to decide how they use that compensation. So if any finance comes, or if there is land ownership now to all existing reserves both agricultural and mineral resources be controlled by the Aboriginal people themselves now. Aboriginal Trusts should be set up where the people are elected by the Aboriginal people themselves and they are given the power to decide how the money is to be used, or how the resources of the land are to be used, in the betterment of their own interest.

WHITE: Now Miss Sykes is talking in terms of the Northern Territory for this kind of development. Are you talking in the same [...]?

COE: I'm not talking exclusively in terms of the Northern Territory. I'm talking in terms of the whole of Australia. To me land rights are just as applicable here in Sydney as in the Northern Territory. Well compensation is more applicable for Sydney. In fact once the land rights are acknowledged, there is compensation paid to Aboriginal bodies, Aboriginal executive bodies, they in fact can decide where the money's to be spent. Now places like Sydney you can use the money to buy up land that exists now to develop the concept of an Aboriginal type of village, where you are in fact [...] have an Aboriginal controlled community, both politically and economically controlled community, which we are now working towards in Sydney anyhow. So regardless whether we get land rights or not we're still working towards this concept of an Aboriginal village.

WHITE: But isn't there a difference here that where Miss Sykes is talking about the association that exists between the Aborigines and the land, are you going to [...] are you working in the same area when you're talking about Sydney? An association between the Aborigines and the land in Sydney?

COE: Well let us say that the people in Sydney—you cannot say that their association with the land *is*, because their association with the land has been destroyed. They're like me—they're people who have got European blood in them and have got some European ancestry, but we are Aboriginal people as such, we still are, and will always remain that, and retain our own integrity as Aboriginal people. We want to relearn and relive [...] relearn the wisdom of our ancestors if possible, learn the cultural, the spiritual values of the Aboriginal people—our ancestors. You could use the cultural values of the old Aboriginal people to develop an Aboriginal community, but the association the old Aboriginal people once had with the land would not be applicable in a highly industrialised, urbanised society. But you could find some way of incorporating the values, the values of that particular society, so that in fact the Aboriginal people feel they have a part to play in that society, that their cultural norms as such are applicable to them as Aboriginal people [...]

...

MOORE: Miss Sykes, can we come back to your thought about the Northern Territory as a, I think you said, as a black state. Is that right? Or didn't I quite understand?

SYKES: No you misinterpreted.

MOORE: Alright, please explain it again then.

SYKES: Northern Territory under control of blacks elected by the communities in the Northern Territory.

MOORE: You mean that the Parliament of the Northern Territory [...]

SYKES: I don't mean that the whole Parliament would necessarily be black [...] you know, because this would be in itself racist. There are whites in the area entitled to vote for whoever they like. But I do think that if you had a voter registration plan carried out in the Northern Territory could certainly put quite a lot of Parliamentarians in, and they would be black.

MOORE: Now supposing that there were a majority of blacks in the Parliament of the State of whatever ... Would you expect that blacks from other parts of Australia would therefore be inclined to go and live there in great numbers, or what?

COE: You'd probably find that the Northern Territory would become equivalent to what it is [...] say Israel is now to the majority of Jews over the rest of the world. It is their spiritual homeland, in fact they've got security, even though they could be in the States, Australia [...] they take this sort of emotional kind of security from it. Some way of giving them strength because they've got some land and some society which they can claim and they can identify with, they feel an affinity with; and as such the Northern Territory could become the Aboriginal's sort of Mecca, if I could use that word.

...

MOORE: ... Miss Sykes ... What is the aim [...] for blacks to join the white society, to change it, or to opt out from it completely?

SYKES: I think that's a matter of personal choice for each and every person to make by and for themselves. But the opportunity to choose any way they want must be made available.

...

NAGLE: But if you choose this separate development [...] I mean, the great difficulty about that is this in fact exacerbates or strengthens the racial attitudes that you say you want to get rid of ...

COE: [...] we don't choose this separate development. It exists, it's a fact, and we've tried to explain it, it exists now. It's a fact, and we want that fact acknowledged. All we want to do now is to take control both of the economical, the political and cultural resources of the people and of the land, Aboriginal people and of the land, so that they themselves have got the power to determine their own future.

...

MOORE: ... what to you is black power? Let's get onto this term which is often used in this context. And I've used it earlier on. And it seems to me it has very different meanings, according to who you speak to about it ...

SYKES: I'm sorry, black power is not a word that I care to use very much.

MOORE: But it is a phrase that's used a lot, isn't it?

SYKES: It is a phrase that I think is misused in this country a lot, yes.

NAGLE: Which phrase would you prefer? Black consciousness?

SYKES: Black action, perhaps. Black people in motion.

NAGLE: What sort of action do you have in mind?

SYKES: The action that you're seeing. The embassy, people making their demands, in fact people starting to demand their rights, which hasn't happened very often in the past and which has been ignored when it has happened. I think now they're making their voices heard [...]

WHITE: What has led to this sort of feeling in Aboriginal people that has come up say in the last 18 months, 2 or 3 years? That at last perhaps white people are starting to notice it more. It might have been there a lot longer.

SYKES: I think it's only been there for a very short time. I think in the past mostly the spokesmen have been what we refer to as good niggers sponsored by whites now who've been making their comments heard and whites have been saying yes, he's a [...] what we think is a good type of black asking for things. And this is not really what we think should have occurred. Now we have a lot of young people coming up with education and not necessarily good niggers by white standards, and they are making what they want heard. I think this is only a very new thing and it has a lot to do with, I think, how much oppression there has been in the past, and people moving away from the reserves into the cities.

...

COE: ... we were just saying that the older type aboriginal leaders ... well it's like building a pyramid, they're a step below, and their time has passed, faded out. There's a time come for a new kind of action, a more positive direct action.

MOORE: Well what's that new action? Just talk about the direct action.

COE: Well, that direct action [...] well, at least the people in Sydney [...] the young group of blacks which I'm a member of is that concerted direct black action. Well we ourselves mix with our own people, know the problems of our own people, and try to find some way ourselves of trying to overcome these problems ... The direct black action that Michael Anderson and the rest of the boys at the embassy are taking, or even the kind of direct black action that Dennis Walker is playing up in Queensland; now they all have got their own fields in which to act, and they're all in doing a very important job. There is [...] all are trying to achieve, I think, possibly the same end, the self-control of communities by black people, black communities. But some of them are going about it in different ways, are advocating different methods.

MOORE: Are any of them advocating [...] here's a very white question [...] are any of them advocating violence?

COE: Well it depends what you mean by violence.

MOORE: Carrying guns.

COE: Well I think to myself [...] this is a personal opinion of course [...] I think it would be stupid for black people in Australia to carry guns because of the fact that the white people are such a majority. Now white people in the past have shown— particularly white police and the white welfare— have shown a total disregard for the feelings and aspirations of the black people. Now I see when black people in Australia pick up the guns, I would think myself that there would be no hesitation whatsoever on the part of the white power structure to wipe out these so-called black troublemakers.

WHITE: Is that not a possibility though, especially with the white reaction, especially using, also using your terminology of the pyramid, the next rung after you mightn't feel this way.

COE: Well let us say, the frustration of a generation of people being promised so much, particularly black people being promised equality and equal opportunity, let us say, and never seeing that promise become a reality, what do you offer these people? I don't know. Can you blame these people if they themselves want to take some positive control in determining the way they shall live their life. Now when you talk about violence I would like to talk about the violence, the legalised white violence that is perpetrating us black people. The legalised white violence that denies us our rights, both human, political, social rights. The classical example again is the Yirrkala people's decision, that one white man has got the sole arbitrary power to decide Aboriginal people should not be given land rights. Now that is to me violence, legalised white violence. The killing of black kids from malnutrition, that is to me white violence. You've destroyed our environment, our way of life, and you've put us in a void; cultural, economic and political void, where the people have got nowhere to go, have nowhere to fill their aspirations, and in such, they're left in a nowhere man's land where you expect them, all of a sudden, once you destroy their way of life, to compete successfully, equally in a white system against white people, on the same terms [...] that the white man [...] the most important point is that the white man dictates those terms. Now when you see these young kids like [...] for every white kid that dies from malnutrition there are six black kids. Now to me that is white violence, legalised white violence, because you deprive these kids, you are depriving these kids of a chance to live. Because the resources are available in this land, when you consider it, that per head of individual, this is perhaps one of the most wealthiest countries in the world; and when you consider that this is one of the most wealthiest countries in the world, per head of population, to me it is a scandal that there are so many aboriginal kids dying from malnutrition, that there are so many blacks living in ghettos and shanty towns, when in fact this is our land, and as such we should have some control or some [...] more or less some slice of the economic and political resources of this land, to ensure that kids, Aboriginal kids, are not dying from malnutrition. But they are dying from malnutrition—that to me is white violence. So when you talk about violence, you take into account the 200 years of suppression that the black people have had to live under, denial of our rights, that has tried to make us become imitation white men, on what absurd justification I don't know, the sort of justification that a white society is more superior and as such we've got to conform to it. Now that to me is white violence, because it denies you the right, the human right, to decide your cultural, your economic, your political beliefs.

MOORE: Well to come to black action, or black power, or whatever we call it. I mean the tactics of your political struggle now. How much does your getting what you want to get depend on instilling some degree of fear in white Australians?

SYKES: I don't know if you could consider it fear. I'd say respect would be more the word. I think that the white Australian has very little respect for the black Australian. The white Australian has got what he calls respect by violence and if we're to take a page out of his book, perhaps we will have to use violence too to achieve some degree of respect from the white man. That's the only language he understands ...

144. *Herald* (Melbourne), 20 July 1972. 120 Fight At Black 'Embassy'. Police Rip Out Tents

Canberra— About 60 police clashed with 60 aboriginals and student supporters in a wild brawl on the lawns opposite Parliament House today. Knives and a spear were drawn and police and protesters swapped punches as police carted off the aboriginal "embassy" tents. The fighting went on for 10 minutes. Eight people were arrested. Police said that four of their men had to go to hospital after being hurt in the clashes. As police tried to drive off with the tents and the arrested protesters, more people lay on the road and blocked the police vans. Hundreds of onlookers— tourists and public servants— watched the battle.

The police acted today less than 40 minutes after an ordinance banning camping on Government land had been gazetted.

The aboriginal "embassy" was set up on Australia Day— nearly six months ago.

The Minister for the Interior, Mr Hunt, said this afternoon: "The police acted with great restraint. One policeman had his arm broken and another was badly bitten" ...

Sergeant John Scougall of Canberra police said that four police were taken to Canberra Hospital. "Three policemen will have X-rays taken and the fourth is suffering from a groin injury. He was kicked," Sgt. Scougall said ...

About 60 uniformed police arrived at Parliament House at 10.40 a.m. and told the aboriginals that they were going to take down the tents ...

29. 27 January 1972: The day after Prime Minister William McMahon declared in an Australia Day speech that Aborigines would not be granted land rights, a small group of Aborigines established an 'Aboriginal Embassy' opposite Parliament House in Canberra. Michael Anderson, chairman of the NSW Aboriginal Lands Board (left of photograph), told a journalist: 'If we destroyed a church we'd be put in prison, but when white men destroy a spiritual place like Arnhem Land we can't put them into prison. I look to Arnhem Land', he explained, 'as a place where we can start to dig in our roots and restore the pride of the Aboriginal culture', adding: 'If they destroy that we have no place.' Other placards at the embassy read: 'Which do you choose—land rights or bloodshed?' *(Courtesy* Age*)*

30. & 31. On 20 July 1972 the Commonwealth government, concerned by the enormous attention the tent embassy was attracting from the international media, ordered police to remove it. This resulted in serious clashes with demonstrators, which were repeated three days later and captured by television cameras and press photographs (above). On 30 July, in a peaceful demonstration, black power advocates (below), including Roberta Sykes (fifth from left), triumphantly reestablished the tent embassy and again raised the new symbol of Aboriginal nationhood—the Aboriginal flag—before these were once more pulled down by the police. (*Courtesy Jeff Cutting Collection, AIATSIS N4540.08;* Sydney Morning Herald)

32. During Easter 1979 Aborigines near Warrnambool, in Western Victoria, blocked the entrance to Framlingham Regional Park which they claimed as 'tribal land'. Descendants of the aged Mary Clarke led the campaign to regain land which had been part of an area reserved to their people in 1861, a meagre 235 hectares of which had been granted them in 1970. Whereas need and historical association had been emphasised in their earlier campaigns, the sacred nature of the land was at the centre of the concerns being expressed by these people, who were now publicly representing themselves by their tribal name, 'Gunditjmara'. *(Courtesy* Age*)*

33. 18 April 1980: Having evicted Amax Petroleum and police from an oil drill site earlier that month, Aborigines, pictured here in buoyant mood, rallied at Noonkanbah in Western Australia to plan the next stage in a protest which had become a national symbol for the struggle for land rights. They were supported by the Kimberley Land Council, the Strelley mob—veterans of the 1946–49 stockworkers' strike and the later Pindan Co-operative in the Pilbara—and trade unionists. *(Courtesy Michael Gallagher)*

34. & 35. 26 January 1988: Aborigines from all over Australia gathered in Redfern, where they began a march through the streets of Sydney to protest the bicentenary of the white invasion. One of the leaders of the demonstration, Galarrwuy Yunupingu, described it as 'the biggest crowd' he had 'ever seen to mourn the injustice of the past'. At Mrs Macquarie's Seat on Sydney Harbour, some Aboriginal protesters erected a tent embassy, and chanted 'murderous dogs' and 'convict scum' at the passing 'First Fleet'. Others, led by Michael Mansell, staged a re-enactment of the arrival of Captain Arthur Phillip in which they repelled the invaders by overturning his rowboat and throwing him and his companions back into the sea. Meanwhile, in Phillip's homeland, Burnum Burnum was preparing to lay claim to 'this colonial outpost' on behalf of all Aborigines. *(Courtesy* Australian *and* Sydney Morning Herald*)*

36. 12 June 1988: At the Burunga festival, near Katherine in the Northern Territory, Prime Minister Bob Hawke witnessed the Pitjantjatjarra, Yolngu and other Aboriginal clans performing traditional dances which testified their 'title to the country', before Galarrwuy Yunupingu and Wenten Rubuntja, chairmen of the Northern and Central Land Councils respectively, presented him with a statement in the form of a painting which called on the Commonwealth to recognise Aboriginal rights. Hawke responded by promising to institute a process which would see 'a treaty negotiated between the Aboriginal people and the Government on behalf of all the people of Australia'. *(Courtesy* Australian*)*

37. In June 1989—seven years after they had initiated legal proceedings—Meriam (Murray Islander) plaintiffs Revd Dave Passi and Eddie Mabo (left of photo) and James Rice (far right), assisted by barrister Bryan Keon-Cohen (second right), presented their challenge to the legal fiction of *terra nullius* at the Supreme Court of Queensland in Brisbane. In 1992 the scales of justice finally tilted in the favour of the indigenous peoples of Australia when the High Court brought down its Mabo judgment, although by this time the man whose name the case had come to bear had died. *(Courtesy Trevor Graham)*

38. 21 December 1993: Lois O'Donoghue (far left), Noel Pearson (far right) and other delighted Aboriginal negotiators celebrate with Prime Minister Paul Keating the conclusion of their negotiations over the government's native title bill, having heard that support from the Greens would ensure its passage through the Senate. Pearson hailed the legislation as a 'very substantial movement in the history of this country and a first step towards eventual, ultimate reconciliation between black and white Australians'. *(Courtesy Australian)*

39. 23 December 1996: Senior Wik woman, Gladys Tybingoompa, dances outside the High Court in Canberra, after hearing its judgment that native title was not necessarily extinguished by pastoral leases. 'It is to me an historic moment', she proclaimed: 'I strongly believe that the spirits of the ancestors were with me and I was doing it for my people of the past, now and the future, and I'm a proud woman today of Cape York'. *(Courtesy* Australian*)*

40. Pat Dodson, Chairperson of the Aboriginal Reconciliation Council, reads the 'Call to the Nation' at the closing ceremony of the Council's 1997 convention, trying to sustain the spirit of this movement in the face of a Commonwealth government which seemed unable and unwilling to recognise, let alone comprehend, past injustices towards indigenous Australians and the 'burden' of these for the present. (*Mark Wilson/Courtesy* Age)

41. The politics of embarrassment: A delegation of the National Indigenous Working Group in Johannesburg—comprising (left to right): Glenn Shaw, Geoff Clark and Michael Mansell—seek the support of the South African government to bolster their fight against the Australian government's '10 point plan' (or 'scam', in Noel Pearson's words) to amend the 1993 *Native Title Act*. They hold a symbol of sovereignty sought by Clark and Mansell's Aboriginal Provisional Government. (*Courtesy* Sydney Morning Herald)

Aboriginals and students linked arms and surrounded the main "embassy" tent, flying two aboriginal flags. A spokesman for the "embassy," Mr Gary Foley shouted to police: "Anyone of you who touches this tent is going to get thumped." Police then started pulling down three other tents ...

The aboriginals and students, arms linked, began singing, "We Shall Not Be Moved," and chanting "Land rights now, land rights now."

Police carried tents, blankets, sleeping bags, stores and clothing to trailers parked on the road. Police then circled the main tent and Inspector J. Johnson said through a loud hailer: "If you fail to move you may be arrested for obstructing police." The aboriginals and students broke into a chant. "We shall not be moved." Then police moved in and the brawl started ...

A Herald reporter saw police pick up three knives and a spear during the struggle. One of the knives was bloodstained. A policeman took a knife from a man and said: "We don't want this sort of thing, or see anyone get hurt."

There were about 30 aboriginals at the "embassy." A few were dressed in all-black—black power clothing. Most of them wore black power badges and land rights badges.

145. *Age*, 24 July 1972. Tent Embassy Sparks Brawl

Canberra— Eighteen people were arrested and several people injured during violent clashes between police and demonstrators outside Parliament House yesterday when Aborigines and their supporters tried to re-establish the "Aboriginal embassy." More that 200 demonstrators and about 250 police confronted each other as police moved in to demolish a tent which the protesters had put up. Eight of the people arrested were Aborigines.

The "embassy," which was set up six months ago to protest against the Government's refusal to grant Aboriginal land rights, was pulled down by police during wild scenes last Thursday. This followed the introduction of an ordinance by the Federal Government making it illegal to camp on unleased land in the Australian Capital Territory.

Yesterday morning the demonstrators, including almost 100 Aborigines, marched from the Australian National University to Parliament House, where they were met by about 50 police. They sat down on the road outside and listened to speeches.

When two policemen walked behind the crowd, the demonstrators ran to the lawn where the embassy had stood. They erected a tent, and formed a human guard around it. About 200 police marched in from the gardens adjoining Parliament House and surrounded the demonstrators. As the police moved in on the crowd around the tent, there were violent scuffles and several policemen and demonstrators were bleeding from the face.

Five policemen and nine demonstrators were treated for injuries at the Canberra Hospital. All were allowed to leave later. A spokesman for the Department of the Interior said two policemen were treated for bites, two for cuts and abrasions, and one for a suspected broken shoulder. He said two of the demonstrators arrested were treated by a Government doctor. One was treated for a stomach pain, and the other for a bleeding nose.

The charges against the 18 people arrested include insulting language, hindering police, and obstructing and assaulting police. The demonstrators arrested will appear in the Canberra Court later this week and next week. One of those arrested yesterday was also among the eight people who were arrested in last Thursday's demonstration.

While the melee was going on outside Parliament House, the Prime Minister (Mr. McMahon), the Leader of the Country Party (Mr. Anthony), the Treasurer (Mr. Snedden) and the Minister for Primary industry (Mr. Sinclair) were inside finalising details of the Federal Budget.

Two busloads of Aborigines—one from Sydney and one from Brisbane—travelled to Canberra to take part in the protests against moving the embassy. Other Aborigines travelled by car or hitched rides. Black Panther leader Mr. Denis Walker was among the demonstrators.

The Aborigines are likely to hold another demonstration next weekend. Miss Bobbi Sykes, one of the Aboriginal leaders, said yesterday: "The actions taken by police against us are creating militance for us. People would come from all over Australia to support us if they had the money to get here." Some of the Aborigines were going back to Sydney to raise funds, Miss Sykes said.

A group of Aborigines on Friday took out a writ against the Minister for the Interior (Mr. Hunt) requiring him to defend the legality of the new ordinance. They have also sought a temporary injunction asking that no action be taken under the ordinance. The temporary injunction will be heard in the Australian Capital Territory Supreme Court tomorrow.

In Brisbane, Queensland's Aboriginal Senator Neville Bonner appealed to militant Aboriginal demonstrators "to obey the law and give me the opportunity to bring this matter before Parliament". He said he would ask the Government to provide Australia's indigenous people with their own permanent lobby.

146. Joe McGinness, President, FCAATSI, letter to the editor, *Nation Review*, 12-18 August 1972

Ms Bobbi Sykes is well entitled to set out her opinions; but in respect to FCAATSI *(Review,* August 5) she has slipped into errors of judgment because she is not aware of all the facts. It is sad to see Ms Sykes using the press to divide the aboriginal movement.

The Federal Council for the Advancement of Aborigines and Torres Strait Islanders is certainly not a "white-run" body. That word implies that white people have the authority, and make all the decisions. This is not so. The president, Mr J. McGinness, is an aboriginal, the general secretary is an islander, and the full executive comprises a majority of black people to white people, not the other way round.

Not only are the black people quite free to speak their minds—and we certainly do!—but we are aware that such white people as we have on the executive, have realised the importance of listening to blacks. They really think about what we say, listening and talking back as equals. We have a common ground in aboriginal and island radical politics. They do not think they are better than us; nor do we necessarily regard them as our inferiors. All members are democratically elected; none are appointed.

Apart from that, there is a closed black caucus at conference, founded in 1960. In Alice Springs, for example, in 1972 (Ms Sykes was not present), some 300 elected blacks from missions and cattle stations met in closed session and aired their grievances. Their decisions were ratified by the open sessions, and sent straight to the relevant government departments. So public servants are *directly* aware of black people's debated decisions.

As for FCAATSI "having very little grass roots support", or being "not fully representative of the people"—every state secretary on the executive is a black person, including representatives of Northern Territory and Torres Strait Islands. This is not meaningless "tokenism" either, for state secretaries who accept nomination are normally "well clued-up" in local aboriginal or island politics, and have a wide personal influence, and following.

Various levels of black radical politics are represented, too, from age to youth. Without FCAATSI the isolated areas of Australia, such as Alice Springs or Thursday island, would be forgotten. All can speak freely, and do.

FCAATSI did not capitalise on the activities of the black embassy. The embassy tent was placed on the lawns at federal parliament house, because FCAATSI forced the federal government to be responsible for aboriginal affairs. That took ten years!

If Ms Sykes were to study the history of the black movement in this country, she would learn that prior to the 1967 referendum, blacks came under six separate laws. She may have found that— if it were not for FCAATSI— campaigning about the referendum there would need to be six state embassies.

It is impossible in the short space to list all the campaigns, all the reforms, all the victories chalked up. Legal battles for civil rights (the Namatjira appeal, the Stuart case, the Hope Vale flogging, the Nancy Young case); repeals of discriminatory laws (in NSW, SA, NT, WA and even in Queensland); land law (SA); the rights to drink and vote (all states, and federal); equal wages, decent industrial conditions (all states but Queensland and NT).

In 1958, when federal council was born from state organisations affiliated in the previous year, the aborigines were outcasts, segregated either in reserves or out of sight on riverbanks. From the first, we were dedicated to the eradication of black injustice, not just ameliorating conditions. We fought to rub out all discrimination from the statute books both state and federal. Since 1967, with commonwealth finance available, the children of the blacks are emerging in high schools and universities.

For many years FCAATSI has affiliated to it many white organisations who are expected to seriously interest themselves in black affairs, and to leave their white political and religious ideas at home, Notably, interest has fallen away among trade union officials; but church and humanist leaders, and politicians, are now actively concerned in aboriginal rights. Through these white organisations, FCAATSI has won growing interest for aboriginal affairs overseas.

Since 1963 FCAATSI has been pestering federal governments for a "national lobbying place" in Canberra. All the negotiations with Mr Hunt since May were made by blacks, and this is quite acceptable to the FCAATSI whites.

147. *West Australian,* 12 August 1972. Aboriginal Leaders Want Federal Control

Canberra, Fri.— A national conference of Aboriginal delegates today voted unanimously for the Commonwealth to take over control of Aboriginal affairs throughout Australia. They called for a full ministry of Aboriginal affairs staffed and run by Aboriginal leaders.

Mr David Anderson, of Victoria, a former vice-president of the Aborigine Advancement League, said "It's criminal that the Government won't let us run our own affairs. If the New Guinea natives can get a House of Assembly, surely we can run our own department. All State Aboriginal departments should be abolished; Commonwealth control would be far better than State control. The States are always saying they are short of money."

'Embassy'

The conference called also for the Aboriginal "embassy to be set up again on the lawns of Parliament House."

The secretary-treasurer of the "embassy", Mrs Pat Eatock, said the issue centred around the claim for land rights. "This was a means of telling the world the way Aboriginal people live," she said. "We were on the front pages of newspapers in New York and England. While the tent was there we were being heard more effectively than we are being heard at this conference today."

Police

Another motion agreed to unanimously called for Aboriginal police who would be responsible to the Aboriginal people who elected them. They would be similar to the New Zealand Maori wardens. This was proposed by a W.A. delegate, Mr Jack Davis, who said Aboriginal law enforcement officers were very necessary, particularly in the North-West. "There are, many white men going to mining camps and they don't have their women with them," he said. "Many young girls are being raped. They are girls aged between 11 and 15 who are being assaulted in these areas. The police officers who are white protect the white women but don't give a damn about the black women."

The conference decided to ask the A.C.T.U. to establish a black trade union to deal with wages and conditions of black Australians. The originator of this motion, Mr Denis Walker, said that problems would be better brought to the attention of the public if a 5,000-

member-black trade union could call on the A.C.T.U. to support
them. With the A.C.T.U. machinery behind them the Aborigines
could do a lot of research on wages and conditions. "Black people
have not got any confidence in the trade union movement at the
moment," Mr Walker said.

In another motion the conference condemned the A.C.T.U. for
hypocrisy in its protest against apartheid in South Africa. It claimed
the trade union movement had done nothing to protest about the
plight of the Aboriginal people.

148. *Canberra News*, 26 November 1972. Violence Coming: Perkins

Aborigines' spokesman, Mr. Charles Perkins said this morning more
trouble could be expected from militant aborigines. "The problem
has been building up for quite some time", he said. "It is obvious
that if they did not get a better [deal] this was the only resource left
in this element of the Aboriginal people. Aboriginal affairs are in a
shocking state, you can't blame them for taking action into their
own hands."

Mr Perkins said black people were sick and tired of waiting for
the Government and white people to do something. "It is obvious
even to a blind man that Queensland is one of the worst States for
discriminatory acts and practices," he said. "I don't condone violence
but I can understand our people acting this way when they have ex-
hausted every avenue for improving their conditions."

Mr Perkins said the Commonwealth Government did not emerge
blameless from the shameful treatment of Aborigines. "The Northern Territory is worse than Queensland in many cases", he said.
"The high infant mortality rate and the grim health conditions
prove that."

He said he had warned the people of Australia five years ago that
violence would erupt unless something was done to improve conditions. "The Queensland demonstration was only the beginning of
more such militant and violent action on the part of many groups
who are sick and tired of waiting", he said. "They are sick of seeing
their children dying or living in a vicious cycle of poverty". Mr Perkins said everybody had laughed when he had warned them of what
could happen.

"There are too many white people in Aboriginal Affairs", he said.
"To them Aboriginal Affairs are big business. They should keep out

of it and let the Aboriginal people look after their own affairs".

149. *Age,* 17 January 1974. Blacks To Tell China

Sydney.— A group of Aborigines flew off to China yesterday to "embarrass" the Australian Government as part of its land rights campaign.

Mr. Garry [Gary] Foley, leader of the 10-member group, said at Sydney airport the Government was "ignoring" Aborigines. "We have now a situation where we no longer have any reasonable sort of Opposition we can depend upon and the Government is ignoring us," Mr. Foley said. "So our next strategic move must obviously be to take the entire case of Aboriginal land rights in the international sphere and embarrass Australia that way."

He said the invitation for the five-week, expenses-paid visit was extended to his group by the China Peoples' Association for friendship of Foreign Countries.

"Generally speaking, most people are under the misconception that Aborigines are extremely better off under the Labor Government. Rest assured we don't intend to make any glossy statement in China about the Labor Party. We have a Minister at the moment who is extremely paranoid about 'white backlash', and as a result has done very little for Aborigines."

He said his group was taking to China films showing the destruction of the Aboriginal embassy in Canberra and "other evidence of how the Government was treating minority groups in Australia".

Mr. Foley said it was hoped to convince China it should send a delegation to Australia as guests of Aborigines.

150. Senator Neville Bonner, Parliamentary Debates, 12 March 1974

... In view of some of the things which have happened recently, I have become rather concerned particularly in relation to the problems which are facing members of my race. As the first and only, to date, elected Aboriginal member of Parliament, I seek the indulgence of the Senate for I feel compelled at this point in time, because of what is happening to my race with threats of violence and the inevitable backlash which will take place, to refer today to 3 sections of the Australian community. My first appeal would be to those of my race who are young, frustrated, eager and impatient for change and who, I feel, have been led to believe that violent demand is the answer to the present problems facing our people. I do not believe that threats of violence nor the kind of violent actions, a sample of which we have seen recently in Canberra, will achieve what is needed to right the wrongs of the past or of the future. We, the Aboriginal people of this nation, need to gain the support of this Parliament, the support of the State parliaments and most importantly the support of the general Australian community.

There has been and still is talk of black power. If the young of my race mean the kind of black power which says that I am proud of my race and I am as good as the next person, and if they get out and help themselves in the white man's environment and beat him at his own game, I say that is good black power. I warn my young friends that I will have no truck with the other kind of black power which, I know, brings in its wake violence, and I warn against it as I have done previously and as I will continue to do. I say to those of my race who are young, who have had the advantage of an education and who are articulate: 'Use these God given talents to influence the thinking of non-Aboriginal communities'.

Many of them have had the opportunity of working within the system. Many have had the opportunity to become members of various committees, and they can do much for the Aboriginal race and the Aboriginal cause. Many, through hard work and study, have attained important positions in the community, and they have grave responsibilities. Their task is a very important one. There are times, I know, when they will become frustrated and impatient, and they will ask themselves what the heck is the use. I say to them that the attitudes of a lifetime cannot be changed overnight. I know that these changes must come. Many young people of my race can do much by working within the present system because I believe that the present system can be made to work for Aborigines by Aborigines. I warn again the young and impatient of my race not to let themselves be brainwashed into believing that violence can solve the problems which are of concern to all members of the Aboriginal race because those people who encourage them along this course are evil and have no true concern for the benefit or the cause of the Aboriginal people.

Through the forum of this Parliament let me now address myself to the older members of my race— those who, like me, have suffered so much because of past discrimination and prejudice; those who, because of the attitudes of the past, have lived in squalor on the banks of creeks and have seen the destruction of their culture, yet have been able to fight back and to give their children the best education that those conditions would permit. Like me, they have a responsibility that is perhaps greater now than ever before. We have seen many changes; some good, some perhaps not so good. We have seen changes of government and changes in attitudes of the people towards the Aboriginal cause. I believe that we are now seeing genuine concern for the advancement of our people, although much remains to be done. We must ensure that the genuine problems of health, housing, education and employment, along with the associated problems, are solved satisfactorily.

I say this to my race: Whilst we remember the bad things and endeavour to rectify them, let us also put on record our appreciation of the good things, such as the hand of friendship that has been extended and the opportunities that are now being offered. We must become involved. We must speak so that we can be a steadying influence on our younger people who speak of black power and violence. We who have crossed so many dry gullies and have known hunger, despair and discrimination in its worst form have paved a much smoother way for the younger members of our race. Now we see the light at the end of the tunnel and I hope that we will not allow it to be blocked by irresponsible actions by our young people and by non-Aborigines who would use them for their own political gain. There are within our community people who are doing that very thing at this very time.

Finally, I address myself to the non-Aboriginal section of the community. Mr Deputy President, your forefathers have a lot to answer for—the poisoned flour, the shooting, the destruction of hunting ranges and hence the destruction of Aboriginal culture. Whether this was done through ignorance or greed or for whatever reason, nonetheless it is history. Although we should not dwell upon it, I believe that you, the descendants of the conquerors, should learn from history in arriving at guidelines for the present and future. I believe that you have much to put right.

There is talk of a white backlash. As an Aborigine, I cannot help asking why this should be. We, the Aborigines, are now being given opportunities that hitherto were denied to us. Surely this is just when one considers the past. I am conscious of the fact that there are in the community non-Aborigines who are in need of considerable assistance, but I do not believe that that is any reason to knock what is being done for the descendants of the conquered. This is our right by birth. I plead with those of the non-Aboriginal races who are part of the so-called backlash to try to understand that what is being done by governments is the true entitlement of the indigenous people who have been dispossessed of what was truly theirs. I say to them that their intolerance can only add fuel to the fires that have been kindled by those who want to see racial unrest in our wonderful nation ...

Mr Deputy President, I felt that I should say the things that I have said because this is the first time that the voice of the Aboriginal people has been heard in this chamber. I realise that I have responsibilities to all sections of the Australian community, but I feel also that I have a particular responsibility to people of my own race.

151. *Hobart Mercury*, 1 May 1976. Truganini To Be Disturbed No More

"We come today on behalf of all the aboriginal people of Australia to pay tribute to Truganini." So began the oration given by Mrs Rosalind Langford, former secretary of the Aboriginal Information Service in Tasmania, at the cremation ceremony for Truganini at Cornelian Bay cemetery yesterday.

A hundred years after her death, and after years of agitation and controversy, the ashes of Truganini, Tasmania's last surviving full-blood aboriginal, will be scattered today in D'Entrecasteaux Channel, close to the heart of her tribal ancestral territory.

Mrs Langford spoke to a small gathering which included relatives of Truganini, members of the Tasmanian aboriginal community and the Acting Premier, Mr Lowe. Mrs Mary Clarke, who claims to be a great grand-daughter of Truganini, travelled from Warrnambool [Victoria], to attend. She expressed relief that the bones of Truganini were "finally laid to rest". It has been a source of concern among many aboriginals that Truganini had been denied burial, and her bones kept for scientific purposes.

... Truganini's remains [were] cremated, because many of the aboriginals involved feared that her bones might be exhumed at a later date. As Mrs Langford said in her oration: "The degrading of her body has brought the aboriginal race together for one cause—to have her rest in peace."

152. *Hobart Mercury*, 11 August 1982. Anger Voiced Over Fate Of Skeletons

The Tasmanian aboriginal community yesterday expressed outrage at the trustees of the Tasmanian Museum and the State Government's non-involvement over the fate of aboriginal skeletal remains held by the museum [The Crowther Collection].

The State secretary of the Tasmanian Aboriginal Centre, Mrs Rosalind Langford, said yesterday that the trustees of the museum had stated that they saw the destruction of the skeletal remains as an irreversible action which would prevent any study of the material.

Mrs Langford said: "The museum's proposal of joint responsibility for the collection, to set an example to other States on the possibilities of co-operation between a museum and the aboriginal people is a farce. How can a body such as the museum expect to set examples of co-operation when it is dictating to the aboriginal people conditions which it sees as being in the best interests of aboriginal people. The Tasmanian aboriginal community is sick and tired of such paternalistic attitudes and has made its decision in relation to the aboriginal remains at the museum. The collection was obtained illegally and is being kept illegally. The desecration of aboriginal dead will not be tolerated for much longer."

Mrs Langford said aboriginal people in Tasmania called on all churches and individuals to support their stand for the return of their dead, or once again are they, too, going to be non-committal and leave the aboriginal people to fight alone once more?

4 1970s - 1998

The last three decades of the twentieth century saw not only striking change but also continuity in Aboriginal politics. The relationship between the Australian state and indigenous peoples assumed a new dimension, and at the same time many of the forms and methods of protest which had characterised the struggle for Aboriginal rights since the 1920s largely fell into disuse while other ones emerged. The focus of indigenous activists continued to shift from their emphasis on citizenship rights to one which favoured Aboriginal rights, and these were increasingly extended beyond demands for 'land rights' to encompass calls for the recognition of Aboriginal nationhood and sovereignty.

Aboriginal politics and government in the 1970s

The election of Gough Whitlam's ALP in 1972 marked a turning point in Aboriginal politics in the sense that it was to be the first in a succession of federal governments that were committed to a major change in their approach of Aboriginal politics. On the one hand, it undertook to address the historic disadvantage of indigenous peoples and restore their lost power of self-determination by means of new government programmes, a considerable increase in the level of expenditure, the granting of land rights (in the Northern Territory), and the founding of Aboriginal legal and medical services which were to be managed by local communities. On the other hand, through the establishment of the first nationwide representative body, the National Aboriginal Consultative Committee (NACC), and recruitment of Aborigines to the bureaucracy, it sought to include Aboriginal leaders in the process of government.

The consequences of these developments for Aboriginal politics were profound. First, many of the objectives for which Aboriginal activists had fought since the 1920s, such as overturning racially discriminatory laws and practices and pleading the need for programmes to enable Aboriginal advancement, ceased to be of immediate relevance (although the former continued to be a matter of the utmost importance in Queensland (**156**)). Second, the locus of Aboriginal politics began to shift from protest to management as many Aboriginal leaders were charged with the responsibility of implementing new policies, and so became incorporated in the task of administration, either as employees of the federal government or of the agencies established to deliver services to Aboriginal communities.

As a result of the new approach by the Commonwealth, the force which Aboriginal protest had in the late 1960s and early 1970s was severely blunted. It was not entirely stilled, as black power advocates like Denis Walker showed (**154**), but such militancy was increasingly marginal to Aboriginal politics, in part because the advent of black power had not led to the establishment of strong national organisations. At the same time, FCAATSI, the organisation which had dominated the campaign for Aboriginal rights since the late 1950s, went into decline as a result of the split in its ranks between Aboriginal and non-Aboriginal campaigners. This left the indigenous struggle without the organisational power that had provided much of its coherence in the previous decade or so.

By the mid-1970s it was already evident that Aboriginal protest was increasingly coming from a new quarter—government and quasi-governmental bodies and, in particular, figures like Charles Perkins (**153**).[1] Their voices were raised as it became apparent that federal government was unable to meet the expectations it had raised among Aboriginal people. Increased expenditure on Aboriginal programmes failed to bring much in the way of rapid improvement in the lives of Aboriginal people and their communities, and 'self-determination' did not see a transfer of real power to Aboriginal organisations, causing enormous frustration (**155**).

The attempt to induct Aboriginal leaders into government did not still radical demands. The campaign for land rights continued to gather strength, as was evident in major battles over land in the late 1970s in places as far apart as Noonkanbah (**159** and **160**) and Framlingham.[2] With increasing consistency and force, Aboriginal groups put forward the position that they had rights stemming from prior occupation of the continent that had never been abrogated by treaty or any other legitimate means. Former tent embassy leader Paul Coe tried to use the courts to test these claims (**158**), but his lack of success, like the failure of the Yolngu in the Gove case in 1971, seemed to deter any further recourse to the law, at least until Eddie Koiki Mabo and other Murray Islanders began their campaign to overturn the fiction of *terra nullius* in 1982 (**162** and **163**).[3] Instead, the proposal of a treaty or Makarrata, to be negotiated between the Commonwealth and the Aboriginal people, attracted much attention among Aboriginal bodies and organisations, such as the National Aboriginal Conference (NAC), the successor to the NACC (**161**).[4]

New forms of Aboriginal politics in the 1980s

The NAC also sought to represent Aboriginal protest against the deep-rooted structural inequalities and continuing racial discrimination in Australia, but on this front, as well as on others relating to the key issues of land, other customary rights, Aboriginal heritage and self-determination (164), it failed to establish its primacy as the centre for Aboriginal politics. This is partly attributable to the fact that government defined its role and starved it of funds, but the more fundamental reason for its failure lay elsewhere. This representative body was not grounded in Aboriginal culture but had a form imposed upon it by whites who continued to believe that they knew what was best for Aborigines (168).[5] This caused immense frustration among its officebearers, such as Rob Riley, and this was especially evident when governments broke promises relating to Aboriginal demands like those for national land rights legislation (166).

The organisations which gained greater acceptance among Aborigines and provided many of the most effective Aboriginal leaders during the 1980s were those based on local communities. Unlike their predecessors in both the nineteenth and twentieth centuries, these organisations received government funding and had administrative functions and the responsibility to deliver services. In urban areas Aboriginal legal services, with officers like Michael Mansell and Paul Coe, were an important basis for mobilisation, while in rural areas it was land councils— most notably the Northern and Central Land Councils, founded in 1973 and 1977 respectively— which served this function, with leaders like Galarrwuy Yunupingu, John Ah Kit and Michael Dodson assuming prominence. Cooperation between and coordination of these organisations on a national level was minimal; a federation of land councils was formed and there were coalitions of organisations working in the areas of health, legal aid and other services, but membership was fluid and they had few mechanisms by which they could implement the decisions they made.

In this decade ad hoc organisations were established to tackle specific issues. A major concern in country towns and urban centres, such as Roebourne and Redfern, was the poor relations that continued between Aboriginal communities and police. This led to a Committee to Defend Black Rights being founded in 1984 to demand a royal commission into the death of a young man in police cells (165 and 167), a call which widened to one for a national inquiry into Aboriginal deaths in custody. Such organisations expressed the deep-seated frustration and bitterness that was common in many Aboriginal communities., although some saw reason to emphasise achievements since the 1967 referendum (171).

At the same time, and in the context of the coming bicentenary of white colonisation, issues of Aboriginal nationhood and sovereignty became increasingly central to the agenda of Aboriginal organisations and bodies of various political persuasions (**170**). Of particular importance was the renewal of calls by Yunupingu, Kevin Gilbert and others for a treaty and/or constitutional change that would recognise Aboriginal rights and the status of Aborigines as prior owners of the country (**172 173 175** and **178**). This was also to be central to the concerns of the Aboriginal Provisional Government, founded by Michael Mansell and others in 1990 (**179** and **180**), coinciding with a new government initiative which had, as one of its objectives, the incorporation of Aborigines in the Australian nation state— the establishment of the Aboriginal and Torres Strait Islander Commission (ATSIC), a body that was to be granted political and administrative functions denied to its predecessors (**177**).

In the years leading to the bicentenary, activists like Mansell sought to take Aboriginal politics onto the international stage, whether in the form of appealing to the United Nations and its associated agencies or to renegade governments like Libya (**170**). Although this was a risky strategy in as much as it could alienate potential non-Aboriginal supporters, as well as dismay fellow Aboriginal activists (**169**), it was often used in the 1980s (and the 1990s) (**176 181** and **197**), especially when the eyes of the world might be on Australia, as they were during international events like the Commonwealth Games in Brisbane in 1982 and the Bicentennial in 1988 (**174**).

Native title, reconciliation and a new future?

As well as seeking change by trying to apply pressure through international forums, indigenous people continued the avenue of legal redress, finally achieving success when the High Court delivered its Mabo judgment in July 1992. This overturned precedent and rejected the fiction of *terra nullius* by finding that native title had survived the assumption of British sovereignty unless specifically extinguished by an act of government, notably the granting of freehold title. The ruling was greeted with dismay in many conservative circles, but was seen by Aboriginal people as no more than justice finally delivered.[6] Communities in southeastern Australia eagerly welcomed the Court's decision as an opportunity to regain remaining parcels of unalienated crown land (**182** and **183**) At the same time the historic ruling provided further impetus for recognition of Aboriginal rights in any revision of the Australian Constitution (**184**).

In 1993 ATSIC representatives and some land council leaders set themselves the task of negotiating with the Keating government the terms of the legislation that would give effect to the High Court's Mabo judgment

(185). The success of these pragmatists— described by ATSIC Chairperson Lois O'Donoghue as a new generation of Aboriginal leaders— was hailed as a historic outcome for Aboriginal Australians (186). It was also greeted as a basis for furthering national reconciliation between Aboriginal and non-Aboriginal Australians (186-188).

It soon became apparent, however, that it was Aboriginal communities in remote Australia, rather than those peoples who had been most dispossessed by colonisation, which were most likely to make gains under the native title regime, as evidenced by the Carpentaria Land Council's successful battle with a multinational mining giant— a development which nevertheless suggested that there had been a telling shift in the balance of power between indigenous peoples and the interest of capital since the routing of the traditional owners at Noonkanbah in 1979-80 (194 and 195). For other Aborigines, despite the social justice package being demanded by ATSIC (191), there a mounting disappointment as their fears that the Native Title Act would provide them with little if any reparation were realised (189 and 190). This was one of the reasons why ATSIC was subjected to attacks by Aboriginal leaders like former Black Panther Gary Foley (192).

Radical Aboriginal voices grew louder following the election of the Howard government in March 1996 (194 195 and 197), especially as it became evident that the Coalition was deeply unsympathetic to Aboriginal rights and the history which had given rise to the demands for these. This became even more apparent as the government increasingly revealed its determination to amend the 1993 Native Title Act. When it ignored the High Court's Wik decision of December 1996, which recognised the rights of both pastoral leaseholders and native title holders, the cause of reconciliation looked destined to founder (199). This was especially so because of the Prime Minister's refusal to apologise to the 'stolen children' in the wake of the Human Rights and Equal Opportunity Commission's inquiry into the separation of Aboriginal children from their families (198), despite the best efforts of Patrick Dodson and the Council for Aboriginal Reconciliation (193 and 196). The hopes that had been encouraged by the achievements of the previous few years were quickly being dashed. The pragmatic Aboriginal leaders who had been able to negotiate with Keating could do little but bemoan the Howard government's failure to respect Aboriginal rights, denounce its plans to extinguish native title rights, and contemplate a return to the direct protests of black power (199 and 200).

NOTES

1 See Peter Read, *Charles Perkins: A Biography*, Viking, Melbourne, 1990, chapter 6.

2 See Steve Hawke and Michael Gallagher, *Noonkanbah: Whose Land, Whose Law* Fremantle Arts Press, Fremantle, 1989.

3 See Nonie Sharp, *No Ordinary Judgement: Mabo, The Murray Islanders' Land Case*, Aboriginal Studies Press, Canberra, 1996.

4 Prominent white activists also campaigned for a treaty; see Judith Wright, *We Call for a Treaty*, Collins/Fontana, Sydney, 1985.

5 See H.C. Coombs, *The Role of the National Aboriginal Conference*, AGPS, Canberra, 1984.

6 See Murray Goot and Tim Rowse (eds), *Make a Better Offer: The Politics of Mabo*, Pluto Press, Sydney, 1994, and Bain Attwood (ed.), *In the Age of Mabo: History, Aborigines and Australia*, Allen & Unwin, Sydney, 1996.

Aboriginal politics and government in the 1970s

153. *Advertiser* (Adelaide), 17 January 1974. PS Man Hits At Ministers

CANBERRA— A senior Federal public servant is expected to be sacked following a severe attack against his own Minister and another Cabinet Minister. He is Mr. Charles Perkins, an assistant secretary in the Department of Aboriginal Affairs.

Mr. Perkins, a part-Aborigine strongly criticised the Minister of Aboriginal Affairs (Senator Cavanagh) for not understanding his portfolio. He also attacked the Minister of Northern Development (Dr. Patterson) for making statements which he said could incite violence between Aborigines and whites in the NT.

Mr. Perkins said Senator Cavanagh had been moving too slowly on Aboriginal programs. "I don't think he has the experience or the depth to be able to understand what we want to the extent that we would be satisfied," Mr. Perkins said. Asked if his Minister needed more time to come to grips with Aboriginal affairs, Mr. Perkins replied: "I think he's had enough time. I think enough research has been done on Aboriginal affairs." All the Royal Commissions, Auditor-General's reports and enquiries proposed by the Government were just "fruitless exercises," Mr. Perkins said.

Statements like those of Dr. Patterson on Tuesday laid the foundations for violence. Dr. Patterson said in Darwin on Tuesday that the immediate Aboriginal problems in the NT stemmed from alcohol and from militant stirrers from the south. It was only a matter of time before serious violence erupted in the NT between Aborigines and whites.

He said Dr. Patterson was a Right-wing conservative with a minimal understanding of Aboriginal affairs and his remarks should not be taken seriously. He advised Dr. Patterson to confine himself to his own portfolio and called on the Prime Minister (Mr. Whitlam) and Cabinet exercise some control over the Minister.

The only solution was to take Aboriginal affairs out of politics, turn it into a statutory body and provide it with massive injections of funds to cope with the main problems of aborigines— housing, education, employment— and giving Aborigines decision-making powers in the areas of their own responsibility. A "lead boots" approach by the Government would only cause more discontent among Aborigines and would eventually lead to violent confrontations.

Speaking from Katherine, in the NT last night, Senator Cavanagh said: "The statement made by Mr. Perkins referring to Dr. Patterson and myself is a breach of the Public Service Act. This is one of numerous breaches which have occurred. As a result of the previous breaches, there is at this time an investigation being carried out within my department. When this investigation was arranged, the chairman of the Public Service Board (Mr. A. S. Cooley) advised the secretary of my department in my presence that it was Mr. Dexter's responsibility to lay charges against any person breaching the Public Service Act. (Mr. Dexter is the permanent head of the department). I anticipate that Mr. Dexter now will act accordingly."

The seriousness of Mr. Perkins's attack is understood to warrant dismissal from the Public Service. This would almost certainly raise a storm of protest and criticism from Aboriginal leaders.

154. *Sun* (Melbourne), 11 June 1975. Blacks Clash With Police

Sydney—About 50 aboriginals and their supporters fought a running battle with police yesterday after aboriginal activist Denis Bruce Walker was arrested.

Police arrested Walker, 28, when he attempted to walk into the High Court in Sydney with a .22 rifle slung over his shoulder. Walker struggled as six policemen dragged and carried him 50 metres to Darlinghurst police station. He abused police, calling them pigs. His supporters jeered, booed and waved placards.

Chanting "Free Walker," some supporters charged police and fights broke out. Eggs were thrown and police were kicked and punched. After Walker was dragged inside the police station some supporters tried to enter but were pushed away.

Walker had gone to the High Court for his appeal against an extradition order to Queensland. He has been charged in Queensland with having conspired with another man last August to demand $10,000 from Mr James Barghese, with the threat that if he failed to comply, $2000 would be put on his head. Mr Barghese is president of Queensland University's student union. The High Court refused Walker leave to appeal.

After yesterday's fights Walker was remanded in custody. He was charged with possessing a .22 rifle, resisting arrest and using unseemly words. Six others were allowed bail.

155. Gary Foley, Publicity Officer, Aboriginal Medical Service, 'The history of the Aboriginal Medical Service—a study in bureaucratic obstruction'

... In writing the history of the Aboriginal Medical Service, I have found it impossible to ignore mention of the actions over the years by the Department of Aboriginal Affairs. Indeed it would seem that the success of the A.M.S. has been in spite of, rather than with the help of. the D.A.A. If in the course of this report a less flattering picture is drawn of the D.A.A., it is nobody's fault but the D.A.A. Their actions in minor instances have caused unnecessary hardship and in major instances have endangered not only the existence of the A.M.S. but also the lives of Aboriginal people ...

Conclusion:

In writing this report I have concentrated on our dealings with the D.A.A. in an attempt to highlight the incompetence and outright criminal negligence of certain officers of that agency. From past experience in other Aboriginal organisations, I know that the D.A.A.'s standard excuse for its bungling and inaction is that of incomplete or late audits from the Aboriginal organisations. This criticism can in no way be applied to the A.M.S. Why then have we been subjected to the type of treatment from the D.A.A.? Why has the A.M.S. been forced to operate from virtually ever since its inception, on bank overdrafts?

The answer to these questions can only be supplied by the men responsible, Mr. Barry Dexter, Mr. Laurie Malone, Mr. Barry Powell and their subordinates. The two ministers Mr. Bryant and Senator Cavanagh must also accept the responsibility for failing to ensure that their bureaucrats didn't use Aboriginal organisations in their quest to consolidate and exercise their own power. It seems that ever since the formation of the D.A.A., Aborigines have merely been a pawn in the game of power polities waged between the bureaucrats and politicians in Canberra.

The general public only ever hears of the supposedly enormous amounts of money "handed out" to Aboriginal organisations. They are never told of the way in which supposed self-determination organisations such as the A.M.S. are forced into almost total dependence on the D.A.A. in order to survive. The story of Aboriginal organisations operating on bank overdrafts is by no means a rare one. Apparently the D.A.A. sees this as a sure-fire means of creating dependence and destroying any degree of independence and self-sufficiency.

The Labor Government came to power partially on its promises of self-determination for Aborigines. This slogan today, however, has a very hollow ring for most blacks. The government still has an opportunity to correct the mistakes so far made, but this will require strong Ministerial leadership which will force the bureaucrats to be what they really are. PUBLIC SERVANTS!

156. *The Queensland Aborigines Act and Regulations 1971.* Written by the Black Resource Centre Collective, 1976. Main contributor Lionel Lacey (Fogarty). Other contributors Cheryl Buchanan and Vincent Brady

... Within the black community in Queensland there has been a growing awareness and understanding of the things which affect our lives, and it is through this that we have decided to put the Queensland Act into the minds of every person who wants to change this society. The time has come when all of the racism, racist laws and murders and rapes and every other outrage that is put up to keep us oppressed, are to come out of the closets where everyone can see them and judge them and act upon them.

The Act is very difficult to read because it is in legal terms and it can be twisted by the white authorities to suit their needs.

The Queensland Act is *the* law that makes it *legal* to oppress blacks in Queensland, so we have made this booklet available so that people can *begin* to understand how this Act works.

We say begin, because the majority of whites in Queensland and throughout Australia do not know that this law exists and yet it affects a large black population. If you have ever thought about apartheid in South Africa, you should start to see that the Queensland Act is apartheid in Queensland where there is a separate law for blacks.

Even if this Act were abolished tomorrow it would still not be the answer to our fight for freedom, because there are still so many questions in our minds that need answers— like the questions of land ownership and police brutality. If the Reserves are to be no longer controlled by the State Government through the Queensland Act, there should be a recognition that black communities have a right (morally or otherwise) to make decisions about the land they were born of. You might get a situation where the Act gets abolished and the Director and the Premier decide to move everybody into the cities. You see. So we have to think very carefully about what our demands are.

We want the Act smashed but only if our rights to ownership and community control of Reserve and tribal lands is what follows. With this there would have to be a whole new awareness and respect among the white population of our *rights* as a people who have been oppressed for so long.

There would have to be almost total change in society. Some of us call it *revolution*. For the sake of our children, we must keep on speaking out openly, brothers and sisters, on all issues that cause us hardship— until we can live again, one with the land, as people.

Life Under The Act— Lionel G. Lacey

I come from Cherbourg Aboriginal Reserve, about 200 miles from Brisbane, Queensland. I would like to tell a little story about how the Queensland Acts affect me and my people.

Well, in the Reserve or community there has to be a white manager. We have one on Cherbourg. The people have got to see the Manager if they want a job, because he says and tells you where you will work. When I was little I knew the Manager was the boss because he had an office of his own and I used to see my uncles and aunts or some other blacks sitting outside for hours. They were waiting for him to call them in. Then he would ask them questions like: What can you do? How long did you go to school? Who do you live with ... ? and so on. The people would wait for something like two weeks and then he would give them jobs like Hygiene or some other shit job that pays $24 to $42 per fortnight.

On Cherbourg there are things that are really bad, like the people have only the right to vote for two of the Aboriginal councillors. But the big man, the Director (Pat Killoran), who is white, can appoint three councillors of his choosing. If the Director doesn't like the two Councillors that the people pick he can then appoint all of the councillors.

At Cherbourg there was, and still is, hardly anything to do. There is no pub, no pool tables, no swimming pools. In the law of the Queensland Acts, no grog is allowed on the Reserve anyway. When I got a job the pay was $24 a fortnight. A lot of people will say that things have changed now. Well things may have changed a little bit in the cities, but on the Reserves the country blacks are still pushed down and can't control their own affairs and the wages are still the same. The wages might have been raised by $1 to $2, but this is fuck all. There are still bad housing conditions, and medical and education are not given to us in the way that they should be given. The Queensland Acts are fucking our minds, we don't know which way to move.

When we go away from the Reserve into the city, when we want to come back home the whites put the laws in the way, like you have to have a permit to go back on the Reserve. If you learn something from the city or are involved in the Black Power movement, you will not be allowed back home. Why? Because the white man is scared about blacks learning about how to fight these laws. The white man wants to keep control because there is profit in it for him, and also he thinks that blacks are like kids and cannot control their own affairs.

The white Manager is there to explain to the Aboriginal Council about the laws; in other words, to set up Uncle Toms. Uncle Toms love their controller and will do anything for the white man. The Council on the Reserves are Uncle Toms. Also the Aboriginal Council is there to keep control of the black police. Some of the laws are worth looking at.

One law is "That a person shall not carry tales about any person so as to cause domestic trouble or annoyance to such person". That means to me that I can't joke about my mates or talk about the whites that live in good houses and get good wages and good food, while we have fuck all …

Then there is the law "That a person swimming or bathing shall be dressed in a manner approved by the Manager". What it means is that before a black person can go down to the creek for a swim he has got to stand up in front of the Manager to get approval of what clothes he or she is wearing. We couldn't afford to have good swimming togs anyway because of the wages.

We have got to get permission to use electrical goods, such as a hot water jug, electrical radio, iron or electrical razors. Also no person on a Reserve can ever own their own home; this will always be owned by the Director. So if a wife and husband are asleep in bed, the Director has the power to wake them up if he wants to. One law is "That parents shall bring up their children with love and care and shall teach them good behaviour and conduct and shall ensure their compliance with these By-laws". What right have these bastards got to tell us blacks how to live our lives? When you look into the Queensland Acts it is very hard to understand. Just think how hard it is for us blacks to understand when most of us don't even know what is in these Acts. We are just forced to live under them. We have got no right to the land as far as the Director and others think; they own every square inch of it.

Under the Queensland Acts they even have the right to shift us off the Reserve and our homes, if they want to. And they do it. In North Queensland at Mapoon in the Cape York area, they forced the black people off Mapoon with guns. The people went back last year, though, to reclaim their tribal land. This shows that some blacks are starting to wake up to what is going on and are fighting against it.

When a black person is born in Queensland the Director has the full power to decide everything that will happen to that child. I only just mentioned a few of the laws. There are hundreds of laws just like the ones I said. They have put it in their language and so it is very long. With these Queensland Acts we are never treated like people, we are treated like animals. I remember that we never saw anyone except for the tourist buses full of whites that used to come around to have a gig at us.

Blacks all over Australia have had demonstrations and have written things about these Acts; some people have gone to jail too, over these

Acts. People have fought on almost all angles and got the support of some whites to try to get rid of these Acts, and bring about awareness to everyone about what is happening. But as soon as blacks do these things, the Government sends in the police to jail them or frame them up. I was framed up by the pigs because I was fighting against these Acts and spoke to a lot of people about them.

The Government and all the white bosses don't want the people to know about the shit conditions that blacks are living in. The Queensland Acts are still there. Blacks are getting killed, raped and pushed down everyday because of it.

This is our land. It was taken off us and we want it back. We want to have control over our lives instead of some pig pushing us down or some white Manager or black Uncle Tom telling us what to do. We must push up now. We will keep on fighting anyway. I hope you understand it a bit more too, because it is very hard to write about the Queensland Acts. What I wanted to do was to give you a feeling to get up and fight against them now.

157. *Courier Mail*, 12 June 1976. Black Man Feels The Lash In 3-Hour Rights Protest

Aboriginal civil rights leader Don Davidson was handcuffed to a flag-pole and whipped in King George Square yesterday at the height of a three hour black rights demonstration.

Wielding the thonged and weighted whip was a white youth, Doug Tassai, 21, himself a black rights protestor. The whipping— carried out in the centre of a chanting group of demonstrators wearing red headbands and armbands— shocked many of the crowd of 400. The whip was made of plaited brown leather, about a metre (3ft) in length with leather thongs at the tip.

The lashings, said the demonstrators, symbolised the oppression of black people by white society. After more than an hour of fiery speeches the crowd was stilled as Davidson— on crutches with a broken leg— hobbled from the Aboriginal Tent Embassy. He slowly made his way across the Square to the flagpole, which was flying the Queensland flag. As Tassai flayed his back, Davidson called out for yet more strokes.

Visibly Upset

Raw welts covered has back from the 15 strokes. The handcuffs removed, Davidson hobbled back to the tent, which was later removed by protesters.

After the whipping, Tassai was visibly upset. "I did it because I feel for these people. It disgusts me how they are treated." He said he felt ashamed for every white Australian but if they also felt ashamed of what he did then the whipping was worth while.

Tassai said after he performed the whipping he started shaking. He said he then had a drink. Tassai said he was approached about a week ago to do the whipping but said he only decided on Thursday night to do it.

'Do It Again'

Davidson, surrounded by protestors, sat huddled in a blanket after the scourging. "We are sick of being trodden on and I will do it again until I bleed for my people,' he said. Mr. Davidson said the Lord Mayor (Alderman Sleeman) was a very understanding, sympathetic man. "He has given us a very good go," he said.

King George Square was flanked with police and special branch detectives stood among the crowd. The Police Minister (Mr. Hodges) and three Government medical officers stood at the edge of the square. About two hours after the start of the rally the aborigines began to pull down the tent which had stood for five weeks in the square. The men, women and children cleared the area of all rubbish. They painted a red cross on the bare ground where the tent stood as a symbol of aboriginal land. Mr. Davidson said the tent would be put in storage and a meeting on Tuesday would decide where to erect it again.

The Labor Party's Federal spokesman on aboriginal affairs, Senator Keeffe, told the crowd that the Fraser Federal Government had set out on a programme of cutting financial aid for aborigines "with the pious hope that the aborigines and their problems would just go away". Trades and Labor Council president (Sir Jack Egerton) said the performance of Alderman Sleeman in resisting police pressure to have the Tent Embassy shifted was commendable. He said he supported the movement for black rights but told the leaders that they had to listen to the advice of "people who have been around and who know the ropes."

158. Coe v. Commonwealth of Australia (the first defendant) and the Government of the United Kingdom of Great Britain and Northern Ireland (the second defendant). High Court of Australia, 1978

Amended statement of claim

"1A. The Plaintiff sues on behalf of the aboriginal community and nation of Australia and for the benefit of that community which is a community of more than seven persons.

"1B. The Plaintiff is a member of the Wiradjeri Tribe and has authority from this and from other tribes and the whole aboriginal community and nation to bring this action ...

"1. The Plaintiff is a member of and a descendant of the aboriginal people of Australia and is a member of the aboriginal nation.

"2A. On or about a day in April 1770 Captain James Cook RN at Kurnell wrongfully proclaimed sovereignty and dominion over the east coast of the continent now known as Australia for and on behalf of King George III for and on behalf of what is now the secondnamed Defendant.

"3A. On or about the 26th day of January 1788 Captain Arthur Phillip RN wrongfully claimed possession and occupation for the said King George III on behalf of what is now the secondnamed Defendant of that area of land extending from Cape York to the southern coast of Tasmania and embracing all the land inland from the Pacific Ocean to the west as far as the 135th longitude including that area of land now occupied by the firstnamed Defendant at the Commonwealth Offices, Sydney, Commonwealth Bank Building, Martin Place, Sydney.

"3B. The claims of Captain Cook, Captain Phillip and others on behalf of King George III and his heirs and successors were contrary to the rights, privileges, interests, claims and entitlements of the aboriginal people both individually and in tribes and of the aboriginal community and nation as more fully set out in 8A hereof.

...

"4A. From time immemorial prior to 1770 the aboriginal nation had enjoyed exclusive sovereignty over the whole of the continent now known as Australia.

"5A. The aboriginal people have had from time immemorial a complex social, religious, cultural and legal system under which individuals and tribes had proprietory and/or possessory rights, privileges, interests, claims and entitlements to particular areas of land subject to usufructuary rights in other aboriginal people. Some of the aboriginal people still exercise these rights.

"6A. Clans, tribes and groups of aboriginal people travelled widely over the said continent now known as Australia developing a system of interlocking rights and responsibilities making contact with other tribes and larger groups of aboriginal people thus forming a sovereign aboriginal nation.

"7A. The whole of the said continent now known as Australia was held by the said aboriginal nation from time immemorial for the use and benefit of all members of the said nation and particular proprietory possessory and usufructuary rights in no way derogated from the sovereignty of the said aboriginal nation.

"8A. (also 21A) The proclamations by Captain James Cook, Captain Arthur Phillip and others and the settlement which followed the said proclamations and each of them wrongfully treated the continent now known as Australia as *terra nullius* whereas it was occupied by the sovereign aboriginal nation as set out in paragraphs 5A, 6A and 7A hereof.

"11A. The aboriginal people being as aforesaid a nation from time immemorial to the present day were and are entitled to the quiet enjoyment of their rights, privileges, interests, claims and entitlements in relation to lands in the continent now known as Australia and were entitled not to be dispossessed thereof without bilateral treaty, lawful compensation and/or lawful international intervention.

"12A. On and after the 26th day of January 1788 when Captain Arthur Phillip RN landed at Sydney Cove the said Captain Phillip and others including the servants and agents of the first and secondnamed Defendants and persons claiming through and under the first and second named Defendants unlawfully dispossessed certain of the aboriginal people from their lands and have prevented certain members of the aboriginal community from entering into possession of their lands and from hunting and fishing and enjoyment of usufructuary rights in respect of the said lands and have thereby destroyed the culture of the Plaintiff and the aboriginal people, their religion, customs, language and their way of life that they would have otherwise enjoyed.

"13A. As and from the date of Federation on or about the year 1900 the firstnamed Defendant has purported to exercise sovereignty over the continent of Australia. From the same date the firstnamed Defendant has had the obligation not to prohibit the free exercise of any religion but yet the said firstnamned Defendant has from that date enacted legislation which has deprived the Plaintiff and the aboriginal community and nation of his and its rights, privileges, interests, claims and entitlements in part and in whole from time to time including his and its rights to freely practice his and its religion to his and its hurt, degradation and humiliation.

"14A. Since the wrongful proclamations aforesaid the firstnamed Defendant has legislated to permit by its servants, agents and licensees without the consent of the aboriginal community and nation to plunder the territory of the continent of Australia of its minerals and oil resources so that the complete destruction of certain fuels and minerals being part of lands of religious significance to the said aboriginal nation is imminent.

...

"16A. In 1972 the firstnamed Defendant and the secondnamned Defendant recognized the sovereignty of the aboriginal people and nation by recognising the aboriginal embassy established on that land immediately in front of Parliament House Canberra and subsequently elsewhere always under the flag of the aboriginal nation.

"16B. In 1975 the Senate, the Upper House of Parliament of Australia, passed a resolution accepting the fact that the Plaintiff and the Plaintiff's ancestors, and the aboriginal community, were in possession of the entire continent of Australia prior to 1788 and urging the firstnamed Defendant to introduce legislation to compensate the Plaintiff and the aboriginal community and nation. The firstnamed Defendant has not challenged this resolution and it may be taken as its admission.

"And the plaintiff claims:–

(i) A declaration that all lands and waterways within the continent of Australia presently occupied traversed and/or used by the aboriginal people for the purposes of habitation, hunting, food-gathering, fishing, tribal ceremonial or religious usage and/or tribal burial are and shall remain at the absolute command of the aboriginal people free from interference at the suit of the Defendants or either of them or any person or corporation claiming thereunder whether under colour of law or otherwise.

(ii) A declaration that all legislation of the firstnamed Defendant allowing permitting or facilitating the transfer of land on mining is invalid in so far as it interferes with the religious rights of the Plaintiff and the aboriginal community and nation.

(iii) An injunction restraining the firstnamed Defendant from authorizing any mining or other activity which interferes with the proprietory and/or possessory rights and/or religious rights of the aboriginal people unless and until internationally recognized arrangements are made for the transfer of such rights as may be necessary for such mining.

(iv) An order against the firstnamed and secondnamed Defendants for compensation to be made to the aboriginal people and nation and to such individuals and tribes as have been deprived of their proprietory and/or possessory and other rights in land and religious rights and for compensation for interference with their culture, religion, customs, language and way of life which they would have otherwise enjoyed.

(v) Costs.

(vi) Such further or other order as the court thinks fit.

159. *Age*, 21 April 1980. Blacks Unite: Mining Doubt

DERBY— Aborigines throughout north-western Australia have formed a united resistance movement against mining on sacred sites. Representatives of 26 Aboriginal communities in the Kimberley and Pilbara unanimously supported the move at a bush meeting on Noonkanbah station at the weekend. The decision— taken after months of controversy over Amax Petroleum's plans to explore for oil in a traditional sacred site at Noonkanbah— appears certain to affect the Ashton consortium's giant diamond find near Lake Argyle ...

The 150 community representatives decided to send people to help any group trying to prevent mining on its sacred sites. This tactic was used successfully when Amax contractors were ejected from the Noonkanbah sacred site by about 90 Aborigines three weeks ago.

Noonkanbah's spokesman, Mr Dickey Skinner, said his community wanted to protect its culture and lifestyle by shutting the station gates on white miners. "The State Government says the miners have a legal right to go on to a pastoral lease," he said. "Gudia (white people) talk about their laws which are only 150 years old. Our laws are 40,000 years older. Aboriginal law is stronger. Gudia law is the new law.

"We invite everybody here to become one people with one voice to fight this. We are not going to give up just because the Government says so. We are only going to talk, not fight with rifles or bombs or silly things."

An old man from La Grange, Mr Jack Mularti, said Noonkanbah's Pea Hill area was important for initiations to all Kimberley Aborigines. "If we spoil the man places, we are lost," he said. "Now we are standing together for our land. But we need help" ...

160. *Australian*, 30 August 1980. Ban-Breakers Drill Noonkanbah

The West Australian Government took over a drilling rig at Noonkanbah Station on Friday and started drilling on a site claimed to be sacred to local Aborigines. The shock move pre-empted a negotiated solution being worked out by the Aborigines, the Federal Government and the mining companies.

The chairman of the Kimberley Land Council, Mr Darryl Kickett, said the Government had waited until the Noonkanbah people were away at an annual race meeting at Fitzroy Crossing before starting work. He said representatives of all land councils in the State would hold a protest meeting at the station on Wednesday and plan joint retaliatory action ...

The State Government took possession of the drilling rig on Friday morning, and drilling started at noon ...

161. National Aboriginal Conference Submission to the Senate Standing Committee on Constitutional and Legal Affairs, on the Makarrata, 1982

1. In presenting this submission to the Senate Standing Committee on Constitutional and Legal Affairs, the National Aboriginal Conference submits, in accordance with opinion as surveyed to this date, that since colonisation of this country in 1788 by the British, Aboriginal and Torres Strait Island people have maintained their sovereignty. In asserting this we maintain that our nationhood is a matter both of fact and law.

2. Nothwithstanding what has been said so far by legal experts offering advice, we maintain that our nationhood is fundamental to our bargaining position if we are to entertain a Makarrata (Treaty).

3. In pursuing the Makarrata (Treaty) we assert our basic rights as sovereign Aboriginal nations who are equal in political status with the Commonwealth of Australia in accordance with the principal espoused by the International Court of Justice in the Western Sahara Case that sovereignty has always resided in the Aboriginal people ...

38. Should the Australian Government fail to come to terms with this issue then, according to the consensus gathered through Makarrata (Treaty) seminars throughout this country, the NAC has acquired the mandate from the people it represents, to go and present a case to proper international authorities, namely the Racism, Apartheid, Discrimination and Decolonisation Sub-Committee of the United Nations seeking its support in initiating internationally supervised negotiations through the United Nations with respect to having this country decolonised, thus enabling us to seek reparation under Chapter 11, 12, 13 of the United Nations Charter concerning non self-government and trust territories ...

39. In concluding this submission the NAC expresses its eagerness to come to terms with these negotiations in a satisfactory manner which will not cause unnecessary political wrangles. We are aware of Australian ambition to be one nation, one people. However, this cannot be achieved if our people are denied justice in accordance with international opinion relating to a people's right of self-determination ...

162. Eddie Koiki Mabo, 'Land Rights in the Torres Strait', talk delivered at a seminar, Townsville, 28-30 August 1981

... In the Torres Strait, land ownership is the same throughout. It is different from Aboriginal land ownership on the mainland. Although we have tribal regions, we go much further into the clan area and then to individual or family holdings. This system existed as long as we could remember. When the first white men arrived in our islands they found people as village dwellers who lived in permanent houses and in well-kept villages. They also discovered that we were expert gardeners and hunters.

The land was inherited always by the male descendants just as male children in white societies always retained the family name. The terms we use for the male name-holders are *Neai Borom* or *Neai Lied-Lied.* Girls inherited land only in cases where the couple had no male children. In some instances daughters were given land as a wedding present.

Before the father died, or during his life-time, he would make sure that his family and friends knew his wish as to which one of his sons would be the heir to his land. He would also insist that the heir to his land must not deprive the rest of his sons or daughters of the use of his land. In most instances the decision for the use of their father's land remains at the good-will of the heir. Such was the case of my father allowing his sisters to garden in the land that I now inherit ...

Mer ... is divided into three major tribal divisions ... These are *Meriam Pek, Komet Pek* and *Dauer Pek.* These are divided and subdivided right down to clan groups. The laws relating to land were maintained by the *Aet* of Mer or Dowar. Whenever there was a dispute over boundaries, the *Aet* was called upon to settle the disputes in each of their respective islands ...

Inside our *Piaderam* tribal subdivision of Las village, I own the land handed down to me by my father, and on the right of my clan *(Mabo),* I have *Sagigi* and *Kanieu* clan and on my left are *Sam, Wailu* and *Dawita* clans. The boundaries between us are all distinct and known to us all. From my point of view, we have a similar system to the English, Welsh and Scots. None of the land will ever be sold for cash ...

163. Eddie Mabo and [others] v. the State of Queensland and the Commonwealth of Australia. High Court of Australia, 1982.

1. Since time immemorial, the Torres Strait Islands of Mer (known as Murray), Dawar and Wajer and their surrounding seas, seabeds, fringing reefs and adjacent islets (hereinafter collectively referred to as "the said Islands") have been continuously inhabited and exclusively possessed by people called the Miriam people, who speak a distinct language of their own (the Miriam language), who are known as Murray islanders and who are included in that group of people generally known as Torres Strait Islanders ...

2. The Plaintiffs are Murray Islanders and members of the Miriam

people. The first named Plaintiff is a descendant of the traditional leaders known as the 'Aiets' of the Miriam people. The first Plaintiff is now the head of his family group. The fifth named Plaintiff was the Chairman of the Island Council of the said Islands. The Plaintiffs bring this action on their own behalf, and on behalf of the members of their respective family groups (hereinafter collectively referred to as "the Plaintiffs"). Further particulars are set forth at Annexure C of the Plaintiffs' Statement of Facts filed herein.

3. Since time immemorial, since 1879, since 1901 and since within living memory (hereinafter collectively referred to as "since time immemorial") the Miriam people have continuously occupied, used and enjoyed the said Islands and resided on the said Islands in permanent settled communities with a social and political organization of their own.

Particulars

Since time immemorial the Miriam people have continuously and to the exclusion of peoples other than themselves :–

(a) occupied, used and enjoyed, and benefited from the said Islands;

(b) built and lived in permanent residences, housing individuals together with their immediate families, which were and are built in groups of houses, so as to constitute several villages situated on the islands of Mer and Dawar;

(c) made, planted, tilled, cultivated and harvested gardens permanently situated in particular areas of the said Islands;

(d) hunted wildlife in the uncultivated areas of the said Islands;

(e) harvested the produce of natural plants and vegetable life growing in the uncultivated areas of the said Islands;

(f) fished in the adjacent waters and harvested the natural produce of the sea in the reefs and waters of the sea surrounding the said islands;

(g) used water from the said islands for sustenance, medicinal and spiritual purposes;

(h) dug for and used stones, flints, clays, ochres and minerals on the said Islands;

(i) set aside areas and built shrines on the said Islands for the purposes of sacred, religious and spiritual activities and carried on such activities in such areas;

(j) set aside areas and built meeting places on the said Islands for the purposes of social and political organization of the community;

(k) established and carried on a social and political organization with community leaders and institutions that governed their affairs and that included therein a system of law and, inter alia, laws, customs, traditions

and practices of their own for determining questions concerning
  (i) the ordering of community life;
  (ii) the ownership of and dealings with land, seas, seabeds and reefs;
  (iii) the carrying on of agriculture, hunting and fishing;
  (iv) social relationships;
  (v) religious and spiritual activities; and
  (l) carried on trade, commerce and intercourse with the inhabitants of Cape York, Papua New Guinea, islands in the Torres Strait and other neighbouring islands ...

And The Plaintiffs Claim
  A. A Declaration that the Plaintiffs are –
    (a) owners by custom;
    (b) holders of traditional native title;
    (c) holders of usufructuary rights
  with respect to their respective lands.

  B. A Declaration that –
    (a) the ownership by custom;
    (b) the traditional native title;
    (c) the usufructuarry rights
  of the Plaintiffs with respect to their respective lands have not been impaired ...

New forms of Aboriginal politics in the 1980s

164. A Summary of Concerns of the Aboriginal People of Australia Distributed by NAC Chairman, Mr Roy Nichols, at the World Assembly of First Nations, Regina, Canada, 1982. Compiled by NAC Research Unit

[Following a general discussion of the problem of racial discrimination and racism the following concerns were listed.]

Electoral Rights
  The International Covenant on Civil and Political Rights states there must be universal and equal suffrage, as guaranteed by Article 25(b):
  Every citizen shall have the right and the opportunity, without any of the distinctions mentioned in Article 2 (which included race and colour) and without unreasonable restrictions.

The keyword in this quote is *opportunity*. When polling booths are not located within easy reach of Aboriginal communities the "opportunity" to vote is almost negligible. In Queensland officials have taken little responsibility in the encouragement of Aboriginals to enrol for the elections. In Western Australia the process of enrolment has been made so difficult that Aboriginals are actually deterred from enrolling. Complaints have been lodged that some communities have experienced local interference in the exercise of their rights to vote. One man, for instance, took a barrel of alcohol down to the community the night before the election in an attempt to provide hangovers instead of electors the following day!

Infringement of personal freedom
A large number of complaints have been received on matters of infringement of personal freedom of individual Aboriginals. These related to experiences of discrimination in legislation and in the application of apparently non-discriminatory policies in a discriminatory way. Main areas of concern were policing, housing, health care, social security, social services, education, participation in the elections, the freedom to move in public places, the freedom to travel and the freedom to participate in cultural activities. We are finding, for instance, that an inordinate number of Aboriginals are being convicted for petty crime on the one hand, while the Aboriginal community is being deprived of equal privileges of bodily protection by the police, with that given to the white community. In the country towns Aboriginals are refused service in local pubs and are hampered from receiving an equal share of those services available to the rest of the public ...

Land rights
Land rights are probably the most critical question for Aboriginal peoples today. It is not a question of ownership, it is a question of sovereignty. Contact between European colonizers and Aboriginal peoples presents to us an unfolding saga of systematic physical and cultural genocide against the indigenous inhabitants. They were driven from their native territories, they were hunted and shot as if they were game, and later— when the civilizers became more civilized— they were exposed to an education system which was designed to detach them from their cultural heritage. Even in recent years children of mixed blood were torn from the arms of their mothers to be raised separately from the Aboriginal community.

The fight of Aboriginal peoples today for their land is a struggle for the right to maintain their identity. With a sense of nationhood they have a sense of identity. With legally secured land rights, they have a secure location. With location they have sovereignty and the right to determine, themselves, the developments of the future. Without identity, deculturization is guaranteed. Without possession, dislocation and dispersal is inevitable. Without sovereignty, deprivation and dependency face the majority of Aboriginals for the foreseeable future ...

The Makarrata

In April 1979 the National Aboriginal Conference called for a Makarrata or Treaty to be negotiated between the Aboriginal peoples of Australia and the Commonwealth (Federal) Government. The writing of the Makarrata is presently a major project of the National Aboriginal Conference. Preliminary research by our field researchers among Aboriginal peoples has produced an outline of the following concerns and grievances:

1. *Land:* The Federal Government should acquire all land originally set aside for the use and benefit of Aboriginals since colonisation, or adjacent land where these lands have been usurped, to be handed over to the Aboriginal communities under an inalienable Freehold Title in perpetuity.

2. *Self-Government:* Each respective tribal territory should be allowed to develop self-government to ensure their political, economic, social and educational advancement and to be allowed to pursue this advancement at their own speed, in their own way.

3. *A National Aboriginal Bank* should be established with branches in each State of the Commonwealth.

4. *The Payment of 5% of the Gross National Product* per annum for a period of 195 years, should come into effect upon the date of the signing of this agreement

5. *All national parks and forests* should be returned to those Aboriginal communities under whose territorial jurisdiction they fall.

6. *All artifacts and artworks* located by archaeological diggings for museums and art centres should be returned to the Aboriginal communities from whose territories they were obtained.

7. *Traditional rights* of hunting, fishing and gathering should be guaranteed to Aboriginal peoples on all lands and waterways under the jurisdiction of the Commonwealth Government.

8. *Legal and management rights* over all minerals, timber, waterways, airspace and other resources on lands given to Aboriginal peoples in perpetuity should be maintained by the Aboriginal peoples.

9. *Aboriginal customary law* should receive due recognition in those territories where they reside.

10. *Aboriginal schools* should be established in Aboriginal territories.

11. *Aboriginal medical centres* should be established in Aboriginal territories.

12. *Aboriginal legal aid offices* should also be established.

13. *Aboriginal lands, businesses* and cash compensation derived from the Gross National Product should be *exempt from all taxes* for a period of 1 95 years.

14. *The freedom of movement* across State borders without prejudice should be given to Aboriginals.

15. *One seat in Parliament* per State in both Houses of Federal Parliament should be reserved for Aboriginal and Torres Strait Island representation.

16. *Anthropological and Archaeological research* should not be conducted without full approval from those Aboriginal people whose territorial jurisdiction prevails in the chosen area.

Mining and Aboriginal Lands

Considerable concern has been expressed by our people over growing tensions and conflict between Aboriginal communities and the Mining Companies which are working on their land. This is particularly controversial in Queensland where the government appears more interested in appeasing American multi-nationals than in preventing a disruption of racial harmony. The growing anger of our people over the question of their land rights, the disregard for our sacred sites, the inadequacy of investigation into the problems mining is causing, and the inadequacy of compensation for Aboriginal lands lost to mining threatens, in some areas, to result in an outbreak of open hostility. These grievances are at the root of the movement now in the Aboriginal community to protest during the upcoming Commonwealth Games in Brisbane in September of this year ...

Education and Employment

... The National Aboriginal Conference sees two aspects of the Aboriginal education question. Firstly, Aboriginal children should be taught in schools to cater for their unique needs. They should be taught not only how to cope with modern Western society, but also taught to uphold their indigenous cultural values and identities with pride. Secondly, we would like to see Aboriginal studies become an integral part of every Australian child's education so that an accurate understanding of Australian history and Aboriginal culture may develop. By teaching Aboriginal studies throughout Australian schools we hope to promote understanding and respect for different cultural viewpoints in the public at large and to remove the stigma of racial stereotyping which presently supports wrongful racist attitudes of many Australians.

The education services we would like to see offered should aim at developing in Aboriginals a sound knowledge of, and pride in, their rich cultural heritage. In addition, we wish to see young Aboriginals acquire the technological and academic skills which will enable them to lead our people in the future. We feel that Aboriginals are best able to understand and communicate the needs and aspirations of their people. This requires them being given responsibility for the implementation of policies, funding and administration of programs in Aboriginal education, employment and other development areas ...

The challenge in the education today is to prepare our children so they are able to maintain their own cultural identity as well as to be able to function in the wider Australian community to their own and to their peoples' advantage. We seek the highest possible quality of education for our children.

All research has shown that Aboriginal students are, under the present system of schooling, reaching very low standards of achievement. Instead of meeting the needs of Aboriginals, present schooling attempts to bend them towards the needs of the system. The result of under-achievement is seen in the current high rate of Aboriginal unemployment. Unemployment among Aboriginals is six times higher than that of Australia as a whole. This estimate only takes into account those people enrolled with the Commonwealth employment service. It does not take into account the many Aboriginals in remote parts of the country who are not registered for work. This great problem is largely due to the apparent inability of the current education to transmit educational and vocational skills to our people.

165. *Age*, 8 October 1983. Tension Over Young Black's Death Erupts Into Violence

ROEBOURNE.— About 100 Aborigines angry at the death of a 17-year-old black in police custody, last night wrecked sections of the only hotel in Roebourne. Aborigines crying "murderers, murderers" raided the hotel's bottle department, smashed doors and furniture and went off carrying large quantities of liquor.

The town's policemen were forced to retreat to the end of the street as Aborigines hurled full bottles of beer at a police van during the raid which lasted about 20 minutes. Police had lost control of the riot when the West Australian Minister for Mines, Mr Peter Dowding, the local member of Parliament, arrived and persuaded the people to stop.

The 17-year-old, John Pat, died in custody after a clash between Aborigines and police at the hotel last week.

The trouble started last night when two policemen arrived at the hotel. Soon afterwards an Aboriginal woman was arrested. Senior police in the town last night accused "white stirrers" of fomenting the trouble. Roebourne police said that after the disturbance at the hotel a car was set alight in the town ...

Late last night, police vans were patrolling the town. Glass from broken windows and bottles littered the street outside the Victoria Hotel ...

One of the district's JPs, Mr Bruce Duncan, who regularly presides over the Roebourne court, claimed yesterday that police were terrorising Aborigines in the town. "This is a town on the boil," he said ...

The WA deputy commissioner of police, Mr Ayres, has flown to Roebourne to appeal for calm in the community. Yesterday he faced an emotional meeting of local Aborigines in their local hall. About 100 blacks, many of them relatives of John Pat, packed the hall. Several shouted at Mr Ayers during the meeting ...

166. *Age*, 12 October 1984. Aborigines Losing Patience With Labor: NAC Chief

Canberra.— The Chairman of the National Aboriginal Conference, Mr Rob Riley, yesterday attacked the Federal Government for apparently negotiating compromises on national land rights with mining and pastoral groups without the knowledge of Aboriginal groups and for reversing its stand on Aboriginal veto over mining.

Mr Riley, addressing the National Press Club in Canberra, said Aboriginal tolerance was "wearing thin" and that unless Aboriginal rights were restored by the bicentenary in 1988 "more direct measures may be called for" than continuing consultation. Mr. Riley said this could include embarrassing Australia in international forums.

Mr. Riley outlined what he said was the "Aboriginal bottom line" on land rights, including the right of veto over mining and mineral exploration, recognition of ownership, recognition of customary law, the right to self-determination, the right to compensation, direct access to mining royalties and protection of sites of significance. "Regardless of the type of land rights legislation arrived at in the short term, Aborigines will never relinquish these basic principles," he said.

He said that after the Government took office last year, Aborigines had been "tantalised by the knowledge that we were closer to achieving our aims than at any time in the past 200 years. The achievement of these aims by 1988 is being jeopardised by the Federal Government's retreat from its original commitment".

The Government had been easily intimidated by State Governments and groups opposing land rights and had failed to counter the vicious and constant attacks on land rights by those groups. "We are tired of the ALP cringe from unchallenged attacks on land rights by conservative politicians, by vested interest groups such as miners and pastoralists and by other fringe groups that appear to have intimidated this Government so effortlessly and so effectively," Mr. Riley said. "We are weary of the Government's constant unfulfilled promises that it will respond to these critics on our behalf and in defence of its own commitment and integrity."

Mr. Riley attacked the Government for:

• Failing to provide resources for Aborigines to consult on national legislation in an efficient way and for rendering the Aboriginal steering committee advising the Government on land rights policy "a virtual rubber stamp".

• Issuing a discussion paper on land rights which retreated from its original principles and for proposing a new weaker form of Aboriginal control over mining such as operates in South Australia.

• Deferring its promised public awareness campaign on land rights to undertake attitudinal surveys which amounted to a cynical exercise to suppress debate until after the election.

"Our future well-being should not depend on favourable opinion polls, nor should our rights be jeopardised by the desire of political parties to gain or maintain office," Mr. Riley said.

He said Aborigines were always being told by the ALP not to get upset because no matter how little they ended up with "we could expect a damn sight less from the conservatives. We are constantly warned, never publicly of course, to behave ourselves or end up with nothing". He added that despite reservations about the ALP, "we have no expectations from the Liberals".

He said he could offer politicians three clear justifications for land rights to take the issue out of the "gutter of political brawling ... to the level of legal and moral obligation", historical injustice and resulting disadvantage; the legal fiction of terra nullius that Australia was unoccupied before Europeans arrived; and Australia's international obligations.

167. *Age*, 11 September 1986. On The Road For Black Justice

The utter despair of the five Aboriginal families pervaded the room. All had a member who had died while in police custody or in jail. All were dissatisfied, horrified, outraged and finally worn down by what they consider the inadequate investigations into the deaths, and their inability to take the matter any further.

As one by one they told their stories, a chilling pattern emerged. Bad police–Aboriginal relations, continuous arrests for minor offences, threats, harassment, beatings, mysteriously sudden deaths in police cells or jails, intimidation of black and white witnesses, highly charged racist behaviour, contradictory police evidence, the deceased person's clothing "lost" and, in two cases, the heart and brain "lost" after autopsy.

In 1984, after five police charged with the manslaughter of 16-year-old Aboriginal youth, John Pat, were acquitted, some Aborigines were so concerned to protect the rights of Aborigines that they formed a Committee to Defend Black Rights.

Chairperson Helen Boyle said: "Some Aboriginal deaths in custody get publicity, most don't. We're encouraging families of these victims to speak out, and seek justice. There seems to be a conspiracy on behalf of the police, prisons, pathologists and courts to stop the truth coming out."

The five families today embark on a national speaking tour, beginning in Sydney and ending in Perth on 28 September, the anniversary of John Pat's death. They are seeking support from civil rights groups, the legal and medical profession and others to press for investigations into the deaths.

...

Helen Boyle quotes prison statistics to back the committee's argument that there is one law for blacks and another for whites in Australia.

"The overall imprisonment rate in Australia is 60 per 100,000, but for Aborigines it is 726 per 100,000. Aborigines are jailed 20 times the average rate in WA and die in suspicious circumstances at a great rate in that state also. In South Australia, Aborigines who appear in court are four times as likely to receive a prison sentence as whites.

"When you have the mining industry spending millions of dollars in anti-Aboriginal propaganda, the governments cutting back on Aboriginal welfare, the mood seems to grow that it's open season on blacks.

"What we're trying to get over is this is not only about black rights— it has serious implications for all human rights."

168. Lois O'Donoghue, *An Aboriginal and Islander Consultative Organisation* (1986)

...

Conclusions and Recommendations

Between October 1985 and July 1986 I have consulted with Aboriginal people throughout Australia. I have also sent letters to approximately 900 Aboriginal organisations providing information and seeking views on the form of a new consultative organisation ...

The main points that came out of my consultation are: –

1. The great majority of Aboriginal people wish to see a new national Aboriginal consultative organisation established.

2. The two most popular names for a new organisation are: 'Aboriginal and Islander Congress' and 'Australian Aboriginal and Islander Congress'.

3. There was majority support for the new organisation having the following features:

— incorporation under its own act of Parliament;

— regional assemblies made up of representatives of local community and service organisations;

— selection of national representatives by popular elections;

— electoral boundaries/regional assembly areas, to be drawn up after a thorough review, taking into account Aboriginal peoples' tribal, cultural and language affiliations and population, transport and communication patterns.

4. There is a strong wish on the part of Aboriginal people that the new organisation should be an independent body, able to give a strong expression to a national Aboriginal voice. There was less emphasis on other roles, such as providing advice to the Government and participating in policy development and the administration of programs and services. Majority views reflecting these wishes were:–

— full-time salaried membership for national representatives;

— an advisory role only for portfolio and national Aboriginal service organisations;

— secretariat resources, both at the regional assembly and national levels, separate from the Department of Aboriginal Affairs.

5. There is considerable concern that local Aboriginal communities should have strong controls over their representatives to a national organisation. This includes a wish to have provisions for binding representatives and the national executive of the Congress to the decisions of regional assemblies and powers to have representatives recalled, and dismissed.

The views of Aboriginal people have been considered in relation to the five options and the five principles proposed in the discussion paper. From these considerations it has become clear to me that there is likely to be a considerable gap between what Aboriginal people see as a desirable form for a new organisation and what is likely to be approved by the Government. This gap concerns both the resources which are likely to be available for a new organisation and the form of an organisation which can be expected to provide a satisfactory balance between the roles of providing a political voice for Aboriginal people, advancing self-management through participation in the administration of policy and programs, and providing advice to Governments.

I am also aware of the wishes of many Aboriginal people to continue to be involved in the development of a new organisation. There remains a considerable amount of uncertainty about how a new organisation should be constituted in order to effectively meet the wishes and expectations of both Aboriginal people and the Government.

Recommendations

1. I believe that the Government should proceed with the establishment of a new national Aboriginal consultative organisation by:

a. announcing guidelines within which it is prepared to see a new organisation established;

b. setting a time-table for continued discussions with Aboriginal people on the form of the new organisation;

c. distributing this report, together with the Government's guidelines and response to the report, to Aboriginal organisations and communities, as a basis for further discussions.

2. Regional assemblies should be established throughout Australia, initially paralleling the current DAA Area Offices, through which representatives from Aboriginal communities and organisations would consider the Government's guidelines for a new organisation.

3. After regional assemblies are established a national meeting of an Interim Aboriginal and Islander Congress should be called to consider a national Aboriginal response to the Government's guidelines.

4. There should be a review of the former NAC electoral boundaries with the objective of establishing regional assembly boundaries which reflect Aboriginal peoples' tribal, cultural and linguistic affiliations and population, transport and communication patterns.

5. Once the form of a new organisation is agreed between the Government and Aboriginal people, steps should be taken to have it incorporated in an act of Parliament. This could be part of a legislative package along the lines of a "Makarrata" or agreement between Aboriginal people and the Australian Government.

169. Neville Bonner, 'To My Fellow Countrymen', *Age*, 8 May 1987

It is as the only recognised elder of the Jugarah tribe of Queensland, a recognised Aboriginal elder statesman and a former holder of public office in the Australian Senate that I wish to address my fellow country-men— both Aboriginal and non-Aboriginal— on the question of Libyan support for Aborigines.

Any statement in support of accepting such foreign aid should not be regarded as representing the views of any Aborigines other than those who have made them. No individual Aborigine can speak on such matters for all our race. Contrary to the assertions made by the Premier of Queensland, those statements are not evidence of an Aboriginal-inspired conspiracy against non-Aborigines. No such conspiracy has ever existed and does not now.

It is, however, a matter of grave concern to me as it should be to all Australians, that such a proposal should gain any currency at all— from any section of our community. It can only be understood in the context of the frustration that some younger and impatient Aborigines have endured and continue to encounter in the struggle to fulfil our obligations to our past, our present and our future.

The solution does not and cannot be in accepting alms from another country, and it is truly naive to consider that such an arrangement could be struck without "strings attached". Consequently, any such action cannot be condoned under any circumstances.

The frustrations and sense of hopelessness about the future which underlie any support for Libyan assistance by any individual Aborigine are not of course peculiar to one racial or cultural group. All of us have every reason to be deeply concerned about the future of our families and children as we approach the 21st Century. There is little doubt that if we are to survive the genocidal threats that are posed by the prospect of global terrorism and nuclear conflict; the development of AIDS into epidemic proportions; the prospect of the depletion of the world's economic resources and accompanying famine, death and deprivation, then we must work together and draw upon the collective strength, wisdom and resources of all our cultural heritage.

It is only by working together, sharing our problems and jointly designing responses that all of us may hope to overcome the challenges of the present and the future. The knowledge and wisdom that we have inherited from our disparate cultural backgrounds is our most powerful weapon in this struggle. The promotion of conflict based on race and cultural differences will only serve to defeat us before we begin.

Aboriginal sovereignty is a state of mind which relates to the cultural and spiritual integrity of my people. It is not a doctrine which should be expediently exploited to promote sectarian political interest. Nor does it have political dimensions involving the establishment of a separate nation or state.

The misuse of the term sovereignty by both Aboriginal and non-Aboriginal people should be studiously avoided. It will only serve the interests of those who wish to prey upon social disharmony and dissension for their own reasons. Responsible leaders in the whole community (Aboriginal and non-Aboriginal) must continue to defuse reactions to this debate which are based on panic and irrationality.

Professor Manning Clark has offered sound counsel on the question of resolving conflict between our cultures when he says: "The important thing is to keep talking, not get too worked up about not getting too far in changing attitudes".

Only in so doing, can we hope to achieve a noble future for this great and ancient country and the generations of children and families that it must sustain and nurture.

170. *Age*, 14 May 1987. Mansell Wants Libya To Help Put Case To UN

Colonel Muammar Gaddafi of Libya has been asked to help Aborigines put their case for sovereign power to the United Nations. Michael Mansell, the Aboriginal activist who recently returned from a visit to Libya, said yesterday that he had asked Colonel Gaddafi for the assistance.

Speaking at the Tranby Cooperative College for Aborigines, in Sydney, he said he wanted countries such as Libya and other Arab and African states to support the Aborigines' right to be heard in the UN. He would have no hesitation in doing a deal with Colonel Gaddafi. "I would run up and shake Gaddafi's hand, pat him on the back and say, you're a good bloke, if he agreed to help us."

But he rejected suggestions that dealing with Libya amounted to supporting terrorism. "If any agreement involved violence, I would reject it out of hand." Using Libya as a lever into the UN was, however, too good an opportunity to miss.

"The UN is made up of powerful countries who make up the rules about who can even go and say something there ... and we are not part of that group. So you have to get the support of club members and Libya is one of those members," he said. "If they want to stand up and give us speaking time at the UN, as I understand it, we are able to take advantage of that, whereas at the moment that forum isn't open to us."

Mr Mansell said the result of a Libyan-backed protest to the UN could have even greater ramifications for Australia. "If Libya and a whole range of Arab countries can acknowledge that we are not, in fact, a minority group in this country but a sovereign people, it is possible that we can have relations with those countries, not on the basis of a minority group appealing for help, but on a nation to nation basis."

He refused to say whether he intended to return to Libya at this stage. Strong links had been established between Aborigines and Libya on his last trip and he said he hoped this spirit of friendship would continue.

Mr Mansell also called on the Federal Government to hold public debates on whether the Bicentenary celebrations should be scrapped, since they marked the "invasion" of Australia by white settlers.

171. *Age*, 27 May 1987. Aboriginal Advances Threatened: Perkins

Twenty years after the historic referendum by which Australians finally recognised Aborigines as full citizens, an anti-black backlash threatens many of the advances that have been made, Australia's most senior black public servant has warned. The head of the federal Department of Aboriginal Affairs, Mr Charles Perkins, took the occasion of the 20th anniversary of the 1967 referendum to attack both black activists and white conservatives, whose frustration at the apparent lack of progress by Aborigines had led them to radical "solutions".

Mr Perkins said he believed that white Australians, who voted by a 90 per cent majority to include blacks in the Census and give the Commonwealth power to make laws relating to Aboriginal welfare, had perhaps grown impatient with the slowness of progress. "There is a misconceived notion in the white community that too much has been done for the Aboriginal people," he said.

"And it is very sad to see the Liberal Party pandering to the backlash in its Aboriginal affairs policy." The recently announced Liberal policy would hand most responsibility for Aboriginal affairs back to the State governments, deny land rights and cut special benefits given on the basis of race. "The Liberal Party and National Party policies are so retrograde, they are taking us back into the stone age," Mr Perkins said. "It would cause race conflict.

"It's sad to see them trying to capitalise on that misinformed backlash which obviously exists in the Australian community. White Australians sooner or later have to regard Aborigines as the owners of this country, and due recognition has to be given."

At the same time, he criticised activists, such as Tasmanian lawyer Mr Michael Mansell, who have proposed the radical solution of a black nation. "The problem is a lot of the stirrers around, including Michael Mansell, have not been around long enough to see what is happening," Mr Perkins said.

He pointed to the establishment in 1972 of the Department of Aboriginal Affairs, and in 1983 of the Aboriginal Development Commission (ADC). "There now are more than 118 pastoral properties to which the ADC has the title, and which are being transferred to Aborigines. The Aboriginal people, through the ADC, are the greatest landowners in Australia of pastoral properties," Mr Perkins said. "Hostels provide more than 4500 beds for blacks every night, where they can put their heads down is safety and security." There are now 1200 organisations providing assistance for black Australians, including 53 medical services and 58 Aboriginal legal services. "This is all progress," Mr Perkins said. "Okay, people might say they haven't done much, but they have." There were 280 housing associations run by Aboriginal people and up to 20,000 houses had been provided for Aborigines since 1967. "Infant mortality is not what is was," Mr Perkins said. "We have task forces operating on trachoma."

...

172. Kevin Gilbert, *Aboriginal Sovereignty: Justice, the Law and Land*. A draft written in consultation with Aboriginal Members of the Sovereign Aboriginal Coalition at Alice Springs on 19-21 June 1987

Draft Treaty: Introduction

Let it be clearly understood that the Aboriginal position on Land Rights is a Sovereign Aboriginal Position.

From the Beginning of Time, time immemorial, our people, our culture, our land areas were clearly defined in the law and have so remained. The Aboriginal Law was not available to vagaries of change and 'amendment'. The Law was, and remains, a constant and unchanging law of rights, duties and responsibilities.

The Law governing our ownership and possession of land is such a constant Law and remains, in perpetuity, unchanged. Aboriginal Sovereign Rights in land covers the whole of this land on this continent of 'Australia'.

In 1770, our land was first invaded by Captain James Cook. As the Accredited, lawful representative of the Crown of England, Cook was *legally* bound by his Orders from the Admiralty to 'take Possession with the Consent of the Natives'. He failed to do so, and in so failing to act to that legally binding instrument of Orders, he acted in a criminal, unlawful manner which then allowed the terror and invasion, the massacre and theft of our land.

The instruments of law in Britain recognised Aboriginal Sovereign titles and rights in land. Such rights were an established fact of British and international law at that time. Such recognition of native right was the very legal basis of Captain James Cook's instructions.

From the fact of the instruction, which was a legally and internationally binding order upon Cook, all subsequent duties and rights of a legal standing flowed. So too, the departure from this order, or use of fraud in act or claim by Cook, the Accredited agent of the Crown, made null and void any act or attempt to establish a legal position by the Crown.

The British and Australian 'Government' have no valid title to the Sovereign Root Title of Aboriginal land and cannot acquire a legal, valid title except by entering into a legal, binding TREATY of international status with Aboriginal People of this our country.

Our TREATY encompasses all the lands of this continent. Therefore our Treaty shall insist upon these conditions:
- recognition of our Sovereign Aboriginal Nation State;
- Recognition of Aboriginals as a People;
- Recognition that the 'Federal Government' and the 'State Governments' of Australia have no valid claim or right to title or *compensation* over those areas of land registered as 'Crown' lands, Crown parklands, forest, reserves, national parks, commons.

The Commonwealth and every State shall legally:
- recognise original ownership, possession and Root Title of Aboriginals to land;
- restore immediately all unalienated 'Crown' lands, including State and National Parklands, Aboriginal reserves, travelling stock reserves;
- negotiate Aboriginal State Boundaries;
- recognise that Aboriginal State Lands are Sovereign Aboriginal Lands with title in perpetuity and inalienable;
- agree that the Aboriginal land base be not less than 40% of the total landmass of each 'Australian State' land holding;
- agree to the Aboriginal State being sovereign and autonomous in our community government, development, culture and law.

International Bill of Rights overrides all discriminatory laws and practices throughout the Commonwealth wherein those areas of State; and where Aboriginal traditional law applies that Aboriginal Law prevails.

All hunting, fishing, camping and usufructuary rights continue without constraint to Aboriginals.

A negotiated compensation fund (war reparation fund) be established from a 7% of National Gross Product for the loss of the rest of the land and the social, physical, psychological ravages made upon us.

The 'Australian Government' to enter into a Treaty in good faith in the interest of the Aboriginal people, the other peoples settled within our lands nationally, and the international community of which we all are a part.

Sovereign Treaty: Executed Between Us, The Sovereign Aboriginal People Of This Our Land, Australia, And The Non-Aboriginal Peoples Who Invaded And Colonised Our Lands

1. SOVEREIGN POSITION

1.1 *General*

1.1.1 We, the Sovereign Aboriginal People hold and maintain our Sovereign Root Title to these our lands now known as 'Australia'.

1.1.2 Our Sovereign Root Title inherent, has been held by our forebears since the Beginning, Time Immemorial, and has never passed from us in any way, nor have we lost our inherent Root Title of Sovereign Possession.

1.1.3 Our Sovereign Aboriginal Ownership, Possession and Sovereign Root Title to these our Lands and our People have never been lost, removed or ceded in any form or manner by any *legal* act or claim.

1.1.4 Our Sovereign Root Title is therefore intact and remains intact over all of these our Sovereign Domains of land, now known as 'Australia', and those areas of land off-shore from the Mainland wherein reside Aboriginal People.

1.1.5 We are free to manage our own affairs both internally and externally to the fullest possible extent, in the proper exercise of our Sovereign Right as a Nation.

1.1.6 No other State shall assert or claim or exercise any right of jurisdiction over our Aboriginal Nation State, or People, or area of Land or Sea inherent to us as lands of our Sovereign Domains, unless pursuant to a valid treaty freely made with our lawful representatives accredited of our Nation.

1.1.7 Our Sovereign Aboriginal Nation, fulfilling the criteria of Statehood, having Inherent Possessory Root Title to Lands, a permanent population and a representative governing body according to our indigenous traditions, having the ability to enter into relations with other States, possesses the right to autonomy in self-determination of our political status, to freely pursue our economic, social and cultural development and to retain our rights in religious matters, tradition and traditional practice.

1.1.8 We, the Sovereign Aboriginal People are to be accorded our right and proper recognition as a People and a Nation State, subjects of international law.

1.1.9 Inherent in this Treaty is the immediate Proclamation of our Sovereign Aboriginal Rights of State.

1.1.10 The failure of Britain and subsequently the successional government, Australia, to enter a legally valid treaty with our Aboriginal Sovereign State has resulted in a position of national and international consequences which must be resolved in accordance with the proper standards of principle, good faith and requirements to international law as applies to the validity of States. Australia's claim to 'sovereignty' in root title is not a valid claim.

2. LAND

2.1 *General*

2.1.1 As root title to all such land and territory was unlawfully claimed and assumed as 'property of the crown', those colonial institutions known as 'State Governments of Australia', have no lawful basis of claim of right or compensation for such areas of these our territorial lands to be returned unencumbered to us.

2.1.2 Certain portions of lands will be cedable title under a fully accredited treaty enacted and executed at the direction of the Aboriginal People by and through our fully accredited Sovereign Representatives.

2.1.3 Aboriginal Sovereign Domain shall not be reduced in area at any time under any treaty to an area of the total land mass to a lesser degree or portions than 40%. The total land mass to be assessed on what is presently known and recognised as 'state' boundaries, i.e., New South Wales, Victoria, Queensland.

2.2 *Crown Lands*

2.2.1 There shall be immediate restoration to us of those parts and parcels of land registered as 'crown lands'. These 'crown lands' have no legal justification to being so termed and bear no encumbrance or responsibility upon the local inhabitants or the international States with whom we are most concerned.

2.2.2 All those areas of land that have been gazetted as 'crown lands' such as those areas of our exile known as 'Aboriginal Reserves', state forests, travelling stock reserves, are to be returned forthwith in correct legal status as Sovereign Aboriginal Domain ...

173. Galarrwuy Yunupingu, 'What The Aboriginal People Want', *Age*, 26 August 1987

Australian Governments since Federation have left Aboriginal policy to the states. They hunted Aboriginal people off their land and put them into reserves, which did not acknowledge land rights, but fenced our people up in compounds to stop them from competing with other demands for land, like mining and farming.

Even these reserves only remained our land at the whim of government agencies. They could be revoked if they got in the way of economic activity. This is not history: it is still happening.

This process ignores our rights as traditional landowners. It has created a class of dispossessed urban Aborigines, people who were kicked off their traditional associations and their identity.

Land rights and Aboriginal self-determination are a long way from being achieved. We still suffer from "divide and rule" tactics. For self-determination to become reality, we need constitutional guarantees of our rights to our land. So far, the Federal Government has tried to set the agenda through debate on the so-called Makaratta Treaty. We reject this utterly because it would be inadequate without the proper constitutional backing.

A treaty which is recognised by international convention must state that:

• Aboriginal people are the indigenous sovereign owners of Australia and adjacent islands since before 1770 and as such have rights and treaty rights;

• Their sovereignty was never ceded; and

• The doctrine of terra nullius cannot be supported in international law as the legal basis for European occupation of, and acquisition of sovereignty over, our land.

Recognition of land rights is the key to Aboriginal self-determination. It is the basis for our development of a secure social, cultural and economic base. It gives us the basis for claiming compensation and achieving proper health, education, legal and child care services.

The constitution must restore our rights to land under secure title, guarantee our access to lands and sites of Aboriginal significance on land which cannot be restored to us, give us full control of our own lands and compensate us for our lands which have been alienated. We are not just interested in the concept of you "paying the rent"; we want our legitimate sovereignty recognised.

The constitution should also guarantee the preservation of our social and cultural heritage and compensate us for the way in which they have been eroded at the hands of invaders. It should provide for Aboriginal people to develop a secure economic base. It must be the beginning of true self determination for us.

Next year's celebration of 200 years of European occupation of Australia, as it stands, spits in the face of every Aboriginal and Islander person. You are asking us to stand by while you congratulate yourselves of having stolen our land. You want us to keep quiet while you celebrate the raising of the first British flag in 1788. For us, this was an act of war which led to genocide.

You have the chance to right the wrong. You have the chance to recognise what you have done. If you want us to join you in a celebration for all Australians, 1988 should be the year when you come to us with a real recognition of who we are and a positive vision of our place in this Australia.

174. *Sun* (Melbourne), 27 January 1988. Black Power On The March

The Aboriginal flag flew high yesterday as more than 20,000 black and white Australians joined in a protest march through the streets of Sydney. Organisers were amazed at the size of the crowd, which made its way from Redfern Oval to Hyde Park to "support the Aboriginal struggle for peace, justice and freedom". Traditional tribal dancers came from all over the country to take part in what many called the black alternative to the celebration of a nation.

The march was the largest seen in Sydney since the Vietnam moratoriums. It was designed to focus attention on the black struggle on the day before the Muirhead Inquiry into Black Deaths in Custody begins in Adelaide. None of the expected violence flared during the march as police and rally organisers kept tight control.

Aboriginal activist Gary Foley said the support from both black and white Australians had been overwhelming. "It's been beyond all expectations," Mr Foley said. "Let's hope Bob Hawke and his Government gets this message loud and clear from all these people here today. It's so magnificent to see black and white Australians together in harmony. It's what we always said could happen. This is what Australia could and should be like." The marchers were given support from organisations as diverse as the PLO and the Italian Migrant Workers Families.

A number of tribal elders refused to be photographed as they led the procession. One television news crew was told to have some respect when it tried to film some of the tribesmen performing ritual dances.

A deafening roar erupted when the protest march finally reached Hyde Park just after 2 pm. Hundreds of both black and white families had lined the walls of the park to cheer the procession.

The Rev Charles Harris, a leading figure in the March '88 committee, said it was an historic occasion for Aboriginal people. He said Aborigines wanted the Australian Government and the world to know that they had been victims of gross injustice for too long. He claimed Aborigines had been manipulated and oppressed, their children victims of racism and they were treated as foreigners in their own land. "We are the sovereign people of this land and this celebration is a farce, it's hypocrisy."

Earlier, a procession of 2000 Aboriginals made their way from Redfern to a harborside tent embassy. Organised by radical Sydney activists, the rally attracted a rowdy crowd which included Michael Mansell and Charles Perkins.

Twice the marchers were involved in stand-offs with a contingent of 100 police who tried to block their progress. The tense situations ended without violence when police allowed the group to proceed as individuals. Once at the tent embassy, the group set off flares and turned away from an attempt to recreate the first white landing in Australia, dumping two participants gently, but unceremoniously, into the water.

175. Barunga Statement, presented by Galarrwuy Yunupingu, Chairperson of the Northern Land Council, and Wenten Rubuntja, Chairperson of the Central Land Council, to R.J. Hawke, Prime Minister, at the Barunga Festival, 12 June 1988

We the indigenous owners and occupiers of Australia call on the Australian Government and people to recognise our rights:

•   to self determination and self management including the freedom to pursue our own economic, social, religious and cultural development;

•   to permanent control and enjoyment of our ancestral lands;

•   to compensation for the loss of use of our lands, there having been no extinction of original title;

•   to protection of and control of access to our sacred sites, sacred objects, artefacts, designs, knowledge and works of art;

•   to the return of the remains of our ancestors for burial in accordance with our traditions;

•   to respect for promotion of our Aboriginal identity, including the cultural, linguistic, religious and historical aspects, including the right to be educated in our own languages, and in our own culture and history;

• in accordance with the Universal Declaration of Human Rights, the International Covenant on Economic, Social and Cultural Rights, the International Covenant on Civil and Political Rights, and the International Convention on the Elimination of all forms of Racial Discrimination, rights to life, liberty, security of person, food, clothing, housing, medical care, education and employment opportunities, necessary social services and other basic rights.

We call on the Commonwealth to pass laws providing:
• a national elected Aboriginal and Islander organisation to oversee Aboriginal and Islander affairs;
• a national system of land rights;
• a police and justice system which recognises our customary laws and frees us from discrimination and any activity which may threaten our identity or security, interfere with our freedom of expression or association, or otherwise prevent our full enjoyment and exercise of universally-recognised human rights and fundamental freedoms.

We call on the Australian Government to support Aborigines in the development of an International Declaration of Principles for Indigenous Rights, leading to an International Covenant.

And we call on the Commonwealth Parliament to negotiate with us a Treaty or Compact recognising our prior ownership, continued occupation and sovereignty and affirming our human rights and freedoms.

176. *Age*, 6 July 1989. Black Leaders To Seek UN Action Over Jail Deaths

Aboriginal rights leaders will ask the United Nations to act on black deaths in custody, following the death of a 19-year-old Aborigine in a South Australian police cell and a reported suicide attempt by another man in the same cell block a few hours later.

The Committee to Defend Black Rights, the group representing the families of Aborigines who have died in custody, said yesterday that it would ask the UN to put pressure on the Australian Government for legislation to reduce the high number of Aborigines being imprisoned after they were taken into custody.

The committee's public relations officer, Mr Greg Eatock, said the committee would also seek pressure on the Federal Government for laws that would punish those who failed to follow regulations and procedures when Aborigines were jailed. "Here we are at the close of the royal commission (on black deaths in custody) and our people are still dying," he said. "In South Australia, the commission has handed down reports on seven cases and the strongest thing to come out of it there so far is an internal prisons' system inquiry with a $50 fine. The commission's recommendations will continue to be ignored, as they were in the latest (Ceduna) case, until the Federal Government acts."

He said the committee would send two representatives to Geneva at the end of July for a meeting of the UN indigenous peoples' working group on human rights ...

177. ATSIC, *What Is ATSIC* (1997)

The Aboriginal and Torres Strait Islander Commission— ATSIC— is the peak representative indigenous agency in Australia. It is also a Commonwealth statutory authority responsible for administering many programs for Aboriginal and Torres Strait Islander people.

ATSIC was established in March 1990, amalgamating the former Department of Aboriginal Affairs and Aboriginal Development Commission.

What makes ATSIC different from its predecessors, and unique among indigenous agencies around the world, is its elected arm.

Through ATSIC, indigenous representatives have for the first time been given real authority in the process of government decision-making affecting their lives.

Every three years Aboriginal and Torres Strait Islander people around Australia elect representatives to sit on 35 Regional Councils and the Torres Strait Regional Authority. Regional Councillors and members of the Torres Strait Regional Authority in turn choose 17 Commissioners to make up the ATSIC Board. Two additional Commissioners are appointed by the Minister for Aboriginal and Torres Strait Islander Affairs.

Regional Councils and the Board decide how the ATSIC budget is to be spent.

The Board is also the premier policy-making body in indigenous affairs, the principal advisor to government, and a powerful advocate of indigenous interests across the whole range of government agencies— Commonwealth, State/Territory and local.

ATSIC is still an evolving organisation, coming to grips with the developing and complex relationships between elected indigenous representatives, an administration staffed by public servants, indigenous service-delivery organisations and governments at all levels.

Nevertheless, it is now well-established as a forceful and independent indigenous voice in policy formulation, program design and service delivery.

How ATSIC Came About

ATSIC was the culmination of 20 years Commonwealth involvement in Aboriginal and Torres Strait Islander Affairs, and represented a radical departure from previous bureaucracies and advisory committees.

The Commonwealth's involvement in indigenous affairs dates back only to 1967, when a constitutional referendum was overwhelmingly passed to allow the national government to legislate for Aboriginal and Torres Strait Islander people, concurrently with the States ...

In 1972 Aboriginal affairs began to be administered as a separate area of government, with the establishment of the Department of Aboriginal Affairs. The guiding policy was to be self-determination for indigenous Australians, defined as 'Aboriginal communities deciding the pace and nature of their future development as significant components within a diverse Australia'.

In 1987 the Commonwealth moved to replace the department with a statutory authority based on indigenous representation. The then Minister envisaged the Aboriginal and Torres Strait Islander Commission as a means of 'address[ing] seriously the vital issue of self-determination for Aboriginal and Islander people' by ensuring 'that Aboriginal and Islander people are properly involved at all levels of the decision-making process in order that the right decisions are taken about their lives'.

Another aim was to decentralise the administration of Aboriginal affairs through the division of Australia into regions, allowing 'grass-roots' self-determination.

The Aboriginal and Torres Strait Islander Commission Act was finally passed in 1989, enabling the establishment of the Commission in the following year.

The Legislation

The *Aboriginal and Torres Strait Islander Commission Act 1989* enshrines the goal of empowerment of Aboriginal and Torres Strait Islander people. Since 1990 the ATSIC Act has been amended many times, in response to reviews and changing circumstances, and to advance self-determination for Aboriginal and Torres Strait Islander people.

ATSIC's statutory functions include the formulation of programs, their implementation, the development of policy proposals, providing advice to the Minister, and monitoring the effectiveness of programs for indigenous Australians including programs conducted by other agencies.

The Minister
     The Minister for Aboriginal and Torres Strait Islander Affairs represents the interests of ATSIC in Parliament, in the Cabinet and in the formulation of the Federal Budget by the Expenditure Review Committee.
     Although ATSIC is an independent statutory authority, the Minister has a limited number of powers under the ATSIC Act. For example, the Minister must approve the ATSIC Estimates and the form of those Estimates. The Minister is able to seek information on any aspect of ATSIC's activities, and may issue General Directions to the Commission and Directions about the administration of ATSIC finances.
     A close and co-operative relationship between the Minister and ATSIC is vital to the effective representation of the Commission and indigenous people in Parliament ...

Chairman
     The ATSIC Chairman is currently appointed by the Minister from among the 19 members of the Board. The current Chairman is Mr Gatjil Djerrkura OAM. The Deputy Chair (an elected position) is Commissioner Ray Robinson. After the next ATSIC elections, the Chairman will be elected by Commissioners from among their number.

Administration
     Supporting Regional Councils and Commissioners is an administrative arm, staffed by Commonwealth public servants and headed by a Chief Executive Officer. Approximately 37 per cent of staff are Aboriginal or Torres Strait Islander.
     There is a Central Office in Canberra, State Offices in each capital city, and 27 Regional Offices throughout Australia ...
     Since 1990 ATSIC has decentralised much of its operations, concentrating resources at the regional level.
     It is vital for effective service delivery that a close partnership exists between ATSIC's elected arm and its administration.

Torres Strait Islander arrangements
     The ATSIC Act put in place arrangements for Torres Strait Islanders in acknowledgment of the fact that they form a minority within the indigenous population. Approximately 80 per cent of the 28 000 Torres

Strait Islanders live outside the Torres Strait.

Torres Strait Islander Advisory Board

The Torres Strait Islander Advisory Board provides advice to the Minister and ATSIC on the social, economic and cultural advancement of Torres Strait Islanders living outside the Torres Strait area. The Board is appointed by the Minister. An Office of Torres Strait Islander Affairs within ATSIC's administration supports the TSIAB.

Torres Strait Regional Authority

The Torres Strait Regional Authority was established on 1 July 1994. It replaced the Torres Strait Regional Council and is an autonomous statutory authority under the ATSIC Act, with a 20-member elected board. The TSRA performs similar functions to ATSIC in the Torres Strait ...

178. Kevin Gilbert, Transcript of a speech at the Aboriginal Tent Embassy, Canberra, Day of Protest and Mourning for the 25th Anniversary of the 1967 Referendum, 27 May 1992

It's twenty-five years since we Aboriginal People have had Australian citizenship imposed upon us, very much against the will of the Aboriginal People, for we have always been Australian Aborigines, not Aboriginal Australians.

We have never joined the company. We have never claimed citizenship of the oppressor, the people who have invaded our country.

Twenty-five years after this citizenship, which was supposed to give us some sort of rights and equality we see that instead of lifting us to any sort of degree of place or right it has only given us the highest infant mortality rate, the highest number of Aboriginal people in prison, the highest mortality rate, the highest unemployment rate.

And after twenty-five years we still have Aboriginal children and people dying from lack of clean drinking water, lack of medication, lack of shelter.

We have still had twenty-five years of economic, political and medical human rights apartheid in Australia. And it hasn't worked for Aboriginal People.

At the end of the twenty-five years, we have seen the Australian Government and the Australian people try and get off the hook of responsibility by saying, ten years down the track, we'll have Reconciliation.

And Reconciliation doesn't promise us human rights, it doesn't promise us our Sovereign rights or the platform from which to negotiate, and it doesn't promise us a viable land base, an economical base, a political base, or a base in which we can again heal our people, where we can carry out our cultural practices.

It is ten more years of death! There must be something better.

Australia is calling for a Republic and a new flag, a new vision. It cannot have a vision. It cannot have a new flag. It cannot have a Sovereign nation until it addresses the right of Aboriginal People, the Sovereign Land Rights of Aboriginal people.

You cannot build a vision, you cannot build a land, you cannot build a people, on land theft, on massacre, on continuing apartheid and the denial of the one group of Aboriginal people.

We have committed no crime, we have done no wrong except own the land which the churches and white society want to take from us.

It must change.

And we can never become, and we never will become, Australian citizens. For we are Aboriginal People. We are Sovereign Aboriginal People.

We fly the flag at half mast, in respect for Alice Dixon, the mother of the boy who died in custody, Kingsley Dixon; and for all the Aboriginal people who have died in custody and been murdered in custody. And for all the Aboriginal people in gaol. And for all the children who are dying. A mark of respect and mourning for those who have died in the struggle. Because Australia still has not had the maturity, or the vision, or the guts, or the will, or the humanity, to come to justice, to come to terms, with our rights, as Sovereign Indigenous People.

Today is not a day of rejoicing, not a day of pride for Australia. It's a day when we hold our flags at half mast, in respect for Alice Dixon, and all the people who have died in custody, all the children who continue to die, even as we talk, through economic and political apartheid in this country.

We are still dying. Nothing has changed.

And white Australia and the politicians, are trying to avoid the responsibility, by pushing it off ten years in the future, where it promises nothing.

It has to change.

The Aboriginal vision for this country, Aboriginal Land Rights, is right for everyone. It means you cannot build any nation without integrity. You cannot build it without justice. You cannot build it without humanity. You cannot build it without compassion.

These are things that have to be addressed. We have to go forward with a vision. We have to go forward with a justice for everyone. That vision, that justice, that integrity, must address Aboriginal Sovereign rights, reparation, so we can have an economic and a political voice.

We can't be done anymore. Australia is not going to get away with killing us anymore. This type of apartheid has to be addressed.

If the Referendum hadn't been passed, we would have been further advanced, because white Australia would not have fooled the world into thinking that something positive was being done.

The international world would have looked much more closely at us, much sooner. They are now, but it would have advanced our cause by at least fifteen years.

We are now going to light our international distress flares ... and we are going to signify with these distress flares the position Aboriginal People are in, and we want to signify to the world, that we need international aid, that our arms and legs have been taken from us, and we ask the International World to help restore our legs ... and we need our arms.

179. 'Intellectual Prisoners', *APG Papers*, July 1992

... The APG [Aboriginal Provisional Government] stands for the right of Aboriginal people to have the ultimate say over their destiny. The Provisional Government proposes a model for the Aboriginal Nation— a nation exercising total jurisdiction over its communities to the exclusion of all others. A nation whose land base is at least all crown lands, so called. A nation able to raise its own economy and provide for its people.

This cannot occur over night, but it could be in place within 25 years. That would be dependent on three developments:

1.Through developing within the Aboriginal communities a thorough understanding of how the Aboriginal government will work, how real it can be, and what it would mean in practice. This can only be achieved through meeting after meeting after meeting.

2. Once the Aboriginal community has had chance to think seriously about it, a referendum of Aboriginal people should be held. The question would be— Aboriginal independence, yes or no.

3. Presuming a majority vote in favour of independence, then a timetable agreed upon between the white government and the Aboriginal people could be laid down. The timetable would basically cover the transfer of control over Aboriginal people back to Aboriginal people.

The practical benefits under an Aboriginal government which are not available under a white government include:

1. No Aboriginal person would pay rent. Each Aboriginal family would be provided with housing of their choice. They would have to

maintain it.

2. Every Aboriginal person not able to work or find work will be maintained by the government.

3. There would be free medical service with free access to specialist medical facilities not available within the local services.

4. Complete control over local communities would be put back in the hands of local people.

5. There would be strong encouragement of Aboriginal communities to maintain their strong links with their heritage and culture.

180. 'Towards Aboriginal Sovereignty', *APG Papers*, July 1992

On 16 July 1990 the Aboriginal Provisional Government (APG) was formed by Aborigines in Australia. This article was prepared by the APG to outline its structure, purpose and strategies, and some of the implications of the establishment of a sovereign state for Aborigines.

There has been a lot said about the sad treatment of Aboriginal people in Australia, particularly since the 1960s. As a result, government funded programs have been aimed at giving assistance to Aborigines. Practice shows that the best programs have been those funded by government but implemented by Aboriginal organisations run by Aboriginal people.

Programs aimed at reducing Aboriginal leprosy rates, other health problems, improving access to the goods and services of the community, for example, law, education, housing, and generally upgrading the social situation of Aborigines, have unquestionably benefited Aboriginal communities. With these social benefits have come some minor changes in Aboriginal politics. Until 1967 Aborigines were not regarded as human beings and were prevented from voting. There were too few Aboriginal spokespersons and any organisations acting on behalf of Aborigines were invariably run by whites. Generally speaking, that has changed.

From 1967 to 1976 there have been significant changes. Aboriginal Legal Services were established in every state and territory. In 1976 Land Rights legislation in the Northern Territory was passed by the federal parliament. The establishment and funding of the National Aboriginal Conference (NAC) gave Aboriginal people for the first time an effective voice at the national level.

Since then, however, it is at best difficult and at worst impossible to point to projects of the same magnitude as those mentioned above, apart from perhaps the Royal Commission into Black Deaths in Custody. Just as those initiatives indicated a trend towards better treatment of Aboriginal people by government, the failure by governments to have similar initiatives of significance in the 1980s indicates a trend in the opposite direction. Justice Michael Kirby best summed it up during the 1988 celebrations, by suggesting sadly that the white population had become bored with the subject of Aboriginal justice.

In the meantime, Aboriginal communities are left to suffer the disadvantages which have continued since the halcyon days of the 1970s. There have been few initiatives, with no policy changes likely to benefit Aboriginal people to any significant level, and, even more frightening, no real direction coming from the Aboriginal community.

A Decade of Consultation

When the APG was launched, one of the first outcries from some sections of the Aboriginal community was "lack of consultation" about its formation. For over a decade meetings of the Federation of Land Councils, Coalition of Aboriginal Organisations, National Aboriginal and Islander Legal Services, SNAACC, and even the NAC saw numerous discussions held about the sovereign rights of Aboriginal people in this country. The same people who cried lack of consultation were present at these meetings where there was little action, but much talk.

At these national meetings where, presumably, the national delegates were reflecting the views of their local communities in talking about the sovereign rights of Aboriginal people, the call had long been for Aborigines to begin acting sovereignty rather than continuing to use rhetoric. How much longer would the discussions have had to be held— ten years, twenty years, or even longer before a decision would be made? How many more Aboriginal men women and children would suffer while the debate went on?

There will always be those who oppose change, but not all Aborigines saw it that way. Former Department of Aboriginal Affairs Secretary, Mr. Charles Perkins, probably the most well known Aborigine of recent times, said on 17 July 1990 that some Aboriginal organisations had "died on the vine and needed to change direction and become as creative and dynamic as they were thirty years ago".

Without doubt Charlie was referring to the enormous time spent by Aboriginal organisations and the delegates "discussing" a plan aimed at alleviating hardships for Aboriginal people without any of these plans seeing the light of day. The most embarrassing moment for those Aborigines opposed to the formation of the APG came from the unlikely source of former Northern Territory Chief Minister, Paul Everingham, who said in *The Australian* on 8 August 1990: "the fact is that self-determination will remain a dream until Aborigines show the determination to deal with the realities of Australia today ... "

The Purpose of the Aboriginal Government

The APG plans to change the situation in Australia so that instead of white people determining the rights of Aboriginal people, it will be the Aboriginal people who do it. In previous times, even when government policy was supportive of Aborigines, helpful polices at the same time reinforced white domination of Aborigines. For example, Land Rights legislation in the Northern Territory retains absolute ownership of that land for the Australian government but gives certain rights to Aborigines. If the white government ever repealed the legislation, the land would automatically revert to the white government.

The second important change sought by the APG relates to the status of the relationship between Aborigines and whites in this country. Until now Aborigines have always been regarded as nothing more than a minority group in Australian society. The APG rejects that, insisting that nobody in the world has any greater right than Aborigines to determine what it is that we desire.

Thirdly, the APG believes that, despite the fantastic work done by Aboriginal organisations throughout our country, Aboriginal people still are not able to fully accept responsibility for determining the long term future. Organisations have essentially been service delivery organisations, snowed under with all the day to day crises of a poorly treated people. They have been so busy trying to keep their communities alive that they had little opportunity to sit down, design and implement policies aimed at giving effective control of Aboriginal communities back to the communities themselves. The APG sees itself playing a major role in filling this void.

Fourthly, the APG looked at the current situation of Aboriginal Affairs and saw nothing to indicate that there was ever going to be change from continual reliance upon the white welfare system and being forced to participate in the Australian political system. APG members recognised the need for a body which, by virtue of its name and purpose, would set a new theme and plan for the long term destiny of Aboriginal people. We believe the APG does this.

The Objective of an Aboriginal State

We can anticipate the white reaction to any challenge from the Aboriginal community to over 200 years of white supremacy and domination. What is seen by Aborigines as freedom and independence is for whites a form of apartheid; what has been put forward as the right of Aboriginal people to control themselves has drawn the comment of "separatism"; what the APG sees as self-determination for Aborigines is viewed generally by the white powers-that-be as a dividing up of the country.

Furthermore, whenever members of the Aboriginal Provisional Government talk about an Aboriginal State, the immediate response from our opponents is that "Aborigines are to be rounded up and put on a little piece of land somewhere in the middle of Australia". Clearly, all of these examples indicate the strategy of those opposing the intentions of the APG; namely, by putting *fear* into the discussion it is hoped that more and more Aboriginal people will turn away from the debate and therefore everything will remain the same.

Let it be clearly understood: the Aboriginal Provisional Government wants an Aboriginal state to be established, with all of the essential control being vested back into Aboriginal communities. The land involved would essentially be crown land but in addition there would be some land which would be needed by the Aboriginal community other than crown land.

The test for which lands come under the Aboriginal Provisional government would *be the land needed by Aboriginal communities to survive on.* No longer would Aborigines need to beg governments or judicial bodies for land to be returned to Aboriginal people. At the end of the day, enough land would need to be returned to Aboriginal communities throughout Australia to enable them to survive *as a Nation of people* and the remaining land would be kept by whites and their governments as a basis for them to continue their nation.

There will *not* be a need for all Aboriginal people to live on Aboriginal land. Some may choose to do so, and some may choose to continue to live under the jurisdiction of white Australia. There is nothing wrong with that because, if nothing else, it gives Aboriginal people a choice which we do not have now. We must all subscribe to white jurisdiction at the moment.

Nor would Aboriginal people have to live in a particular small area on Aboriginal lands. The areas would be scattered far and wide around Australia and would be the land needed by local Aboriginal communities. While some have scoffed at the peculiar boundaries such a division of land would create, it is not unusual in international circles. For example, the United States is a nation yet is separated completely from its territory in Alaska. Its territory in Hawaii is halfway around the other side of the world. This has not been seen as a reason to laugh at the jurisdiction of the United States.

At the moment Aboriginal communities have to abide by the white man's law. That would change under the APG because each Aboriginal community would determine its own form of legal system appropriate to its community situation. It would mean, therefore, that some Aboriginal communities would practice "traditional" laws, others who have had much more contact with the white community would have a mixture of white and black law, and even others would have a system which is simply appropriate to their life style in any given situation. Any person from outside the Aboriginal Nation entering Aboriginal land would be expected to abide by that legal system and, conversely, any Aboriginal person going into white cities or towns would be expected to abide by the white man's legal system. Here is one disadvantage of Aboriginal Sovereignty which is conceded: if the basis for Aboriginal self determination is the mutual respect of each others' rights as peoples, then Aborigines cannot expect to carry their own laws onto Australian government controlled areas. By the same token, people coming onto Aboriginal land cannot expect to ignore Aboriginal law. But it should also be recognised that there is scope for both sides to soften the normal harshness of penalties if a white person came onto Aboriginal land and was not familiar with the laws and broke such a law, it may well be that the white person would not be punished as strongly as an Aboriginal person would be. By the same token, we would expect that Aborigines who broke the white man's law would also be treated in a lighter way than white people themselves.

The political control of each local Aboriginal community would be vested in the community themselves. There would be no point in transferring white power to an Aboriginal Provisional Government which simply imposed the same policies from above. The local communities must have absolute control over their day-to-day activities and the direction in which the local Aboriginal communities are to move. The residual powers of negotiating with foreign governments for trade, coordination of some uniformity between Aboriginal communities and so on, would be vested in the Aboriginal Provisional Government. Election to the APG would be via the local community controlled councils.

This then is the basic outline of how Aboriginal people can exercise control over their own communities without hindrance from any other government. The Aboriginal Government would operate alongside all other governments in the world, including the Australian government, and not be subordinate to it. White legislation would have no application whatsoever to Aboriginal communities because absolute control over Aboriginal land would be vested in Aboriginal communities. The laws of the white man would not apply unless the Aboriginal communities wanted it. There would be no right of the police to come onto Aboriginal land unless it was by agreement with the Aboriginal community.

In exchange for Aboriginal people giving up to perhaps half of the country to white Australians, there would need to be some compensation package. It need not necessarily be in the form of money and perhaps ought not to be, so that we become more self sufficient at an early stage. However, having access to specialised institutions such as medical facilities, education facilities and telecommunications systems could be a basis for that compensation for ceded lands. Further, it would be in the interests of the Australian government to prevent Aboriginal land being used as a sanctuary by criminals from its own area, or drug runners evading Australian police by running through Aboriginal land. This could be done by coming to some arrangement with Aboriginal community organisations to allow police access on certain conditions. Both communities would have mutual benefit. There is no necessity for continual conflict provided that the imposition of the white man's will on Aborigines is removed once and for all ...

181. *Sydney Morning Herald*, 29 January 1992. Aborigines Quit House As Four Arrested

Canberra: Nearly all the 100 Aborigines and their white supporters who occupied old Parliament House left the building voluntarily last night, but four who allegedly refused to move were arrested by Federal police. The arrests were made about 7 o'clock following a joint decision by the Prime Minister, Mr Keating, and the Minister for Administrative Services, Senator Bolkus.

The protesters had occupied the building since 5 pm on Monday, calling for Federal Government and United Nations recognition of Aboriginal sovereignty over Australia. Although police ended the occupation, a "tent embassy" remains on the lawns outside.

Police said the four arrested— two men and two women— were taken to the city police station and charged with trespass under the Public Order Act. The arrests fulfilled a goal set by the Aborigines. They hope the arrests will strengthen their sovereignty case in the High Court, and the International Court of Justice in The Hague if necessary.

An Aboriginal flag was lowered from the flagpole, another flag which was draped over a statue of King George V was removed, and mattresses, inflatable mattresses and blankets used to cushion the hard polished floor of the Hall were stacked outside.

The climax to the protest was far different from the last moments of a similar protest for land rights 20 years ago. On the order of the McMahon Government, a rally outside the House was broken up with great violence from both sides.

Yesterday, Mr Paul Coe, of the Redfern Aboriginal Legal Service, was able to present a "Declaration of Aboriginal Sovereignty" to the Minister for Aboriginal Affairs, Mr Tickner., It invoked a claim upon Australian land under the rule of international law, as "we have never surrendered nor acquiesced in our claim to these lands and territories".

Last night, Senator Bolkus said he believed the outcome had the support of both sides. In short, this meant the sanctity of the hallowed halls of the House was restored without force or aggression, and the Aborigines now had more ammunition to pursue their legal claims for sovereignty.

Mr Bill Craigie was one of the original quartet of Aboriginal protesters who set up camp 20 years ago outside Parliament House. He felt yesterday that the Government was refraining from ordering violent action this time because of possible human rights ramifications for Australia. "The Government isn't telling the police to move in, not because they feel guilty for what they have done to the Aboriginal people, but if they do move in it will be an international event," he said. "The whole world is watching."

The Aboriginal poet Mr Kevin Gilbert vowed that his people would not wait another decade for ownership of the land. "We will spread dissent, discord and prove that white Australians do not hold a sovereign title. It is a defective title because we never surrendered our land," he said.

The tent embassy is likely to continue for some time. Aboriginal numbers were being reinforced last night, as members of the local Ngunawal community have joined those from Sydney. Groups from Queensland are expected to begin arriving today.

Native title, reconciliation and a new future?

182. *Age*, 14 January 1993. Tasmanians To Discuss Claim

The community is excited by a new feeling of power as a result of the High Court judgment recognising a form of native title to Australia, the lawyer and activist Mr Michael Mansell said yesterday.

Tasmanian Aborigines' requests for land rights have been rejected by state authorities, including the present Liberal Government. The previous Labor administration failed to get through the upper house of Parliament a bill giving a land council control of 53,000 hectares of Crown land.

Many traditional and sacred areas in that bill could now be subject to the native title claim. Mr Mansell said families could show continued use of such areas for activities such as foraging for bush food, shell-making or, in the case of the islands, a mutton-bird- gathering industry. "On my reading of the case and case law, Tasmanian Aborigines would have no difficulty in proving a claim for more than 20 per cent of the state," Mr Mansell said. "I have been surprised by the number of families who said they could show a connection with particular areas." The Tasmanian Government has not responded to the Mabo decision, and Mr Mansell said if necessary the community could begin a Supreme Court action to have it enforced.

The two-day meeting of more than 200 members of the Aboriginal community next week is to decide tactically which claim to put up and how to pursue it. "There are so many options possible," he said. "The community is very excited. We are so accustomed to getting knocked back: now it's something tangible. We have a new feeling of choice and power."

Mr Mansell said the National Party leader, Mr Tim Fischer, should re-sign over his remarks on the Mabo judgment in which he referred to a "guilt industry" in Australia. "People shouldn't feel guilty," Mr Mansell said. "What they should feel is that injustices were done in the past and are continuing today. They should be ready to rectify some of the damage."

183. *Sydney Morning Herald*, 4 June 1993. NSW Faces Mabo-Style Claim. Aborigines Seeking Native Title Over One-Third Of State

NSW's first Mabo-style land claim has been filed in the High Court, where the Wiradjuri people are seeking native title to traditional lands amounting to one-third of NSW.

In a claim lodged on the first anniversary of the High Court's historic Mabo decision recognising a form of native title, the Wiradjuri people are also seeking billions of dollars in compensation for trespass and dispos-session of their traditional lands. The claim is bordered by the Lachlan River in the north and the Murrumbidgee River in the south, which in-cludes the State's prime agricultural and grazing land. It extends west to the region around the town of Griffith.

According to Mr Paul Coe, the chairman of the NSW Aboriginal Legal Service, which is acting for the Wiradjuri people, the papers lodged in the Sydney registry of the High Court yesterday included a blanket writ cov-ering all land formerly possessed by the Wiradjuri people. They would be represented by the Aboriginal artist Mrs Isabel Coe, who was named as the plaintiff in the writ.

Mr Coe, who is her brother, told the Herald that counsel would be instructed to argue that State laws that effectively transferred title from the land were invalid because the Wiradjuri people never ceded their sovereign title over the land.

In the Mabo decision, the High Court ruled that native title could exist only if it had not been extinguished by the Crown. The court also ruled that the terra nullius principle was invalid. Terra nullius, used by the British to claim sovereignty over Australia, means "empty and unoccupied land".

Mr Coe said that because the High Court had invalidated terra nullius, the Wiradjuri people could argue that their land was taken by people using an invalid principle which later became the rationale of several laws concerning land occupancy and ownership. "There was no consent at the time," Mr Coe said. "The original assertion of sovereignty applied is invalid because terra nullius has been revoked. There was no legal or moral right to take the Wiradjuri land. We're seeking more than native title; we're seeking sovereignty."

The writ says: "The first and second defendants having trespassed upon the lands of the Wiradjuri nation and forcibly, wrongfully and unlawfully dispossessed (had) degraded and devastated the Wiradjuri nation with rape, kidnapping, pillage and murder."

The NSW Farmers' Association's policy director, Mr Terry Ryan, said the area under claim included land regarded as some of the nation's finest agricultural and pastoral land, producing wheat, rice and other crops. The claim brought into question whether 10 per cent of Australia's agricultural production, which came from the land claim area, could be relied upon in future. "I'll give the Aborigines their due— they sure have got fine taste in land," he said. "You are looking at a very large number of people who will affected by this claim," he said. "It is a threat to their security and their ability to use their land productively."

184. Pat Dodson, Chairperson, Council for Aboriginal Conciliation, Welcome Speech to Conference on the Position of Indigenous People in National Constitutions, 4 June 1993

... A century ago, the Australian people engaged in a debate about creating a nation. They held meetings ... They wrote articles and letters in newspapers. Many views were canvassed and voices were heard. The separate colonies, having divided up the land between them, discussed ways of sharing powers in order to achieve a vision of a united Australia.

The result was the Australian Constitution, establishing the Common-wealth of Australia in 1901.

A century later we are beginning a new debate on that Constitution and are considering a republican path. The old links to the crown and the British Empire, once so central, are not so relevant or meaningful to the nation we have today. The old allegiances no longer seem so appropriate. The old anthems and coats of arms no longer seem to fit our sense of ourselves as Australians in this place at this time.

A century ago our Constitution was drafted in the spirit of *terra nullius*. Land was divided, power was shared, structures were established, on the illusion of vacant possession. When Aboriginal people showed up which they inevitably did they had to be subjugated, incarcerated or eradicated: to keep the myth of *terra nullius* alive.

The High Court decision on native title shatters this illusion and Abo-riginal and Torres Strait Islander people have survived to make their contribution to the shape of the nation's political and legal future.

The nation has now woken from two centuries of sleep to become aware that Aboriginal and Torres Strait Islander people were owners of the land and were managers of the country long before the Union Jack was raised and rum drunk, here or elsewhere. While it may seem to be a new dawn for Australia's indigenous people, it has been a rude awakening for others. A moment of truth has arrived. The deeds of the past and present require those who have benefited most to take the steps towards those who have suffered most in the last 204 years. They must reconcile themselves with a new reality and then find the path of restitution that will lead to reconciliation.

No longer can Aboriginal property rights be ignored. No longer can indigenous customary laws and traditions be disregarded. The decision brings the wider Australian community closer to a true reconciliation on honest, negotiated terms with Aboriginal and Torres Strait Islander Aus-tralians.

A century after the original constitutional debate we have an opportu-nity to remake our Constitution to recognise and accommodate the prior ownership of the continent by Aboriginal and Torres Strait Islander peo-ple. But in this new debate there is a danger of history repeating itself. There is a danger of Aboriginal and Torres Strait Islander rights to land and cultural identity being ignored in the rush to establish a republic with minimal change to the Constitution. There is a danger of new arrange-ments to share power being developed without seeing and somehow meeting the Aboriginal and Torres Strait Islander peoples' yearning to es-cape the powerlessness of exclusion and dispossession. There is a danger of a new Constitution being drafted that tries to capture the spirit of a modern Australia, but that denies the spirit of indigenous Australia.

Terra nullius may be gone but the old habits of constitutional drafters die hard. The silences and omissions of the past echo loudly in the present ...

[T]he Council for Aboriginal Reconciliation and the Constitutional Centenary Foundation share an aim of encouraging education and promoting public discussion, understanding and review of these issues. We both encourage the kind of debate of a century ago. We encourage the meetings, the letters, the articles, the arguments if a new vision of Australia is to emerge that is in keeping with our sense of ourselves as Australians, as belonging to this place, as being a part of this time ...

185. Noel Pearson, 'Law Must Dig Deeper To Find Land Rights', *Australian*, 8 June 1993

For many months the Prime Minister has been telling the nation that the High Court's decision is the best opportunity the country has had to build a reconciliation between Aboriginal and non-Aboriginal Australians. Clearly he is right.

But the "Mabo process" also carries immense unavoidable challenges. An insensitive or inadequate response has the potential to set reconciliation back decades with disastrous consequences not only for Aboriginal people but for the nation as a whole.

Indeed, Mabo is quite probably the most complex and testing single issue any peacetime Australian government has had to address. The challenge does not rest only with the Government and Aboriginal groups but extends to all Australians. All Australians must examine the manner in which they relate to Aboriginal people if there is to be a solution that will ensure a just and prosperous future for us all; a solution Australia can hold up to the international community and, most importantly, our regional neighbours, as confirmation of this country's standing as a free and mature participant in the resolution of the problems of others.

Late last year the Prime Minister instituted a consultation process to consider the views of all groups with an interest in the decision. He has undertaken to continue this process until September, when the Commonwealth will spell out its position. As an initial step, an interdepartmental committee (IDC) of Canberra bureaucrats was put together to prepare a report on the implications of the decision. From this report the Government will extract a set of principles it will take to the Council of Australian Governments meeting in Melbourne.

A broadly based group of Aboriginal land councils and legal services has drawn up its guiding principles for responding to the decision. Known as the "peace plan", these principles were put to the Prime Minister at a meeting on April 27.

The IDC's principles have approached Mabo from a very different philosophical perspective to Aboriginal groups.

Aboriginal people see Mabo as essentially about the recognition of indigenous human rights. The IDC sees it as primarily a land management problem. The IDC has approached the issue not from the perspective of building a new Australian identity separated from the country's British colonial past, but has reinforced that traditional colonial outlook by making the issue of secure access by strangers to another's resources the overriding concern.

The IDC's principles offer a continuation of the colonial legacy with whites free to take from blacks as they please and without regard to the relationship to the land developed over millennia that is at the heart of Aboriginal title.

By characterising Mabo as primarily a problem of land management, the IDC not surprisingly sees the Commonwealth's task as helping the States deal with a vexing land and resource question. If however, Mabo is treated as a question of indigenous human rights, which has been the approach adopted by courts and governments in Canada, the United States and New Zealand, the Commonwealth's obligation to take primary responsibility is unavoidable.

This is required by its international treaty obligations and the responsibility it assumed with the 1967 constitutional referendum to make laws with respect to Aboriginal people.

The treatment of Mabo should be located within concepts of indigenous human rights being developed internationally. Principles governing the treatment of aboriginal title elsewhere, particularly Canada, the US and New Zealand, cannot be disregarded. Indeed, Aboriginal people will take significant account of the standards applied to indigenous people in those countries where recognition of aboriginal title has a much stronger history when assessing the Commonwealth's response. The Commonwealth cannot justifiably adopt principles which establish *lesser* positions than those prevailing elsewhere.

Mabo inevitably raises questions of land management. We do not believe that this is an accurate or just characterisation of our challenge. To treat Aboriginal title as a land management issue also ignores the question of the right to self-determination in accordance with the laws and customs the court has explicitly said gives the title its particular form. This form can naturally vary from place to place and over time as laws and customs change.

The IDC has pushed the principle of non-discrimination as an appropriate way to treat Aboriginal title. By "non-discrimination" the IDC means treating Aboriginal title as analogous to a freehold or other interest derived from the Crown.

Yet to compare Aboriginal rights to the rights of others not discriminated against in the past 200 years is not appropriate. So much has been lost that Aboriginal people are entitled to expect special protection for what remains. There needs to be positive acknowledgement of *different treatment* of Aboriginal title which reflects the fact that Aboriginal culture is inseparable from the land to which Aboriginal title attaches. The loss or impairment of that title is not simply a loss of real estate, it is a loss of culture.

The IDC has assumed that to treat Aboriginal title equally and "no less favourably" than other titles means Aboriginal title must be treated like "normal" titles. The fallacy of this approach is that strict adherence to the notions of formal equality compounds inequality because it fails to acknowledge the legitimacy of difference, particularly of culturally distinct minorities.

The High Court exposed this fallacy in the case of Gerhardy v Brown, where Justice Brennan said: "Human rights and fundamental freedoms may be nullified or impaired by political, economic, social, cultural or religious influences in a society as well as by the formal operation of its laws. Formal equality before the law is an engine of oppression destructive of human dignity if the law entrenches inequalities."

The equating of Aboriginal titles with normal titles obscures the very nature of Aboriginal title. Aboriginal title arises out of the customs and laws of the Aboriginal titleholders; nothing in mainstream titles is comparable. The High Court in Mabo clearly stated that indigenous title is *sui generis* (of its own kind) and that it is misleading to attempt to define the title by resort to English property law concepts.

There are clearly no titles under the real property law of Australia which have their origin in laws and customs of a particular cultural group. Being a cultural title, interference with Aboriginal title not only has a legal consequence but also has a cultural consequence. It must be remembered that while Parliament may legislate to save or revive titles where it allows interference, there will still be a real detriment to culture. You can technically save Aboriginal title at Coronation Hill but you can't save culture when the hill is flattened.

There should be no statutory attempt to define Aboriginal title as a title comparable to other forms and we believe that the very nature of

Aboriginal title precludes any correlation being drawn with other titles as a matter of policy. Aboriginal people should not be made to suffer for the conceptual failings of the IDC.

There are titles issued from 1975 to 1992 which may be invalid or for which compensation is due to Aboriginal titleholders owing to the Racial Discrimination Act. The Commonwealth Government has apparently assured people who obtained grants during this period that their titles will be protected and they will not be liable to any additional costs. The underlying rationale is that because Aboriginal title was not recognised then, their conduct was innocent.

To say the takers of title were "innocent" obscures the truth. Many of these titles were obtained in extremely unconscionable circumstances and were the subject of legal appeals (which, before Mabo, were mostly unsuccessful).

The title takers frequently knew of traditional Aboriginal interests. In many cases, they rode roughshod over Aboriginal objections.

The onus is on the Prime Minister to translate his vision for a new national identity for Australia into a principled and just resolution of indigenous claims.

Paul Keating has publicly accepted the challenge presented by Mabo. If he is to meet this challenge, he must reconcile the IDC's approach with the expectations of Aboriginal people.

The process of reconciliation will be determined by the extent to which government responses to Mabo can come to terms with the peace plan. You cannot force reconciliation, nor can you impose solutions. The content of Commonwealth legislation must receive the endorsement of Aboriginal groups if the historic opportunity of Mabo is to be seized.

186. Lois O'Donoghue, ATSIC Chairperson, Opening statement at media conference, 19 October 1993

Very late last night we secured a negotiated outcome that meets the major interests not only of our people but of all Australians and, by so doing ensures that we start off together down the long path to genuine reconciliation.

It is an historic decision.

The decision is historic not because we have gained from the Prime Minister an agreement to everything we sought. We have been willing to compromise in the interests of a truly national settlement. We have, for example, accepted a greater role for the States than we would have preferred and we have accepted greater constraints on our rights to negotiate developments on our land than we would have liked.

It is an historic decision for two fundamental reasons.

First, we have managed in the last fortnight to turn around a decision which, while perhaps satisfying the States. the miners and the farmers, would have failed to address deep-seated Aboriginal concerns.

With the help of our friends in the Labour Caucus; with the help of the Democrats and the Greens; with the strong support of trade unions, church groups and community organisations; and with the strong personal involvement and the understanding of the Prime Minister we have secured a remarkable settlement and historic agreement.

We have secured 10 major goals in the negotiations of last week. Those goals, set out in the document I am now circulating, keep faith with the core principles that have driven our case from the day that the High Court decision on native title was handed down.

The Cabinet decision of last night, which at this very moment is being incorporated into legislation, is in my personal view historic for another equally profound reason.

What you have seen emerge in the last fortnight, building on Eva Valley and other meetings, is a powerful new coalition in indigenous affairs.

ATSIC is working co-operatively, in close alliance with Aboriginal organisations in Australia.

A new political voice has emerged in this country that will have to be listened to. A new political force that will make a major impact on shaping the future of our nation in the years ahead.

You see— with the notable exception of myself— the emergence of a new generation of Aboriginal leadership, speaking with the commitment of the past but with the language of today. Strong, determined, forceful yet able to argue, negotiate and conciliate.

Articulate Aboriginal leaders, supported by professional administrators are able to match Commonwealth and State bureaucrats and advisers and industry representatives in complex legal and administrative argument, in media know-how and in political judgement.

The tired old arguments— that Aboriginal people could not negotiate, that a united front of indigenous organisations could not be achieved, that ATSIC could never gain a political voice independent of Government have been laid to rest. Last night those myths were buried.

Indigenous affairs will never be the same in our nation. All Australians will benefit from the conjunction of forces that has emerged to represent the interests of Aboriginal and Torres Strait Islander peoples. A new future is possible ...

187. Council for Aboriginal Reconciliation, *The Key Issues of Reconciliation*, 1994

The Council for Aboriginal Reconciliation has a clear view of the practical achievements that are necessary to bring about reconciliation between Aboriginal and Torres Strait Islander peoples and the wider community.

It has identified eight key issues which are essential to the reconciliation process. These require a practical response by whole Australian community. Addressing these issues in a committed and effective way is essential to our future.

The key issues are:

Understanding Country: A greater understanding of the importance of land and sea in Aboriginal and Torres Strait Islander societies;

Improving Relationships: Better relationship between Aboriginal and Torres Strait Islander Australians and the wider community;

Valuing Cultures: Recognition that Aboriginal and Torres Strait Islander cultures are a valued part of Australian heritage;

Sharing Histories: A sense for all Australians of a shared ownership of their history;

Addressing Disadvantage: A greater awareness of the causes of indigenous Australians' disadvantage;

Responding to Custody Levels: A greater community response to addressing the underlying causes of the high levels of Aboriginal and Torres Strait Islander people in custody;

Agreeing on a Document: Agreement on whether the process of reconciliation would be advanced by a formal document or documents of reconciliation; and

Controlling Destinies: Greater opportunities for indigenous Australians to control their destinies.

The Council wants to know what the community thinks about these issues and how people have worked at improving their knowledge and understanding about these matters as well as any activity undertaken in a mutually co-operative manner with Aboriginal and Torres Strait Islander peoples over these issues ...

188. Mandawuy Yunupingu, 'Give Back Our Laws', *Herald Sun*, 25 January 1994

With the recent passage of the Federal Government's native title legislation, all Australians can now face the future of this country with a greater degree of optimism. We have a challenge in front of us, but it is one that, with consideration, consultation and respect for the many cultures that make up Australia, we can face with dignity and pride.

We now have the opportunity to get all Australians working together under the new arrangements. Long-sought recognition of Aboriginal sovereignty gives us the framework within which to develop a better awareness within the multicultural society of Australia, engendering respect for all cultures within this country.

I see that Aboriginal people have got a more solid standing now that the vision for contemporary Australia is going to be lifted by Aboriginal Australia. It gives us a basis to start being involved, to actively participate in making this country work in terms of economy, business and social changes ...

Politically, if the reconciliation process results in the negotiation of a treaty, I would like to see Aboriginal politicians elected by Aboriginal people being part of the Australian Parliament.

In terms of land management, I see a lot more interaction between Aboriginal and non-Aboriginal people, both on a federal and state level. Aboriginal people are again starting to get themselves involved in various aspects of land management, such as conservation. I see Aboriginal and non-Aboriginal people working together towards that.

We would include mining companies and all the people who have a vested interest in the resources of this country, and work with them to manage the land. If mining is to be allowed by Aboriginal people on their land, they are obviously going to have to be involved in the management so that precautions can be taken to ensure that conservation is part of the whole process.

Through this involvement, Aboriginal people are going to participate more in today's commercial world. I see that as part of the vision for Australia, that a lot more Aboriginal people are going to think in terms of money, in terms of industry. All these types of things have to be part of the ongoing development of this country, and we have got to get ourselves prepared for it. I see more Aboriginal people being included, being part of the competitive situation.

I think now that we have got a basis on which to operate through the native title legislation, it opens up a new way that has got to get the individual thinking. I see that as very important for the change we have to embark on.

Essentially, we all have to embrace this change because it is part of our Australia. Through developments in the legal recognition of indigenous rights, through the celebration of culture and music and dance, I see that unification is happening. Right now, the sounds of Yothu Yindi are part of that preparation. We see music taking an influential role as part of that.

I see Australia's artistic endeavour changing in terms of taking on board Aboriginal perspectives and the perspectives of the many other cultures that make Australia. And that, I think, is worth celebrating and building on.

189. *Australian*, 6 October 1994. Native Title Isolates Urban Blacks: Activist

The great contemporary Aboriginal milestones of land rights and native title had effectively established Aborigines in the bush as the "real Aborigines" while urban blacks remained ignored, impoverished and culturally isolated, an Aboriginal activist claimed yesterday. And Aboriginal land councils, so often the political vanguard of indigenous causes, had reinforced the injustices by placing barriers in the way of urban Aborigines trying to regain their cultural inheritance.

The claims, by Aboriginal consultant Ms Jaqui Katona, came after another day of soul-searching by the "stolen generation" of Northern Territory Aborigines meeting at the Going Home conference in Darwin. The conference has brought together hundreds of Aborigines who as children were "stolen" from their natural mothers and placed in mission homes to be assimilated into white society.

But yesterday's discussions at the conference arrived at a view that both Aboriginal and non-Aboriginal power structures needed to change if the wrongs of the past were to be addressed properly.

Ms Katona, the conference convener, said there was an overwhelming concern among delegates that land rights and the recognition of native title had left them out of the equation. "What people here are talking about is their birthright." Ms Katona said yesterday. "They were born on country, can prove genealogy, but because of the prescribed legal definitions of traditional ownership they have been excluded from making land claims. It is the same situation for both the native title and the land rights legislation. They rely on spiritual affiliation and knowledge of sacred sites and their boundaries as the test for traditional ownership of country. But when you have been taken away as a child, you just do not have that knowledge anymore."

The result had been the creation of a "separate class of Aboriginal citizen", confined to live in towns without culturally appropriate administrative measures to deal with their needs. It also meant urban Aborigines had been denied a share of the economic benefits that sometimes accrued to "traditional" Aborigines through land claim processes.

Ms Katona said the final conference resolution today was likely to recommend urgent amendments by the Federal Government to its native title and land rights laws to make "going back to country" easier for dispossessed urban Aborigines.

But while the Central and Northern land councils had appeared "supportive", Ms Katona said many delegates remained cynical. "The land councils have put up so many barriers in the past that people do not have faith in them anymore." Ms Katona said. "The (land council) anthropologists had denied many people the right to be involved and consulted about land claims. There are people here who will swear black and blue the land councils are not doing their job properly."

The reason, according to Ms Katona, was suspicion by land councils that urban Aborigines had "exploitative" motives for wanting to re-establish associations with their traditional lands. "People out bush are classified as the real Aborigines, the bona fide ones, while for us there is no fair process to go back to our country. We want a fair process."

190. *Sydney Morning Herald*, 26 January 1995. Mansell Working For A New National Day

Today, the day he calls Invasion Day, the national secretary of the Aboriginal Provisional Government, Mr Michael Mansell, will work in his Hobart office, ignoring the official public holiday and celebrations four blocks away. "Having a public holiday is an acknowledgement there is something good about the day and for Aborigines to take Australia Day is subscribing to a view that is racially wrong," said Mr Mansell, who like many other indigenous community workers takes off Aborigines Day in July instead. "Would the Jews join in celebrations of the Holocaust, or Australians the day the Japanese bombed Darwin?" asked Mr Mansell, who would prefer Australia Day on May 27, the anniversary of the 1967 referendum which gave Aborigines citizenship.

But in Sydney, the Aboriginal group Yothu Yindi, which normally plays at the alternative indigenous-run Survival Day music fest at La Perouse, will tonight be at the heart of the mainstream festivities, performing for the first time at the official Australia Day concert in the Domain. Signs of a sea change in relations between Aborigines and non-Aborigines? "Very much so," said its lead singer, Mandawuy Yunupingu, who was Australian of the Year two years ago. "We will tell people how they can balance things. Now is the time to reconcile." Mr Mansell yesterday called January 26 "a day of shame". Mr Yunupingu's reply: "It is a picture in which people entrench themselves." But he agreed with Mr

Mansell and the NSW Aboriginal Land Council in calling for the Federal Government to consider changing the date.

"At its foundation is invasion and Anglo settlement," said the land council's publicity officer, Mr Aaron Ross. Despite what other Australians might think, many Aboriginal communities had told the land council they favoured January 1, the anniversary of Federation, he said.

The deputy director of the Cape York Land Council, Mr David Byrne, said for Aborigines in remote communities it was just another day. "What do Aboriginal people have to celebrate?" he asked. "The average life expectancy for Aboriginal people is 47 to 48 years and the imprisonment rate is still 22 times per head of population that of others." The co-ordinator of the Trade Union Committee for Aboriginal Rights, Mr Kevin Tory, said it was understandable that those who had migrated to one of the richest countries and enjoyed a high standard of living and political stability would want to celebrate.

"But the sad fact is, they don't give recognition that the nation was developed for thousands of years." Amid rumours of a possible demonstration against the $10 entry charge for the Survival 95 La Perouse concert, organisers believe more non-Aborigines than ever will be among the 20,000 expected to attend an alternative event with historical roots in the 1938 Day of Mourning.

"One of the wonderful things about the Mabo legislation is that non-Aboriginal people feel they can give more open support and can show it on the day to Aboriginal people and organisations— and that is something more effective than a reconciliation committee," said an organiser, Ms Bronwyn Bancroft.

191. *Koori Mail*, 5 April 1995. ATSIC Lays Its Cards On The Table Over Social Justice Deal

A formal claim has been lodged on behalf of all indigenous Australians for compensation and reparations for past dispossession of land and the dispersal of the indigenous population since white settlement 200 years ago. The issue was put on the table when the Aboriginal and Torres Strait Islander Commission (ATSIC) presented its submission to the federal government on its social justice package for Aborigines.

The social justice strategy will form the third part of the government's response to the Mabo High Court decision, following the native title act and the Aboriginal land fund. The ATSIC submission, based on the views of indigenous people, said reparations for the damage done to Aboriginal society and culture must form an essential part of the strategy.

But it made clear that compensation should be over and above money directed to Aborigines to redress disadvantages in areas such as health, education and housing. "Development of national compensation principles should include investigations into accessing revenue derived from the use of land by non-indigenous Australians, including applying a proportion of mining royalties and property taxes or the equivalents," the submission said.

ATSIC said discussions about reparations could be held in the context of the need for a treaty for indigenous Australians— another major demand in the submission. ATSIC also called for:

* Reserved seats in the federal parliament for indigenous people;
* The creation of official parliamentary observer status to the ATSIC chairperson with the right to speak in parliament on indigenous issues;
* Official recognition of the Aboriginal flag;
* Recognition of customary law; and
* Making certain Commonwealth grants to the states conditional on the improvement of Aboriginal living conditions.

ATSIC officials acknowledged that the call for reparations along with some other measures recommended were likely to create controversy. But ATSIC chair Lois O'Donoghue said the submission was not about dividing the nation. "It is about the recognition of the unique place of Aboriginal and Torres Strait Islander people in Australian society today and the realities of our history and our dispossession," she told Prime Minister Paul Keating at the official handover of the submission. "The emphasis is on indigenous rights and citizenship entitlements."

192. Gary Foley, 'Tragedy For Another Aboriginal Generation In Waiting', *Age*, 20 July 1995

In 1990 the Federal Government unveiled the cornerstone of its Aboriginal Affairs policy by announcing the creation of the Aboriginal and Torres Strait Islander Commission, ATSIC.

The then Aboriginal affairs minister, Gerry Hand, announced a grandiose plan envisaging that ATSIC would take over the functions of the old Department of Aboriginal Affairs and be an administrative body, controlled by the elected representatives with a mandate from the Aboriginal people. These elected representatives would make funding decisions, advise the minister, consult with communities and control the actions of the Aboriginal affairs bureaucracy.

But today ATSIC is in crisis and faces growing criticism from Aboriginal communities. It experiences one public relations disaster after another, with Koori health statistics and imprisonment rates worsening, and vast amounts of monies spent to no avail.

A dithering, besieged Aboriginal Affairs Minister, Robert Tickner, falls back on the line, "I have no power any more, it's now ATSIC's responsiblity". This is akin to a ventriloquist saying that the dummy controls the show. So, why has ATSIC ended up the inept and controversial body it is today?

The answer rests in the manner in which the Federal Government created ATSIC in the first place. The fact is that ATSIC is yet another failed attempt by non-Koori bureaucrats to decide what is best for Kooris. To understand why ATSIC failed we must understand the nature of its conception and birth.

The year is 1990, and the inaugural ATSIC elections are about to be held. The minister and the public service hype-machine have been working overtime, claiming this is "a great moment in Australian history" and that Aboriginal people would at last have a real say in their own affairs.

A compliant media of the day (and today) parrots ministerial press releases and conducts promotional interviews with a range of government-approved Aboriginal spokespeople, most of whom are long assimilated into the Canberra bureaucracy or some other form of government position.

But while ignored by media, the anti-ATSIC forces were well-organised, especially in south-eastern Australia. In Melbourne, an alliance, the ATSIC Review Group, ARG, produced information material distributed widely in Aboriginal communities in south-eastern Australia. They advocated a boycott of the ATSIC elections because of the "fraudulent nature" of the new body.

The ARG pointed out that the public servants of the old Department of Aboriginal Affairs had been offered lucrative contracts in the new ATSIC, and that these three-year contracts were signed, sealed and delivered months before the ATSIC elections.

Then there was the requirement that to participate in the ATSIC election, a Koori needed to be on the Australian electoral role. This single rule disenfranchised a significant segment of Aboriginal Australia.

Meanwhile, desperate that ATSIC have credibility, Gerry Hand made brave predictions about voter turnout but knew that anything less than a voter turnout of 50 per cent could be a political disaster.

By the time the November 1990 elections were held, there was such widespread cynicism in Koori communities that fewer than one third of eligible voters nationally participated.

While in parts of the Northern Territory voter turnout reached 80 per cent of those eligible, across the nation the participation rate averaged only about 30 per cent. In the big metropolitan communities voter turnout was low a mere 10 per cent in Sydney, the largest Koori community in Australia.

Members of ARG and similar anti-ATSIC groups throughout Koori Australia hailed the results as a success for the boycott campaign.

Perhaps a reasonable claim, with only a 17 per cent voter turnout in Victoria and a mere 33 per cent eligible voters participating nationally. But media reports locally and nationally focussed obediently on the ministerial press releases that claimed the result as a "great victory for democracy".

Self-congratulation ensued among politicians, bureaucrats, media superstars, newly-elected ATSIC reps and ministerially-appointed chairperson. They had contrived with careful stage-managing to create an illusion; a fraud, against all Australians and Koori peoples. The ATSIC House of Cards had been established. Dissenting voices had been silenced, courtesy of an obedient parliamentary press gallery, handicapped by their own ignorance. The scene was set for a slow disaster to engulf the administration of Aboriginal Affairs over the next five years and which is in the beginning of its final stages now.

The tragedy is that the long-suffering Aboriginal community are the big losers, yet again. It seems that most Aboriginal communities south of the "Brisbane Line" will have to wait another generation before they see genuine self-determination, economic independence and local community control.

193. Patrick Dodson, 'Reconciliation Misunderstood', *Australian*, 13 September 1996

For those of us who are involved in promoting reconciliation between indigenous Australians and the wider community, it is good to see letters from people supporting, debating and questioning the process. Reconciliation must be seen as a people's movement.

While research conducted recently for our Council indicates strong support for reconciliation, there is still a high level of misunderstanding about its goals and implications.

The Council's vision is of "a united Australia which respects this land of ours; values the Aboriginal and Torres Strait Islander heritage; and provides justice and equity for all".

Reconciliation can mean many different things. But, above all, it must involve some form of agreement that deals with the legacies of our history, and takes us forward as a nation. It means achieving practical and demonstrable outcomes through recognising indigenous cultures and achievements, and through improving the lives and circumstances of indigenous people.

One of your correspondents asked whether reconciliation requires present generations of Australians to take on the guilt of their forebears. It doesn't. But nor should today's indigenous Australians continue to suffer the legacies of the past because the nation has not yet found the ways to overcome them.

The inquiry by the Human Rights and Equal Opportunity Commission into the stolen generations is drawing the nation's attention to the relationship between past mistakes and ongoing disadvantage. Recognising and addressing this connection is one of the central strands of reconciliation.

The same correspondent was concerned that he was being asked to "embrace someone else's fairy stories". My grandfather taught me that the river is the river and the sea is the sea. Each has its own complex patterns, origins and stories, and even though they come together, they will always exist in their own right. Non-indigenous Australians cannot be expected to learn or understand the lessons of my grandfather, but simply to respect that they are central to my identity. This acceptance of diversity is another important element of reconciliation.

194. *Sydney Morning Herald*, 6 July 1996. One Man's Gulf War

"I believe Australia is still illegally occupied," says [Murrandoo] Yanner, whose critics call him an extremist. "This is my land and I honestly believe we are in the 208th year of occupation and we have never been given any justice or any rights. John Howard and Rob Borbidge are extremely racist—they would pass laws to hang us if it was socially acceptable."

He has also demonstrated that Aborigines are facing the bitter prospect of seeing their leaders exchanging fierce attacks with each other. The most degrading insult one Aborigine can trade with another is "Jacky Jacky"—referring to the Aborigines who sided with the police, while their people were being massacred or moved, earlier this century.

"He (ATSIC Commissioner Terry O'Shane, who sided this week with the Government and Century Zinc) is a Jacky Jacky. In the olden days I would have been the one with the spear getting shot and he would have been the one behind the troopers with their carbines."

Yanner's people are the traditional owners of the land between

Burketown and the Queensland/Northern Territory border and, as the co-ordinator of the Carpentaria Land Council, he represents the interests of more than 5,000 Aboriginal people.

This week he told anyone who would listen that if the Century Zinc mine went ahead it would lead to Australia's equivalent of the Bougainville conflict. He has received letters of support from the Bougainville Revolutionary Army.

But Yanner— the second-oldest in a family of six boys and two girls— says that people have misinterpreted his claim that the Queensland and Federal Governments' determination to see the mine opened would lead to bloodshed. "I didn't say we were going to go out and kill every white honky ... My gun is my head, the barrel is my mouth and my bullets are truth and justice," he says, with the same calm oratory skill as shown by one of his heroes, the former executive director of the Cape York Land Council, Noel Pearson.

"I love Noel. I look in the mirror and I see me as a younger version of Noel. He has given me a lot of wisdom. I am an intellectual parasite. I will take the best out of anybody and use it for my own purposes— for my people" ...

195. *Age*, 20 February 1997. No ATSIC Funds For Aboriginal Mine Fight

The Aboriginal and Torres Strait Islander Commission has decided not to fund legal action by Aboriginal groups to delay further the $1 billion Century Zinc mine. The decision not to provide funding shows the growing pressure on the six native title claimants who walked away from talks late last week. They have refused to sign a negotiated agreement on the project.

There is considerable anger in the Aboriginal community over the breakdown, much of it directed at the Carpentaria Land Council activist, Mr Murandoo Yanner, who is believed to have encouraged the collapse. The halt in talks jeopardises a $90 million compensation package being offered to Aboriginal people by the mine's developer and the Queensland Government, and damages the indigenous advocacy of regional agreements as an answer to the High Court's Wik decision.

However, sources said the decision against funding the contest was not politically motivated, despite Mr Yanner's recent call for the head of ATSIC, Mr Gatjil Djerrkura, to resign. The native title claimants in the case were warned in December that funding would not continue after the 13 February deadline. Mr Yanner had been advised that money would be available while the claimants were negotiating, but not if action was initiated against Pasminco ...

196. *Sydney Morning Herald*, 29 May 1997. A Call To The Nation. Delegates' Closing Address Reconciliation Summit

We, the participants at this convention, affirm to all the people of this nation that reconciliation between Australia's indigenous peoples and other Australians is central to the renewal of this nation as a harmonious and just society which lives out its national ethos of a fair go for all; and that until we achieve such reconciliation this nation will remain diminished.

We further declare that reconciliation and the renewal of the nation can be achieved only through a people's movement which obtains the commitment of Australians in all their diversity to make reconciliation a living reality in their communities, workplaces, institutions, organisations and in all expressions of our common citizenship.

This convention has been a profoundly moving experience for all of us privileged to take part and has renewed the spirit and determination of all participants to carry on their work for reconciliation. The commitment and the spirit we have all witnessed here demonstrates that the principles and values of reconciliation have become embedded in the hearts and minds of many Australians.

This convention has put reconciliation firmly at the centre of the national political agenda. Despite the airing of differences on specific issues, the convention also witnessed some profoundly unifying statements from political and community leaders who all affirmed support for reconciliation and found common ground in recognising some requirements of reconciliation. These included coming to terms with our intertwining histories, better human relationships and the addressing of disadvantage.

We note that leaders across the social spectrum promised their own personal apologies and sorrow for the treatment of indigenous peoples; this was itself an historic moment. We call on all parliaments, local governments, organisations and institutions to follow this lead with their own form of apology so that we can all move forward together to share responsibility for the future of this nation.

We call on our fellow Australians to join together across this land to build a people's movement for reconciliation of sufficient breadth and power to guarantee that Australia can truly celebrate the centenary of its nationhood in 2001, confident that it has established a sound foundation for reconciliation.

We commit ourselves to leave this gathering determined to work with all those prepared to join us in this movement. We call on all Australians not to stand on the sidelines but to demonstrate a commitment to reconciliation by becoming personally involved in reconciliation activities in their neighbourhood, their communities and their workplace.

This will ensure that Australians can walk together beyond the centenary of Federation into the next millennium towards the vision of a united Australia which respects this land of ours, values the Aboriginal and Torres Strait Islander heritage and provides justice and equity for all.

197. *Sydney Morning Herald*, 2 August 1997. Now The World Watches

In Geneva this week, on the first day of the annual United Nations meeting that gives the whole world a chance to see how nations are treating their native peoples, the leader of Australia's indigenous delegation, Geoff Clark, wore a T-shirt advertising the Aboriginal Provisional Government. For the next four days, Clark discarded this symbol of an organisation that does not recognise Australia's sovereignty, in favour of a suit.

"We've got a lot more sophisticated in our tactics," he explained. A vice-chairman of the APG, arguably Australia's most radical black organisation, he is also an elected board member of the Aboriginal and Torres Strait Islander Commission (ATSIC) in a very modern indigenous political melding of the radical and respectable.

Clark was not the only such chameleon in Geneva. Josie Crawshaw, a fellow APG office-bearer and ATSIC commissioner, was there in a delegation that has learnt how to play by the rules of international diplomacy.

The APG's secretary, Michael Mansell— also at the Geneva meeting— said the new, sophisticated tactics included asking European countries that were shocked at Australia's apparent global backsliding on human rights issues to put economic pressure on the Australian Government. Mansell said four nations (which he refused to name) were close to agreeing to move at the European Parliament in September for mandatory human rights clauses to be included in any contracts between European and Australian companies involving governments. This would be similar to moves the United States made over Burma to get companies to put pressure on the generals to improve their human rights behaviour, he said. "It has an economic effect. It can make the difference between an Australian company getting a contract and not getting one. It's the difference, for instance, between a company buying Australian beef and buying beef from around the world."

If you think this spectre of Australia as an international pariah over its treatment of indigenous people, as the former South Africa was, is just the pipe-dream of Mansell— a man who lost credibility over his flirtation a decade ago with Libya's Colonel Gaddafi— you are wrong. Other indigenous activists this week foreshadowed to the Herald that, as a result of lobbying by a group that includes the conservative head of the NSW Aboriginal Land Council, Aden Ridgeway, Australia may also be castigated at the Commonwealth Heads of Government Meeting in Edinburgh in October. "Nigeria was expelled because of its human rights record," said one.

While trade sanctions are not an option in their diplomatic manoeuvrings, Aborigines taking their native title fight to the world are also considering— further down the track— asking sympathetic tourists, who name indigenous culture as one of the main magnets, to boycott Australia.

But Europe is the target now. As Clark pointed out, Aboriginal lobbyists had welded their factions together for a European thrust that had gained urgency as the Federal Government tried to push through its controversial 10-point Wik native title plan before year's end.

Olga Havnen claimed that when she visited Brussels, Bonn, The Hague and London as executive officer of the Canberra-based National Indigenous Working Group on Native Title last month with five others, European bureaucrats, political advisers and NGOs were asking what they could do to put pressure on Australia. The Europeans, she said, were up to date on the Pauline Hanson phenomenon and the native title debate. They were astounded when Australia, formerly an international human rights hero, refused this year to sign a European Union trade agreement because of its human rights clause. "When we talked to people about the Human Rights Commission budget being cut by 43 per cent, they couldn't believe it had been cut to that extent at the same time that the Race Discrimination Commissioner was reporting a three-fold increase in discrimination complaints," Havnen said. "In Europe, there is a strong sense of bipartisan support for human rights issues. Maybe this is a legacy of the horrors of World War II. It is something the Europeans take very seriously, not only at the political level, but at the personal level."

Her delegation has been invited back to address the European Parliament's human rights committee in September and by Norway's government to attend a summit on indigenous people's human rights in Oslo.

In Geneva on Thursday, the Federal Aboriginal Affairs Minister, John Herron, was forced to rebut a damning report by Dr Erica-Irene Daes, the chairwoman of the UN Working Group on Indigenous Populations. Daes wrote: "Despite the provisions of the 1993 Native Title Act, there remains great difficulty in bringing claims to land due to the criteria established which are wrought with discriminatory and colonial biases." Herron said her paper was inaccurate, out of date and misleading. But this may not be Daes's final word.

Mansell this week called for an independent international arbiter to visit Australia to report on whether in its handling of native title and land rights the Federal Government "is really acting in a fair and equitable manner in dealing with Aboriginal people, or whether its policy is simply racist". He favours Daes, but for a formal UN visit the Federal Government must agree. Herron told the Herald he had no objection to her visiting and reporting. "It's a free country and I'm certainly happy with anybody coming in because I think we've got a proud record in Australia," he said. On the other hand, he said, "we're a parliamentary democracy. We don't need the United Nations coming and telling us what to do ... I don't think we need anyone coming from outside telling us how to run our country."

198. Mick Dodson, 'We All Bear The Cost If Apology Is Not Paid', *Age*, 18 December 1997

The Commonwealth Government has finally responded— in part— to the National Inquiry into the Separation of Aboriginal and Torres Strait Islander Children from their Families. While there are some laudable initiatives that will have tangible effects, there exists a matter of much greater significance, which the Government's response fails to grasp.

In its response, the Government fails to appreciate that the way forward for all Australians has as much, if not more, to do with spiritual repair as with material programs.

Australians cannot escape the uncomfortable truth that policies and practices of the past were inherently racist. "Half-caste" children, and others, were taken from their families for no reason other than the color of their skin.

Despite the best motivation of the individuals involved in administering these policies, or their belief that what they were doing was in the best interests of the children, the facts remain that the aim was the destruction of a group of people— the Aboriginal people. No amount of welfare or well-modulated phraseology can remove this reality.

The package announced by the Minister for Aboriginal Affairs, Senator John Herron, focuses principally on the welfare-related recommendations, insultingly dismissing as "not applicable" the fundamental principle of self-determination. It excludes any indigenous organisation from participating, in any formal way, in the monitoring of government application of the recommendations.

The package omits any attention to fundamental issues of compensation and it excludes the recommendations on training and learning that would ensure schools' curricula include compulsory modules on the history and effects of forcible removal. This flies in the face of the minister's statement that "we must learn from the past so that we do not allow such circumstances and policies to happen in our community again". If we don't teach, how can we learn?

Indigenous people repeatedly told the inquiry that an apology would make an enormous difference to their ability to overcome the traumas they have suffered. Without an expression of real regret evidenced by a national parliamentary apology the package is fundamentally flawed.

The justifications for refusing to offer an apology are spurious straw-clutching. There is no legal impediment to stop such an initiative. Further, the Government's argument that a national apology is untenable, given the large proportion of Australians who have arrived in the past 20 years, is fallacious and does not reflect the views of many Australians.

Today's Australians are not being asked to accept individual guilt, but collective responsibility. Ethnic communities have offered their apologies to indigenous people. Their mood is captured in the remark of Mr Randolph Alwis, the chairman of the Federation of Ethnic Communities Councils of Australia, who recently said that "we are part of the current society and society is a continuum. Anything we can do to help the reconciliation process, we will do".

Above all, the Government's refusal to apologise stands in sharp contrast to the plethora of formal apologies from parliaments around Australia, churches, community groups, ethnic organisations, schools, local governments, unions, leading non-government organisations, and the thousands of individual Australians who have signed petitions, written letters and declared their sorrow. Indeed, these groups, and many individual Australians, have felt compelled to make it clear that they directly endorse the Human Rights and Equal Opportunity Commission's recommendation that there be a national apology.

The Government also has reasserted its rejection of indigenous people's right to compensation. The Government made it clear in its initial submission to the inquiry that it did not consider compensation appropriate. The national inquiry considered this, along with a wealth of expert advice, and concluded that an essential component of reparation for past wrongs was monetary compensation.

It is regrettable that the Government's view has not changed. An absence of any statutory compensation fund is already resulting in recourse to the courts at significant legal cost to taxpayers and potentially significant compensation payments.

However, there are some positive initiatives. In targeting health, counselling services and family reunion, the Government shows that it appreciates the long-term impact of removing Aboriginal and Torres Strait Islander children from their families, on the wellbeing of those families and communities.

Programs to expand indigenous link-up programs will provide much needed practical support for the bringing together of families torn apart by past government policies. The provision of more than $39 million to enhance counselling and mental health services for people affected by separation also will help.

Aboriginal people know what it means to be poor— and know that material assistance is not irrelevant. But we also know it is not material wealth that makes a family. If there is a lesson to be learned from our families being broken apart, it is about love, understanding, and the seeking and giving of forgiveness.

These are values that could make an Australian family of all people within this country. Many know this. The Commonwealth Government's failure to understand has resulted in a failure at the heart of its response. As a consequence, we are all the poorer.

199. *Australian*, 1-2 November 1997. Racist Scum: Pearson Blasts PM

Prominent Aboriginal leader Noel Pearson lashed out yesterday at the Howard Government, describing it as "racist scum" and its Wik 10-point native title plan as "absolutely obscene".

His comments came as a shock, with Mr Pearson widely regarded as a moderate negotiator for Aboriginal people and acknowledged as one of the architects of the Keating government's 1993 native title law.

Mr Pearson said the Howard Government's plan defied the High Court's majority Wik decision last December that found native title could co-exist with pastoral leases. "These people who've concocted the 10-point scam, who call themselves true liberals, are not true liberals," he told a luncheon in Sydney. "They are racist scum. No less. So it is absolutely obscene for racial discrimination to again re-emerge as a policy we would even contemplate" ...

200. *Age*, 24 January 1998. A Black View Of Howard's Way

Ten years ago, Galarrwuy Yunupingu and other Aboriginal tribesmen sat with Bob Hawke on the sand at Barunga in the Northern Territory and talked of a treaty. In the year of the bicentenary, the meeting was powerfully symbolic.

Yunupingu, the chairman of the Northern Land Council, recalls the day a prime minister came to a home of indigenous Australia as part of a seminal year for relations between black and white Australia. Everybody, he says, was trying to make the relationship more believable. "I believe we got a practical commitment from Bob Hawke and his Government in 1988. It marked the turning point towards better relations, to unite this nation as one and to kill off discrimination."

While the treaty plan eventually evaporated through lack of political will, the year was the springboard for the formation of the Council of Aboriginal Reconciliation in 1991. By the end of 1988, the Royal Commission on Aboriginal Deaths in Custody handed down its interim findings.

A decade on, Yunupingu sees a dramatic change in the way the national government is approaching his people. Since the election of the Howard Government, he talks about a lack of commitment and an absence of real leadership. "We have lost faith in the false promises, bad faith and discriminatory law of a Government which acts against indigenous rights," he says. "We no longer feel that we are able to negotiate with this Government. It has undermined our respect for the Parliament of this country" ...

At the start of 1988, there was an expectation or hope that the year could be significant. Almost 10 years ago to the day, the New South Wales magistrate and former head of the NSW Aboriginal Affairs Department, Pat O'Shane, reflected on what the year might end up meaning. "Whatever happens after the bicentennial, things can never be as bad as they were before," she said. O'Shane today still believes that to be the case, but argues strongly that the position has slipped since the election of the coalition and the prime ministership of Howard, who she savagely criticises. "There is no empathy in the man, there is no sympathy in the man. He just has nothing. He is really quite lacking in any kind of skills whatsoever in regard to those kinds of issues" ...

There is a consensus that the relationship is at a contemporary low-point. But some Aboriginal activists go further. A long-time campaigner who was at Barunga in 1988, Professor Marcia Langton, describes the current atmosphere as appalling. "It's probably the worst it's ever been," she says. "I don't think there's ever been such ill-will about the administration and policy development in Aboriginal affairs ever in the 20th century, having due regard to previous historic periods and different ways of thinking. I mean, these blokes are reinventing the 19th century."

In 1988, Charles Perkins was at the centre of the Aboriginal bureaucracy, occupying the most senior public service position ever held by an Aborigine, as a controversial secretary of the federal Aboriginal Affairs Department. Since then, he says he has seen improvements in Aboriginal health, education and housing, but believes the past 18 months have been disastrous. "I think we've slipped back, at least 10 years, in terms of race relations (and) the psychology of Aboriginal people in terms of looking at themselves and their own position in Australian society," he says. Perkins also believes Aboriginal Australia is running out of options and may have to return to direct protests. "I think that we're moving towards taking to the streets again, which is a bit sad," he says. "Why should we have to do that again?" ...

Tasmanian Aboriginal lawyer Michael Mansell ... says today he did not share the same optimism in 1988 as many other Aboriginal activists and leaders. But at the same time, he says there was a mutual respect between indigenous Australia and, particularly, the Keating Government. "With this new Government, I think it's the opposite," he says. "There's hardly any sign of respect for Aboriginal people at all, let alone people [who] are trying to represent Aboriginal people. On top of that, they don't give anything."

Mansell argues there is a need for a return to black radicalism, and particularly looks towards the 2000 Sydney Olympics on the issue of native title. "If the same old tactics of going in and using flowery language doesn't work, then you've got to do things that focus on issues that are harmful, that strike a raw nerve with the Government." In terms of the Olympics, he believes the only effective protest would be the boycotting of the Games by other countries ...

Galarrwuy Yunupingu, meanwhile, is searching for more lasting solutions that will reflect the spirit and commitment of 1988. He argues for the protection of Aboriginal interests in a way that can't be altered by governments of the day, by enshrining rights— including native title— in the Constitution. "We need something in whitefella law which is strong and lasting and faithful to our law. The closest whitefella law which can do this is the Constitution."

Sources: documents and illustrations

Document number

1. George Augustus Robinson Papers, Mitchell Library, State Library of New South Wales, MSS A7073, part 4, CY reel 825
2. Tasmanian Aborigines, Mitchell Library, State Library of New South Wales, MSS A612
3–5. Colonial Secretary's Office, General Correspondence CSO11/26 file 378, Archives Office of Tasmania
6. *Herald* (Melbourne), 8 March 1859
7. National Archives of Australia (Melbourne), CRS B312
9. Report of the Board Appointed to Inquire into Coranderrk Aboriginal Station, 1881–82, pp. 8–9, Victoria, Legislative Assembly, *Votes and Proceedings*, 1882–83, vol. 2
10. Report of the Board Appointed to Inquire into Coranderrk Aboriginal Station, 1881–82, p. 60, Victoria, Legislative Assembly, *Votes and Proceedings*, 1882–83, vol. 2
15. *Daily Telegraph* (Sydney), 5 July 1881
16. *Riverine Herald*, 20 July 1887
17. Colonial Secretary's Correspondence, 1/2667, Archives Office of New South Wales
19. Mortlock Library of South Australiana, State Library of South Australia, SRG94/W83/13
20. State Records of South Australia, GRG 52/1/1888/158
21. Enclosed with Mr Blackmore, Acting Trustee, Church of England, Poonindie, to the Minister of Education, 5 February, J.D. Somerville Papers, Mortlock Library of South Australiana, State Library of South Australia, PRG 15
22. *Register* (Adelaide), 21 February 1894
23. Mathew Blagden Hale Papers, Mortlock Library of South Australiana, State Library of South Australia, PRG 275
27. & 28. Premier's Department Correspondence and Special Bundles, 9/1957, Archives Office of New South Wales

30. National Archives of Australia (Canberra), CRS A659/1, 1943/1/1451
31. National Film and Sound Archives, Melbourne
32. A.P. Elkin Papers, University of Sydney Archives, P130, 12/68/144
33. Select Committee on the Administration of Aborigines Protection Board, 1937–38, pp. 62–64, New South Wales Parliament, *Joint Volumes of Papers*, 1938–39–40, vol. 7
34. Premier's Department Correspondence and Special Bundles, 12/8749, Archives Office of New South Wales
36. P.R. Stephensen Papers, Mitchell Library, State Library of New South Wales, MSS 1284
37. The Publicist, Sydney, 1938, pp. 1, 3, 5–6
38. & 39. Mitchell Library, State Library of New South Wales
40. State Library of Victoria
41. A.P. Elkin Papers, University of Sydney Archives, P130, 12/68/149
42. & 43. Mitchell Library, State Library of New South Wales
44. Kevin Gilbert, *Because a White Man'll Never Do It*, Angus & Robertson, Sydney, 1973, pp. 13–17
45. Home Secretary's Office General Correspondence, 23/593, HOM/J453, Queensland State Archives
47. Jack Horner, *Vote Ferguson for Aboriginal Freedom*, Australian and New Zealand Book Co, 1974, between pp. 88 and 89
48. & 49. Mitchell Library, State Library of New South Wales
52. Progress Report of Royal Commission on the Aborigines, pp. 113–16, 119, 120, South Australia, Legislative Assembly, *Votes and Proceedings*, 1913
54. State Records of South Australia, GRG 52/32/61
55. State Records of South Australia, GRG 23/1/1935/317
58. State Records of South Australia, GRG 52/10/1938/5
59. Public Records Office of Western Australia, AN 45/1, Acc. 1497, file 4259/1914
62. Public Records Office of Western Australia, AN 1/7, Acc. 993, file A/94/1928
64. A.P. Elkin Papers, University of Sydney Archives, P130, 12/68/144
65. Public Records Office of Western Australia, AN 537, Acc. 987
66. Public Records Office of Western Australia, AN 1/7, Acc. 993, file 55/35
67. Anti-Slavery Society Papers, Rhodes House, Oxford, MSS Brit. Emp. s. 22, G953a/4
69. Public Records Office of Western Australia, AN 1/7, Acc. 993, file 305/47
70. Riley & Ephemera Collection, State Library of Victoria
74. E.R.B. Gribble Papers, Australian Institute of Aboriginal and Torres Strait Islanders Studies, MSS 1515/11/66
75. State Library of Victoria
76. National Archives of Australia (Canberra), CRS A1, 1935/3951

77. Premier's Department Correspondence and Special Bundles, 12/8749, Archives Office of New South Wales

78. National Archives of Australia (Canberra), CRS A659, 1940/1/858

80. National Archives of Australia (Canberra), CRS A431, 1945/1591

81. Public Records Office of Western Australia, AN 1/7, Acc. 993, file 75/1936

82.–84. Premier's Department Correspondence and Special Bundles, 12/8749, Archives Office of New South Wales

85. State Library of Victoria

86. National Library of Australia

89. Donald Thomson Papers, Museum of Victoria

90. National Archives of Australia (Canberra), CRS A431, 1949/1591

98. Gordon Bryant Papers, National Library of Australia, MS 8256/182/2/3

99. & 100. Gordon Bryant Papers, National Library of Australia, MS 8256/182/Miscellaneous Correspondence and Papers V

101. Gordon Bryant Papers, National Library of Australia, MS 8256/184/1/3

102. Riley & Ephemera Collection, State Library of Victoria

103. Gordon Bryant Papers, National Library of Australia, MS 8256/182/3/3

104. Gordon Bryant Papers, National Library of Australia, MS 8256/184/2/3

105. Gordon Bryant Papers, National Library of Australia, MS 8256/182/2/3

106. Methodist Overseas Mission Papers, Mitchell Library, State Library of New South Wales, MSS MOM 465

107. Council for Aboriginal Rights (Victoria), *Ownership and Development of Reserves by Aborigines*, leaflet, 28 June 1963, Council for Aboriginal Rights (Victoria) Papers, La Trobe Collection, State Library of Victoria, MS 12913/7/3

110. Gordon Bryant Papers, National Library of Australia, MS 8256/182/2/3

112. Select Committee on Grievances of Yirrkala Aborigines, Arnhem Land Reserve, Minutes of Evidence, pp. 29, 30–31, 32, Commonwealth of Australia, *Parliamentary Papers*, 1962–63, vol. IV

113. Barry Christophers Papers, National Library of Australia, MS 7992/10/No folder no.

116. Joint Committee of the Legislative Council and Legislative Assembly Upon Aborigines Welfare, Minutes of Evidence, pp. 82–83, 84, 92, New South Wales Parliament, *Joint Volumes of Papers*, 1967–68, vol. V

117. Gordon Bryant Papers, National Library of Australia, MS 8256/175/3

119. Aboriginal Welfare Board Correspondence Files, 8/3002.1, Archives Office of New South Wales

124. Barry Christophers Papers, National Library of Australia, MS 7992/28/15

125. Barry Christophers Papers, National Library of Australia, MS 7992/9/no folder number

126. Rod Hagen, Personal collection

127. Riley & Ephemera Collection, State Library of Victoria

128. *Australian Argus Law Reports*, 1972–73, Part 1, Butterworths, Sydney, 1973, pp. 67–71

129. *Identity*, July 1971

135. *Smoke Signals*, September 1969

136. FCAATSI Papers, Mitchell Library, State Library of New South Wales, MSS 2099, Y600

137. FCAATSI Papers, Mitchell Library, State Library of New South Wales, MSS 2099, Y600

138. *Smoke Signals*, September 1970

139. Riley & Ephemera Collection, State Library of Victoria

142. *Newsletter of Aboriginal Affairs*, April 1972

143. FCAATSI Papers, Mitchell Library, State Library of New South Wales, MSS 2099, Y599

150. Commonwealth of Australia, Senate, *Parliamentary Debates*, n.s., Vol. 59, 1974, pp. 197–99

155. *Identity*, July 1975

156. Koorie Research Centre Library, Monash University

158. (1979) 24 *Australian Law Reports* 118, pp. 120–23

161. *National Aboriginal Conference Newsletter*, May 1982

162. Erik Olbrei (ed.), *Black Australians: The Prospects for Change*, Students Union, James Cook University, Townsville, 1982, pp. 143–46

163. High Court of Australia, Brisbane Registry, B12 of 1982

164. *National Aboriginal Conference Newsletter*, September 1982

168. AGPS, Canberra, 1986, pp. 41–44

172. Treaty '88, Canberra, 1988, pp. 52–55

175. Galarrwuy Yunupingu (ed.), *Our Land is Our Life: Land Rights Ä Past, Present and Future*, University of Queensland Press, St Lucia, 1997, pp. 226–27

177. ATSIC, Canberra, 1997

178. Elie Gilbert, Personal collection

179. & 180. Koorie Research Centre, Monash

184. *The Position of Indigenous People in National Constitutions*, AGPS, Canberra, 1993, pp. 6–8

186. Aboriginal and Torres Strait Islander Commission

187. *Australian*, 30–31 July 1994

Illustration number

1. Lyndall Ryan, *Aboriginal Tasmanians*, 2nd edn, Allen & Unwin, Sydney, 1996, chapters 14 and 15.

2. Diane Barwick, *Rebellion at Coranderrk*, Aboriginal History, Canberra, 1998, p. 62, note 16.

3. *Ibid.*, pp. 20-25, 33, 41, 66, 295.

4. *Australian Board of Missions Review*, January 1912.

5. *Encyclopaedia of Aboriginal Australia*, Aboriginal Studies Press, Canberra, 1994, p. 75; Heather Goodall, *Invasion to Embassy: Land in Aboriginal Politics in New South Wales, 1770-1972*, Allen & Unwin, Sydney, 1996, photographs, p. vi.

7. Anna Haebich, *For Their Own Good: Aborigines and Government in the Southwest of Western Australia, 1900-1940*, University of Western Australia Press, Nedlands, 1988, pp. 274-76.

8. *Argus*, 17 April 1936.

9. William Cooper to Premier of New South Wales, 9 May 1937, 12/8749, AONSW; *Smith's Weekly*, 16 October 1937; *Argus*, 13 November 1937; P.R. Stephensen, Secretary, Aboriginal Citizenship Committee, to A.P. Burdeu, President, AAL, 14 December 1937, P.R. Stephensen Papers, Mitchell Library, State Library of New South Wales, MS 1284.

10. *Man* Magazine, March 1938; Jack Horner, personal communication to the authors, 28 August 1998.

11. *Man Magazine*, April 1938.

13. *Sydney Morning Herald*, 13 and 15 February 1949.

14. *He, too, is an Australian!*, Victorian Aborigines Advancement League leaflet, 1957, Riley & Ephemera Collection, State Library of Victoria; *Analysis of Mr Rupert Murdoch's Article*, leaflet, 1957, Gordon Bryant Papers, National Library of Australia, MS 8256/182/3; *Tribune*, 20 March 1957; *Smoke Signals*, May 1957, pp. 2-3.

16. *Sun* (Melbourne), 24 December 1958; *Smoke Signals*, December 1958, p. 1, April 1959, p. 3, July 1959, p. 2.

17. *Herald* (Melbourne), 22 May 1963; *Age*, 23 May 1963; Eric Onus, Secretary, Save Lake Tyers Committee, Circular Letter, 15 May 1963, Council for Aboriginal Rights (Victoria) Papers, La Trobe Collection, State Library of Victoria, MS 12913/7/6; Council for Aboriginal Rights, Ownership and Development of Reserves, leaflet, 28 June 1963, CAR (Victoria) Papers, MS 12913/7/3.

18. *Age*, 5 and 15 August 1963; *Sun* (Melbourne), 28 August 1963; Gordon Bryant testimony, in Faith Bandler, *Turning the Tide: A Personal History of the Federal Council for the Advancement of Aborigines and Torres Strait Islanders*, Aboriginal Studies Press, Canberra, 1989, p. 42; Edgar Wells, *Reward and Punishment in Arnhem Land 1962-1963*, Australian Institute of Aboriginal Studies, Canberra, 1982, p. 80.

19. *Tribune*, 20 May 1964.

20. *Sydney Morning Herald*, 17 February 1965.

21. *Outlook: An Independent Socialist Journal*, no. 2, April 1965.

22. *Tribune*, 19 October 1966.

23. Frank Hardy, 'The Tribe That Went on Strike ...', *Australian*, 6 June 1967; Frank Hardy, *The Unlucky Australians*, Thomas Nelson (Australia), Melbourne, 1968, photograph facing p. 213.

24. *Sun* (Melbourne), 27 May 1967; see Bain Attwood and Andrew Markus in collaboration with Dale Edwards and Kath Schilling, *The 1967 Referendum, Or When Aborigines Didn't Get the Vote*, Aboriginal Studies Press, Canberra, 1997, chapter 5.

25. *Australian Women's Weekly*, 28 June 1967; *Aboriginal-Australian Fellowship Newsletter*, September 1967, Aboriginal-Australian Fellowship Papers, Mitchell Library, State Library of New South Wales, MSS 4057, box H5058; Attwood *et al.*, *The 1967 Referendum*, p. 58.

27. *Sydney Morning Herald*, 30 April 1970.

28. *Sunday Australian*, 5 December 1971.

29. *Age*, 28 January 1972.

30. *New York Times*, 8 March 1972.

32. *Age*, 16 April 1979; *Australian*, 1 September 1980.

33. See Steve Hawke and Michael Gallagher, *Noonkanbah: Whose Land, Whose Law*, Fremantle Arts Centre Press, Fremantle, 1989, chapters 12 and 13.

34. & 35. *Australian*, 27 January 1988; *Sydney Morning Herald*, 27 January 1988.

36. *Australian*, 13 June 1988; *Sydney Morning Herald*, 13 June 1988.

37. See Nonie Sharp, *No Ordinary Judgment: Mabo, the Murray Islanders' Land Case*, Aboriginal Studies Press, Canberra, 1996.

38. *Australian*, 22 December 1993.

39. *Australian*, 24 December 1996.

41. *Sydney Morning Herald*, 20 October 1997.

Index